DIVIDED

Divided

Aimee Aumock Missy Kampa

Copyright © 2024 by Aimee Aumock and Missy Kampa
All rights reserved. Printed in the United States of America
Morning Stories Publications LLC
Lewiston, MN 55952
www.MorningStoriesPublications.com

Library of Congress Cataloging-in-Publication Data

Names: Aumock, Aimee, author; Kampa, Missy, author.
Title: Divided / Aimee Aumock Missy Kampa
Description: First edition. | Lewiston : Morning Stories Publications LLC, 2024.
Identifiers: Library of Congress Control Number: 2024919892 | ISBN 978-1-965528-00-6 (paperback) | ISBN 978-1-965528-04-4 (hardcover) | ISBN 978-1-965528-02-0 (ebook)

Edited by Holly Stoddard and Tracey Barski
Cover art and heading illustration by Madison Szmurlo

Dedicated to everyone
who thought they knew everything
but soon discovered they didn't know anything

New Characters. New names to figure out how to say.

Let this little guide help you along your way.

Arisanna (Ari) — are-ih-SAUN-uh (ARE-ee)

Lunagarde — LOON-uh-gard

Torren — TORE-in

Callan — CAL-in

Lachloren — LOCK-lo-rin

Edric — EE-d-rick

Cyran — SEER-uhn

Alterria — all-TARE-ee-uh

Lyra — LEER-uh

CHAPTER ONE

FOLLOW THE PUP

As I peered over the top of my book, a pair of golden eyes stared at me from the deep shadows of the trees.

"Stay away from the woods, Arisanna," Mom would say. "Especially without your father. You never know when the wolves will find you."

I flipped from my stomach to my knees and dropped my book next to a clump of purple wildflowers.

Dad and I often paused our hikes and lessons to drink in the musical howling that sporadically floated amidst the trees, but we'd never had a wolf make its presence known.

So what were those eyes? I left the story of Wonderland behind and crept forward.

A tiny golden-eyed wolf pup loped out of the tree line, tongue lolling to the side.

The fear Mom still harbored hadn't taken hold in me. Instead, my heart took flight.

"Hey, little one. Did you come to wish me a happy birthday? I've never met anyone like you." Though still far away, I reached my hand toward him.

He gave a shrill yip and sped his pace, adding a playful leap as he met me. More surprising than his presence was that, like me, he lacked fear.

Circling my ankles when we met, he allowed me to run my hand through his dark gray fur, but when I stroked his muzzle, he coated my fingers with slobber.

"Gross," I said, wiping the goo on my jeans.

He yipped again, then rubbed his head against my knee and headed back the way he'd come.

"Don't leave," I pleaded.

He paused and looked back as though beckoning me.

Should I follow my "white rabbit" and see where he goes?

I glanced back at my house, its three levels and ten bedrooms better suited for a family larger than my parents and me. The wraparound porch could accommodate a lot of company, yet we never had any. A set of angled double doors jutted off the side of the house, an unwelcoming entrance to the cellar where my parents had been working for hours. They could be done at any time.

I took a step forward, my mind and heart at war. If I were to continue, I would break my parents' trust and their only rule: never enter the woods alone. But like Alice following *her* white rabbit, curiosity got the best of me.

A cool breeze swept through the trees, putting its arm around my shoulders, tousling my long brown hair, and pulling me toward the adventure my heart suddenly craved. The pint-sized pup pranced back and tugged the hem of my shirt with his teeth, urging me forward.

Having made my choice to continue, I remembered my dad's warning during one of our daily nature walks: "The woods can be disorienting, Rissy, and knowing how to navigate them is vital." He scratched a star into the bark of a tree. "Everything will begin to look the same until you can't find your way back."

Heeding his advice, I slid my hand into my pocket and gripped the cool metal of my pocket knife. Pulling it out, I stepped to the tree in front of me and carved an upside-down triangle that matched my little wolf friend's marking. My feet hesitated as I left the safety of my backyard. Even as my heart commanded me to continue, it stuttered, knowing the rule I willfully broke.

"Keep walking, Rissy." Step by step, I continued on until my house disappeared from view.

Far ahead of me, deep in the woods, a chorus of wolves howled. The pup's ears perked up, and he sniffed the air. I scratched a mark into the bark of another tree. As the howling faded, the pup loped further into the woods.

Keeping my eye on him as I trailed behind, I appreciated the way the canopy above blocked the intense heat from the meadow but let the sun's soft rays filter through. A fresh breeze whispered through the leaves, and I felt at home surrounded by the songbirds' melody, crickets' harmony, and the low humming bass of the bullfrogs near the river.

I snapped my head forward as an unfamiliar sound cut through the forest's melody. It wasn't wolves, frogs, or birds. No. It was a voice. A girl's voice, not much different from my own. I froze, confusion fluttering in my mind. Our property stretched on for acres. No one else had ever been in these woods, so where had this girl come from?

"Torren!" The girl's cries grew more fervent as I pushed my feet forward, still scratching a mark into every fifth tree.

"Hello?" I called out as the pup trotted behind me.

"Torren, where are you?"

My heart raced as I followed her voice into a small clearing.

She stood in the center of the grove of giant trees whose large roots littered the ground around her. With hair the color of gold, she reminded me of Alice.

"Who are you looking for?"

"Have you seen a boy?" Her soft gray eyes sparkled as I approached, and fresh tears threatened to spill into new streams on her already tear-stained cheeks.

By the time I reached her, my head had grown heavy, and the verdant world spun around me. I took a deep breath to steady the sickening vertigo before I managed to reply, "I haven't seen anybody but you."

"I can't find my uncle."

"Your uncle?" I don't know if she explained because the pressure in my head weighed heavier with each moment, forcing me to press my palms to my temples and squeeze my eyes shut. I couldn't stay.

My foot caught on a gnarled root as I twisted away and dropped to the ground. Attempting to brace myself, my elbows bent with the force of my fall, and my head slammed against a buried boulder.

The girl gasped and reached for me. Tiny sparks danced when her hand folded around mine. A sharp burning sensation followed, and we broke apart, knocking me back on my butt.

Her hands flew to her mouth. "Oh, no! You're bleeding."

Still sitting on the ground, I gently pressed a finger to my head. The sudden sting made me flinch, and I pulled my hand away. "I need to get a bandage from my house. Come with me. It's not far, and my parents could help you find your uncle."

She shook her head and took a step back.

A small, blue, circular light began to form where I'd been standing. This couldn't be an illusion stemming from the knock to my head because it drew the girl's attention too.

As the light grew, she whispered, "I knew I'd find it again." She glanced around and yelled, "Torren! It's here!"

When no one responded, her face fell.

Torren. The name sparked a funny feeling, like I'd heard it before. I opened my mouth to ask if we'd met, but she spoke first.

"It's so beautiful." A smile played on her lips as her eyes met mine.

The light stretched out in front of her, wide enough to swallow her whole. Her fingertips brushed against the blue glow, and as she smiled, she leaned closer, like Alice must've done when she discovered the rabbit hole.

Before I could tell her to be careful, Dad's hoarse voice cut through the thickness of the woods.

"Arisanna, where are you?

"That's my dad. He can help you," I said, but she only took a step forward. My heart thumped against my chest as I turned toward my dad's voice and shouted. "Dad, I'm over here. There's a—"

A bright light flashed behind me. By the time I returned my focus to the girl, both she and the mysterious light had disappeared.

"Hey!" I yelled.

"RISSY!" Dad's voice grew closer, more frantic.

"Dad? Dad, I'm over here!"

"Stay where you are, and keep calling for me, Rissy. I'll come to you!"

"Dad!" I shouted again, following his instructions.

Branches snapped and crackled as he burst into the small clearing and crouched beside me. He held my book in his hand, pressing it into my back as he drew me close.

"You had us worried," he breathed against my hair.

"I'm sorry I frightened you. It all happened so fast."

He sighed and held me away from him, his hands firmly on my shoulders. "You *must* be careful. If anything were to happen to you—" His eyes widened as he brushed his thumb against my temple. "What happened?"

My cheeks flushed and I hung my head. "I tripped."

"We told you never to come into the woods alone. What possessed you to break the rules?"

"The wolf pup..." I glanced around the clearing, disappointed by the pup's absence. "And a girl with golden hair. I think she was my age, and she sure was upset."

"You saw a girl? Here? What did she say? Where did she come from?"

"She asked me if I'd seen her uncle."

"Was someone else here, too?" His amber eyes darted around.

"Just her and a glowing blue light. But right before you reached me, they both disappeared."

His head snapped upwards. "Riss, I need you to check. Is that shimmer still in the sky?"

I wrinkled my brow, unsure what that had to do with the blue light. "Why? Can't you see it?"

He tugged on the ends of his ash brown hair. "You're the only one who can." Dad rarely showed signs of nervousness, but something about this situation had him on edge.

My heart thudded against my chest. I'd asked him about the shimmer many times, but the conclusion had remained the same: it must have been a mirage. If that were true, why would he be asking about it now?

I glanced up. The golden shimmer still flickered high above us. "Then it can't be a mirage like you once told me. The sun shines in town, too, but the shimmer's only around our property, like a shelter. What is it?"

He pulled in a deep breath and slowly released it before he smiled. "Shelter is a good word for now. When the time is right, we'll explain more. Let's get you home and fixed up." He stood and set me on my feet, reaching for my hand.

I wrapped my fingers around his and led him along the path I'd carved.

"Riss." Pride filled his voice. "You marked your trail."

I straightened my shoulders. "Of course I did. You taught me it was important to always be able to find my way home."

A smile tugged at the corners of his mouth. "I did."

I took my book from his hand and flipped through the pages. "If Alice had marked her trail, maybe she wouldn't have gotten lost. I'm about halfway through, but I bet she misses home soon."

"A girl with golden hair disappearing into a rabbit hole. An ironic connection," he mused, chuckling softly.

Did he think I confused what I'd seen with my book?

We broke through the tree line, and from this view across the wide-open expanse encircled by endless trees, our spacious home looked like a cozy cottage nestled against a backdrop of firs.

We were a few yards from the front door when Mom barreled out, nearly knocking me off my feet as she held me close. "Why did you wander off? You know not to go into the woods alone." She leaned back and brushed my hair away from the cut on my head.

"I'm fine," I assured her before she could ask.

"She marked her trail." Dad hesitated a moment, locking eyes with Mom. "It's time she earned a little more freedom."

Chapter Two

Into Alterria

Nearly six years had passed since the girl in the wood vanished with the flash of bright light, but every night her disappearance replayed while I slept.

Since then, my parents allowed me freedom to explore the woods, so I spent my days following the trail I carved into the trees, hoping to find her again. Except for the throbbing in my head when I stood where the light had formed, there was nothing to assure me she'd ever been real.

As the weeks passed, the rush of the river implored me to explore further. It was there I met Kai, the day after my thirteenth birthday. He quickly became my best friend, my only friend, and two years later, we became a couple. With him by my side, my days were no longer lonely.

Until last month when he became only an addition to my nightly dream.

I shifted in my bed, fighting the wakefulness that began to wash over me. I didn't want to lose the chance to see him smiling at me again, even if it wasn't real.

The bright light flashed, and the girl was replaced by a foggy haze. Kai's boots came into focus first, but he became clearer with each step until finally he stood in front of me, his lopsided smile stretching the scar on his bottom lip.

"Until we meet again." His steel gray eyes bore into my soul as his smile fell, and he brushed a kiss on the back of my hand like he did every time we said goodbye. Then the fog swallowed him up, and I was left with the reminder he wouldn't be coming back again.

The bright afternoon sun broke my dream into pieces. I swiped a tear from my eye as I sat up and swallowed back the bile that rose in my stomach. As if the pain of his abandonment wasn't torture enough, I had to lose him again every night.

Despite it being lunchtime, I shuffled to the kitchen and poured myself a bowl of cereal. I kept hoping that sleeping the days away would make the remaining hours easier to bear, but that hadn't proven true so far. My heart felt heavy, as it had for the last few weeks.

Mom pulled out the chair beside me and tucked her sandy blonde hair behind her ear. "How'd you sleep?"

Instead of answering, I shrugged and swirled the milk with my spoon.

"Well, we're ready to listen when you're ready to talk, sweetie."

The corners of my mouth turned down, and I looked away so she wouldn't see my eyes fill. "You and Dad didn't believe me before. Why should things change now?"

It wasn't anyone's fault Kai had never met my parents. Every time we tried, something got in the way—rain, schoolwork, a no-show—until finally, we stopped trying.

"Ari, we do believe you." Her deep brown eyes that matched my own pleaded for me to confide in her, but I couldn't.

"You believe me now that he's gone." Scowling, I shoved my chair back and dumped my untouched bowl in the sink.

"Arisanna." My dad walked in, his voice stern. "Don't hurt your mother just because you're hurt."

Dad was right. I wasn't normally contradictory, but my dream had underlined how much I had lost.

"I'm sorry, Mom." Letting my tears fall, I snuggled against her when she drew me to her lap. Even weeks away from eighteen and nearly as tall as she was, I relished feeling like her little girl. The pain didn't go away, but it hurt a little less knowing she loved me.

Dad claimed the chair I'd just left. "Ari, there's a lot we need to talk about. Your mother and I still have some work to do, but meet us in your clearing around dusk. Okay?"

"If you finish before then, I'll be in the meadow." My voice cracked.

His eyes narrowed as he tried to read my face, but I quickly averted my gaze. He helped me to my feet and hugged me instead. "Love you, honey. See you tonight."

While Mom and Dad worked, I stuffed a black backpack with an old blanket, a flashlight, and a childhood favorite from the bookshelf. My growling stomach led me to the kitchen for water, snacks, and a sandwich before heading to the meadow.

It hadn't rained in weeks, and I missed the usually tall, soft grass. I spread the blanket on the ground beneath me to protect the backs of my legs from the scratch of the dry, stubby grass that had taken its place. Out of habit, I searched for Kai. We'd spent hours here together over the years, but he wouldn't be coming today. Instead of succumbing to the disappointment of his absence, I attempted to lose myself to fairyland.

The heat of the summer sun and the river's soft murmur lulled me to sleep. I woke to the howling of wolves. The blue-gray of dusk had replaced the brightness of day. I pushed myself up and listened for the howling to resume. When it did, I jumped to my feet and shoved my book and blanket into the backpack. I hadn't heard the wolves in ages, and I needed to get a closer look.

As I walked, shining my flashlight on the tree trunks, the upside-down triangles I had carved six years ago guided my path. I'd gone to the clearing more or less daily, futilely hoping I would find the girl again. Would the wolves be there instead?

The howling stopped abruptly as I broke through the last of the trees and entered the clearing. I stared in amazement. The light I'd been searching for had returned—though different this time. Instead of a bright blue circle, a shimmering gold pillar carried endlessly into the evening sky until it became one with the dome around our property.

In a severe case of déjà vu, the same heaviness that weighed in my head as I stood in the exact same spot nearly six years ago, knocked me off balance and I tripped on the gnarled root. My head scraped against the rough bark of a fallen tree, and the flashlight flew from my hands. A warmth slid down my forehead onto my cheek as I rose to my knees. I flinched as I touched a cut under the warmth, my fingertips red with blood.

Enclosed within the light, red and white napkins lay scattered on a checkered blanket. Someone had left in a hurry. A picnic basket lay tipped on its side next to three crystal bottles, all half full. Green, red, and blue.

I hesitated for a moment before I crept forward and reached toward the light for a handful of napkins. As my fingertips met the glow, tiny sparks jumped toward me. I flinched back, but the blood kept dripping down my cheek, urging me to try again.

This time, I ignored the sparks and grabbed the napkins poking out of the basket. Sitting back, I pressed them against my forehead to stem the flow of blood.

Take the blue bottle.

"Hello?" How hard did I hit my head? Not only had I heard a voice, but I'd actually responded to it.

Take the blue bottle.

Logically, there was no reason to obey the girl whose voice echoed in my head, but I took a sharp breath and shoved my hand through the pillar of light again. My long brown hair slid over my shoulder as I leaned forward. Painless sparks jumped off my skin every place the light touched. I grasped the bottle and pulled it from the light.

"Now what?"

Receiving no response, I placed the corked bottle into the front pocket of my backpack.

The woods were too silent. No chirping or croaking or hooting.

I grew nervous and stood to follow the path back home. Why weren't Mom and Dad here?

My heart faltered as thick ropes of black and white fog looped around my ankles like lassos and dragged me into the forest's darkness. Fear clogged my throat. Where were my parents? They said they'd be here. Were they trapped in this strange fog, too?

In the blink of an eye, I found myself toe to toe with a brute of a man who was probably around the same age as my dad. He seemed familiar, yet I'd never seen him before. He towered over me, which would've been threatening had his steel gray eyes not flashed such worry as his gaze met mine. The fog wrapped around us both, climbing like a vine, and I struggled to disentangle myself from its hold.

"Try to relax. This won't be comfortable." His muscles tensed in contradiction to his own advice, the ropes of smoke shoving us into each other. Neither of us had any kind of control.

"What's happening?" I asked, endeavoring to raise my hands between us.

"It will be over in a minute."

When the fog finally dissipated, we were no longer in the woods.

My head spun, and I staggered back a couple of steps before regaining my balance.

The man took quick steps away from me. He turned around and stared at me as I stood in place. "Are you coming?"

I couldn't control the way my face contorted as I tried to make sense of what had just happened and why this stranger expected me to follow him. Did he trap random people in the woods frequently? As I shook my head, several loose strands of hair fell across my face, and I brushed them away.

His eyes flickered to my forehead. "You're hurt."

"I'm fine." Pressing my fingers to the cut, I winced. "What was that?"

The man frowned and squinted at me. "It's late, and you're not safe."

"What do you mean I'm not safe?"

"You're an Outsider, and we don't have much time. You'll have to come with me."

Outsider? What did he mean? I swallowed the knot in my throat. "No way. Take me back to my parents."

"I can't. Those woods are forbidden."

Confusion overpowered the fear that crept to the surface. "Those woods are mine, and you were just there. Why can't you take me back?"

The man mirrored my expression. "They're not of our world. You're in Alterria now."

"World? We're literally across the river from my home." My heart sped up. Across the river. Maybe he knew Kai and I could finally ask him why he left so abruptly.

"Didn't your parents know?" His eyebrows drew together.

I tried ignoring the clawing fingers that gripped my insides like a vice but met with no success. My breath was shallow, and sandpaper scratched over my words. "Know what?"

"About Alterria."

"What's Alterria?"

His eyes darted around as he scanned the area, then cleared his throat. "I'll explain, but we have to get indoors."

My head and my heart were in turmoil. On one hand, I'd been taught that focusing on emotions in a tough situation would make things worse. On the other, being ripped from my home—by fog, of all things—set my anxiety on edge. On top of all that, I'd been thrown together with some man I'd never met who insisted I follow him to his house. This whole situation tied my stomach into knots.

I had to address this logically, lest my fear and the uncertainty of this situation left me stranded in the middle of nowhere with no way back home. "I don't know who you are," I insisted.

"I'm Callan."

Tentatively, I accepted his extended hand, and heat radiated between our palms. "Arisanna. I'm still not going anywhere with you."

You can trust him.

"Did you hear that?" I asked. It was her again.

Callan pursed his lips. "I don't hear anything, but it's dark, and the wolves have started to prowl."

Trust him.

The words were reassuring, but how could I take advice from a disembodied voice?

Callan must have sensed my indecision. He gestured around. "I understand your hesitation, but where else will you go?"

Vast woods lay beyond the flowing river, but everything looked so unfamiliar bathed in darkness.

"You really can't help me?" My voice wavered, and tears threatened my resolve.

Callan shook his head. "That's not my gift. My transporter's no longer here, but my brother could get you home. You'd still have to come with me. Come on. My wife will have dinner ready."

Heat crept into my cheeks, and my jaw tightened. Why was he talking about gifts? I just wanted to get home. "There's no bridge, no boats?"

He responded to my questions with a sigh, the gruffness in his voice softening. "There's only one bridge, but it's on the other side of the city. I can bring you if you think you could make your way home from there."

We rarely ventured from our property, except when we went to town for supplies, and the marketplace was nowhere near the river. I shook my head. "Boats?"

"Outlawed."

I furrowed my eyebrows. "Why?"

"Too many accidents." He shrugged and turned away. "Are you coming?"

Between the voice and the mention of a wife, trusting Callan had to be a better choice than wandering in the dark, so I followed him, leaving plenty of space between us.

"Tell me, Arisanna," my name rolled off his tongue as though he had said it many times before, "what brought you to the woods?"

"I live right outside of them. I was supposed to meet my parents."

Show him the bottle.

"You don't know what this is, do you?" I removed the bottle from my backpack.

Callan's eyes grew large. "May I see that?"

I stepped closer and handed him the bottle.

"Where did you find this?"

"At the picnic, the one surrounded by a strange wall of glittering light."

He held the bottle above his head and stared as the moonlight shone through the liquid. "It sounds like you saw a barrier. They're constructed to hide the items they surround. They're not meant to be seen. But you saw it—all of it?"

Wiping my clammy palms against my jean shorts, I swallowed at the knot in my throat and forced myself to speak above a whisper. I had just been dragged here by fog but worried *I* may not be normal. "Is that bad?"

His eyes narrowed as he handed the bottle back to me. "As far as I know, it's never happened before."

Keeping my eyes down, I placed the bottle back in my backpack.

"Everything will be okay. We're nearly there."

Clouds had covered the moon by the time we arrived at a dilapidated building. The dead flowers in the window box, crumbled stones in the walkway, and weathered paint on the front door told me Callan was either at the wrong place or setting me up to be murdered.

I crept up the front steps, my heart racing as he led me inside.

We stepped into a darkened entryway, and the fear that clenched my chest was soon replaced by the comforting smells of fresh-baked bread and roasted tomato basil soup, my mother's favorite.

Callan guided me into a cozy kitchen. "Deborah, she's hurt."

A thin woman, her honey-brown hair slicked back into a bun, set a kettle on the back burner of the stove and reached into a cupboard for a first-aid kit. She glanced at me with a questioning tilt of her head but didn't ask for an introduction. "May I?"

"It doesn't hurt much." The same glint of familiarity I had sensed with Callan took me by surprise. Had we seen them in town? How hard had I hit my head?

"Still, it needs to be cleaned up. Is that okay?"

I nodded, and she took care of the cut on my head.

"Where's Torren?" Callan asked, approaching the sink on the adjacent wall. He washed his hands and toweled them dry.

Deborah hesitated. "I haven't seen him since he left this morning. He'll be home to sleep, I'm sure."

Callan threw the towel into the sink and rubbed his temples. "He needs to be careful." He leaned back against the countertop and drew in a deep breath. "Did you go to the hospital today? How's the girl?"

Deborah's face bunched up in concern as she finished applying the bandage. "She's not well. She doesn't belong here. There has to be a way to get her back home."

"Not well," I repeated in a whisper. I didn't belong here, either.

Deborah motioned to the dining room table. "Have a seat. Soup is nearly ready."

The scraping of the chair was a thin disguise for the rumbling my stomach decided to start singing. My cheeks burned as I sat, hoping neither of them had noticed.

"Callan, you haven't introduced our visitor."

"Deborah, this is Arisanna."

"It's so nice to meet you, Arisanna." She shared a knowing glance with Callan before clearing her throat and smiling. "Are you thirsty, dear?"

Disoriented by the sudden change in conversation, I nodded, but by the time she returned with the two mugs she'd filled from the kettle, comfort had replaced my confusion.

I leaned over the mug she placed in front of me and breathed in the sweet, fresh scent. The image of a white bunny on the side of the mug implied it belonged to a child. As I placed my hands around the warm cup, every muscle in my body became paralyzed.

Deborah jumped, knocking her chair to the floor. "There were no signs." She wrung her hands frantically. "If only we had the elixir."

Though my body was frozen, my mind raced. Elixir? What kind of elixir? Did this kind of thing happen in Alterria often?

Callan placed his hands over hers and spoke calmly. "No. This is different. You gave her Celia's cup."

Deborah froze, and I imagined her suddenly bloodless face mirrored my own. "Just like he said."

More mystery. Who was "he," and what did he say?

Callan dropped to his knees and removed contents from the lower cabinets one by one. "C'mon. It has to be in here." His upper body all but disappeared as he crawled into the back corner of the cabinet.

"Yes!" He scurried out of the cabinet, emerging with a palm-sized green bottle.

"It's time to find out what this will do." Callan shook the bottle vigorously and then splashed the liquid onto the cup.

As Celia's cup faded into nothing, my ability to move returned.

I pursed my lips and forced myself to speak calmly, though I wanted to do anything but. "I have a few questions. Who are you? Who is Celia? What just happened to me?" My voice rose, and the words tumbled out faster than I could think of them. "What happened to that cup? Where am I? What happened to this mystery girl?" I took a deep breath and shouted, "WHAT IN THE WORLD IS GOING ON?"

"Callan." Deborah's voice broke, and she covered her mouth.

He stepped toward her with open arms, and she fell into his embrace. While holding her, he looked at me. "Celia was–is– our daughter."

"Why did you say 'was'?" I asked, glancing from him to Deborah, my frustration fading to bewilderment.

"She's been missing for six years. With the help of Council–" he spat the word– "we've been unsuccessfully searching for her. A couple of weeks ago, a young girl showed up the same way you did. It nearly killed her, so Council told us they were giving up."

"Then why am I here?"

"I wish we could tell you." Callan cleared his throat. "What were you doing in the woods?"

He'd asked this before, and I'd made sure he knew my parents would notice my absence, but it wouldn't hurt to elaborate a little. "I followed the sound of the wolves."

"Wolves? You should have taken her to the hospital right away, Callan."

With light circles, he rubbed the small of her back and whispered, "This might be different. Calm, Deborah."

"Yes." She breathed in deeply, and her shoulders relaxed as she exhaled. She filled a fresh cup for me and sat back in the chair, folding her arms across her chest. "Following wolves is dangerous."

"The wolves have never bothered me. Tonight reminded me of the first time I'd been in the woods alone," I said, eyeing the cup with suspicion.

"I promise it's safe this time," Deborah assured as Callan took the seat beside her.

A pleasant warmth flowed through me as I sipped the tea.

Deborah smiled. "What happened the first time?"

Comforted by both the drink and Deborah's voice, I thought a moment before deciding to summarize. "On my twelfth birthday, I followed a small gray wolf into the woods. After a while, I heard a girl calling for someone." The name had long since left my memory, a ghost in my mind.

Deborah gave me a sideways glance. Her knuckles turned white as she gripped her mug. When she saw me eyeing her hands, she loosened her hold.

I took another sip. "I kept walking until I found her. She looked scared. Then my dad called my name, and I shouted for him, but when I turned back around, she'd completely disappeared. I've searched for her nearly every day since."

Deborah squeezed Callan's hand and began firing questions at me. "Disappeared? How? Did you see fog?"

I shook my head, my voice drifting as the memory of the day filtered back into my mind. "There was a strange blue light."

"Arisanna," Callan's deep timbre, gentle and soothing, cut into my memory. "How old are you now?"

"Almost eighteen."

Deborah's mug shattered on the floor, and her face drained of all color. "Celia."

CHAPTER THREE

MEET TORREN

The bright sunlight shining through the small window roused me from a heavy sleep. I sat up and scanned the room, trying to remember where I was.

Dolls lined the shelves against the pink walls, and frills adorned the bedding. Framed pictures filled the nightstand.

I picked up one that showed Callan and Deborah with a young boy and the girl from the woods. Deborah was right. I *had* seen Celia.

Then another picture caught my eye. An old man cradling a baby with emerald green eyes stood beside a younger Callan who held another baby with bright blonde hair. The old man had a thin, vertical scar on the right side of his lower lip, identical to Kai's. I wondered about the coincidence until heavy footsteps passing outside my door drew my attention.

I swung my legs over the edge of the bed and walked to a child-sized chair in the corner. It held a T-shirt, black leggings, and a note.

Picked out some clothes I thought might fit you. There's a fresh toothbrush in the bathroom. Help yourself to some food. -Deb

After getting ready for the day, I sat at the kitchen table to nibble a granola bar I'd found in the cupboard. Soon, I became lost in my thoughts.

Two male voices tugged me back to reality as Callan entered the living room, followed by a slightly taller man with tousled brown hair.

Could this be the brother that could get me home?

Callan took a seat on the plush sofa, facing away from where I sat.

The stranger paced in front of him.

"Torren! Please calm down."

"I was getting closer to her. I could feel it. And then that cursed fog pulled me away." He tugged at the ends of his hair as he wore a hole in the carpet.

"Pulled away? Are you telling me you still don't have control after all these years?"

"Of course I do," came Torren's frustrated retort, then more quietly, "Most of the time."

"This isn't good. What happened?"

"I was afraid." He stopped pacing.

"Of what?"

"Of what? Of the wolves, for one thing. You know what they do." Torren lowered himself onto the couch and muttered, "And that strange wall of light."

He saw the light, too? I leaned forward to focus on their conversation.

"Let me get this straight. You heard wolves, saw a light, and got pulled away?" Callan quirked his eyebrow.

"Basically."

"Edric already has it out for us. If he finds out you were traveling again…" Callan rubbed the back of his neck. "You need to be careful."

Torren grunted. "Tell me something I don't know."

Callan's voice cracked as he spoke in a hushed tone. "Torren, I'm so sorry."

"Sorry for what?"

"The formative years that you needed a mentor, I failed you." Callan took a heavy breath. "I was too focused on Celia."

"You didn't fail me, Dad. You taught me so much. The control issues are nothing to worry about." After a long pause, he asked, "Where did you search this time?"

Dad. So Torren wasn't the brother.

I deflated a little and wondered when I'd meet this brother that could supposedly help me. I didn't want to be trapped here any longer than necessary. All my life I wanted a little more adventure, and now that I'd been literally dragged into a whole new place, I only wanted to go home. My lips curved into a smile at the irony.

"Across the river from our meadow," Callan admitted in a low voice.

Anger laced Torren's words. "Why would you search the Outside? I *told* you there was nothing there."

"But there was, Torren. A young woman got caught up in the fog when Thomas brought me back."

My breaths came rapidly, and my heart raced as Torren's face reddened.

If Callan was talking about me, why was Torren getting angry?

Torren sat up straight and dragged his hand through his hair. "Who is she? Is she okay? Is she going to be stuck here like the last girl?"

Callan placed his hand on Torren's shoulder. "I think she may have a connection to our world."

"What makes you say that?"

"She didn't need the elixir. Only people with Alterrian blood can survive without it."

"Where is she?"

Pieces of their conversation spun in my head. Stuck. Connection. Elixir. I stood and approached the two men, hoping for some clarification to the mounting confusion that was about to overwhelm me.

When Torren turned toward me, my confusion compounded as his half-raised smirk mirrored Kai's, and I couldn't help but whisper his name.

"Ari." His bright emerald eyes searched my face, a spark igniting and burning out so quickly I must have imagined it. He shook his head, his scowl causing my chest to tighten.

He wasn't Kai, so how did this stranger know my name? I reached for the back of the sofa to support myself, but it was too far away.

Callan twisted and caught me under my arms, pulling me over the top.

I fell onto Torren's lap, and for a moment, I felt safe.

"No. Not you." Torren looked down at me with a mix of fear, anger, and regret. He stood abruptly, dropping me to the floor, then without hesitation, offered his hand to help me to my feet.

As our hands connected, my vision became hazy for a few seconds before returning to normal. Shaking off the after effects of whatever just happened, I could do nothing but watch him stalk out of the room.

His booted footsteps faded as he left, and the walls vibrated with the slam of the door.

Callan glared after Torren.

A few hot tears slid down my cheeks, and I turned to brush them away.

"My grandfather was known as Kai." Callan let the name sit between us for a moment. "Who's Kai, Arisanna?"

His gentle question caused my mind to wander to laughter-filled summer days and autumn nights in Kai's arms, dancing in the mist beneath the moonlit trees. "I loved Kai, but he left. If it's all the same to you, that memory is too painful for me right now."

"Torren seemed to know you."

"I've never met Torren."

Callan sighed but didn't push me.

"You mentioned Torren last night. Why does he need to be careful?"

"Because Council called off the searches."

Was he being intentionally vague? "I'm sorry. What?"

"Torren is my youngest brother, and–"

"Brother? But he called you Dad."

"When our parents died, I raised him, so Torren and Celia grew up together. As you must've heard, Torren feels responsible for her disappearance–"

"And he doesn't want to listen to Council."

Callan nodded.

A shrill ringing sounded in the small kitchen. It repeated, and then Deborah mumbled in the distance.

"What was that noise?" I asked.

Callan tilted his head, and a smile tugged at the corners of his mouth. "The telephone?"

"Oh, of course." My cheeks burned. I knew what was coming. I hated this nervous tick of mine. "We have one at home. No one ever calls us. We only went to town occasionally. It was a long walk. Took close to a day to get there and back. I don't really know anyone other than my parents." In my anxiousness, I spilled more than I intended. I glanced away, suddenly homesick. "Last night, you said your brother could get me home. Did you mean Torren?"

"I did, but we'll need to find him first."

"And quickly," Deborah stated as she joined us. "That was Ronin. He needs Torren before the meeting begins. Arisanna needs to come as well. They know."

"Wait. What do you mean they know? About me?"

"I'm afraid so." Deborah's eyes were sympathetic.

"And this meeting is *because* of me?"

Her voice soothed me. "No, sweetie. Council meetings happen every month."

"And they're mandatory." Callan heaved himself up. "When do they need us to appear?"

"The meeting time didn't change," Deborah said.

I glanced between them. "I still don't understand. Who are *they?*"

"Council probably doesn't know about you specifically, but with the Council transporter tracking how many people come back, they know I didn't return alone."

"With no ill effects, they *should* send her home," Deborah said.

Callan cocked his head. "Edric would never approve that."

The clock on the wall chimed and drew Deborah's attention. "If we're going to get there before it starts, we have to leave now."

"How? Who knows where Torren's stormed off to this time."

"He didn't go far." She peered out the window, and gave Callan's hand a squeeze. "I think you need to talk to him."

I looked out, too.

Torren paced the yard, kicking at stones, his face stormy.

Callan sighed. "I'll be right back."

I'd had my fill of eavesdropping this morning, so I shut myself into the bathroom. Once again, my tears failed to wash away memories of Kai, especially with the reminder of him so fresh in my mind.

Too soon, I heard Torren and Callan come back into the house.

I splashed cold water on my face, blotting it dry with a towel before I joined them in the living room.

"Let's go." Callan said, breaking the silence that filled the room.

Torren looked everywhere except at me. What had I done to anger him so?

My thoughts were cut short as white wisps of smoke wrapped around all of us from the ground up. I closed my eyes, bracing myself for the uncomfortable closeness, but it didn't come.

"And here we are," Torren said with a note of pride that prompted me to open my eyes. "Council Hall, the heart of Alterria."

Chapter Four

First Meeting

Torren took on the same scholarly voice Kai often used while we mulled over my history lessons in the meadow. "Alterria was ruled by the royal line until several of them were born without gifts, which caused an uproar in the land. Civil war transformed the glory of the Alterrian palace into ruins, like it mourned the people it lost to banishment, or worse."

I tilted my head, observing him closely as he spoke, his passion evident in the way he focused on the building as though he'd been present during its destruction.

"Those who remained had to come up with a new way to govern to protect its people and avoid another war. High Councilman Robert accepted the responsibility, and Alterria rebuilt and thrived. Over the years, he restored both the original castle's architecture and our country's pride and hope for the future."

I eyed the towers of stone in front of me. It could've slipped off a page of my Medieval history book, turrets, drawbridge, and all.

I glanced back to Torren, his smile mirroring a ghost of my past. If Kai had shared about where he was from, would he have told me its history as enthusiastically as Torren did?

"About thirty years ago, High Councilman Robert opened the library and the courtyard to the public. None of the books could be removed from Council premises, but everyone was welcome to study Alterria's laws, folklore, and tradition inside a piece of its own history."

"That's such a great idea." As a newcomer to Alterria, that would be a perfect way to satiate my love of learning. "I'd like to do that, too."

His smile turned to a frown. "Good luck. Current leadership locked a lot of those books away, and though no one officially banned people from the courtyard, the atmosphere isn't as welcoming as it used to be. Look around. Everyone's got the same worn-down expression because none of us want to be here at all. And *that* guy is part of the reason."

A man dressed in black robes walked toward us, a scowl on his face. His salt-and-pepper shoulder-length hair hung wild. From this distance, I couldn't make out much of his features, but his eyes were full of contempt.

"Who is he?" I asked.

"Thomas," Torren spoke the name with disdain, "Council transporter and his royal highness's right-hand lackey."

"Careful," Callan growled under his breath as Thomas shifted away from us.

Torren groaned. "I have to go."

Deborah grasped Torren's elbow as he started to walk away. "Find Ronin," she stated.

He responded with a nod and took a few steps forward. Suddenly, he spun on his heel, his eyes connecting with mine, full of desperation and maybe a bit of hope.

"Until we meet again," he whispered as he reached for me, and my heart faltered. He brushed a kiss onto my hand before flashing me a crooked smile, as though Kai had stepped out of my dream. Then Torren disappeared with a pillar of smoke.

I stood stunned for a moment. Who was this familiar stranger? I didn't have time to dwell.

As Council Hall loomed closer, the crowd grew thicker.

Deborah's eyes darted around, and she smiled and nodded at a few people who passed us. "We left early enough. I thought we'd be able to avoid this crowd."

"What good would that do? Aren't we all going to the same place?"

Callan kept his voice low as he answered my question. "After Celia disappeared, it didn't take long before people ran out of things to say. Pity is a look you can only stomach for so long, so we try to get here before everyone else."

"Even after all these years?" I looked around, but he was right. Most people glanced over at us but refused to make eye contact.

"What more can you say to the family shrouded in tragedy? It got worse when the townspeople became fed up with the disruption the searches caused to their daily lives. For the most part, it's easier to keep our distance and encourage them to do the same. You saw our house."

"That was on purpose?" I thought back to my initial reaction upon approaching their house.

Callan nodded. "I blame this summer's drought for the flowers, but the hanging shutters, the chipped paint, yes." He glanced around the sea of people. "The point is we got sick of overhearing the gossip."

As if on cue, a voice sounded loudly behind us. "I know they're good people. *He* is too hard on them, and I don't care if he hears me say so or not," an elderly plump woman said defiantly to the man beside her before bumping into Deborah.

"Oh, good day, dear," the woman said, mock surprise in her voice.

"Good afternoon, Doris," Deborah responded with a tentative smile.

Doris and her companion nodded, hurrying over the drawbridge and through the tall, thick wooden double doors that swallowed the townspeople as they filed in.

A train whistle sounded in the distance as we followed them, joining the crowd in a cavernous room.

"What is this place?" I asked.

"The Assembly Room," Deborah answered. "It's where all the town meetings are held."

A long table sat on a dais in the center. A single archway in the background framed a seemingly endless hallway.

Callan, Deborah, and I stood against the back wall waiting for the meeting to begin. Soon, four middle-aged men in matching black and red uniforms entered from the doorway and took their places at the table, a stoic look on each face. Thomas stood and cleared his throat, and all laughter, whispers, and chatter ceased. "All rise for the Honorable High Councilman, Edric Agnar."

The High Councilman sauntered into the room, a swagger in his step until he reached the center of the table, Thomas on his right-hand side. The High Councilman stood tall, back straight as he scanned the room. His beady eyes held a hint of malice. His graying hair swept in whisps across his forehead. An intimidating air hung around him as he remained standing, his voice booming through the crowded room, carrying all the way to the back, "Bring up the miscreant."

Two guards stepped forward from a row up front, each holding a young man's arm.

Deborah gasped.

"So good of you not to run this time, Torren," Edric said, seating himself.

"Kinda hard to." Torren raised his arms to showcase the metal bracelets that adorned each wrist. "You might be able to bully everyone into doing what you say, *Edric*, but you'll never have our respect!"

"You will be silent."

Torren's voice was strangled.

Edric smirked. "You have broken our laws and criticized our authority by traveling without permission. Again. You have been given much latitude due to your youth and your…family connection. No longer. I hereby sentence you to the Glass House."

Deborah softly cried as she placed her hand on Callan's shoulder and shook her head.

He dropped his head, deflated. "No."

Whispered arguments spread across the Council table until a man with Torren's broad shoulders and Callan's nose stood. "High Councilman, you have no right to make an executive decision."

Thomas offered up a snakelike grin that sent a chill through my body.

"And yet, it is done." Edric stood and snapped his fingers.

Two wolves rose from their haunches at his feet and leaped from the platform. The sheer size of the creatures startled me, but I was not afraid of them. With quiet growls, they nosed Torren through the archway and out of my sight.

Helplessness overwhelmed me as he disappeared, but what good would my protests have done? I shook my head slightly, confused by the strong sense of protectiveness I held for someone I had just met.

Edric turned to the man who had stood against him. "Now, Ronin, Council has questioned your loyalty since we voted to cease the search for your niece."

Ronin glanced at each Council member in turn. Only Thomas would meet his eyes, a smile slithering across his face.

"Some say you should spend a few days in the Glass House yourself." Edric's eyes traveled to the archway Torren had just been led through.

Ronin grew pale and eased back into his seat.

Edric must have sensed Ronin wouldn't argue further because he turned to face the crowd, and his voice reverberated around the room. "Bring me the girl."

A shiver rushed through me when Deborah pressed her hand into mine. She didn't look at me, but she squeezed my palm again and tipped her chin up, indicating that I ought to walk forward.

I took hesitant steps. On my right, a wolf nudged against my leg.

Smaller than the others, his back was the right height for me to rest my hand. He had a patch of white fur shaped like a handkerchief on his back, much like the pup I followed six years ago.

As I stopped in front of the platform, Edric smiled kindly, which invoked a trembling that I tried to hide.

"My dear, you found yourself here unexpectedly. Do you have any questions?"

"Hundreds, sir." Averting my eyes, I combed my fingers through the thick fur on the animal still at my side, and the corners of my mouth twitched. Everything I'd been hit with in less than twenty-four hours begged to be analyzed and explained. But nothing about the High Councilman invited me to ask those questions.

"I see you've settled in with the Lachloren family. I hope our prisoner hasn't begun to fill your head with stories." He looked at the other Council members, and they nodded—all but Ronin, who stared at me intently.

"I do not know Torren," I said steadily, meeting the High Councilman's gaze.

"Best not to associate with people such as him. Someone could get the…wrong idea…about you." The High Councilman still smiled, but the feigned kindness vanished.

Anger boiled in my chest. We had never met before, and he was trying to dictate my choices.

Tread carefully.

The invisible voice influenced my reply. "I suppose you would know best. This world and your people are all so new to me."

Edric glanced at the wolf still nuzzled up to my side. The High Councilman's eyes narrowed, and his jaw pulsed. "What did you say your name was again?"

I raised my eyebrows, feeling uncooperative. "I didn't."

A smile toyed at the edge of Ronin's lips, replaced in an instant by a subtle shake of his head and slight glare.

My heart thudded against my chest, and my sudden boldness shriveled away. I glanced down at the wolf at my side and swallowed hard against the lump forming in my throat. "Arisanna," I stated barely above a whisper. I brought my gaze back to the High Councilman.

His eyes burned as he stared me down. "Your full name, child."

I could feel all eyes on me. "Arisanna Morganfire Lunagarde."

A hiss spread through the room, but I dared not to move my eyes from the High Councilman's gaze.

He leaned back against his chair and placed his hands on the table in front of him, his fingers intertwined. "A unique middle name. May I ask its meaning?"

"It was my mother's maiden name, sir."

His cheeks flushed, and he leaned forward, his voice returning to the gruffness it held prior. "Arisanna. Your parents—"

"Sir," Callan's resonant voice spoke from behind me, "she hasn't been here long. Perhaps this interrogation can wait until she's had a chance to settle."

The High Councilman glared, his eyes flashing as he spoke. "She does not belong in our world."

"She's had no ill effects."

"Interesting." Edric drew out the word. "There must be further inquiry. She'll be admitted to the hospital for testing. Our priority is to make sure she's safe."

I didn't like the snide drip with his final word.

Callan clenched his fists. "Sir, please allow my wife and I to bring her back to our home. You know Deborah will give her the care she needs."

Edric considered this request. "Very well. I shall send for her soon. The wolf must accompany her."

Callan stiffened and glanced at the creature. "Yes, sir."

"Meeting adjourned." Edric disappeared within a plume of smoke.

As we left Council Hall, Callan remained tense. He shook his head as I opened my mouth to speak. "Not here."

I followed the pace Deborah and Callan set as we trudged silently through a bustling town, a stark contrast to the scene we had left behind at Council Hall.

I'd often gone with my parents to the edge of our town, but we never went to the heart of it. Everything we'd needed had been right outside at little roadside stands.

Here, people smiled and laughed as they went in and out of the busy shops opening up after the meeting.

"What's that?" I pointed to a singular building with space for maybe three people inside, stationed at the start of an overgrown path.

"That's a transport booth," Deborah stated.

Excitement bubbled through me. "Is anyone there? They could get me home."

Callan shook his head. "I'm sorry. Those transporters don't have that ability."

Were they trying to prevent me from leaving? I lowered my voice to mask the sudden anxiety flaring in my chest. "But Torren does?"

"That's something that can't be discussed in the open." Callan glanced behind him, his gaze landing on the wolf. "Or around *that*."

My breathing became shallow as I realized my only way home had been taken away from me.

We continued along the path, and I tried to memorize the way, to maybe come back later, but the twists and turns we took all the way to their house made me dizzy and disoriented.

Deborah hurried me inside while Callan led the wolf behind the house. Once the front door snapped shut, she threw her arms around me and held me close.

Tentatively, I patted her back. "Are you okay, Deborah?"

She pulled away and held me at arm's length. "We suspected last night—her eyes, his nose—but we didn't want to overwhelm you. Now that I know for sure, let me get a good look at you."

"What are you talking about?"

"We knew your parents. Your mother and I were best friends."

First Vision

Deborah busied herself in the kitchen and set a bowl of soup in front of me. Though it was reheated from the night before, the aroma of garlic and fresh basil made my mouth water.

I took a tentative bite, then, overcome by hunger, began shoveling it into my mouth.

Deborah chuckled. "I suppose everything is finally catching up to you." She slipped a book from the shelf behind her and placed it on the table, running her hand across the leather cover.

I pushed my bowl to the side when she slid the book toward me. "What's this?"

"It's a history book."

Images of the High Councilman's burning eyes when I told him I didn't know Torren filled my mind.

I shook my head and pushed the book back toward her. "I shouldn't know any of this." My eyes fell on a cluster of photographs as she opened to a page in the center. "I thought you said this was a history book."

"It is. *Our* history." She smiled as she ran her fingers across a photograph. "With the right gift, these can come alive."

Did she mean the photographs could come to life? The front door slammed and made me jump.

Callan's heavy steps echoed in the hall as he walked toward the kitchen.

I stared at his muddy boots.

"Where's the wolf?" Deborah asked, a bit of nervousness playing in her voice.

Callan brushed his hands down the sides of his jeans. "He's at the edge of our property. I secured him to a tree. They won't be able to spy from that distance."

"How can a wolf spy?"

Deborah responded. "Those creatures are genetically mutated to transmit everything they hear. This one seems different than the others, though. He acted more like a pet. I wonder if he's defective."

"We can't take any chances." Callan's deep voice was filled with conviction. "The fact that Edric insisted the wolf come with us means he's interested in you and will try to get as much information about you as he can."

"Why would he possibly be interested in me?"

"He knows you couldn't have had the elixir, and you haven't reacted like the other Outsiders." Callan began fixing himself a plate.

"Which means you belong here." Deborah rested her hand on my shoulder.

Did I belong here? Did everyone in Alterria get bossed around by invisible people? The corners of my lips rose. Without any good reason, I'd even taken the advice. "The bottle I had last night, where did I put it? Could that be the elixir?"

Callan stood from the table and left the room. He returned, twisting the container of dark-blue liquid I'd pulled from behind the shimmering barrier. "The elixir is green and has gooseberry seeds in it." He held the bottle out to me. "This isn't from Alterria."

"Cal," Deborah said sheepishly. "It is. Izzy and I invented it when we were twelve. We called it the Crystal Ball Potion. She must have taken the last of our store with her when she left."

He looked at his wife with awe. "You never cease to amaze me." He blew her a kiss, which she caught and held to her heart.

I smiled at their affection and then turned my attention to the bottle. I tilted my head and squinted at the dark liquid that danced within. It sparkled like the stars in the night sky.

In the light of day, I realized I had seen this before, when I was very small. Mom had tucked herself away into the cold, damp cellar at the back of our house. The walls were lined with cubbies and shelves, all filled with objects that seemed like ordinary household items but held a little bit of something that made them stand out as anything but ordinary. She had this same liquid in a tall pitcher and poured it into a crystal bowl.

I knew what to do. "Do you have a crystal bowl, something you might crush medicine or herbs in?"

Deborah's mouth curled up in a grin as she reached into the cupboard and took out a bowl nearly identical to the one Mom had used all those years ago.

I poured all the liquid into it and waited, but nothing happened. My shoulders slumped. "I'm sorry."

Deborah smiled. "Is there a reason you asked for that bowl in particular?"

"When I was little, I saw my mom pour this liquid into a dish similar to this one."

Deborah placed her hand on top of mine. "What happened when she did that?"

"I thought I'd imagined what happened next. A pale blue mist rose above it, and then people appeared inside the mist. Almost like a movie scene."

"Try to remember if she did anything before the scene appeared." Deborah said.

I closed my eyes, envisioning my mom pouring the sparkly blue liquid into the crystal bowl, and my thoughts transferred to the now-empty bottle in my hand. "Who was that set up for?" I didn't mean to speak my thoughts out loud.

"Good, Arisanna. We can see them." Deborah's voice reminded me of my mom's when I finally figured out fractions. "We can hear them, too. You're getting it."

My parents' voices surrounded me.

"Lucian, are you sure this is the right time?"

"She's ready, Izzy. She needs to know where she came from." Dad's deep voice echoed in the small room.

I opened my eyes and watched as a scene unfolded above the bowl.

My parents were in the clearing, setting up the picnic blanket. A soft howl sounded in the distance.

Mom glanced around nervously. "Lucian?"

Dad ran his hand down Mom's back. "It's far away. We hear them all the time. There's no reason to be nervous."

Mom removed the three bottles from a shoulder bag slung across her body and lined them up on the blanket. "I'm not sure I'm ready." She squeezed her eyes shut.

Dad wrapped her in a tight embrace and planted a kiss on her head. "But *she* is. We've seen Ari going in and out of these woods every day for the last five years. Most of the time, she comes out smiling."

"But last month..."

Dad sighed. "I know. I miss her happy smile."

"Do you think she got pulled into our world? What would they do to her if they discovered she's a Morganfire?"

White fog swirled at my parents' feet, and Dad's voice shook. "Izzy! Do something. If they find this..."

Mom nodded and grasped the pendant around her neck. She closed her eyes and whispered, "Ocultar." As she spoke the word, an incandescent wall surrounded the picnic area, and everything inside disappeared. The fog at their feet siphoned away from them. "No," she whispered. "Something's wrong. The concealment, it's shimmering."

"But the picnic is still covered. No one will see behind the shimmer."

The howling intensified, and Mom twisted around, searching for the source of the sound. "Lucian!"

Dad reached out his hand, and Mom's fingers curled around his. "It's getting closer, Iz. We have to go."

"But Lucian, the fog. What if it already took her?"

"She's a Morganfire. She is brave and strong, like her mother." He kissed her forehead, and they ran back toward our house.

The scene above the bowl faded away.

I gritted my teeth and brushed away an angry tear before it slipped down my cheek. "What were they hiding from me?"

Deborah and Callan looked at each other, seemingly at a loss for words.

"You're hiding something, too," I quietly accused.

Deborah turned to me, her eyes begging me not to push the subject. "All I can tell you, Arisanna, is that your parents weren't safe here, so they did what they had to do."

"And what was that?" I asked, my skepticism evident.

Deborah grasped both my hands in hers. "Isadora Morganfire and Lucian Lunagarde disappeared."

CHAPTER SIX

A WARNING

"Disappeared," I repeated, the word hanging between us. It tasted wrong on my tongue. "But they didn't," I said childishly. "They've been with me."

Deborah gave my hand a squeeze. "They brought us hope, especially Izzy. I can't tell you how hard the years have been since that day."

I offered her my napkin and the hint of a smile.

Deborah dabbed her tears, her wavering breath interrupted by three heavy thuds.

Callan massaged the back of his head and groaned before trailing dirt through the kitchen on his way to the front door.

Deborah rose and began to wash the dishes as I grabbed the broom leaning in the corner to clean the dirt he had left behind.

In less than a minute, he returned with Ronin in his wake.

"Arisanna, I'm Ronin. It's a pleasure to meet you." His handshake was firm, but an unnatural heaviness traveled through my body, then disappeared as quickly as I'd noticed it.

Before I could respond, he strode to the window and yanked the curtains closed. "We're being watched."

"I thought as much and made what accommodations I could," Callan said.

Ronin nodded once. "Even so, I hesitate to speak freely." He peeked through the drapes before turning to face us. "But I must deliver my message before I run."

"Run?" Deborah asked.

Ronin ignored her. "Please sit." His eyes lingered on the book still lying on the table.

The three of us exchanged glances, but we did as he said.

Ronin remained standing near the window. "This is heavy, but I need to prepare you—Torren is being devoured and lacks the strength to fight back. Recovery will be more difficult this time around."

"It's Celia's disappearance," Callan explained, sounding worn. "He continues to bear the full burden."

"We've never blamed him, Callan," Deborah said.

"He knows that, but it changes nothing for him."

"I've been given the honor," Ronin spat the word, "of examining the transmissions from the Glass House. I've witnessed his suffering through his memories. He feels responsible for more than just Celia." Ronin's eyes connected with mine again, but I quickly looked away. "Finally, there's the matter of our new visitor. The presence of yet another Outsider has caused great concern."

"I don't even know why I'm here. My parents never shared any of this world with me."

Ronin sighed. "When Isadora and Lucian disappeared, Council voted on whether or not to seek them out. Since Brayden—our brother—and Lucian were friends, Brayden lobbied hard to find him and bring him home. Other members of Council thought we were better off without your parents. Personally, I thought your mother and father were better off without us."

Ronin paused to pinch the bridge of his nose. "At the time, there had been a shift in leadership, and I couldn't afford to step on Council's toes. I felt pressure to prove my independence from

Brayden, as we were the first set of twins to be Council members, so I voted against him. Brayden hasn't forgiven me for that."

"Ronin," Callan interrupted. "You can't—"

Ronin held up his hand and continued. "When Celia went missing, Council voted again. I had nothing left to lose at that point. Everyone could be convinced that Izzy and Lucian left of their own accord, but what would happen to a Council who refused to search for a child? Still, they wanted to make it difficult. If you didn't follow their guidelines, you would visit the Glass House."

I still didn't know exactly what the Glass House was, but it sounded bad. My heart ached for Torren, though I barely knew him.

"Brayden argued the restrictions, but I'd been too weak to go against the High Councilman. He claimed concern for the safety of all, and he fooled nearly everyone." Ronin paused again.

A stream of questions rushed to my mind, but his pause was too brief for the words to leave my mouth.

"Callan and Torren received authorization to be part of all Council-approved searches because of their family connection. Council couldn't see a feasible way to deny them. Brayden and I were prohibited because of our positions. When Edric threw Torren into the Glass House for going on an unaccompanied search, Brayden walked away and hasn't spoken to any of us in years." Not breaking eye contact, he spoke in a low voice. "Arisanna, may I speak to you alone before I leave?"

I trailed behind him, and we stopped at the front door where we would be out of earshot. Running water from the kitchen further drowned our conversation.

Ronin closed the gap between us. "Your wolf has me a bit concerned. Wolves are only attached to specific people if they're trained to be, and yours isn't. While he yearns to protect you, he will betray you against his will."

Though I didn't understand his warning, I pursed my lips and nodded.

"I have one final message for you, Ari."

My heart dropped at the use of a nickname I had yet to share here.

"Remember, Torren is real." Ronin checked his watch, and his next words thundered through the cozy house. "I must go."

"Where?" Callan asked as he and Deborah joined us.

Ronin shook his head. "I'm not exactly sure, but there's a lead I need to follow." With a quick goodbye to Deborah and me, he strode out of the house.

Callan followed him.

Deborah's mouth formed a thin line. "Ronin has put himself in danger to warn us."

Callan returned inside, his face drawn. "Arisanna, would you mind checking on your wolf? I need to speak with Deborah alone for a moment."

He picked up where I left off with the broom while Deborah gave me a one-armed hug and shooed me out.

Knowing the fresh air would help clear my head, I walked around the back of the house.

The wolf had been secured to a tree on the opposite side of the yard, and he appeared content despite being bound by the chain.

"Hello," I said quietly, lowering myself beside him and stretching my legs.

He laid his head on my lap, and I stroked his fur, humming a lullaby my mother had taught me.

Several minutes passed before Deborah appeared beside me. "Callan is on his way to speak with Council now."

I looked up in alarm. "Is that safe?"

Deborah motioned for me to follow her.

I patted my wolf's head before stepping away.

His tongue hung out, and he rested his head on his paws.

Once we reached the door, Deborah continued. "He was summoned. It would be far more dangerous to ignore the request."

"Oh."

Rainless clouds drifted lazily in the sky while the birds chirped in the trees. They were oblivious to the darkness I felt creeping up on me.

CHAPTER SEVEN

PASSING CALM

"Hopefully this will cool the house a bit," Deborah said, pulling the curtains shut. She sat beside me on the overstuffed couch.

I squeezed my interlaced fingers against each other, trying to calm my jittery nerves. "Should Callan have been gone this long? It's been a full day."

"Council runs on their own time. Once, he waited at Council Hall an entire week before being seen." She placed her hand gently on top of mine and a wave of calm flowed through me. "Feel better?"

My anxiety had relaxed, and I found it easier to breathe. "Yeah. How did you do that?"

"It's my gift." Trembles ran through her body as they rolled out of my own.

"What do you mean by gift? Is it magic?"

"No. Not magic. Most Alterrians have one."

The door slammed open, startling us. We glanced up at a tall dark shadow that loomed in the doorway.

"Callan!" Deborah ran to greet her husband.

He wrapped his arms around her and pulled her close, kissing the top of her head.

With a pang of homesickness, I smiled. They reminded me of my parents, and I wondered if Mom and Dad would think to look for me here.

"What happened?" Deborah asked softly, leaning back without loosening her grip around Callan.

He glanced up, and his eyes connected with mine.

A million questions raced through my mind, each one of them making my palms sweat, but something inside told me to pay close attention.

"They want me to bring her. Tonight." He broke away from Deborah and sank into the spot beside me.

"Deborah, what could they possibly want me for?"

She was my mom's best friend, and she'd already brought me peace, but she simply shrugged and sat in the armchair to my other side. The way she fiddled with the hem of her shirt brought another round of questions, so I focused on Callan.

He took a deep breath. "There's more. Torren's been taken to the hospital. As long as he cooperates, he'll be able to come home. They brought up Ronin, too." He squeezed his fists and stood to pace the length of the living room.

"Callan?" Deborah's calm voice was full of concern. She placed her hand on his as he passed by. "What did they say?"

"Ronin voted against them. He was the *only* vote against them."

"Against what?" Deborah's voice raised.

"They're going to send Arisanna to the labyrinth."

Deborah brought her hands to her mouth, her eyes wide. "No. Not there."

I watched as they went back and forth. Though my lack of knowledge and Deborah's gift subdued me, adrenaline built up, bubbling within my veins. "What's going on?" The force with which my words left my mouth startled even me.

Deborah took a deep breath. "The labyrinth," her voice cracked. She cleared her throat and began again. "The labyrinth was once used as a training ground to help people from our world learn how to hone their gifts. More recently, Council used it to discover the gifts of our young. As the child works their way through…" She pursed her lips and swallowed. "Callan, we can't let them take her there."

"There's nothing we can do."

Involuntarily, I bounced my knee. It didn't do anything to relieve my nerves. "Why's it bad? If it's just meant to show gifts, I don't have any."

Deborah and Callan exchanged worried glances as he sat on the arm of her chair.

I dropped my shoulders. "What aren't you telling me? Please don't send me somewhere blind."

Deborah spoke, her tone reassuring. "You're a Morganfire *and* a Lunagarde. You have a gift. It just hasn't shown yet."

"The problem?" I squeaked.

Callan cleared his throat. "First, no known Alterrian has been born and raised on the Outside. For all we know, it could take ten years for your gift to fully activate. Second, Alterrian children have had two years to learn to use their gifts. Their specific gift activates the different challenges in the maze."

"But if I have no gift? What does *that* activate?"

Deborah leaned back in her chair and bit her lip. "That's what makes us nervous for you. It's said to drive the giftless mad, and most end up leaving the labyrinth unconscious in the arms of their parents. There's no cure, so the family leaves Alterria shortly after."

"You're nervous?" My voice squeaked. "I'm terrified!"

"Knowing your family, you shouldn't be worried. Still, the labyrinth will mess with your mind. Just remember, nothing is real in there." Deborah's smile was probably meant to reassure me, but Callan's hands were balled into fists and his jaw was set in a rigid line.

"I know there's something else," I challenged.

He nodded. "You come from two pure lines that both depend on other people's gifts."

I took a shaky breath. "And that's what puts me in danger?"

A sharp knocking interrupted the conversation.

I jumped to my feet. "They're here now?" I screeched. The shrillness sent shivers through me.

Deborah stood in front of me and grasped both my hands, her gift of Calm surging through my body. With a shudder she collapsed into the chair. "I hope that will last long enough to get you through the first couple of rooms." She beckoned me closer, and I crouched beside her.

Callan strode to the door as the banging became more incessant.

Her words poured out under her breath, "Don't let them break you. Remember, what you experience is not always real. We'll see you again soon. I promise."

The door flew open, crashing against the wall as a trio of men burst into the room.

"Where is he?" bellowed the largest of the three, as he strode closer until he stood nose to nose with Callan.

"I'm not sure of whom you speak." Callan wrinkled his eyebrows in confusion.

"Don't play me for a fool." The words reverberated around the room as a smaller man came in from behind the brutes, the largest retreating. Thomas, the lackey Torren had pointed out yesterday, patted the large wolf at his side. "If you won't tell me where he is, give me the girl."

Callan shook his head. "I was told to bring her tonight."

"High Councilman doesn't believe you will bring her. Especially with your brother going missing."

"Ronin?" Callan acted surprised.

"Torren," Thomas spat.

Deborah gasped, and I stood from my crouched position.

Thomas jerked his head toward me. "I'm taking her now."

"Don't do this," Callan growled. "Thomas, don't send her. Your little girl isn't much older. Would you put *her* in this position?"

"Don't bring my child into this," Thomas snarled, jerking his head toward Callan to pin him with a cutting glare.

Callan's voice lowered. "Arisanna didn't grow up in Alterria. You're signing her death sentence, and you know it."

Thomas didn't break my gaze as he responded. The way he stared at me sent shivers up my spine. "The High Councilman seems to think otherwise."

Black and white ribbons of smoke coiled up my body and swallowed me whole.

Thomas's glowering eyes and eerie smile remained visible for a moment, but then even those disappeared.

I was alone in the fog.

CHAPTER EIGHT

ENTER THE LABYRINTH

The smoky tendrils slithered away from my body, breaking into wisps before dissipating into the ground. From the dim light of the single hanging bulb, I saw only myself reflected in a mirror leaning against one of the stone walls.

I took in my surroundings. Adjacent to the wall with the mirror stood a heavy wooden door. As I crossed the room to go through it, the door got further away, so I spun around to go back the way I came. Then the mirror disappeared, and darkness bathed the wall behind it. I turned toward the door, but it too was gone.

My heart beat at a normal pace, but it thudded in my ears. Scared but calm, thanks to Deborah's gift. I took a deep breath and closed my eyes tight, afraid to let the ever-changing room drive me mad.

"Ari!" Kai's voice broke through the darkness as though he stood beside me. "Ari, come with me."

Upon opening my eyes, a vision of fireflies danced above Kai.

His steel gray stare drew me into the illusion, his outstretched hand so close, I could grasp it if I tried.

I smiled. Illusion or not, I desperately wanted to play along. After all, this was my favorite memory.

With his hand still extended, Kai approached me. "Come on. You don't want to miss this."

His smile made my heart skip a beat.

I reached toward him, the vision so real, his fingers warmed my palm and brought me peace.

He leaned in and whispered in my ear, breath brushing against my cheek. "Close your eyes."

I squeezed them tight, following him blindly. If the illusions here were all like this, I would never leave.

"Open." He grabbed both my hands and pulled me closer, my body matching the sway of his.

We were back in our meadow, and the river seemed to sparkle. Fireflies floated around us, and the forest creatures serenaded our moonlit dance.

He rested his cheek against mine and sang, "Dancing so close, beneath the sky so starry. Together forever, Kai and Ari."

With a sigh, I rested my head against his chest to discover our hearts beat in unison. I wished we could stay like this forever, but our time together never lasted long enough.

This moment was cut short as misty black and white fingers filled the forest floor and climbed up Kai's legs.

Heat scorched my cheeks, proving this wasn't part of my memories.

"Ari!" His voice filled with fear as he was forcefully dragged away. He reached out to me, and I ran to him, collapsing to my knees as our hands came together.

A tear ran down his cheek as he knelt and brushed a soft kiss on the back of my hand. "You have to let me go."

This couldn't be goodbye.

"No, I already lost you once." I lowered my head and brought our interlaced hands to my heart. "You can't leave me again."

His voice shook as he turned away from me. "I don't love you anymore."

The most painful words I'd ever heard spoken stabbed me in the heart for a second time, and I dropped his hand before the black and white fog wrapped around my ankles.

As the tentacles of fog climbed his body in a separate lasso, my palms began to burn.

I pressed them against the cool stone wall, attempting to soothe the searing heat. It didn't help. The burning blazed across my hands as a primal roar burst from my chest.

"Kai! Don't leave me!" The fog yanked my feet from beneath me, and I landed on my elbows, clawing at the dirt-packed floor as I slid across the ground.

The moment the fog swallowed Kai whole, the misty fingers that had wrapped around me disappeared.

I squeezed my eyes shut, trying to shift the illusion back to the beginning. "Go back. Please, go back." My pleading fell flat in the vast empty space. The more I fought my anguish, the more the heat grew around me.

The faint sound of his voice echoed in my head. "I'm so sorry."

Tears slipped down my cheeks as I opened my eyes.

The room, composed of four metal walls, had shrunk and was completely engulfed in flames. The heat smacked against me and intensified.

My head clamored, and my rapid heartbeat rang in my ears. I was going to die here.

Surrounding me on all sides, the flames licked the walls of the narrow room, like a greasy piece of meat on the grill. I could hear the echoes of Kai's voice from my memory calling out to me. Close, but still so far away.

"Kai," I whimpered, "help me!"

Smoke filled the room, forcing me to cough with every breath. The heat became unbearable. The flames seemed to grow with my fear, closing in on me as they danced around the room. Sweat dripped down my back as I twirled, searching for an exit.

"Kai!" I cried out, my tears drying as they hit my cheeks.

Arisanna. Calm down. I know you're afraid, but I need you to trust me.

"Who are you?"

That will be revealed in time, but for now, I need you to listen.

Something about her soft voice reminded me of home.

Close your eyes. Take a deep breath, and slowly count backward from ten.

"10...9...8...7...6..." Was it in my head, or was the room cooling down?

Keep counting, and don't open your eyes.

"5...4...3...2...1."

You did it.

"It's okay." A deep, comforting voice spoke in my ear. "The flames are gone now."

I flinched as strong arms wrapped around my waist, and someone rested their chin on my shoulder. I turned to face the person behind me.

"I'm so happy you're safe." Torren's smile reminded me of Kai's, and my heart ached.

He wasn't Kai.

Kai wasn't here, only illusions of him toying with my heart and mind.

I wriggled from Torren's grasp. "You moved us with fog yesterday. Did you bring me here? To Alterria?"

He shook his head vehemently. "I know what happens to Outsiders who come here. I never would have put you in danger. Though had I known..."

Jerking back an inch, I glared at him. "Why would you care? We just met."

Sadness flashed in his eyes. "Am I really that different?"

I let out an exasperated sigh. "They warned me things would mess with my head, but I don't understand why you're here. I don't even know you."

He twisted a silver ring on his right pointer. A dome surrounded us, a barrier, glimmering much like the one I had seen the night I arrived in Alterria.

"Ari. Look at me."

He'd called me Ari when we met, too. Only my friends called me by that name, and I only had one friend.

I stepped closer to really look at him for the first time. Struggling to fight off the terrible mind tricks I'd been warned about, my stomach turned.

He squeezed his eyes shut, and as he did, his cheeks began to plump. His brown hair took on a darker hue, nearly black. A faint scar appeared on his lips. When he opened his eyes, the brilliant emerald green had been replaced by a steel gray to rival Callan's.

"Kai?" I gasped and shook my head as Torren's face quickly reappeared.

How many more illusions were they going to throw at me? Did Torren work for Council? How did they know about Kai?

Dizziness overtook me as my thoughts swirled.

Torren rested his palm on my shoulder. "Are you okay?"

My jaw went slack as he came back into focus. "How did you do that?"

"The dome?" His voice had a tone of uncertainty and apprehension.

I shrugged. "Well, that, too. But how…you were Kai."

He took a hesitant breath.

"You know what? No. Don't answer that. Why does it matter, anyway? They already locked me in this maze of torture. You're nothing but an illusion meant to torment me. Don't bother. I'm not revealing any secrets." I stepped back.

"I'm *not* an illusion," he said sadly.

I wanted to believe him, but how could I? "The High Councilman accused me of knowing you. Perhaps that's why they're throwing your two faces together."

"Ari, it's me. I'm real."

Ronin's final message resurfaced. Had it been a ruse he planned with Torren to mess with my mind? "Kai never played tricks on me. Kai loved me...for a while."

Torren dug the tip of his boot into the ground. "I never stopped loving you, Ari. I had to leave to protect you. They called off Celia's search and watched travel extremely close. Especially between worlds. Especially when I traveled."

"But why?"

"They knew I blamed myself for her disappearance. That I searched for her every chance I got. They didn't know I had no hope and had given up. Until I found something amazing. Something that kept drawing me back."

Our eyes connected, and my heart skipped a beat.

"Someone I couldn't stay away from." He dropped his eyes to the ground.

Was he ashamed of what he'd done to me as Kai, or was he trying to mislead me? I couldn't tell fact from fiction in this place.

I stared at the dome surrounding us. The way it shimmered brought me back to the concealment in the clearing. "Hey," I said sharply, "you mentioned a shimmering light when you were talking to Callan before you got mad at me."

He sighed and looked up. "I went back to the woods that night to find you. To explain why I left. Dad's search was the first cover I had since…"

My heart sank. Since he left me.

"When I heard voices, I thought you might be nearby. Guess I was right about that, but it didn't matter. The first howl sent my mind into a panic, and I couldn't stop my fog. Before it took me away, the shimmering light caught my attention, but it was too late. I never found out what it was."

Electricity raced through me as he wrapped his hand around mine.

"I never wanted to leave you, but I didn't know how to stay. By going back, I made everything worse. I wasn't mad at you yesterday. I was mad at myself. It's my fault you're here. I keep hurting the people I love. I was supposed to keep you safe."

I waved, indicating the dome he'd created. "Is that what you're doing now?"

He let out a long breath and tapped the ring on his finger, the same ring I'd seen Kai wearing since I met him. "My brother, Brayden, gave this to me before he left us. It represents his gift. He told me it would give me cover and fool anyone watching me."

"Why would you need to hide like that?"

He shrugged as he rubbed the silver band. "I had two brothers on Council. They told me my gift was special and that if Council ever found out *how* special, I'd be invaluable to them." He glanced around nervously. "Ari, I know you're angry with me and you have every right to be. I promise we'll discuss what happened in depth, but this is not the place. The illusions may start off with a moonlit dance, but once the heartache breaks through, it will feed on that and amplify it. This place thrives on negativity. The dome will protect us but not for long."

I glared at him. His sudden shift from explanation to warning made me uneasy. "And how do I know you're telling me the truth? That this dome isn't just another trick to make me lower my guard? How do I know you aren't working for *them*?" I took a shaky breath, and my lip quivered. "And how did you know Kai's face? What's your gift? Deceit?"

"I would *never* work for Council," he spat. The corners of his mouth twitched downward as he lowered his voice. "That face is a part of me, but that's all it is. A face."

"How am I supposed to believe *that*?"

He looked at me, his eyes pleading. "Ari, I would never intentionally hurt you."

I scoffed and folded my arms across my chest. "You *intentionally* lied. You didn't think that would hurt?"

He reached toward me, then second-guessed himself. His voice, deep and hushed, filled with remorse. "I don't know what I would do if anything happened to you. Everything I've done was to protect you." His pain—pain I'd seen in Kai's eyes but never understood—touched my heart.

I swallowed back a lump and reached out to him. "Kai..."

Torren. His name is Torren.

I dropped my hand at the sound of her voice.

Rely on him. He's real and wants to help you.

My heart raced. "Torren, why did they send me here?"

He cocked his head to the side and betrayed the hint of a smile. "They're trying to discover what you're capable of."

"I don't have any gifts. I wasn't born here."

Torren gestured to the torched walls.

My eyebrows jumped up my forehead. "Are you telling me I caused that fire?"

"Almost certain of it. I can't control flames."

"And you're really here with me? I'm not on my own?"

He's real, Arisanna. See for yourself.

He reached out, and I grabbed his hand.

I squeezed, and he squeezed back. As the voice and Ronin had assured me, he was real. "I was alone."

He furrowed his eyebrows. "You weren't alone. I've been here the whole time."

My mind flickered to the dance and the confusion that overcame me when my illusion felt so real. "How did you find me?"

"I had no idea where you were. Last I remember, I was in the hospital recovering from the Glass House."

"Then how are you here?"

He shrugged. "My guess is Council sent me."

"Okay," I drew out the word. Had Ronin known that was the plan? "Why would they do that?"

"Most of the time, Council does things for their own selfish reasons. Since I just left the Glass House, I'm guessing I'm a pawn in their game to somehow get more from you." He took a deep breath. "I think they're trying to exploit you. I'll try my hardest to make sure they don't."

"Exploit me? In what way?"

"I'm not sure, but why do you think you're here? You're the first Outsider to show no signs of Alterria affecting you."

"So that makes them believe I belong here."

"It's more than that. You're an enigma, and they want to take advantage of you in any way they can."

"They know my parents were special, which means I must be different."

Torren gave one quick nod.

The silence that fell between us hung in the air until he cleared his throat and smirked. "Why'd you call me Torren?"

My cheeks burned. "What do you mean?"

"You called me Kai before and then switched to Torren."

"That's your name, isn't it?" I raised my eyebrow and cocked my head, but the corners of my mouth twitched.

He mimicked my movements.

I had something I *needed* to tell—even if it was simply to reassure myself that I still had a grip on reality—and he knew it. Like always, I couldn't hide the giveaway twitch. "Don't laugh."

He straightened up and drew an "x" over his heart, exactly like Kai did whenever I had something important to tell him. Underneath it all, Torren really was Kai, and I trusted Kai with everything.

I closed my eyes and sucked in as much air as my lungs could handle. Exhaling slowly, I shared the one thing that had brought me both peace and anxiety over the past several days. "Since I got swept up in the fog, I've been hearing a girl's voice. She seems to be guiding me. Protecting me."

Torren grasped my hands and looked into my eyes, but he remained silent, his face devoid of expression.

I pulled my hands away. "Council's right. I am different. And now *you* think I'm crazy."

"Not in the slightest."

"Is it… an Alterrian thing?"

"Voices? No." He leaned in and spoke confidentially. "I've heard a voice before, too, though. A man's. The day Celia disappeared."

"Were you afraid of it?"

"No. For some reason, I felt comfort."

I swallowed the knot in my throat. "Did you believe you could trust him?"

Torren nodded.

"Is it bad I keep hearing her? Is this what happened to the girl Deborah visits in the hospital?"

"There has to be a reason you're hearing a voice, but you're not going to end up like that girl."

My chin quivered. "How can you be sure?"

Torren leaned in and pressed a kiss to my forehead. "Because you do belong here, and now even I'm intrigued about how powerful you truly are."

"Powerful?"

"Most kids who start to show their gifts have control issues for the first two years. You didn't know you had a gift, yet you filled a room with flames and—just as quickly—made them disappear." He smiled. "I've never seen him use it, but apparently, Dad has the gift of Flame. Maybe you got it from him."

"Are you saying I stole it?" I worried aloud.

"No. There are certain gifts that can copy, but we were taught those gifts disappeared from Alterria a couple of decades ago. I don't know what your gift is, but I know it's rare."

I let everything Torren said sink in. "So, I *do* belong here?" My whispered words seemed to spin around the dome's intimate space until my thoughts circled back to the fog that broke us apart. "You think Council put you here as some kind of attempt at espionage? What happens when they find you helping me?"

"We can deal with that when the time comes. They will likely delight in my suffering as well. All I know is I'm not leaving your side if I can help it." He lowered his voice as he dropped his hand to his side. "The barrier is fading."

"Do we need to hide that we know each other?" I was afraid of his answer.

He pursed his lips and shook his head. "They already know."

"What does that mean for us?"

"Things are going to get a little harder, but I'll try my best to protect you."

The barrier dissolved, and Torren stood facing me.

I reached out for him, and he laced his fingers with mine.

"Are you ready for this?"

A smile, frown, and knit eyebrows all smashed together on my face. "Nope."

He gazed deep into my eyes. "It's just the two of us in here. Just you and me. Together, we can handle anything."

Chapter Nine

The Trials

We stepped lightly through the long corridors, exhaling in relief around every corner, then tensing up again at the next bend. We exchanged glances every few minutes, one of us seeming to ask, "When will the next trial begin?" and the other answering, "I don't know."

After the fourth or fifth pause, Torren turned to face me. "Ari, you're going to be okay." He ran his fingertips over my cheek, and the tenseness gave way to butterflies.

My heart and my head warred with each other. How could he be so different, yet the same all at once? I met his gaze and became lost in his emerald green eyes. Though a different hue from the steel gray I was used to, they were still the same eyes I had seen so often throughout the last five years.

He brushed my hair behind my ear. "Trust me."

"I do," I whispered, thrilled to find that I meant it. "I'd follow you anywhere."

"You would?" he leaned away from me, and the corner of his mouth flicked up. "Would you follow me here?" He stepped back. "Or here?" Another step.

Memories of being silly together rushed in. I moved toward him as he continued walking backward. "Yes, Torren." I giggled. "I'll follow you."

"Would you stay by my side?" he asked, wiggling his eyebrows at me and pivoting around to walk next to me again.

"Yes," I said, feeling at ease.

"What about now?" he asked, grabbing my hand and beginning to skip-walk. I had no choice but to join him.

"Even now," I said, laughing.

"What if I closed my eyes?"

"Torren, no!" I laughed. He had to be teasing, but I tugged him to a stop in case he wasn't. "You might run into something."

He uncurled his fingers from mine, and then closed his eyes searching the air for obstacles. He patted my head, my face, and my shoulder.

Joy bubbled through me when he grabbed me by the waist and spun me around.

"Oh, no," he said, "I've run into something, and now I'm falling." He dramatically pulled me to the ground and drew me into his lap, his arms still around me. As our laughter died down, he rested his chin on my shoulder. "Wasn't the worst thing that could happen in here."

"No," I said, "definitely not the worst thing." For a moment, I doubted he had ever walked away from me.

"Why did you come here?"

My heart clenched, and my grin vanished. Was his erratic behavior a trick of the labyrinth? I decided to guard my heart and shrugged. "They kind of forced me in here."

Torren gave me a little push off his lap and then helped me to my feet. "We'd better keep walking," he said quietly. "How did you get *here*? To Alterria."

Anxiety overwhelmed me with his sudden mood change so I started talking for no other reason than to fill the void. "I got forced into Alterria. I was in the woods, same as I used to be nearly every day until recently. It hasn't exactly been my favorite place lately, even though it used to be."

Torren's hand tensed in mine as he dragged in a deep breath.

My words spilled out of their own accord. "Then I heard the wolves. I followed their calls but stumbled upon a picnic instead. There was something wrong with it, something surrounding it. And then the fog came."

The memory wove itself through me, and climbing, clawing fog filled my mind and the floor at my feet.

My eyes widened as I tried to break free from the fog, but the smoky tendrils were still there, still climbing. "What's happening?" I tried to kick the fog away, shoving at the misty blanket now up to my knees, to no avail.

"Ari, stop. Look at me." He grasped my arms above my elbows. The sharpness in his voice eased to a gentle lull. "Look in my eyes and tell me about your happiest memory."

As I focused on his eyes, my racing heart slowed. I slid my hands behind his back, and he pulled me close. "My happiest memory is when I met Kai."

I'd been searching for the girl like I had every day since I'd seen her a year before. And like every other day I'd searched, the woods held their secrets. It was the day after my thirteenth birthday, and eventually, the river called out to me. I saw myself leaning back, my elbows on the narrow strip of sandy beach. I could practically feel the cool, refreshing water washing over my toes. I heard branches snapping behind me, which scared me at first, but when I turned around, I met my best friend.

The memory of Kai walking through the trees pushed away the memory of my transport into this world, and the fog dissipated. My heart raced.

Torren loosened his hold and stared at me, his eyes wide. "That fog wasn't mine. I think *you* did that."

"I don't understand what's going on here." My voice reverberated off the walls.

He pressed a finger to my lips. His eyes flicked upwards pointing out a small camera. "They're watching. They can't hear too well, unless we're loud. Or still for too long."

I lowered my voice in response. "How can I make fire and fog? None of this makes sense."

"It does, because you *do* belong here." The way he gazed into my eyes made me believe him.

The floor was clear of fog, but my mind was a different story.

The warmth of his gentle kiss on my forehead brought back old memories, and I wished we could remain in that moment.

"We need to keep moving." Torren's fingers once again wrapped around mine, and I brushed my thumb along the back of his hand. As we left yet another corridor behind, he kept throwing me glances but didn't speak.

I cleared my throat. "What about you? What's something you've never shared?"

He hesitated for a moment, but then in a low, mechanical voice, he surprised me. "I'm the reason my niece is missing. It all started on her tenth birthday, the year our gifts tend to reveal themselves."

"You were a kid. In what way could you be responsible?"

"I'm a transporter. That fog you saw moves people from place to place. Not many transporters can move other people, and the ten percent that can are either in Council or on their payroll. The trick I played on Celia proved I could move others, too."

"What kind of trick?"

"I created a fog, teasing her. When she walked into it, she disappeared. She was only gone a few minutes, but when she returned, she rambled on about a blue light."

I squeezed his hand, hoping to send him comfort.

Torren's jaw tensed, and he stared straight ahead. He let go of me and massaged the back of his neck. "After that trip, she kept begging me to take her back to that place. When she was twelve, I gave in. It was my gift to her, but she never returned."

Then his words rang in my ears. He *was* the ten percent. Did he know the stakes, or was he part of their game? "So you *do* work for Council."

He leaned close to whisper in my ear, "I can't share any more about my gift right now." He gave me a light squeeze and shook his head, acknowledging that he had an audience. "They don't recruit until sixteen, and by that time, we were all concentrating on finding Celia."

"How long have you been searching for her?"

"Six years."

My heart stopped. I met Kai five years ago.

He came to my woods searching for Celia, just like me.

All this time, Celia's disappearance had brought us together—and I was grateful. A pang of guilt tightened my chest, but I shook it away and placed my hand on his. "It's not your fault." I bit on my lower lip as I debated whether I should tell Torren I'd been looking for her too.

"We need to flip the negativity. Tell me about your friends. Who were the people lucky enough to know such a remarkable girl?"

"How quickly you forget my multitude of friends." I teased, though my heart was heavy. "Especially this one friend in particular."

"Ah, the elusive best friend. What was he like? Super handsome, I'm sure, though not as handsome as I am."

Even though his smile didn't reach his eyes—proof of the effort he made to put himself into a happy place—I laughed.

I laughed harder when he wriggled his eyebrows. "*Very* handsome."

At the turn of another bend in the maze, I slammed into a wall of contempt I couldn't fight off. "Unfortunately, I lost him. Though, I guess he never really existed, did he?"

Torren paused a moment before catching back up to my side. "Arisanna, I'm…" On a soft exhale, I could make out a single word. "Sorry."

The slump in his shoulders and dip of his chin when he apologized reminded me of the guilt I'd heard when he told me about Celia.

"Why did you never mention Celia?"

Torren froze in his tracks and stared at his shoes. "I came to the woods to escape my guilt. And in doing that, I met you. You gave me the opportunity to be someone other than the boy who made his niece disappear. I didn't want to ruin what we were building."

The truth behind the lie showed his vulnerability, but he still lied. My heart fluttered and ached all at once. Anger boiled uncontrollably in my veins and startled me. The force in this part of the labyrinth was too strong—or I was too weak. I couldn't fight the way it affected me.

I had to escape.

Grabbing his hand, I ran. When we hit the next bend, the force lifted, and I stopped short, causing him to stumble into me. I took a quick breath and planted a kiss on his cheek before wrapping my arms around his neck.

He buried his face in my hair. "We are severely failing at keeping this adventure lighthearted."

Torren kept me focused in here, but those twelve-year-olds didn't have a good luck charm like this. They had to navigate this nightmare on their own. How did fear not swallow them whole? Or did it? Is that what happened to Torren?

I strained to hear something in the distance. "Shh. Do you hear that?"

He released me and stepped back. "I don't hear—oh."

Wolves. The howling intensified, coming from every direction. We were surrounded.

Torren glanced back at me and screamed. "No! I won't let them get you."

Before I could react, a cloud enveloped me, then disappeared as soon as it deposited me in an alcove, alone.

"Torren?" His name broke apart before leaving my throat. I tried again, fighting back the fear that made speaking difficult. "Torren!"

"Ari!" His voice volleyed around outside an opening to my left.

I ran through it and tried his name again.

"Stay where you are," he yelled. "Let's play a game. Pretend we're hiding in the woods, like we used to."

Though my heart thudded in an indistinguishable pattern, my lips curled into a smile. "Marco," I called.

Footsteps echoed in the cavern, and I couldn't tell which direction they were coming from.

"Polo," he responded a few seconds later. His footsteps halted.

"Marco."

I waited for his response, but it never came.

Arms wrapped around my waist and a chin rested on my shoulder. The voice in my ear was unrecognizable. "Polo."

I twisted out of the hold and came face to face with an old man, a scar running from cheek to chin. I wriggled from his grasp and stepped away.

A smile slid across his face revealing a mouthful of snaggled, yellow teeth. His voice, as ragged as his clothes, rose above the howls that filled every hollow in the maze. "Run."

The breath caught in my throat, and I spun around to put distance between us.

Where did Torren go?

Before I could call out for him, a snarling laugh echoed around me, filling the gaps between the howls. I ducked into a room on my left. Dim light filtered through pebble-sized holes spattering the ceiling, pinpricks of light pointing at the archways that speckled the walls that stretched into the darkness.

I pressed my palm against the solid wall. If only I could find a safe space.

Behind my fingers, a gap formed, and a soft golden glow beckoned me. Within seconds, I managed to squeeze through the gap in the wall, ending up in a brightly lit room.

This is a safe space, Arisanna. You may speak freely, but you don't have much time. She spoke through the relative silence.

"Where am I?"

This cavern has been lost for many years, all but forgotten. Look around.

The walls were covered in markings that I began to trace with my fingertips, and I smiled. "These symbols are familiar."

My mom had shared a piece of her world with me after all.

Whispering, my smile grew as each line I translated revealed the words of the lullaby my mother sang to me as a child, though I'd never heard the third verse.

Arisanna, I can't hold this space open much longer. You must go back into the labyrinth.

I inhaled sharply with the warning and pictured Deborah, the calmness she had transferred to me earlier filling me once more. I stepped back into the room of caverns.

The howling again filled the air, not sounding any closer than before, as though time had stood still.

Behind me, the passage to my sanctuary had disappeared. Shivers traveled up my spine as the darkness engulfed me. I tucked into a crevice along the wall, concealing myself even more.

Footsteps echoed nearby as the snarly laughter entered the room.

"Ari." The gravelly voice made my heart claw its way up my throat.

He knew my name.

Deciding to use the darkness to my advantage, I stepped out of the hole to dash past him. The attempt was futile.

He caught my arm and pulled me into him, my back against his chest. "Ari. Stop."

The man now sounded exactly like Torren. "I'm trying to protect you. Please don't run."

I swallowed hard against the knot forming in my throat as I struggled to break free. "It's a trick. You aren't Torren."

"It *is* me." He loosened his hold, and I took a step away.

My heart paused. Was this another twisted illusion? How many faces could one person have? I fell to my hands and knees, causing a cloud of dirt to blow into my nose and mouth. I coughed violently.

The man took my hand and pulled me to my feet, and the labyrinth's illusion broke.

Torren's face shifted back into his own, and he wrapped his strong arms around me.

"Torren," I whispered, melting against his chest. "I don't know how much more of this I can handle."

The howling dissipated.

Sadness filled his eyes. He brushed my hair behind my ear before scooping me into his arms.

Cradled against him, my tears fell unchecked. I had reached my limit.

He walked out of the cavern and set me down lightly.

I reached out to lace our fingers together as we stepped around the next corner.

A chill spread through the air as the space around us filled with a stoic, hollow voice. "We found Celia. You must go now, or she will be lost forever."

The labyrinth had turned its attack on him.

I shook my head furiously as desperation crossed his face, and I reminded him,. "It's not real."

A golden orb dipped into the cavern in front of us.

"Ceely?" Torren's voice cracked as he took off after the illusion.

"Torren!" I chased after him. Maybe I could help him like he helped me.

"Where did you go, Ceely?" The orb disappeared, and he dropped to his knees, his face buried in his hands.

As I stepped closer to him, the floor disappeared under pillows of fog. "Torren, look at me."

He looked up and reached out his hand.

We grasped onto each other, but black ribbons intertwined with the white tendrils that continued to swirl and billow around Torren.

"What's happening?" His eyes widened as he struggled against the misty chains that dragged him away. "This isn't me!"

Despite fighting to keep hold of him, I stumbled away like an invisible magnet forced us apart.

"Torren!" My panic rose.

The smoke swallowed him up and then evaporated, leaving no trace of him behind.

I found myself on my knees again, sobbing into my dusty hands. "You said you wouldn't leave. You lied." My heart shattered.

A large palm warmed the space between my shoulder blades. "There now, child." Edric's voice brought on an intense queasiness.

"Why are you doing this to me?" I refused to meet his eyes.

"I have done nothing, child. The labyrinth exploited your weakness. Not me."

My weakness. Was Kai...Torren my weakness? Did Edric intentionally use him to make the labyrinth work better?

Not wanting to give him anything else to use against me, I pressed my fist against my heart, trying to hold back my tears.

"You are upset over the boy. The one you just met?"

Sobs tore through me once more as confusion settled with his words. I hadn't just met Torren, and according to him, Council knew that.

"I have seen the connection you believe you shared with the boy. You should be aware, though, you will always be second best with him," he hissed into my ear. "You were nothing more than a distraction. Look how easy it was for him to leave you when he believed he could bring her home."

I straightened my back and wiped muddy tears from my cheeks. "He yelled for it to stop. Said it wasn't him."

"A fantastic actor, no doubt. You see, the fog is a piece of his power. He can transport himself anywhere by simply picturing it. There are many like him."

"He chose to leave?" I refused to cry anymore tears, but Torren had told me himself of his gift. I was heartbroken, yes, but also quite angry. Angry with him and myself. How could I have trusted him so easily? I looked at Edric.

His smile made me shudder. "Council has voted to allow you to join us. We are all impressed with your strength and resilience through this labyrinth. We have a sudden vacancy that needs to be filled." The way his lip twitched as he said vacancy made me nervous.

"I can't do that. I don't belong here."

"Lucian Lunagarde."

I swallowed the lump that formed in my throat. Why did everyone keep throwing my parents' names at me?

Edric smirked. "Son of Cyran Lunagarde. Your father and his family before him worked alongside us. You belong. Your grandfather would be especially proud to see you follow in his footsteps. With the blood that runs through your veins, you are in a prime position to someday become High Councilor."

I didn't know anything about my past, and I certainly had no interest in becoming a High Councilor. I stood and brushed off my knees. "If it's all the same, I'd like to go home."

"Yes, home. Do you know the way?" An edge of eagerness crept into his voice.

"I don't. Could you take me back to Deborah and Callan?"

"If you believe they wouldn't give you up just as quickly as Torren did to get their Celia back, you are sadly mistaken."

My shoulders slumped, and I dropped my head.

"You have no one here for you. Once you join Council, you are family. You'll have the opportunity to learn everything your parents kept from you about Alterria." His bony fingers curled around my shoulder. "Come with me."

I followed him out of the labyrinth, down winding trails until we eventually reached the river.

He pointed to an old bridge a short way down the path. "That bridge is where our two worlds meet. If you ever change your mind and decide you want to try to find your way home, this is the only way back." Smoke materialized behind Edric.

For a moment, my heart soared believing Torren had come back for me. Instead, Thomas stepped out from mingling ribbons of black and white fog, a large wolf at his side.

Edric placed his hand on my shoulder, and I flinched at his touch. "No need to fear, child. All Council members travel with a wolf at their side. They keep us informed."

"Sir," Thomas interrupted, "he tried to transport to the other side, but we intercepted him."

Edric nodded. "Where is he now?"

"Back in the Glass House."

A chill spread over my body with those words, freezing me in place.

The smile that snaked across Edric's face made my stomach drop. "Want to see what the Glass House does?"

He didn't wait for an answer before turning to the small man. "Thomas, transport us to the Observatory."

Confusion

Black and white fog engulfed Edric and me, and as it slid back down into nothing, we were left standing in a wide room with a large glass window making up an entire wall.

"What is this place?" I turned in a circle, taking in the room.

"The Glass House Observatory. We can watch the transmissions from up here." Edric's voice boomed as he stood in the center of the room, a control panel in front of him. "Look for yourself."

I walked up to the window. A soft click filled the room with sounds of nature. Where I'd expected to find stony walls in the cavern below us, moving pictures filled the space. A gentle breeze tickled the leaves upon the trees. The sun peeked out from behind a cloud, and the song of birds flying overhead filled the air.

On the edge of the single chair in the room, Torren struggled without success to remove the iron bracelets that now adorned his wrists. "Let me out!"

Curious as to why he wasn't trying to leave if he wanted to so desperately, I glanced toward the door where two wolves sat guard.

"I need to help her. She's going to think I left her. Please. Please…" His cries faded as the images on the wall shifted, and my eyes were drawn to the girl with the golden hair dancing across the wall. They weren't merely moving pictures…they were memories.

"Uncle Torren?" The girl froze as a shadow passed over her. "Where are you going?"

Torren's voice floated in, young and laced with annoyance. "Ceely. I've told you before. I'm two months older than you. It's weird when you call me Uncle."

"Why can we hear Torren in these movies but can't see him?" I pressed my fingers against the glass.

"The Glass House draws out the memories that have the strongest emotions attached to them. You're seeing things the way he did." The smile on Edric's face never faltered.

"Does it display the strongest emotions first?"

"No, the memories are chronological."

None of this made sense. "How are we able to see *his* memories?"

"The Glass House was built from stone in the caverns that have that unique ability. You experienced some of that in the labyrinth."

I flinched in disgust. "Why would you put someone through this torture?"

"You ask too many questions."

"But where are you going?" Celia asked.

"To my thinking place. I need to be alone." He plucked a stone from the riverbed and tossed it into the thick tree line.

"Wait! Dad said we shouldn't be separated."

He looked back as he ran ahead and ducked behind the trees. "You'll have to catch me, won't you?"

Celia slipped when she ran toward him. As

she regained her footing, he sent out fingers of fog that wrapped around her body. She tried to run away, but it was too late.

Torren ran toward the spot she had just stood, and smoky whiteness surrounded him. When it faded away, he stood in the middle of a clearing. "Ceely?" The pounding of his heart flooded the room each time the forest swallowed her name. "Celia!"

Another cloud wrapped around him and transported him into a different clearing where he called out to no avail. When yet another cloud rolled up and then disappeared, the clearing where *I* had first seen Celia came into view.

She stumbled into his arms, excitement radiating from her. "Torren, do it again. Please, make the light come back!"

Not wanting to intrude, I tore my eyes from the visions. Torren's head fell back against his seat, but the walls still echoed his memories.

A shift drew me back to his story.

"Why won't you send me back, Torren?" Celia asked him.

"I don't want to send you back, Ceely. We aren't supposed to separate."

"Come with me then."

"Maybe tomorrow."

"You always say that." She dropped to the

ground, arms folded across her chest.

Another shift. Torren gripped the chair.

Celia paced her bedroom. "I'm scared to go into the labyrinth, Torren. I haven't figured out my gift."

"Maybe the Council will help you at your twelfth-year ceremony this evening."

"I hope so." She stopped pacing and stood in front of him. "Now will you take me back?"

"I'll be in so much trouble if anyone finds out I let you go the first time, Ceely."

"I know." Her eyes filled with tears.

"This is the only rule you've ever asked me to break. Why's this so important to you?"

"It's calling me. I can't stop thinking about it."

He let the request hang for a few moments. "Fine, but we'll have to be quick. I'll really be in for it if you're late."

She clasped her hands in front of her heart. "Oh, thank you!"

With a flick of his hand, his gift awoke. Wispy strands of smoke lifted from the ground, growing thicker and faster as they rose, dancing around them.

Celia's joy spilled out in laughter. "This is it!" She held her arms out wide as if embracing the woods that now surrounded them.

"We'd better go back," Torren said, looking over his shoulder.

"I haven't shown you the best part." She let her arms fall to her sides.

"Something doesn't feel right. Let's try again another time."

Celia sighed but didn't argue.

Torren reached for her as the fog swirled.

She grabbed his hand, but their fingers slipped apart.

The fog grew thick and engulfed him alone. "Stop!" he cried.

"Torren! Torren!" Celia's calls faded as she disappeared from view.

He stood by the river. Alone.

Another soft click made my ears ring with the sudden silence. The scene shifted again, and my face appeared on the wall.

My heart dropped. That's how they knew.

Drawn into this memory of us, I saw myself through his eyes as I lay beside him in our meadow. Briefly, happiness replaced the sinking feeling.

The picture shifted to a thick line of trees across the river. My woods.

I heard a soft click and then recognized Ronin's deep timbre.

"You know that Council is calling for an end to the searches."

Torren looked at his brother. "Okay. And you're telling me this why?"

"Torren," he said as he sat, "I know you have not been searching for her. I have seen the look on your face when you come home." He smiled. "You are in love."

Torren focused on his hands as he plucked at the blades of grass.

"I know where you go, Torren."

"I don't understand the correlation of me being in love and Council ending searches." He crossed his arms and took on a mocking tone. "I'm a big boy now. I can make grown-up choices."

"You will be watched. She will be in danger if you continue to visit her."

"Why would Council care who I spend my time with?"

"There is no easy way to help you understand—"

"Understand that you want me to abandon Ari the way Brayden abandoned us? With no reason, just saying it's to keep us all safe."

Ronin flinched before continuing. "It *was* for your safety."

"Don't act like you haven't been as angry with him as the rest of us. Even more. He's your twin, and he left you to deal with Edric's Council alone."

Ronin closed his eyes and responded with a grunt. "Council disapproves of cross-world relationships. They will use her to hurt you."

"Why?" Torren's voice seethed with anger.

"Outsiders cannot survive in our world."

Torren glanced back to the woods. "What if I just stay over there with her?"

"You need to let her go."

Another soft click and Ronin's mouth continued to move, but there were no more words.

On the wall, the images shifted to a piece of paper in Torren's hand.

Impostor. Liar. A third word was scribbled out.

He crumpled the paper and disposed of it into the river.

I heard the soft click again, and Kai's voice filled my ears.

"Alright, Kai. Let's go destroy it all."

My stomach knotted as I braced myself for what came next. Movement in the Glass House caught my attention.

Torren slid from his seat and collapsed as the click made the room silent again.

I stared at him lying on the floor, wondering if his glazed eyes saw the images dancing around him. He was my focus. Everything else faded into the background until Edric sidled up beside me.

"Who is that, Arisanna?" His oily presence made me shudder.

"It's Torren, of course," I replied, aware of how hollow my words sounded in the vast Observatory.

Edric paused. "You don't trust me. There are many challenges to overcome, and—together—we can make a difference. But you have to put your faith in me."

The gulf that stretched between us somehow narrowed.

Be true, Ari. Danger lies ahead.

I dismissed her, my insides sinking as Edric's words continued to wash over me.

"Who is that?" Edric repeated.

"Kai." Why bother denying it? He already knew.

"That's right. And you read the paper. You saw what he truly thought of you. Impostor."

I saw the paper, but I didn't understand why Kai would believe that about me.

But it must be true. Kai had worn a stone-cold expression as he spoke the words that haunted my dreams: *"I never loved you."*

"He *never* loved you." Edric's words plunged the knife into my soul. "He wouldn't have left you if he did. Twice."

I had fallen down a rabbit hole, losing my grasp on reality. "He wanted to protect me."

"You mean by using glamour to change his appearance?"

"Yes," I asserted, clinging to the lifeboat Edric provided, even though it made no sense. "That's proof."

"We all have that ability. That's not special. When you first came here, did it ever once cross your mind to pretend to be someone else? He wasn't protecting you. He was protecting himself. That's not love."

I tried to argue, but his words rang true.

The images above Torren's head came into focus, and I watched myself break.

I remembered well the way I had crumbled, and I turned away, tortured by my *own* memories.

Kai had walked away, shoulders straight and head high. He'd never really loved me.

Hot tears streamed down my cheeks, and I roughly brushed them away. Anger and pain fought a silent battle within my heart.

Edric's cold fingers wrapped around my shoulder, his words whispering the truth I could no longer fight. "His love was a lie."

Chapter Eleven

Lost in Council

I sat in the library surrounded by books after my failed attempt to get home. When I had woken up this morning, I wandered back to the bridge Edric had shown me the afternoon before. Once I crossed over, I realized the lay of the land was unfamiliar, and I would end up lost well before I found my way home. While the Council position didn't entice me, my parents had raised me to make the best of a bad situation.

Baffled by this world that was somehow a part of me, I decided to discover answers for myself. What better place to start than the library of Alterria's Council?

I sat alone at a wide table in the center of the room. Even surrounded by books, concentration eluded me as my thoughts swirled.

"He never loved you…" the words that spilled from Edric's mouth two days ago, *"He never would have left…"* the ones that made me doubt everything, including my own heart, *"His love was a lie…"* played on a loop in my head.

Torren disappeared from the labyrinth when Edric dangled the promise of Celia before him. I had seen his betrayal fleshed out on that cold stone wall. That *should* have given me all the closure I needed from that particular chapter of my life, but I couldn't stop the aching of my heart as my thoughts flashed to him collapsing on the floor, his body stiff as a corpse. That was the moment I knew that if his love for me had ever been real, it was now dead.

Away from the Glass House and Edric's prying questions, I had more control over my mind, and it was anything but clear. While it had been unnaturally easy to believe the narrative Edric fed me, what I knew of Kai planted a seed of doubt.

"He feels responsible for more than just Celia." The way Ronin's eyes bore into mine as he spoke those words gave weight to the conflict that was weaving through my thoughts.

My stomach heaved as I wondered if Torren still suffered in the Glass House. My heart stuttered at the thought of asking Edric again, as he hadn't been too receptive the last couple times, but I needed to try. For Torren. And myself. I stood and slung my backpack over my shoulder.

As though he had read my mind, Edric strode into the library, Thomas and a wolf trailing behind him. Edric stopped in front of me, a smirk playing on his lips, and glanced at the books piled on the table I had been occupying. "Finished with your studies already?"

The heat rose in my cheeks. "I can't concentrate, sir."

"I truly hope you aren't going to ask me about the prisoner again. His punishment is being observed by Council personnel. The doctor will be checking on him shortly." Edric's features softened as my lip quivered.

He turned to Thomas, waving his hand in dismissal. "Go take care of that."

Thomas narrowed his eyes at me, his disdain palpable. "Yes, sir," he said before leaving the room, his wolf following close by.

Edric pulled out a chair and gestured for me to sit. Taking a seat in the chair across from me, he took a deep breath. "I'm sorry,

Arisanna. My intent has never been to cause you pain, but I feel you need some...gentle reminders."

I winced, awaiting the pain he'd certainly remind me about. "Yes, sir."

"Who have you had conversations with since you arrived in Alterria?"

"Callan, Deborah, Torren, and you, sir." I intentionally left out Ronin's name to protect him.

He nodded. "They *seemed* like they cared when they were in front of the entire town, but where are they now? And who is helping you through this confusing time?"

Gritting my teeth, I thought of them. All of them. Though loath to admit it, I couldn't deny he was right. None of them were here. While Edric indirectly answered through books and research, no one else provided me with *any* answers. "You, sir."

"Don't you forget it." He cleared his throat. "I'm going to share something that may come as a bit of a shock. Council has discovered some unsettling secrets that Ronin has been hiding. As you're aware, he's now on the run, trying to escape the consequences of past decisions. Prior to running, he devised a plan to remove his brother from medical observation and place him in the labyrinth with you. The boy was still under care and unstable."

Edric stood and removed a key from his pocket, placing it in my hand. "This key opens that glass cabinet in the back of the library."

I twisted my body to see the dusty cabinet tucked in the corner of the room. "What does that have to do with Torren?"

Edric shot me a sharp look. "He comes from a family who has broken Council's trust. I've given the key to you. You've earned our trust. Remember that, too."

He walked to a low shelf and pulled out a leather-bound book. "At one point, your father worked with Council. You may find some interesting bits of your family history within the pages of this tome."

"Thank you, sir." I didn't like Edric, but he had provided me a home and a chance to learn the truth of my past, a consideration my parents had denied me.

"Now, I have some duties to attend to. I shall leave you to your studies." He tapped the cover of the book he had placed on the center of my table before walking out of the library.

I picked up the book, *A Past Untold*. A photograph drew my attention when I opened to the first chapter. The caption read "Creation of Council: Cyran Lunagarde, Damond Morganfire, and Robert Weiss." Cyran and Damond both appeared to be in their thirties.

Damond had stubble on his chin, and dark blond hair parted neatly at the side. The way his left eyebrow lifted, it seemed he had something amusing to share.

Cyran looked like my dad. Black hair, black beard, black eyes. I guessed that, like Dad's, they weren't actually black up close. Unlike Dad, Cyran had a crease on his forehead that matched his frown.

Robert, with wavy, gray hair a few inches too long, appeared older than the other two men.

Below the caption, strong words caught my eye. *Damond Morganfire was a thief and a true villain.* My stomach turned. I placed the book into my backpack. This would need a bit more time to digest.

I glanced at the locked cabinet. While the contents intrigued me, I had no desire for more secrets. If I truly wanted to understand what my parents hid from me, I needed to understand where I was. I needed to start with the basics: Alterria's founding.

Deep in the book, I jumped when one of the library's double doors creaked open and a short, stout woman wearing head-to-toe blue wheeled in a cart.

She eyed the books I had spread across the table, and, with a shake of her head, she sighed. "These books aren't what they used to be."

My eyebrows scrunched together. "What do you mean?"

Her cheeks went as red as the apples on the cart, standing out against the white curls framing her face. "Pay no mind to me, dearie. This mouth of mine will get me in trouble one day." She cleared her throat and pushed the cart a little closer. "The High Councilman suggested you may be hungry after the hours of study you've completed this morning."

"Thank you so much," I replied, rising immediately to claim a sandwich.

Her face lit up with the friendliest smile I had seen in a long time. "I'm Mrs. Chapman."

I returned her smile. "Arisanna."

"Well, Miss Arisanna, if there's anything else you'd like or a special request for supper, I'd be happy to accommodate you."

My exchange with Edric had left me tense. It wasn't like me. I always pressed for more information rather than blindly accepting statements as fact. "No special requests. Where do you go to relax? I need some fresh air."

She pointed toward the window. "How about the courtyard?"

I copied her directions down on a piece of paper and thanked her.

She nodded once and wheeled the cart out of the room.

I finished my sandwich and packed a volume of history and a map of Alterria into my backpack to study later.

After a quick scan of the directions, I left the library, following the twists and turns until I reached a corridor filled with plate glass windows that provided a view of the garden below.

When I reached the end of the hall, expecting to find a stairwell to get to the ground floor, I found nothing. I consulted my directions and realized I'd made a wrong turn somewhere. I was lost. My heart thudded against my chest, and a knot lodged in my throat.

Not knowing where I'd gone wrong, I wandered, not bothering to investigate any of the arched wooden doors I passed in the maze of hallways. They resembled the one leading to my bedroom, and I didn't want to risk disturbing anyone.

In a hallway identical to all the others, I began walking on a decline. Disoriented like I'd been in the labyrinth, I brushed away the irrational thought that I would never get out of here. Maybe my fear made me more aware of my surroundings, but I believed I heard the soft cry of a child.

I followed the sounds of suffering to a new wing, pushing through swinging double doors. Fluorescent lights reflecting on the tile floor made this hallway brighter than the others. I stopped in front of the unstained wooden door that hid the crying, and my knock echoed in the empty hallway.

"Are you okay?" I called.

No one answered.

"Can I come in?"

When there was still no reply, I decided to open the door.

I expected to find a bedroom like mine. Instead, I found a hospital room.

Against the wall, a little girl laid on a raised, railed bed. In addition to the IV hooked to her arm and a monitor that tracked her vitals, a single strap hugged her waist, holding her on the bed.

I took a deep breath, and sterile air assaulted my lungs.

In the center of the windowless room, a large overhead light hung suspended from an arm that could focus the beam in any direction. A cupboard in the corner was labeled "supplies." There was also a short round table in the corner beside the door, barely visible under the dozens of cards and flowers spilling off the surface. This girl must be deeply loved.

I stepped over to her. "I'm Ari. What's your name?"

Tears spilled silently from her closed eyes, and she shook as she gave a tiny groan, but she didn't speak.

"Is there anything I can do for you?" I asked.

"It hurts." Her voice croaked as though it hadn't been used in quite some time. Her tiny hand reached up, and I wrapped my fingers around hers. With her touch, my palm prickled.

"You have a visitor," a familiar voice said behind me.

I dropped her hand and stiffened briefly. To my surprise, I turned around to a face I didn't recognize.

He was tall, fit, and couldn't have been older than twenty-five. The mess of brown curls at the tips of his hair offset the sad smile fixed on his face. His white coat told me he must be this girl's doctor. "No one but me has visited her for weeks."

Relief rushed through me. I had thought Edric came to reprimand me for being in this part of Council Hall. "No visitors?" I asked, caught off guard by the abundance of gifts.

"Ah, those. Even the most serene visitors will lose patience with a stranger who doesn't improve. But now she has you. What's your name?"

"I'm Arisanna. I got lost and heard her cry. I'm sorry if I disturbed her, but there was no one else who could help."

"Edric told me about you. You're training to fill the vacant Council position."

"There's a lot to learn."

The doctor stood at the girl's monitor, jotting down notes.

"Who is she?"

"We don't know her name. We only know she's from the Outside, like you."

The memory of Deborah's voice flitted through my mind. *"She's not well. She doesn't belong here. There has to be a way to get her back home."*

"You all keep saying 'the Outside'. We call our city Veillis Grove." I took a breath and finished my thought. "Why don't you send her back if being here is hurting her?"

"It's not that simple," he said. "She needs to be healed before she can go home, and we don't even know how to slow down the illness. If we could put her on pause somehow, maybe we could buy some time. As it is, she doesn't have much left."

The beeping equipment was hypnotizing, and I simply stared at her, a tightness growing in my chest. She was so young, and his words hit me hard.

"I'm finished here for now," the doctor said, breaking my trance. "Would you like me to show you back to the main hall?"

"That would be great, but are you sure there's nothing I can do for her? Would it help if I sat by her so she's not alone?"

He stared at me silently for too long. His hazel eyes bore into my soul, sending a wave of uneasiness that forced me to look away. "It wouldn't matter. If a human presence could help her, I wouldn't leave her side."

I sighed.

"Hot," she said, her eyes remaining shut.

I reached out to stroke her head, hoping my cool hands would bring her relief.

When I brushed her forehead, the beeping of the machines went crazy, then flattened to a monotone drone.

I had killed her!

The doctor rushed to his patient, and in my haste to get out of his way, I fell against the supply cupboard.

My heart beat fast as I scrambled to my feet and bolted from the room. Halfway down the hospital corridor, I skidded to a stop when someone called my name from behind me.

"Arisanna, wait!"

Where did Edric come from? I stood frozen in fear. What would they do to the person who killed a little girl?

"Look at me, Arisanna."

I had no choice but to face him. As I turned, I covered my face with my hands and sobbed. "Alterria is making me a criminal. I've never done anything dangerous in my life, and now I've killed a child!"

"No, you didn't. I'll show you." Edric walked back to the girl's room, and I trailed in his wake.

She lay perfectly still.

"She *looks* dead."

"Your touch did exactly what we've been trying to do for her. She's in a deep sleep. We now have time."

"Is that what the doctor said? Where is he?" I searched for him.

Though Edric betrayed nothing but confidence, a shadow of tension flitted across his jaw when he spoke. "Yes. With this development, he felt it urgent to begin his research anew."

Did Edric not see eye to eye with the doctor?

"Okay," I said uncomfortably. I turned my attention to the sleeping girl, but I didn't know what to think.

Edric headed for the door. "I'd like to point out that your decision to stay has already been beneficial." He let silence linger briefly between us.

What would have happened to her if I hadn't been here?

"You've given her a gift, Arisanna. We should let her rest."

The sound of our footsteps filled the empty halls until we came to the corridor with a view of the garden.

"Edric," I said. "How do I get out there?"

He smiled. "I enjoy the courtyard too."

As he led the way, I committed the route to memory.

"It's even more beautiful from out here," I exclaimed when we reached the courtyard's entrance.

It had been built around a pond shaded by a willow tree, as though no one had wanted to disturb its natural beauty. A fountain bubbled at its center, and I'd never seen grass as Kelly green as the blades that grew around the edge of the cyan water. Vibrant paths of flowers lined the walkways, and a bench swing in the center called my name.

"I have a Council meeting I must attend," Edric said abruptly.

"I thought they were monthly."

"Mandatory town Council meetings are monthly. Members of the Council have daily meetings."

"Should I be there?" I asked apprehensively.

"Not yet."

"Thank you," I said, looking forward to the garden's peacefulness.

"I have something for you, though. I'll send it along shortly," he said as he left me alone.

The daffodils brought me a calming peace as I meandered through the garden, stopping to admire the ones most in bloom. A honey bee buzzed by, ignoring me for the wildflowers. Before long, I made my way to the bench swing where I sat and closed my eyes.

I must have dozed off because I awoke to humid breath on my face and shouted in surprise.

My wolf cocked his head to the side, tongue hanging out.

"Are you okay?" the doctor asked.

"Startled, but yes. I'm okay."

"Edric asked me to deliver this gift. Apparently, before Ronin left, he hinted you'd find comfort with this wolf. I don't know that I would, but Edric said you trusted Ronin."

After the labyrinth, how could I trust anyone? Ronin said the wolf would betray me. Why send him to me? And why would Edric consider any of Ronin's advice after he abdicated his position?

"I can take him away if you'd like," the doctor said.

The wolf and I locked eyes, and I knew he must stay whether I wanted him or not. I shook my head.

"May I join you for a while?" the doctor asked.

"By all means."

He sat beside me. Close.

I wished he was Torren—but Torren didn't love me anymore. He never did. My stomach twisted as those words stabbed into me.

Another long look from the doctor reminded me of his intense gaze earlier.

I focused on my wolf, scratching between his ears.

"I never introduced myself. I'm Charlie." He rested his arms along the back edge of the swing, one hand dangling over but not touching my shoulder.

I leaned away.

"I'm sorry, Arisanna. I didn't mean to make you uncomfortable." He removed his arm from around me and shifted further away.

I'd hurt his feelings. "This is all just… a lot."

My wolf rested his head on my knee.

Charlie crossed his arms in front of him, relaxed. "Would you like to talk about it?"

"No. Let's start over. It's nice to meet you, Charlie. You seem like a great doctor. How's the girl?"

"I checked on her before I brought the wolf down. She's still sleeping soundly."

"I'm so relieved. I thought I'd given her a death sentence."

Charlie shook his head slowly. "Arisanna, you are an amazing person. The way you've been thrown into this new experience and are dealing with things no one should have to think about…I find that inspiring."

"Thank you," I said, turning my body toward him.

He had inched closer to me while he spoke, and his hand covered mine.

I didn't want to hurt his feelings again, so I didn't pull away. Besides, it was comforting to feel like someone cared.

"There's no one like you," he whispered, leaning in. He pressed his forehead gently against mine.

Panicked thoughts raced through my mind, but my body froze. Even though I'd just watched myself die inside the day Kai left me, *he* remained the only person I'd ever wanted.

Charlie softly brushed his thumb down my cheek.

"No, Charlie," I managed to squeak out.

He tilted my chin and leaned in, just a fraction of an inch, but my heart jumped to my throat.

I turned my head away to avoid what came next, but it wasn't until my wolf howled that Charlie lowered his hand.

"Arisanna, forgive me. I feel so at home with you, but that's no excuse. I'll go." He rubbed the back of his neck and stood.

Something about him didn't sit right with me, but I was compelled to accept his apology. "I'm sorry. I have a lot on my mind right now."

"That's something I can relate to. I must get back to my patients. Will you visit sometime?"

"Of course."

"Until then." He left the garden, waving his hand once he reached the entrance.

I patted the swing for the wolf to jump up, and he placed his head in my lap. I absorbed his warmth, took strength from his presence, and pushed Charlie out of my mind. Stroking my wolf's fur, grateful for his interference, I began humming the lullaby again.

I recalled the symbols I had seen in the cavernous labyrinth. The secret verse.

Secrets.

I desired to put at least a few secrets to rest before night fell.

"Let's go," I said to my wolf.

He jumped off my lap and stood beside me, once again bringing me comfort and support, like a friend.

"I'm going to call you Cade."

Cade and I found our way back to the library, where he curled up under the table. I strode to the locked cabinet and took the key from my pocket. It was time to learn more about Alterria's secrets.

Chapter Twelve

Secrets Revealed

The locked cabinet concealed a single vial, and I had no idea what I was supposed to do with it or how it could contain any of the answers I searched for.

I closed my eyes and took a deep breath. It was late, and the day had been long. I scooped the vial from the box and retreated to my room, pushing the door closed behind me as Cade curled up on the couch beneath the curtained window.

The cavernous walls absorbed most of the light that emerged from the single bulb on the ceiling as sunset filled the room with a fiery glow.

Reminded of my experience in the labyrinth, I shivered. Reaching for the thin Council robe I'd been given, I wrapped it around me like a blanket, keeping the chill at bay.

My feet dragged as I approached a large bookshelf across the room. On the top shelf, I noticed a small crystal dish, much like the one from Deborah's kitchen. Perhaps this vial's silver liquid would work similarly to the crystal ball potion.

I grabbed the dish and placed it on a small table beside the bookshelf, popped the cork off the bottle, and poured a scant amount of the contents into the dish. It settled for a moment before the solution bubbled, and a thin layer of smoke rose out of the bowl.

Voices filtered in before any images appeared.

"You show great promise. Council would be lucky to have such a talent on board."

Within the haze, images flitted in and out.

Three men huddled close to each other before the image faded.

"What makes Brayden better?" The voice sounded like Edric's but younger. "Why should he be the next High Councilman? I'm stronger than him, more respected by most of the elders."

The image flickered.

A young woman with golden brown hair appeared, pale and unmoving on the grassy creek bed.

A young Edric watched, eyes wide. "Harmony! What is happening to her?" he whispered.

Another flicker.

Edric stood beside Robert at a round table filled with eleven men.

Robert spoke, his voice ragged and slow. "Members of Council, I hereby announce that Edric will be named new High Councilman, effective immediately. I am officially retiring as of today."

A chorus of voices rose, and Brayden's name echoed around the room.

Cyran observed from across the room, a smirk dancing across his lips before falling to a straight line.

Flicker.

Edric and Damond faced each other, both holding onto a pocket watch. Edric's face drained of color as the watch emitted a pale green glow. "What's happening? What are you doing to me?"

The scene went black. When it came back, Edric was gripping his chest. "My gift, it's weakened."

Flicker.

Edric and Thomas walked toward the giant oak tree near the river. A lifeless body lay on the shore.

Edric ran up to the body and checked for a pulse. He shook his head.

"High Councilman Robert?" Thomas dropped to his knees.

Flicker.

"They are still our citizens. If any of us were lost on the Outside, would we not do anything to find them?"

Edric's voice rose above the chaos that erupted, "Council member Brayden, please settle. They have chosen to leave, as evidenced by the burning of the Morganfire family home."

"You believe the home was intentionally set ablaze so they could run?"

Edric made a motion with his hand, and the room fell silent. He spoke, and his voice filled all the empty spaces within the room. "All in favor of seeking out the rogue lovers?"

Brayden raised his hand.

The infamous smile I'd come to know all too well slithered across Edric's face. "Opposed?"

Flicker.

Edric and Ronin sat in the Observatory.

"Council member Ronin, the Glass House is the only way we can show this child how serious his actions are. No one defies Council's orders and escapes punishment."

Ronin clenched his fists, and his jaw twitched. "Sir, he is but a child, as you stated. He already shoulders full responsibility for her disappearance. Doesn't the Glass House seem a bit extreme?"

Edric stood and walked to the door. "You'd do well to learn your place." The slimy smile slid across his face. "You'll be the one to watch his transmissions. Step out of line again, and you will join him."

Flicker.

A young Torren with tears streaming down his face stood in front of Council. "Please, sir. It's my fault she's missing. Let me help find her."

Edric's gentle tone contradicted his words of accusation. "How is it your gift caused her disappearance, yet you don't know where she went?"

"I'm twelve, sir. I still don't know how to control my gift as well as I should. It was irresponsible to practice with her so close."

Edric looked down his nose at the boy. "I suppose an exception can be made to allow you to search for your niece."

Flicker.

A wall of fog fell. Callan stood beside the crumpled body of a young girl, the same girl I had seen in the hospital this afternoon.

She immediately began screeching, "It burns! Make it stop!"

Flicker.

Someone shuffled around the supply closet in the hospital room while the young girl lay motionless in the bed. Glass clattered against glass, and Edric emerged, mixing different things into a liquid form, and then injecting them into her IV.

"Something has to give. What was in that elixir?"

Flicker.

Deborah leaned over the hospital bed and placed her hands on the writhing girl's temples, singing a melody I didn't recognize.

The girl relaxed, only the fluttering of her eyelids and an occasional whimper indicating any discomfort remained.

"I don't know how long this is going to help. We need to find a way to get her home, sir," Deborah pleaded.

Edric stood beside her with his hands clasped behind his back. "I'm afraid crossing over to our world may have made her return all but impossible. She needs to be healed, but I don't know how." A trace of regret dotted his voice.

When a burst of light indicated that all the liquid had disappeared, I rinsed the empty bowl in the bathroom. The images that had flooded the small space above the bowl exhausted me. Drying the dish, I placed it on the bathroom counter, shuddering at the thought of something possibly appearing while I tried to sleep.

I flopped on my bed, my thoughts spinning. Why did all Alterria's secrets seem to revolve around Edric?

Cade jumped onto the mattress beside me and curled into my legs. His nearness relaxed me, and my eyelids fell shut. The darkness swallowed me whole.

I awoke to an incessant tapping at the door.

Cade stiffened, and his breathing slowed.

The air around me became heavy, and since it was still a far cry from dawn, I could hardly see. One more sharp rap on the door drew me from bed.

I pressed the switch on the ceramic lamp on the nightstand and tiptoed to the door, my bare feet chilled by the stone floor. An empty hallway greeted me, the lights on the wall flickering sporadically. As I crept forward, my toes hit something hard. I glanced down to find an old book, its brown leather cover worn and faded. I scanned the empty hallway again before picking up the book and heading back to my bed.

Cade rested his head on my lap.

I opened the book. Though the inscription on the inside cover had mostly worn off, I could make out little bits.

To be given to the descendant of the House of Morganfire. Born of this world, not within.

A shiver raced up my back. Had those words been written specifically about me?

Hoping I held answers in the palm of my hand, I flipped through the pages.

They were all blank.

Frustrated, I closed the book and turned out the bedside light as I crawled into bed.

Cade curled against my stomach, his breathing slow and rhythmic.

I matched mine to his and fell into a well of disturbing dreams about the empty book spitting out vivid repetitions of the enigmatic flickers from Edric's vial.

In the background of this nightmare, the haunting whisper of Torren's voice tearfully called one thing over and over.

My name.

Chapter Thirteen

Rescue

All night, the bad dreams taunted me. I had hoped to discover Alterria's secrets, not more questions.

I rolled out of bed, resolving to find Edric and make him give me answers. Before getting dressed, I stowed the wordless book under my mattress to hide it from prying eyes until I had a clue where it came from. And why it had been given to me. While I kept blindly chasing answers, how many of my own secrets had I created?

I slung the backpack over my shoulder and set off to find Edric with Cade by my side. On the way, I decided to swing by the hospital to check on the little girl.

Charlie met me at her door with a grin spread across his face. "I'm glad you're here. She's still asleep, but she's so peaceful."

I peered around him and smiled. "That's practically a different girl."

"Thanks to you."

I could feel his eyes on me, and I averted my gaze. "I'm glad she's doing so well, but I can't stay. I have some questions for Edric."

"Oh, of course. He doesn't visit the hospital normally, but I believe he planned on stopping by later. You could wait here."

"I'm kind of impatient right now. Maybe I'll check the library." I waved as I made my way out of the hospital.

I took my time, peeking into a few of the open doorways I passed. One room looked like a clothing store where Mrs. Chapman stood organizing a rack full of suits.

Another room overflowed with office supplies on one side and stacks of chairs and folding tables on the other.

A third room featured rows of desks lining the walls. Each seat was occupied by a man in a blue uniform—much like Mrs. Chapman's—wearing a headset. The man closest to the door had red hair, and freckles splashed across his nose and cheeks.

As I paused outside the room, he stood and stretched, tugging the headset cord out of the control panel in front of him. Instantly, Thomas's voice filled the room, and Torren's name captured my attention.

Cade growled when I gasped, and the man's gaze lingered on Cade before turning to me and scowling.

The man stepped to the door and closed it before I heard anything more.

I decided not to peek into any more doorways. Snooping would only get me into trouble.

When I reached the library, Edric stood at my table, the research I'd been doing the day before still covering the whole area.

He looked up at me and gave me a thin smile. "You've been working hard."

I stopped short. At home, I always left my desk full of open books. My dad said an open book welcomes a mind eager to learn, but maybe Edric's priorities differed. "I apologize for the mess," I said, closing the books closest to me.

He watched me with arms crossed. "You used the key."

"Yes," I replied hesitantly.

"And now you have questions."

"I do." The corners of my mouth twitched. The vial contained snippets and glimpses of carefully chosen memories. Would he tell me the truth?

He gave a curt nod and pulled out a chair for each of us.

"My parents first. No one ever told me about the Morganfire home burning. Knowing my history would mean a lot to me."

"I know very little about the arson. I know even less about your parents' disappearance."

"Why didn't you seek them out? If their home had been burned down, they could've been in danger."

"I sensed that they wanted to be alone. Young love and all."

Young love. Like Kai and me.

"I want to see Torren," I blurted out.

"We're done with him, Arisanna," he said flatly. "Next question."

The image of twelve-year-old Torren crying for his niece filled my mind. I went silent.

Edric sighed. "*Why?* We've established that he makes choices that benefit no one but himself."

I remained still, my jaw clenching.

"Well, if that's all, I have some tasks that I must attend to. When you're ready to discuss your other questions, I'll make time." He stood and strode out of the room.

My eyes blurred as, one by one, I gathered up the notes I had left behind the previous day, stuffing them and a couple of books into my backpack. My heart wasn't into studying at the moment.

"It would be in your best interests to watch your step around Edric," Thomas announced in a voice that grated my nerves. "In fact, maybe you should consider going home."

Before I could determine whether his statement was a warning or a threat, he left the shadow of the doorway, and I shrugged as I continued clearing my study area.

When I had finished, I called to Cade, "Let's go back to the courtyard, boy."

Thankfully, I didn't get lost this time. As soon as we arrived, Cade dashed away, nipping at insects flitting around.

I threw my backpack on the ground and stretched myself on a patch of grass near the large willow tree beside the pond. My mind wandered to carefree days in the meadow with Kai as I lay staring at the clouds drifting far above.

What was happening to Kai...or Torren? After five years, I found it hard to believe the person I loved was someone else, but I forced my mind to accept it. After all, I'd seen myself in Torren's memories on that wall.

"Ahem." Charlie stood near me, clenching a handful of dandelion puffballs.

I scrambled to my feet. "Hi, Charlie."

"You know," he said as he kicked at small rocks on the ground, "I have a few hours off. Want to grab a bite to eat?"

"Are you asking me on a date?" My face flushed, unease creeping into my gut.

"I'm hungry and thought you might be as well." With one breath, he sent a whirlwind of white floating around us. "Join me?"

"Okay." Relieved he wanted nothing more than company, I followed him out of the courtyard.

"There's a café in town I'd love to take you to, but I hope the dining room will do for now." He opened the door to the Council cafeteria and nodded toward the seating area.

Sitting across from each other at a table for two, it didn't take us long to finish our meals.

I looked at Charlie and smiled.

"What?" he asked. "Do I have something on my face?"

"No, no," I laughed. "I was just thinking that I'm glad I'm not alone."

He wiggled his eyebrows at me, and I laughed again. He distracted me from my loneliness, but only temporarily.

I had never been lonely with Kai. Was he still being tortured by his past? My smile faded.

"You're thinking of him, aren't you?"

The tears came in a flood, and I put my head in my hands. "I loved him."

"You *still* love him."

I couldn't deny it. I wiped my cheeks and glanced up. "He lied to me and used me, but all I can see is him lying on the floor of the Glass House. I won't be able to move on if I spend the rest of my life wishing I could save him."

"I checked on him last night. Medically, he's fit to carry out the remainder of his punishment."

"How long will that be?"

"Another day or two, to the best of my knowledge."

I bit my lip.

"By the look on your face, I haven't eased your worries." Charlie kept quiet for a moment. "Edric owes me a favor. What if I can get him out early?"

"You could do that?" I brushed the tears from my face.

"I can't make you any promises, but I'll do my best."

"Then what? He's broken."

"I'm a doctor. I can ensure he gets what he needs to forget the past."

Our eyes locked. "You would do that for me?"

He nodded and reached for my hand.

"Thank you," I whispered gratefully.

"Come with me," he said, intertwining his fingers with mine. "I need to evaluate the prisoner before I make my request."

Kai used to hold my hand like that.

Uncomfortable with the intimate gesture, I tried to pry my hand away, but his grip remained firm. It didn't take us long to arrive. Entering the Observatory, I broke free from Charlie and rushed to the window. Gasping, I raised my hand to my mouth.

Torren lay face-up on the floor, his eyes glazed and unblinking, his clothes damp. A stream of water unexpectedly whooshed out from grates in the wall, spilling over him.

"What's going on? Are they trying to drown him?" Anger boiled in my chest, and a burning sensation traveled through my palms. I took a steadying breath and clenched my hands into fists until the burn subsided.

"No. Sometimes the experience is so stressful for people they become sick. No one can go in without being subject to their own memories, so this is how the room gets cleaned."

I imagined him lying there for days with no way out. No one saw to it that he was washed or fed.

His back arched, and he unleashed a piercing scream.

I cried out, too, my heart reaching for him.

"Oh, Arisanna," Charlie whispered.

I spun away from the window and fell to my knees, sobbing into my hands.

He gathered me close and stroked my hair. "Shh. It's going to be okay."

"It's not okay!" I moaned. "He might've never loved me, but I can't take this. They're killing him."

"You're right."

I slowed my breathing and leaned back, my eyes heavy. "What?"

He loosened his hold. "This is killing him. Edric sends me to verify the prisoner handles the visions accordingly every night, but he's not anymore. This isn't Council's objective. He must be removed."

Charlie pressed a buzzer, and a few minutes later, a man in a black uniform showed up at the door. "I need the wolves to remove the prisoner."

The man saluted and turned on his heel.

I leaned against the window, still seeing a random array of Torren's memories blinking on the wall. None of them were complete. I saw my face more than I saw anything else. It hurt too much to think about. I was about to turn away when two wolves entered the room.

Each of them grabbed a mouthful of Torren's pant leg, one on the right and one on the left, and dragged him out.

His memories stopped playing, the wall as blank as Torren's eyes.

Sadness and fear fought for dominance, and my head throbbed. Since arriving in Alterria, I had discovered I'd been lied to by everyone I loved. How much more could I take before overwhelm put *me* in a hospital bed?

I doubted everything. Everyone. Even Torren.

Charlie sat beside me. "I need to assess him. He'll need medication."

"But he'll recover?" Despite my doubt, I still loved him.

"I told you I'm a doctor. I know how to help people. He'll get what he needs to forget the past."

"If it's okay, I'd like to go back to my room for a while."

He helped me to my feet. "Shall I walk with you, or do you know the way?"

I rested my hand in Cade's fur, my trusted companion. "I have an escort, but thank you."

"Meanwhile, I have some tasks to attend to," Charlie said, reminiscent of Edric's words earlier.

When I reached my room, I tossed my backpack on the floor and threw myself on the bed. "I'm going to get up in a second,"

I told Cade, who had curled up on the floor. "I have a lot of reading to do."

***

A sharp rap at the door startled me, and I jolted up. The shadows on the wall told me the sun had begun to set. I'd slept the afternoon away.

"Yes?" I rubbed the sleep from my eyes.

"It's me, Charlie. Would you like to do rounds with me this evening?"

"Oh, yes. Give me a moment to freshen up."

I hurried to the bathroom, splashed some water on my face, and ran a comb through my hair. Maybe this meant Torren was ready for visitors. Butterflies stirred, and I pushed them down.

"Stay, Cade," I instructed, patting him on the head. "I'll be back later."

Charlie waited at the end of the hall. He took my hand when I reached him. "What is it?" he asked when I stared at our intertwined fingers.

I shook my head and pulled away, clasping my hands in front of my chest. "I can't," I said, not wanting to hurt his feelings.

He stepped in front of me and placed his hands on my shoulders. "I'm not asking you for anything. You're in pain, and the doctor in me wants to heal you." He ran his fingers tenderly down my arms. "Everyone needs a hand to hold. It only means what you want it to mean."

I looked into his brown eyes. What did I want it to mean?

"What do you say?" The way he gazed at me sent a jolt through my stomach. Though I wasn't sure what to make of that, I hesitantly let him take my hand the next time he reached for it.

"There's my girl," he said, smiling. "Let's go do rounds."

I was lost in my thoughts as we walked to the hospital wing, anticipating seeing Torren now that he was free from his torture.

We stopped by the girl's room first. She lay still and quiet, a peaceful expression on her face.

After Charlie finished checking her monitors and making notes, he smoothed her covers. It was sweet how much he cared for her.

I stood at the door to Kai's room—Torren's room—and the butterflies returned. The tortured look I'd last seen on his face had been replaced by the peacefulness of slumber.

Charlie finished jotting down notes for him and walked back over to me. "Would you like to speak to him?"

"No. He's asleep."

Charlie wrapped his arm around my shoulder, guiding me in. "I know how important knowing your history is to you. He's part of yours. Sometimes it helps to speak to people when they're sleeping. You don't have to worry about what they're going to say. Just tell him how you feel and put it all behind you."

I couldn't recall talking to him about my history, but there was wisdom in his suggestion.

As I made my way to Torren's bedside, Charlie stepped back and leaned against the wall. I sat at the edge of the bed, reaching for Torren's hand. My fingertips brushed against his, but I drew back when I remembered he wasn't mine.

He breathed in deeply and smiled, and my heart leaped for a moment. His eyes flickered behind his lids. He must've been dreaming.

"I love you," I told him quietly, and although my throat tightened when I spoke my next words, I forced myself to continue. "But I have to let you go now."

Torren's eyes flew open at the sound of my voice, and he looked at me confused. "Where am I?" he exclaimed, struggling to sit up.

"You're in the hospital," I said, startled, swallowing the pain my own words had brought me.

"I need to find Celia. Get me out."

And there it was, Celia again. Always Celia. It shouldn't still hurt, but it did.

My stomach hardened and my chest burned, irrational jealousy consuming me. I was right here in front of him, and he didn't want me.

"Right now, you need to get better." I stood.

His demand had provoked a simmering anger in my chest. At least he used to pretend to care.

"Who do you think you are?" he asked scornfully. "You don't look like a doctor to me."

"Torren," I said, searching his face. "Your love may have been a lie, but don't pretend you don't know me."

"Know you?" Torren clamored, desperately clawing at wires and tubes. "I've never seen you before in my life."

Chapter Fourteen

Help the Girl

Standing still as a statue, I faced the hospital doors, my heart clawing against my chest and up into my throat. I swallowed against it and let a slow breath escape my lips. Adjusting my backpack over my shoulder, the weight of the research sat uncomfortably against me.

Last night, I had tried to concentrate in the library and even my own room, but my mind kept drifting back to Torren's wide-eyed fear.

At first, I was convinced Torren was playing some kind of game, maybe to keep his secrets safe from Council. Then I realized he had unwillingly exposed his secrets on the cold stone walls, over and over again. Playing games was pointless. Could it be true that he really didn't know me?

I closed my eyes and tried to steady the tremors traveling through my body. One more deep breath and I resolved to walk into the hospital.

One step closer to confronting the fear beating in the back of my mind, I rested my fingers on the cool metal handle outside Torren's room.

My heart raced again. Why did I keep putting myself through this? Because he was my only way home, of course. But no...it had to be more than that, even if it hurt to admit.

"Hey." A hand rested on the small of my back. "Are you okay?"

I glanced over my shoulder to see Charlie standing behind me. My lips quivered, and I pressed them together. "Fine," I managed to squeak out.

He nodded, and though his lips moved, no words came forth. Finally, he took a deep breath. "I've never had so many patients needing such intense care simultaneously. Nearly every room is full. Perhaps you could help me out?"

A faint smile crossed my lips. "I would love to help. What can I do?"

He eyed the way I uncomfortably shifted the bag. "Well, the girl had a fitful night. I think she needs your touch again."

He opened Torren's door and peered inside. "Still here," he grumbled under his breath.

Had I misheard him?

He slid the bag off my shoulder and placed it in Torren's room beside the door. "He's still resting. The medicine I administered to calm him last night will take some time to wear off. He could be asleep for a few more hours."

"Let's help the girl," I said.

Charlie stopped outside her door and faced me, his brows wrinkled together. "That thing you did to calm her. How'd you do that?"

"I don't know how any of this works. When I touched her head, I hoped I could bring her a little peace."

Glancing back at Torren's door, I brought my thumb to my lips and chewed at my nail.

Charlie tugged my hand away from my mouth and brushed my hair behind my ear. "What's on your mind?"

The corners of my mouth twitched. "Nothing. Nothing at all."

I opened the door to the girl's room, and Charlie flicked on the overhead lights.

The girl's sheets were rumpled, and her hands held chunks of blanket in tight fists. She moved her head from side to side and moaned.

I dashed to her side and sat in the chair by her bed. When I placed my hand on top of hers, every muscle in her body seemed to instantly relax as her eyes fluttered open.

"Oh," Charlie breathed. He rushed to her other side. "Oh, child! This is the first time you've opened your eyes! Do you need anything?"

The girl cleared her throat. "Popsicle?"

Charlie checked the IV hanging next to her bed and consulted her chart. "Your blood pressures are good. Hydration appears to be normal. Yes, of course." He smiled and hastened to the door.

The girl twisted her hand and gripped mine. Her eyes searched my face, and her bottom lip trembled. "Do you know where my mom is?"

I shook my head.

Tears brimmed in her eyes, and she pulled her hand away, her hospital band loose on her wrist with *Outsider* as her only identification.

"What's your name?"

"Lyra," she whispered, her voice hoarse.

"Hi, Lyra. I'm Ari," I said while digging through my backpack. I found a bottle of water and handed it to her. "How old are you?"

"Ten. I think," she said after taking a sip.

"What do you mean?"

"Well, last I remember, it was nearly my birthday."

"Anything else?"

She hesitated and bit her lip.

Be careful in whom you put your trust. Some secrets must still be kept. Keep her safe.

The voice was back and nausea washed over me. Could Lyra be in danger?

"I won't tell anyone." I drew an "x" over my heart and gave her a faint smile.

She returned my smile and drew in a deep breath. "Mom was in the kitchen, yelling at some man. Then she started throwing things at him and waved her hands at me like she wanted me to run. So I did." Lyra closed her eyes tight.

I pressed her hand and concentrated on helping her feel calm.

When she spoke again, her voice trembled. "But I saw his face before I turned around. His smile scared me. I couldn't run fast enough."

"Oh, Lyra," I whispered.

She steadied herself and continued. "I only made it to the walking path before he caught me and threw me over his shoulder. Mama was screaming to let me go, but he didn't listen. He just kept walking. I tried to get away, but every time I moved, he held on tighter.

"We went over a bridge I'd never seen and when we were halfway across, it hurt so bad. Like my skin was on fire and my head was going to explode. All I could do was scream. But he kept walking, and I must have fallen asleep because the next thing I remember is waking up right now. That's all." She sucked in a breath, and her eyes widened. "Where did he go, Ari? What if he comes back for me?"

"Your doctor has been taking good care of you. He wouldn't let anyone hurt you." I drew my eyebrows together. "How are you feeling now?"

"All the hurt melted away when you touched my hand."

"That's interesting," a voice spoke from the doorway, and Lyra tensed.

Charlie walked over, flashing his charming smile as he presented Lyra with her popsicle, then motioned me toward the hall with a slight flick of his head.

I patted Lyra's hand. "I have to go. Are you going to be okay?"

"Will you come back and visit me, Ari?"

"Of course I will."

She sank into her pillows. "I'm okay right now. You can go. Thank you."

I met Charlie in the hallway, and he leaned in close as he shut the door behind us.

He placed his hand on his forehead. "That is absolutely incredible, the total change in the girl."

"Lyra," I smiled. "Her name is Lyra."

He shook his head, his eyes wide. "Wow, just—I don't know what else to say, but wow! Can you show me how you calmed her?"

I raised an eyebrow. Torren said his brothers warned him not to share too much about his own gift, but Charlie had already seen me calm Lyra. What harm could it do?

"Please?" He placed his hand into my palm, and I concentrated on sending a wave of serenity. He wove his fingers into mine and pressed my hand to his chest. "Ari, you've taken control of my heart in more ways than one."

"Charlie." I yanked my hand away.

"Don't forget, it only means what you want it to mean." He leaned forward and kissed my cheek. His touch made my skin crawl.

I didn't want it to mean anything, but he obviously did.

"I'm truly impressed by you. You have some unique gifts. Are you sure you weren't born here?"

I laughed nervously. "I mean, pretty sure, but who can actually remember their own birth?"

His eyes twinkled when he flashed me a smile. "Funny, too." Then he lowered his voice. "What about your parents?"

I sighed. "I honestly don't know anything about their past aside from the fact they were married young and lost all their family shortly after. I'm hoping the books I brought with me today can help me discover a little more."

"Before you get started with all that work, why don't we head to the dining room for breakfast?"

"Thanks for the offer, but I'm not hungry."

I doubted my churning stomach would allow anything to stay down for long, and I wanted to steer the conversation away from myself. "Lyra seemed quite confused about being here, and I don't know enough about this world to offer her any comfort. Perhaps you could help put her at ease."

"I do need to monitor her and chart her changes." He glanced toward Torren's room. "You said you wanted to move on."

I nodded.

"With the way things were left yesterday, you two have much to discuss. Will you be okay on your own?"

Rolling my shoulders back, I forced a smile. "I'll be fine." My vision blurred as tears flooded my eyes. Traitors.

I turned my back to Charlie and swiped the two tracks from my cheeks. Taking a deep breath, I braced myself and knocked on Torren's door.

HISTORY

Silence answered my gentle tapping. Not wanting to wake Torren, I let myself into his hospital room and padded toward the bed. The face I saw belonged to a stranger, one I had met only a few days ago. My gaze fell to his scar-less bottom lip, so similar to Kai's.

Watching him sleep peacefully, I let myself remember when Kai welcomed my kisses with his crooked smile. My heart beat faster, and I shook my head. Those thoughts would do me no good. Kai wasn't here. He wasn't even real.

I tore myself away from Torren's bedside and walked over to the table in the corner, where a selection of granola bars, graham crackers, and fruits sat on a plate in the center. A slip of white paper leaning against the plate caught my eye.

I figured a little food couldn't hurt. Good luck with everything. —C

I sat, my back to Torren's slumbering form, and reached into my backpack, pulling out a book titled *Council Creation*. Leaning back, I kicked my feet up onto the chair beside me and cradled the book in my lap. Mindlessly grabbing at the fruits on the plate, I became immersed in another world, oblivious to the space around me.

A warmth surrounded me, and a hand reached for the plate. I lowered my feet to the ground, holding my breath as I turned.

"Do you work in the hospital?" Torren quirked his brow and rubbed an apple against the sleeve of his hospital gown.

Surprised by his nearness, I shook my head. I hadn't even heard him get out of bed.

"What are you doing in here, then? Didn't you cause enough trouble yesterday?" The corners of his mouth flinched.

My cheeks burned. "I'm sorry. I should go. I should've known this wasn't a good idea."

He didn't love me. Whatever love existed between us was clearly only in my mind.

As I twisted to grab my backpack, the book on my lap slipped to the floor.

Torren swooped down to pick it up the same time I did, and our heads collided. He lifted the book and placed it on the table as I sat up and rubbed my head. "*Council Creation?* Didn't you learn enough 'bout that in elementary school?"

A knot formed in my throat, and I stared at my feet. "I'm not from around here."

Our eyes locked as I looked up to gauge his reaction.

"An Outsider? I'm guessing I have something to do with you being here."

I spoke softly, "Why would you think that?"

"That little girl is here because of my mistake with Celia, so I assume another Outsider showing up is my fault, too."

Why did everything always come back to Celia?

A frown overtook his face. "I don't know who you are, but you seem to know me. Which is a bit unsettling, if I'm being honest."

"Unsettling. Yeah, I can relate to that." I chortled at the thought. "I'm sorry I made you uncomfortable. I didn't mean to. I'm working through a lot of stuff right now."

He pressed his lips together. "And I'm part of that stuff?"

Resisting the urge to reach out for his hand, I nodded.

"Is that why you're here today?"

"Sort of. I couldn't concentrate anywhere else."

"But here you can? Near me?" His eyes softened, causing my heart to flutter.

I responded with a slight nod.

"Got a lot to learn?" He tapped the book.

"So much. I don't even know where to start." I twisted the chair to sit under the table.

"What do you have so far?"

Grabbing my notebook from my bag, I flipped through the scribbled nonsense. "I can't make heads or tails of any of it. It's interesting, but this world is so immense, I feel like I get swallowed up in it all."

He slid out the other chair, then froze. "Do you mind if I sit with you?"

"Of course not. You should rest. You've been through a lot." I stared at his wrists, now free from the silver bands. "What happened to your bracelets?"

Rubbing his wrists, he shrugged. "They only had them on me at the meeting and in the Glass House."

His eyes seemed to sparkle as he smiled and sat. His knee rested so close to mine I could feel the heat from his body. "I can help."

My breath shuddered, and my words came out barely above a whisper. "Help?"

Chuckling, he nodded toward my notebook. "With making heads or tails of all this."

Heat climbed into my cheeks. "I should be helping you. The doctor said you have quite a bit to recover from."

"This could be just what I need." He locked eyes with me, and when he smiled, my heart stuttered.

"Let's start off on a different foot today." He reached for my hand, and butterflies swept through me.

I expected him to brush his lips against the back of my hand as Kai had always done, but when he gave it a gentle squeeze instead, the fluttering evaporated.

"Hi. I'm Torren."

Torren. Not Kai.

"Arisanna," I breathed as he let go of my hand.

He stared at me, his mouth twitching as though he couldn't decide whether to smile or frown. "Ari."

My heart skipped a beat. "You remember?"

"No," he said, flinching at the disappointment he must've seen. "You look like an Ari."

I bit my lip. "What's the last thing you remember?"

"I assume you don't mean waking up to you saying my love was a lie."

My cheeks burned, and I couldn't control my foot as it slipped and knocked against his shin.

Feigning pain, he rubbed his leg and laughed.

I raised my eyebrows at him and squared my shoulders. "Not. Funny."

"Sorry." He cleared his throat. "I know I'm in the hospital because of my stint in the Glass House. The medicines they give you afterward bring comfort, but they also make a person a bit foggy for a little while."

My heart thudded against my chest. "So you could start to remember things you've forgotten once the medicine wears off?"

"I doubt these medicines could make me forget an entire person, especially someone I could've known long enough to develop deep feelings for." The corners of his mouth drooped.

Deep feelings. It was strange hearing that statement from *Torren*.

I took a shaky breath as my heart shattered once again. Maybe this was proof that I was nothing but a game to him. "What about Celia. Who is she to you?"

"She was my niece, but we were more like siblings. My brother and sister-in-law raised me."

"What happened to your parents?"

"My father died before I was born, and my mother died shortly after. Dad...and by Dad, I mean Callan...said something went haywire in our father's gift when the shift in command happened. It got to be more than he could handle. Eventually, his body shut down." He took a long breath. "Mother died from a broken heart. I just wish I could've been enough to heal it."

I wanted to hold him, but I had to restrain myself. He didn't know me.

His chin quivered before he forced a smile. "Let's get to the nitty gritty of this world. What do you need help understanding?"

"Glamours." The words left my mouth without a thought.

"Everyone has one."

"Just one?"

"Yes and no. A couple of years before we learn our gift, we're taught how to form and access our glamour. We're supposed to focus on perfecting one, and when our gift appears, that's the one that locks in."

"What do you need to perfect?"

"Facial features, eye color, body type, and what you want your voice to sound like."

"If you start practicing before your gift comes, wouldn't glamours look and sound like eight-year-olds?"

"Nope. Your glamour grows the same way you do, including changes to the tone of your voice. It's like a second, altered version of yourself. Once your gift arrives and the basic glamour is set, only cosmetic changes can be made. Makeup. Hair length and color."

"Can you change your clothes?"

"What? Isn't this flattering on me?" he asked, standing to model his hospital gown. "I'd spin for you, but—ya know."

Laughing, I blushed.

"Not clothes," he said as he sat back down. "And it's a shame."

"So how does it work? Are there rules or restrictions to it?"

"There are certain rules, but it's not one size fits all." His eyes sparkled as he spoke and reminded me of days in our meadow telling each other silly stories.

"There's a story behind that look."

His Adam's apple bobbed as he swallowed before a smile grew. "There are certain gifts that can alter glamour beyond the setting period. These people could have glamours that are drastically different day to day. They could even appear to be a different age."

"What kind of gifts can do that?" My words came out in a whisper.

"Gifts that affect the mind, like my brother, Brayden's." A grin spread across his face.

I smiled back. "And here's where the story comes."

He shook his head. "I don't know how you're doing this, but it's making my head spin."

"Doing what?"

The left side of his mouth rose into the crooked grin I loved. "Reading me."

Maybe he wasn't as much of a stranger as I'd originally thought. I fought back the blush that threatened to overtake me.

"When Celia and I were learning our glamour, Brayden showed us how his gift differed from others. So, while we were playing around with how we wanted our glamours to look, Brayden mimicked each iteration as we formed it. It was like looking in a mirror. We found it amusing until he became very serious.

"He warned us there were Alterrians who could manipulate their glamour well beyond their tenth year and some of those people might do it to hurt us. I never understood that. Still don't, but it's something I'll never forget."

The conversation had shifted, and I could tell the words he spoke weighed heavily on him.

But something weighed heavily on me as well. "Does everyone know what their own glamour looks like?"

"Yes. Want to see mine?" Torren's childlike excitement at sharing his glamour made up my mind, and I nodded before I paused to consider the consequences.

In the blink of an eye, Kai smiled at me, and my heart broke. He was my Kai, but he shared none of our memories.

I missed him so much it hurt, but—to him—it was like we'd never existed.

His smile shifted to a frown, and he became Torren again. "Sorry."

My face must've betrayed my emotion, but he'd apologized without knowing why. Guilt tore him apart, and I wondered how long he'd been suffering with Celia's disappearance to make that knee-jerk reaction.

I cleared my throat. "So what are they used for?"

Concern filled Torren's eyes.

Drawing in a breath, I pulled my shoulders back. I wouldn't cry and be the source of more guilt. "I'm fine. Really."

He hesitated before continuing. "They're mainly used if our gifts take us outside of our world and may put us in danger."

For some reason, that answer angered me, and my words came out sharper than intended. "But how does glamour protect you? I don't understand. It's not like Outsiders just walk into your world and can point you out."

He forced out a soft chuckle. "There are other ways into your world that don't involve gifts. We don't use glamour then. If we use our gifts to get to your world, we use the glamour to protect us if an Outsider happens to see the gift being used. Then, if we walked into your world, we would still be safe."

My mind trailed back to when I first met Kai. He had snuck up behind me as I dipped my toes in the river. "Would it be used to deceive a person?"

"Depends. Some use glamour to get closer to people so they can exploit them. But most of the time, glamour's a form of protection and nothing more."

How badly I wanted to ask where he fit in that spectrum, but my heart couldn't take any more today. The corners of my mouth twitched. "Tell me about Celia."

He raised one eyebrow and flashed the same smile I'd seen over the course of the last five years, minus the scar. It still made my heart skip a beat. "She had golden blonde hair and loved an adventure, but she was also a people pleaser—the biggest daddy's girl. She was my best friend before…"

"I'm sorry. I shouldn't have asked."

When he spoke, his voice held a hint of annoyance. "Why all the questions about my family? How long have we actually known each other?"

"Five years."

His eyes went wide as he leaned back in the chair. "Five years and I never told you anything about Celia?"

I shrugged, unsure how much I should share. What if I made him angry? "We didn't really talk family stuff, just that you were raised by your brother and his wife. The topic always made you sad, so I left it alone."

He leaned in a little, his fingertips nearly touching mine. "Then what did we talk about?"

I couldn't control my smile. "Oh, all sorts of stuff! I'd have my school books with me, and we'd learn about economics, and geology, and even a little algebra. We pored over history the most, and you claimed it as your specialty. My favorite was when I brought my literature and you'd ask me to read aloud to you. Besides all that, we'd talk about our favorite things, our hopes and dreams." I blushed. "Our future."

His cheeks turned red as he tried to hold back a smile.

The cloud of memory I'd been floating on disintegrated. We had no future, not anymore.

He drummed his fingers on the cover of the book on the table. "If you plan to read this whole thing, that'll be your future for the *next* five years. Want a summary instead?"

My shoulders relaxed. "If you wouldn't mind."

"What're all the notes and studying for, anyway?"

"I've been asked to join Council, but High Councilman told me I needed to know the history. Plus, I'm a bit curious about it all myself. I feel connected to this world and want to know why."

Torren shot me a sideways glance, opened his mouth to say something, and then shook his head. "Council, huh?"

"Yeah..."

"Well, I see this situation as one of two things. You're either being used to spy on me, or they're looking to get something out of you." He studied me as I processed his words.

I blinked a few times. I just wanted to get home. "Oh. Why do you say that?"

"Future Council members have to follow certain protocols. Making friends with the current prison population is not one of them."

I'd been sent here to discuss things, not make friends. Confusion mingled with hope. Did he think of me as a new friend?

He shrugged. "I could be wrong. I am the kid they keep throwing in the Glass House." He cleared his throat and leaned his chest against his folded arms on the tabletop. "You don't seem to want to join Council."

I shook my head.

"Then what *do* you want?"

"To go home."

His voice softened. "So why don't you?"

How would I answer a question like that after everything I'd learned?

They watched his Glass House transmissions, so they knew our connection and kept throwing us together.

Would going home put my family in danger? Would it endanger him? Something about *just* going home seemed too easy.

A chill ran up my spine as I sensed we weren't alone, so I chose my words carefully. "I don't know the way."

His eyes met mine. "I could help you."

Slight movement of the door caught my attention, and my heart crept into my throat. "How?" I snapped. "You can't even remember me."

Torren's face fell, and he leaned away from me.

"Sorry about that," I whispered before getting up to check the hall, then closed the door behind me. "We were being watched."

He gave me a quick wink and forced a smile. "Council was formed not too long ago by a few old men."

I furrowed my brows. "Really?"

Leaning back into the chair, he threw his arms up. "Hey, I'll tell you the truth, but I have to make it interesting."

I rolled my eyes. "Well, by all means, proceed."

"As I was saying, these old men weren't so old when they came up with the idea of Council. Our little portion of Alterria had recently finished a brutal civil war. Our people were divided into Wilds and Puritans.

"Wilds believed our gifts were good and should be used for such. They also believed the divide between Outsiders and Alterrians was unnecessary and wanted to work to break it down.

"The Puritans wanted to exploit the gifts of others, and some even tried to find ways to make them stronger. These people believed purity made Alterria stronger. They believed in the ideals of past generations.

"Some of these generations went so far as to keep their own bloodlines pure and would only marry a person with gifts that matched their own. Two of the most well-known were the Morganfire and Lunagarde lines."

A cold wave rushed through me, and time seemed to stop.

"Are you okay? Should I keep going?"

Try as I may, I couldn't force any words from my mouth, so I nodded very slowly.

"Ari, if this is too much, we can take a break," he said, his voice soothing me.

I took a deep breath. I needed to hear this from him now before I had to go another night with confused dreams. "No, I want to know more. Please."

He leaned back in his chair again, his hands folded in his lap. "These three old men, who weren't old at this time, embodied both sides. Damond Morganfire and Cyran Lunagarde were both alchemists. Damond believed gifts were meant to be used for good. Cyran wanted purity.

"Their mutual friend, Robert Weiss, embodied both ideals. He believed gifts were inherently good but that working to enhance those gifts could lead to great things. Robert had the gift of Foresight, so he could see a future where both sides worked together to create a perfect unity of good power. He also saw a future where

Alterrians and Outsiders could live again in harmony." He looked at me and grinned. "You following so far?"

I nodded once, my eyebrows drawing inward. "Morganfire: Wild, Lunagarde: Puritan. Robert saw the benefits of both sides."

"Good. The people loved Robert so much that they decided he should be High Councilman. Damond and Cyran never saw eye to eye, but both were asked to join Council. Robert saw how both men could bring a great balance. Cyran jumped at the opportunity, and Damond politely declined. It's believed this is what triggered the Morganfire and Lunagarde feud."

My teeth clenched so tightly that my ears pulsed with pain. I would have fallen over if I were not sitting. On top of everything I should have known and didn't, my grandfathers had been locked in a feud. Was my family this world's Montagues and Capulets, with my parents headlining as Romeo and Juliet? Except instead of embracing death, my parents disappeared.

Torren reached over and placed his hand on top of my clenched fist. "Hey, I don't think you're okay."

A tremble ran through my body.

"We can stop." He grasped both my hands. His touch, strange yet so familiar, redirected my focus. All of that was in the past, and it was important that I know my history.

I took a deep breath. "How long ago did all this take place?"

"Damond, Cyran, and Robert were a little older than my parents. So not long ago. Maybe fifty years?"

I pressed my hands to my eyes. "What happened to the men?"

Torren paused before speaking, like he was ensuring he had his facts straight. "Robert died shortly after transferring power to Edric. Damond died before his daughter disappeared without a trace with her new husband, Cyran's son. Cyran died a little over a decade ago. Poison, I believe."

"I don't understand. I've read so many books in the library that didn't go into any of these details. This is the most I've learned about any of these men."

He pursed his lips. "The ideals of our former High Councilman and Edric clash. I grew up being taught both. I assume if you've been getting your literature from the Council library, it's the history that leans toward Edric's ideals."

I tried to slow my breathing but could feel my head getting lighter.

His eyebrows drew. "Can I help?"

"No." I closed my eyes and steadied my breathing. "I'd been trying to learn more about my family, but I hadn't expected this. Edric knew who I was all along."

"Now I'm confused. I thought you were an Outsider."

"Torren." I took a deep breath. "I'm a Lunagarde."

He nodded, his expression softening.

"And a Morganfire."

Chapter Sixteen

A New Gift

Tossing and turning all night, I wondered what the implications of my name might mean in this new world. As the sun rose, I wandered to the courtyard, attempting to put together the shattered pieces of my mind. I stretched out on the bench swing, the summer heat lulling me into a dreamless sleep.

A gentle tap on my shoulder brought me back to reality.

"Would you like to go to town with me, Arisanna?" Charlie asked.

I looked up, shielding my eyes from the sun. "For what?"

He chuckled. "We had a birthday this week, so I need to make a visit."

"Birthday?"

"A little girl turned ten." He paused and tilted his head. "You know that's when gifts begin to reveal themselves, don't you?"

"Of course. Why do you want me to come with you?"

"Well, you could use a change of pace, and I wouldn't mind the company."

"What about Lyra?"

"She'll be fine. Mrs. Chapman introduced her to a deck of cards. Go Fish evolved to Rummy faster than you can say 'Gin'."

My eyebrows jumped to my forehead. "You're kidding."

Charlie shrugged, a twinkle in his eye. "Can't promise I won't join for a couple rounds later on myself. She seems like she knows what she's doing. In the meantime, what do you say?"

"Sure. Why not?"

When I stepped outside Council Hall, a brisk, hot summer wind blew my hair into my eyes. The courtyard was outside, too, but its walls provided more protection than I'd given them credit for. I tied my hair back and fell into step beside Charlie.

"Have you had a chance to tour Alterria?"

"No. I've only been to Council Hall and Callan's house. I wonder…"

"If you should visit while we're out?" Charlie sighed. "Edric cautioned you'd ask that. Considering what they put you through, he doesn't think it's a good idea."

"What do you mean?"

He stopped and put his hands on my shoulders. "I'm sorry. He didn't tell me any details. If they truly wanted to, they could always visit. Deborah used to come see Lyra all the time."

I hadn't thought about that. They hadn't even tried. So much for being my mother's best friend. I was less important than a little girl they'd never known.

Charlie pulled me in for a hug, keeping one arm around me as we walked, and I reminded myself it only meant what I wanted it to. "Let's put that behind us for now. I'm sure the people we're going to meet will love you."

He removed his arm from around my shoulder as he paused at the end of a row of houses and pointed down the lane. "Look straight through here."

I squinted. "What specifically should I be looking at?"

"That willow in the distance."

The willow stood alone, but the longer I stared, the less normal the tree appeared. Was it fading? No…That was impossible.

I smiled to myself. Was anything impossible in Alterria?

"Some say it marks the old Morganfire home."

"I wonder how many secrets are buried within that rubble," I responded.

"Rubble?" He shot a sharp glance in my direction, then shook his head and continued walking.

"Charlie! Charlie!" a young voice cried as we approached a one-story cottage near the edge of the lane. "Do you have any candy?"

"Candy?" He put a finger to his chin. "Hm."

The little girl pounced on the oversize pockets of his doctor's coat and dug around until she extracted a lollipop as big as her hand.

"Rachel, what do you say?" A thin woman stood in the doorway. Shadows under her eyes suggested she'd had a few sleepless nights.

Rachel moved her fingertips outward from her chin. Her bright almond-shaped eyes sparkled as she enjoyed her treat.

"You're welcome, Rachel. Do you mind if I talk to your mom?" Charlie asked.

"Can I play outside?"

"You know the rules," her mom said.

When Rachel grinned, her top lip covered her teeth, and the corners of her mouth stretched ear to ear.

"Do you mind if I join you?" I asked her.

"Sure," she said. "Do you want a lick?"

"That's okay. Why don't you show me what kinds of things you like to play outside?"

"Hey, do you wanna see a trick?"

"I'd love that."

Rachel shut her eyes tight in concentration.

My heart dropped when she suddenly disappeared. "Rachel?"

Giggling sounded behind me, and when I turned around, there she stood. "Wow, Rachel. I'm impressed."

"I know," she said and proceeded to run around the yard. She appeared and disappeared as she ran, the sucker clutched in one hand. "Do you see?"

Her gleeful laughter was contagious, and I couldn't help but join in.

"Catch me!"

"What?" I spun in place. "Where are you?"

"Rachel, honey, that's enough now." Her mother appeared on the porch step, her voice kind but strained. "Charlie would like to see you. And I mean he'd like to actually *see* you."

Rachel popped into view.

"Arisanna, Mrs. Jones has a freshly baked batch of cookies. I'd suggest you try one. They're delicious."

"Yes, come on in." Mrs. Jones led me to the kitchen table and motioned me to an empty chair. "Charlie said you might be hungry, so I made this for you."

"Thank you, Mrs. Jones," I said, accepting a sandwich, a double chocolate chip, and a glass of cold milk.

She sat beside me and leaned back with a sigh. "No need to be so formal, Arisanna. Please, call me Cora."

"And you can call me Ari."

She pressed her lips together. "Your mom and I were friends once upon a time. You remind me of her. She was good with kids, too."

I glanced out the window and saw Rachel playing her version of hide and seek with Charlie. "She's enjoying her gift."

Cora smiled. "Yes, she's enjoying it immensely. But sometimes she forgets how to bring herself back. I'm so anxious she's going to get stuck that way or that she's going to get hurt. I haven't slept well in two weeks."

"Charlie said she just turned ten."

"It's not uncommon for the gifts to show up a little early, and some don't develop until a little later. It's not an exact science."

Rachel's laughter caught my attention again as Charlie used his stethoscope as a microphone.

Cora followed my gaze. "Charlie's a good doctor—a good man—and the kids love him. When the old doctor retired and we were told Edric would be choosing his replacement, I became concerned."

"You don't trust Edric?"

"I wouldn't say that. I wasn't sure what would happen to anyone who didn't meet his ridiculous standards, but I have to admit he seems to have made a good choice in Charlie."

Charlie poked his head in from the back door. "Arisanna, would you come out here for a moment? There's something I think you could help me with."

"Go on," Cora said. "I need to tidy up."

"It was nice chatting with you."

I went back outside and watched Rachel popping in and out of view. "Her mom seems so worried. I wish there was something we could do to ease her mind."

"Have you learned about the formation of gifts yet in your reading?"

"Torren mentioned some people wanted to keep bloodlines pure and married people with gifts that matched their own. I didn't fully understand."

He gave me a tight smile. "Well, then, I get to teach you a little something today. Gifts are passed down through the generations. If great-grandpa could start fires, there's a chance his great-granddaughter could do the same."

"So a gift must appear somewhere in the family lines?"

"Sometimes an unexpected gift will appear, but chances are the gift will be familial. Rachel inherited her gift from her father."

"That's wonderful. She'll have someone to teach her."

Charlie shook his head. "About eight years ago, someone from Council hired Mr. Jones to do a job that required his skill. Unfortunately, he sustained injuries in the process and didn't survive."

I slapped my hands over my mouth. "Poor Rachel."

"And poor Mrs. Jones. You may have noticed Rachel is a little different from other children. She was born with Down syndrome."

"I've heard of it but don't really know what it means." I looked across the yard.

Rachel had put her gift aside to build a castle in the sandbox. Her tongue stuck out of the corner of her mouth, and she concentrated on putting little twigs in the top of each turret.

"It's more complex than this, but as a generalization, children who have Down syndrome develop at a slower pace. Rachel communicated mostly in signs until the age of four. Even now, she often reverts to signs instead of using words, and sometimes she's a little hard to understand."

"She doesn't seem slow," I said, confused. "She developed her gift two weeks early."

"She's doing great," Charlie said. "Everyone learns at a different pace, and people with Down syndrome are no exception. Some overcome challenges more easily than others."

"Are those challenges why Mrs. Jones is so tired?"

"Without her husband, she's had to raise Rachel alone. But this new disappearing act has been quite stressful for Mrs. Jones."

I looked over at Rachel, still engrossed in her task. Her two braids hung over her shoulder as she dug a moat around her castle. "Is there any way I can help?" I asked, my heart aching for Cora.

"That's actually what I wanted to talk to you about. Mrs. Jones could use a break. She's not ready to let Rachel out of her sight—so to speak—but if you would be willing to visit sometime, spend a couple of hours with Rachel so Mrs. Jones could relax, that would go a long way."

"Rachel is a sweetheart. I would love to."

"I thought so. I'm going to say goodbye, and then we'll head out."

Rachel squatted in front of her creation, sand covering her hands and bare feet. "Do you see?" she asked, proudly pointing when I walked over.

"I do, and it looks wonderful."

"Do you want to play?" She held up her pinkies and thumbs and wiggled both hands.

"I have to go, but I'll come back another time."

"Sure." Rachel smiled and went back to playing.

When Charlie and I left the house, he took my hand again. It made my skin crawl, but I didn't pull away.

"I need to stop at the pharmacy. Do you mind?"

"Of course not," I assured him.

As we walked, he pointed out some of the unique shops, and I took the opportunity to slip my hand away from his.

"Charlie!" called a woman in her early twenties. She wore high heels and a short red dress that intensified her fiery curls.

"Madeline," he replied.

She approached us and cooed up at him. "That lotion you gave me is amazing. My skin is so smooth." She placed her hand on his cheek.

"Indeed it is." He carried an unexpected hint of affection in his voice.

She let her hand linger before stroking his chin. "I'd like to thank you, Charlie. Dinner at my place. Bring champagne."

"I'll check my schedule and get back to you."

"Don't make me wait too long, Charlie." She pouted before giving him a peck on the cheek and then looked at me pointedly, her red smile pasted on. She walked away, auburn curls bouncing on her shoulders.

"Madeline might have a bit of a crush on me," he said sheepishly.

"Clearly," I responded, bewildered by her boldness.

"Here come the Newmans."

A family of three headed toward us. The father was tall with black hair and a beard to match. He wore a permanent glare. The oldest son, a few inches taller than his dad, had dark brown hair and deep chestnut eyes. The shorter boy looked like a younger version of his brother.

Charlie took my hand again, and we continued walking. "Good morning, gentlemen," he said as we approached.

The little boy waved.

"Kyle, no. That's a Morganfire." The father turned his glare to me.

My heart stopped as short as Charlie did.

"What did you say, Mr. Newman?" he called.

I tugged on Charlie's arm. "Please don't. Let's keep walking."

He gritted his teeth but let Mr. Newman continue on his way. "Kyle will be ten in a couple of months. Leif is eighteen. I believe he is apprenticing with his father. Mr. Newman is a Council advisor and has high expectations of his children."

"And everyone else, apparently." I'd never considered that people might not like me because of my last name. It hurt, but I decided not to let it get to me.

"Opinions like that aren't worth your time."

"What's that?" I pointed to a pastel blue building with purple shutters.

"That's the café I told you about. I'd take you, but Mrs. Winterly closed it for renovations this week."

It appeared welcoming and friendly from the outside. I imagined myself drinking a cappuccino at one of the cozy round tables in front, with Kai smiling across from me.

No, not Kai. Torren.

"Here we are." Charlie nodded toward the pharmacy. "Would you like to come in?"

Toward the center of town, directly across from the pharmacy, my gaze settled on a multi-tiered fountain surrounded by four park benches. Hedges lined the grassy, tree-shaded area beyond it.

"Do you mind if I wait out here?"

"Of course not," he said, kissing me on the cheek. "I'll be out soon."

It only means what I want it to mean, right? I released a long breath and dropped onto a bench in front of the fountain.

Two old women beamed at me as they ambled by. "It's nice to see Charlie so happy," the one with a cane whispered to her white-haired friend.

Strangers saw him kiss me. What did it mean to them?

A man stood in front of me, blocking the hot afternoon sun. "Ms. Lunagarde?"

I glanced up at the stranger and squinted against the backlight surrounding him. "Yes?"

"I was told I would find you here. My name is Cedric." He held out his hand in greeting, and I accepted it.

A sudden falling sensation came over me, so I yanked my hand away and gripped the edges of the bench to steady myself.

He didn't seem to notice as he continued talking. "Your grandfather and I were friends. He was quite insistent that we meet." He glanced around nervously before resting his palm on my shoulder and leaning closer. "I must go, but be wary of who you trust." And with that, he disappeared into the crowd.

With my confusion, my lack of sleep the previous night hit me full force.

"Let's get you home." Charlie's sudden appearance startled me.

I wanted to refuse his offer of help when I stood, but my energy was low. Before my knees buckled, he tucked my hand into the crook of his arm, and I allowed him to escort me back to Council Hall.

Once inside, out of the glaring brightness, my strength slowly returned.

"You need to lie down." Charlie's eyebrows furrowed. "The sun took a lot out of you today."

"I want to check on Lyra first."

Once outside her room, he turned to me. "Before you go in, I want to thank you for coming with me today. I enjoyed our time together."

"I appreciate you showing me around." I stiffened as he stepped closer to me.

He slid his hand up my arm to my shoulder, then curled his fingers to brush my hair back. He placed a gentle kiss near the corner of my mouth, then disappeared down the hall.

I remained frozen in place until the urge to scrub my cheek overwhelmed me.

I hadn't expected that, and my stomach twisted. I didn't ask for any of Charlie's advances. I didn't even want them.

As I stepped into Lyra's room, I glanced back to Torren's with a pit settling into my stomach. His door was ajar.

CHAPTER SEVENTEEN

After Town

Lyra's hands were balled into little fists, knuckles white, and she tried kicking off her blankets. A whimper escaped her lips, compelling me to rush across the room.

I sat on the edge of her bed and ran my hand gently across Lyra's forehead, brushing a few strands of hair from her face. Focusing on slowing my breathing, I placed my hands on top of hers and exhaled.

As tremors rolled up my arms and through my body, she stilled. I relaxed and planted a kiss on her head as a small smile formed on her now peaceful face.

"Wow."

I jumped up and spun around.

Torren leaned against the door frame, his hospital gown replaced by running pants and a plain white t-shirt. His crooked smile greeted me, and my heart raced at the sight of him.

Smiling back, I smoothed Lyra's blankets before exiting her room, easing the door closed so as not to wake her.

I nudged his shoulder. "You scared me."

"Didn't mean to." He stared at me, still smiling.

"What are you doing here?"

"I saw you walk past my room." He ran his hand through his hair, and a pit of anxiety settled in my stomach.

What had he seen through his cracked door?

"I missed you," he breathed.

Maybe I had nothing to worry about. I tilted my head up to meet his eyes. "Yeah?"

"It's a bit lonely here," he said with a mischievous grin.

My heart sank. "That's the only reason you followed me? So you wouldn't be lonely?"

"Hey, I was just joking around." His voice was less playful as he reached for my hand. "I really did miss you."

I placed my hand within his and sighed as the butterflies took flight. What did *he* want this to mean? "I missed you, too."

"I'm starving. Want to go get some food?"

"Are you allowed to leave your room?" I looked around to see if anyone was watching.

"As long as I don't leave the building, I don't think they care."

My stomach growled, and I pressed my hands against it, my cheeks warming. "I haven't eaten much today. Food sounds amazing."

When we reached the cafeteria, I took a deep breath, inhaling the warm aroma of freshly made spaghetti that drifted in the air."

Torren grabbed two trays, and I followed him to a table.

He glanced at me. "So, where have you been all day? Hitting the books in the library?"

I shook my head. "I went into town and met some of the people. A little girl just started learning her gift, so we made a house call."

"We?" His voice cracked a little as he spoke.

"Charlie asked me to come along with him."

His jaw pulsed. "Charlie."

I stopped eating and looked at him. "Are you okay?"

He forced a smile and spoke through clenched teeth. "Fine."

We finished eating in silence and brought our empty trays to the counter before heading back toward his room.

"So, you and Charlie..." His voice seemed to curdle as he spoke the words, "You like him?"

"He's a friend. I don't have many of those."

"Am I a friend?"

I thought for a moment. "Kai was my best friend. I've only just met Torren."

His head sank.

I placed my hand on his cheek and guided his eyes to mine. "I didn't mean that in a bad way. I've just met Torren, but he's becoming someone I trust as much as Kai."

He smiled and leaned a little closer.

With Kai fresh on my mind, my heart raced. What would *he* think?

A man and woman turned the corner at the end of the hall. As they passed by, the lady scoffed. "Can you believe she's with that Lachloren boy?"

I happened to *like* that Lachloren boy.

As Torren's smile faded, I glared after her before tugging him into his room and closing the door.

Sliding the chair away from the table, he sat, resting his elbows on his knees, his head in his hands. "You'd be better off with someone like Charlie. Everyone seems to love him."

"I don't." I knelt on the floor beside Torren. I wanted to tell him I was falling for him, but I couldn't.

The way he looked at me when he woke up after the Glass House replayed in my mind. Torren didn't know me, and I was still in love with Kai.

His eyes met mine.

"Just so you know, I don't care about what anyone else thinks. I make my own decisions about who I spend my time with."

He sat up a little straighter. "People may get the wrong idea about you."

"I'm a Morganfire and a Lunagarde. They already have ideas about me." Especially Mr. Newman. But who cared about *his* opinion?

I walked toward a vanity on the other side of Torren's bed. Inspecting my reflection, I pinched my cheeks and pressed my palms to my eyes, then lowered my hands and frowned.

"You okay?"

From the mirror, I could see him staring at me. "Do you think I have a glamour?" I asked, twisting my head to look at him.

He shrugged. "Usually, kids have more or less figured it out by the time they get their gift."

I leaned closer toward the mirror and squinted my eyes, willing them to change color. They refused.

"You're going to hurt yourself," Torren said, relaxed in his chair, leaning his head back on his intertwined fingers.

I whipped around in embarrassment to meet his crooked grin. I couldn't help but laugh. "Well, show me how you do it, smarty pants."

"Well, Callan is the better teacher, but I'll give it a try." He stood and took a deep breath. "You start with your eyes," he said, crossing them. "Then your nose." He pinched the bridge while keeping his eyes crossed.

I folded my arms across my chest and raised my eyebrow.

"Pucker your lips a little, and then spin around in a circle. Make sure it's clockwise, or it won't work." He spun, and when he stopped, he was Kai.

"You've *got* to be kidding me."

"Yeah, I am." He grinned as he shifted back into Torren. "And the look on your face was worth it."

As I dropped back into the chair, I slammed my elbows on the table and leaned into my fists, finishing my fit with a scrunch-faced growl.

He leaned close and ran his thumb across my cheek. "I may need to tease you more often. You're pretty cute when you get frustrated."

Rolling my eyes, I folded my arms on top of the table. Try as I may, I couldn't fight the smile that overtook my frustration. "Stop."

"So, what's next?" he chuckled as he sat.

I held up my palms, a smile spreading across my face. "Should we continue practicing?"

Torren's hands covered mine in haste, his eyes wide. "Not here," he warned in a hushed tone. "Never here."

I slid my hands onto my lap. As much as I relished his touch, I couldn't bear the thought it meant more to me than it did to him. "Okay."

"Are you tired?"

"Not really. Are you?"

"Nope. So, what's on the agenda for tonight? Anything you're itching to learn about?"

I pulled in my bottom lip. "Since the glamour experiment didn't pan out, maybe we should do what we were never able to all those years."

He glanced at me nervously. "What's that?"

"Talk about our families."

"What do you want to know?"

I shrugged. "Anything. Everything. I want to get to know as much about you as possible."

"Well, you know about my parents, being raised by Callan and Deborah. And Celia."

"Has Callan or Deborah come to see you?"

He brushed his thumb down the side of his nose. "Glass House *guests* don't get the privilege of visitors. Or phone calls."

"Oh." I glanced around the room. It seemed so bare compared to all the flowers and gifts crowding Lyra's.

I placed my hand within his and shifted the conversation. "I bet you had a lot of friends growing up."

"I did…but once Celia disappeared, none of them wanted to be around me anymore." He attempted to smile. "Who would want to be friends with someone who could make you disappear into thin air?"

I scooted my chair closer to his, our eyes connecting.

He entwined his fingers with mine.

"I would have," I whispered.

"I doubt you would've stuck around had you known the truth."

All those years of hiding the truth about Celia, he was afraid he'd lose me. Did our conversation spark a memory for him?

"Ari, I still don't remember."

"Why did you say that?"

"That look in your eyes. I've seen it from Dad every time he would leave on a search. Hope looks the same on everyone." He cleared his throat. "Your turn. What was it like for you growing up?"

"Well, I'm an only child, so I spent most of my days with my mom and dad." I shook my head, beginning to understand the reasons behind their choices.

"What about school?"

"They taught me themselves. I loved learning from them and never imagined I missed out on anything. Knowing what I know now, they were probably afraid my gift would show up when they weren't there to protect me from what other people might say or do."

"But it didn't show up?"

"Not until I got here."

Torren reclined in his chair. He opened his mouth like he wanted to ask something but held back.

I looked down at our hands still wound together. "My favorite lessons were the ones that brought us into the woods. Those were Dad's lessons." Summer days spent in the trees, nothing but nature surrounding us, brought a smile to my face.

"Share the memory?" Torren smiled.

I leaned in closer, our knees touching. "There was this one time we were learning about plant life in the woods. We were further out than we'd ever been before. I could hear the river running nearby, but we were still too far away to see it."

Closing my eyes, I watched the memory play in my mind. "Dad had been in the middle of explaining what poison ivy could do when the most beautiful sound I'd ever heard filled the air around us." I stopped talking and listened to the chorus playing in my memory.

"What was it?"

I opened my eyes to find Torren had leaned in closer. Did his lips feel like Kai's? My cheeks warmed at the thought, and I sat back a little, my heart thudding against my chest.

I licked my lips and spoke softly. "Wolves. It sounded like they were serenading us."

"I've never heard of someone who enjoys the sound of wolves. Most people are frightened of the ones around here."

My thoughts flashed to Cade, how his presence brought me comfort. "My dad loves the sound, too."

His eyes widened. "Have you seen one? They're huge! And they've been altered to spy."

"All of them?" I croaked.

"The ones roaming Council Hall, for sure. They were one of Cyran's pet projects."

My grandfather. "Was he a really bad man?"

Torren brushed a strand of hair out of my eyes. "Any history I've learned about Cyran has always felt wrong to me, and I haven't figured out why. All I know for sure is that Edric trained under him."

"I feel like I'm trapped in a storybook, but the middle keeps throwing all these hurdles, and I can hardly keep up. One of these days, I'm going to hit one head-on and crumble into a million pieces."

Torren tugged my hand, his other arm stretched out for me.

I slid off my chair and into his lap, my head resting against his shoulder as he relaxed into me and closed his arms around me. The weight I had been carrying began to slip away.

"I'm here with you. Any hurdle that knocks you down, I'll be there to pick you up."

I looked into his eyes.

"Still no memories. It just feels right."

I sighed and laid my head against his chest. "Too bad true love's kiss can't bring them back."

His heart sped up as he swallowed back a laugh. "This world might seem like it's full of magic, but this isn't a fairy tale."

"I guess not."

His voice softened. "I mean, we could always give it a try."

My breath hitched, and I pressed my lips together as he leaned his head ever so slightly toward mine. My hands trembled as Kai's scar came to my mind. Torren wasn't Kai. I leaned back a little, my mind in a tailspin.

He rubbed the back of his neck as he looked away, his cheeks a cherry red. "I'm sorry. I didn't mean to make you uncomfortable."

The clock above his door caught my attention.

"Torren," I said as I stood, "it's three in the morning. We should probably try to get some sleep." I turned to leave the room when he caught me by the wrist and spun me around.

He grinned, one side higher than the other, just like Kai. He lifted my hand to his lips and brushed on a kiss, just like Kai. And then, just like Kai, he ended with, "Until we meet again."

My heart soared. It was almost like having him back.

With that thought, my heart sank. Although I knew they were the same person, I wasn't being fair to Torren. I couldn't expect him to be Kai, so there was only one thing I could do. I had to bury Kai in my heart.

CHAPTER EIGHTEEN

A LOVE STORY

I didn't sleep. The harder I tried to forget Kai, the more I clung to his memory. I fought a battle in my mind to give myself permission to fall for Torren because—in reality—I already had.

Maybe Kai had a different face and a different voice, but his carefree personality was just the other side of the coin.

Torren seemed to carry the weight of the world on his shoulders, and who wouldn't want a break from that every now and then?

Torren and Kai had the same quick wit and ability to make me smile. Shouldn't that be evidence enough that when I fell for one, I fell for the other, too?

My stomach rumbled, and I decided to head to the cafeteria. Upon opening my door, a book fell at my feet. Picking it up, I flipped through the pages, releasing a long breath when I saw it was filled with words and pictures. I placed it in my backpack and glanced down the empty hall. Following a quick breakfast, I went to visit Lyra.

As I made my way down the Council hallways toward the hospital, I passed several townspeople. Most gave a friendly wave or smile. Some, however, avoided eye contact altogether. I could hear their whispers, barely below a normal tone. They landed on certain words as though they were profanities. *Morganfire. Lunagarde. Lachloren.*

Adjusting my backpack, I kept my head lowered as I proceeded. Never before had I experienced the searing disappointment that came with such hatred of my name.

I shook my head to clear the negative thoughts and focused on Lyra as I entered her room. "Looks like someone is feeling better."

A pair of jeans and a yellow t-shirt covered in bright butterflies replaced the hospital gown, and her long brown hair had been tied up into two French braids. Her bright green eyes lit up with her smile.

"Do you like my hair? Mrs. Chapman did it after my shower. She even got me a cute outfit." She jumped off her bed and spun in a circle. "I love butterflies!"

"You're gorgeous." I watched her dance around the tiny room, her newfound boundless energy making me feel like dancing, too.

She stopped twirling and grasped my hands. "Guess what? Charlie said I get to move into a bigger room now that I don't need needles in my arm anymore."

"That's fantastic!" I placed my backpack on the bed. "I brought you a surprise."

Her eyes widened as she began bouncing. "Really? What is it?"

I pulled out the storybook I had found outside my room.

"Ooh! I've never seen that book before." She took a seat on the bed, patted the space beside her, and snuggled into my side as I sat.

"Once upon a time, there was a bridge that connected two worlds," I read.

"Oh, a fairy tale. My favorite!"

"Mine, too."

Illustrations filled the pages, and the edges were decorated in curlicue designs.

A man named Ronin lived on the magical side of the bridge and was one of the few who dared cross it. One day, he went Outside and met a beautiful woman named Harmony who sold gooseberries at a roadside stand. Before long, the two of them fell in love.

When Ronin tried to bring Harmony to his side of the bridge, she crumpled in pain and fear. After several attempts, Ronin successfully created an elixir that allowed her to be in his magical world for a brief period of time, but the pain and fear always returned.

Ronin sighed, the bridge behind him. "I don't want you to ever come back here. It's not worth the risk. I can't stand to see you in pain, knowing nothing I can do will fix it."

"I'm going to miss you," Harmony said, her eyes dropping to her feet.

"Harmony, you don't understand. I love you too much to walk away. I want to build a life with you. Out there." He gestured to her side of the bridge.

Harmony wrapped her arms around him, and with a kiss, they began their future.

"The end." I closed the book.

"No, wait. You missed a page." Lyra took the book from my hands and flipped to the back. "Look."

I peeked over her shoulder. Sure enough, there was a poem on the back. Not a poem—the lullaby my mother sang to me. I smiled. "I know this song. My mom used to sing me to sleep with it every night."

"Could you sing it to me?"

"Of course."

The mist and the meadow, whenever they do meet
Speak of the young, dancing and free
Glamour in the moonlight, true love so sweet
Sharing ambition, never meant to be

The forest calls my name, I must leave it all and go
In the shadow of the leaves, past the river I will roam
Others will not understand, I can't teach what they don't know
Forever with my guardian, the forest is my home

Born of this world but not within, missing link from far away
Faith expands, protection grows, whatever price must be paid
A power once thought lost revealed, Enlightenment dawns today
From a world once dying to itself, a new life will be made

"I've never heard that last verse. Did you make it up?" Torren once again leaned against the frame.

A giddiness rushed through me. "I didn't hear you come in."

He grinned and brushed his hair from his forehead. "The singing drew me in like a siren song. That was beautiful."

I glanced away. "Thank you."

"What are you reading?"

"A story about an Alterrian and an Outsider who fell in love." My cheeks burned as I spoke, nervous energy pulsing through my veins. Sensing Torren's intense gaze, I couldn't meet his eyes.

"My mama used to tell me a story just like this one," Lyra piped in.

"She did?" My eyebrows raised in surprise.

"Mm-hmm, but I've never seen the pictures before." She smirked at Torren, a sparkle in her eyes. "Do you believe in true love?"

His eyes connected with mine. "I'm starting to."

The tenderness in his voice threw my heart into overdrive. Could we go back to what we once had?

He cleared his throat as he straightened from the door frame. "Do you mind if I steal Ari from you for a bit?"

Lyra cocked one eyebrow, lips upturned in a mischievous smile. "Can I keep the book?"

"How could I say no to a face like that?" I handed it to her and picked up my backpack. I turned at the door to give Lyra a little wave.

Her smile grew as she settled in to reread the book.

I backed out of the room and stumbled into Torren. "So," I stuttered, stepping away, "what did you have in mind?"

His eyebrows drew closer. "Where did you learn that extra verse?"

I froze, unsure what to say. "You're going to think I'm delusional."

"Maybe," he shrugged, a smirk playing upon his lips, "but I'd never tell you."

My mouth fell open.

Bursting into laughter, he gently pushed my shoulder. "I'm joking."

The "x" he drew over his heart put me at ease, and I was more willing to share. "In the labyrinth, a wall opened up under my touch, and I entered a cavern covered with strange symbols. I wish I could show you..."

His eyes sparkled, and I smiled.

I knew that look all too well. "What are you planning?"

"Want to get out of here for a bit?"

I kept my voice low. "How? You're a prisoner. They're not just going to grant you a day off."

He whispered in my ear, "If I can sneak us out, I can sneak us back in."

Chapter Nineteen

The Caverns

Torren grabbed my hand and led me into a linen closet across from Lyra's room. When he shut the door, we were bathed in darkness. His arms wrapped around my waist, and I couldn't control the flutter in my stomach as he pulled me closer.

What if we got caught? What would they do to him? Another stay in the Glass House so soon would surely kill him.

"Hold on tight," he whispered.

Resting my head against his chest, the pace of his heartbeat quickened against my ear, and I squeezed his torso. In a matter of seconds, I became weightless, and then my feet hit solid ground once more.

"Stay like this for a minute," he whispered, his hold on me remaining tight. "You may start to feel a bit dizzy."

My head spun, but I wasn't entirely convinced it was from the transport.

We stood in front of a huge stone structure. A natural cavern system with a large opening took up half the space.

My eyes lingered on the other half that looked like a building had been carved out of it. "Where are we?"

He loosened his hold, and I missed his nearness. "That's the labyrinth. It doesn't look scary from the outside, but you know what it's like on the inside."

"I don't understand. Why build the labyrinth into only one side?"

"Ready for a history lesson?"

"Of course."

"These caverns were whole at one point. Sometime during the civil war, the soldiers used them as shelter. Unfortunately, they started having illusions that enhanced their emotions, which caused their gifts to go haywire. They discovered that half of the caverns focused on positive emotions, half on negative."

Torren paused to dramatically showcase the labyrinth. "Negative emotions make it impossible to control your gift, so people wound up exposing all the quirks they wanted to hide. Council saw the usefulness in the negative side, and instead of sealing it off completely, they constructed the little maze of horrors to train Alterria's military."

"So, no matter what, you can't stay positive in the labyrinth?"

"Yup."

"Well, that explains why we had such a hard time keeping it together in there."

"Don't worry. We're not going back into the labyrinth. We're going to work on you today."

"What do you mean 'work on me'? Am I broken?"

His smile brightened his entire face. "Miss Morganfire-Lunagarde, I am dying to know what you can do."

"Excuse me?"

"There were so many theories about what would happen when two pure lines of gifts would cross for the first time in recorded history. Would the child get one or the other like everyone else, or would it create something never before seen?" His voice bubbled with excitement. "Your gift. It's really awesome, isn't it?"

I shrugged. "I don't know anything about it."

"You must've had *some* time to get to know your gift. No one gets sent to the labyrinth completely unprepared."

"I did."

Torren's face paled. "How did you get through?"

I let the question hang between us.

"Oh." He frowned. "I was part of that 'we' earlier, wasn't I?"

A painful reminder that we no longer shared the same memories, even from a few days ago. "What was it like for you in the labyrinth as a kid?"

"I knew my gift. Even with practice, the labyrinth was still difficult. I was so nervous I would give away too much."

"Too much?"

"My brothers were on Council. I overheard them talking to Dad after we'd spent a long day practicing my gift to prepare for the ceremony."

"The ceremony?"

"When kids are twelve, they're put in the labyrinth to show off their gift to Council. Edric developed a database to track each child and their gift. The kids with strongest gifts were being recruited right out of the labyrinth."

"You told me before they didn't recruit until sixteen."

Sadness flashed in his eyes. "That's what concerned Brayden. The in-depth records didn't start until a few years prior. Brayden asked him about their purpose, but Edric brushed him off. When he pushed again, Edric got angry."

My heart raced. "What was he looking for?"

"Maybe the question is *who* was he looking for?" He led me into the cave opening and twisted his ring, activating the dome again.

When I brushed my fingers across the shimmering surface, tiny sparks of electricity jumped and kissed my fingertips.

His eyes widened, and he ran his hand across the surface, too. "Why did that react to your touch and not mine?"

"Should I be worried?"

"Depends. Does Edric know that happens?"

I shook my head. "It's been happening a lot lately. The other day, when I pulled a bottle from a barrier in my woods, the sparks started jumping out at me."

His eyes narrowed. "How'd you know there was a barrier?"

"I saw the shimmer around the picnic."

He scratched his head and spoke slowly. "I saw a shimmer like that a few days ago but nothing inside it. You saw what it was supposed to conceal?"

"Not normal, huh?"

"You're exceptional." He reached for my hand, and I gladly gave it to him. "If Edric's been looking for a kid our age, you're most likely the one he wants."

Could that have been why my parents kept me out of Alterria? Was it even safe to go home?

A shiver ran up my spine. "He saw me in the labyrinth. That's why he asked me to join Council, isn't it?"

"I can't say for sure, but I'll tell you this: whatever *His Highness* does, he does for his own benefit."

"What should I do?"

"Keep playing along. You're safe as long as he doesn't suspect you're on to him. But, to give you a better advantage, you should probably practice your gift." He rubbed his hands together, and a smile filled his face. "What *did* you discover in the labyrinth?"

Hesitation slowed my response. "Well...I made a room fill with flames."

"Dad's a Firestarter, too. Never seen him use it, but I bet it's magnificent." He looked at my hands in anticipation.

I cleared my throat. "I also made that space open up in the cavern wall."

"Oh, that's right. Wow, a dual gift? Someone won the genetic lottery." He paused and narrowed his eyes. "The Morganfire and Lunagarde lines were some of the last pure lines. How'd they produce a kid with a Firestarter and Manifestation gift?"

I looked into his eyes. "That's not all. I calmed myself down, like Deborah did for me before Thomas sent me in."

"THREE? Wait, like Mom and Dad. Did you somehow take their gifts?"

"At first, I thought I had, but you assured me that wasn't possible. You said people could copy, but my gift was rare."

"Well, I was right," he said, chest thrust out and a gleam in his eye.

"Also, I can make fog, and you just transported us here."

He stood with his mouth hanging open as the dome dissolved. "Well," he said a moment later, "this is the best place to practice away from Council's prying eyes. These caverns hold the same powers as the labyrinth, but this side focuses on the positive emotions, so no scary illusions here."

He led me deeper into the intricate cavern system, the twists and turns confusing me in the same way the Council Halls had when I searched for the courtyard.

I stopped walking. "Are you purposely trying to disorient me?"

He turned on his heel. "I wouldn't do that. I just wanted to get us further in. I've been exploring these caverns for years, so I know them like the back of my hand. Besides, even if we did get lost, I could get us out at any time." As he said that, the fog swirled at his feet.

"So, why did we need to get so far in?"

Smiling, he pointed to an opening in the wall.

Overcome with déjà vu as we walked into a small cavern, I ran my fingers across the symbols. "This is the same room I fell into from the labyrinth."

I met Torren's eyes, and he grinned as he pointed to a symbol. "I know this one. Meadow. The rest..." he shrugged. "Ancient Alterrian symbols aren't something taught in our schools. How did you know what this said?"

"I guess that's a benefit of being taught by my parents. This is my mom's specialty. She's a great teacher." Running my hands over the cool stone, my fingers dipped in each engraved symbol. I froze as I landed on a section I hadn't seen during my first visit. "Tread carefully?"

He grasped my hands. "Ari, you need to be extremely careful about who knows this information."

"What information?"

"I know they put me in the labyrinth with you. Depending on what they saw, they can probably only pin you as a Firestarter, maybe a Manifester as well."

I nodded, though I didn't understand what he was getting at.

"The more gifts Council believes you have, the more valuable or threatening you become to them."

When the blood drained from my face, he brushed the back of his hand against my cheek.

"What's wrong?"

"I did something that helped Lyra—just by touching her—but I thought I'd killed her. Charlie saw. And then, minutes later, Edric chased after me to let me know she was okay, so he must know, too." My breathing quickened.

"Hey." Torren's voice soothed me as he stroked my hair. "Slow breaths. You're going to hyperventilate."

I buried my face in my hands, counting to ten to slow my breathing. "How do I hide gifts I don't even know I have?"

"We'll figure it out. I promise. I brought you here to help you."

Lowering my hands, I looked into his eyes. "You've got your work cut out for you."

A sparkle in his eye made me wish I could stretch out our time together today.

He chuckled. "I like a challenge."

A challenge. I recalled the conversation I'd overheard between him and Callan. "Is it difficult?"

The smirk he flashed made me blush. "Is what difficult?"

I inhaled sharply, nervous I would make him upset. "Controlling your gift."

He looked away, and my chest clenched. "It can be. If you don't have proper mentorship during the formative years, handling intense emotions can cause things to go a little haywire."

"So if someone is scared or angry..."

"Their gift could get out of control."

I thought of Torren's confusion and fear as he left me on the couch, and the unspoken sadness that rested in his eyes as he spoke to Callan. "Would sadness affect your gift?"

"It could if you were unable to focus on a happy moment. The happy thoughts are the ones that can help regain control." His gaze settled on his feet, the toe of his shoe digging into the soft sandy floor.

When I hesitantly rested my hand on his shoulder, his eyes met mine, and I smiled.

"So." He smiled back and brushed his hands against each other. "What shall we start with?"

"You choose."

His smile grew wide. "Fire."

"I don't know if I can get that one to work."

"Why's that?"

"So far, it's only been activated when I'm really angry." I shuffled my feet, and small puffs of dirt rose from the ground.

"That's great. You already learned a trigger. That usually takes a few weeks of practicing. Now that you know the trigger, you can work on ways to counteract it. Learning this can control the intensity of whichever gift you're using."

I quirked an eyebrow.

"We don't have to make you angry for you to channel that energy. Close your eyes."

I followed his instructions, placing my complete trust in him.

Positioning himself behind me, his breath warmed my ear as he guided me. He slid his arms beneath mine, and I rested the back of my hands in his palms, my skin tingling with his touch. "Now think of something that made you just a little angry and concentrate on the feeling in that moment."

I imagined him dropping me on the couch at Callan's my first day here. Heat rose in my palms.

"Good," he said, his lips brushing my ear. "Hold that feeling and open your eyes."

When the room came back into focus, fire danced in my palms and goosebumps rose up my neck.

As Torren rested his hands on my shoulders, my breath quivered in response. "Try this. Think of something that made you even angrier."

I shook my head. "That'll be too dangerous."

"I'll guide you through it. Just try."

I thought back to the labyrinth as Torren disappeared into the fog at the promise of Celia and Edric's frightening smile when he knew I believed Torren chose to leave me.

The room filled with flames licking the walls and choking the air. We were surrounded.

Torren ran his hands down the sides of my arms and hugged my waist tightly.

My heart raced, and the flames died down as I relaxed into him.

He took a step back, creating a small gap between us, and I instinctively turned to meet his gaze. "Ari?" he whispered, averting his attention to his feet.

"Yes?" Our eyes met, and I couldn't figure out the look in his.

"I, uh…" He rubbed the back of his neck. "I don't want to give you the wrong idea."

My heart sank, and I bit my lower lip.

"Listen." He turned his eyes to the ground. "I'm enjoying getting to know you."

"Okay…" I drew out the word.

He lifted his head but couldn't make eye contact. "I just get the impression you feel something much stronger than I'm able to at the moment. You have years of memories…years of us. I only have days."

Brushing my fingers against his hand, I turned my face away. I couldn't look at him while I bared my heart. "I know I should forget our past, and you, but I can't. I think about you more than I should. And my heart breaks with every thought because I know I'm not in yours the same way."

My voice cracked, and I paused to draw in a breath. "But something else keeps pushing through. You forgot me, but no matter how hard I try to push you from my head, your smile always comes back, and I reach for what we had. It's crazy, I know, but I can't stop this incessant merry-go-round no matter how hard I wish to get off."

"I'm so sorry if I've been confusing you. I'm just as confused. You're basically a stranger to me. I shouldn't feel this intense pull to you, but I do. I'm lost, but with you…" He placed his hand on my cheek, guiding me to look at him. "With you feels like the right place to be. I just need time."

My chin quivered in response.

Wrapping me in his arms, he held me close. "I don't want you to think I'm playing games. Because I do like you."

I shook my head, my eyebrows drawing together.

"I'm confusing you, aren't I?"

"Always." I took a deep breath and held on a little tighter. "But this feels safe."

He stiffened. "Safe. Ari, we need to go back. They'll notice. We've been gone too long."

I nodded as the fog swept us up and delivered us back into the linen closet.

We opened the door a crack to make sure the coast was clear before stepping out.

As I made my way toward Lyra's room, a sudden pressure on my wrist made me stop in my tracks and turn around.

Torren brushed his lips on the back of my hand, followed by a crooked smile. "Until we meet again."

My heart faltered at the words he spoke each time we parted in the woods.

Though he claimed he couldn't remember me, I was in his mind somewhere—I had to be.

He slipped into his room, and I shook away my thoughts before I knocked on Lyra's door.

"Hey," I whispered as I walked in.

Lyra peered over the top of the book I had left with her, a massive grin on her face. "What are you doing back already?"

I drew my eyebrows together. "Lyra, we've been gone all afternoon."

"No." She pointed to the clock above the door. "You left thirty minutes ago."

CHAPTER TWENTY

THEY'RE BACK

As we visited, Lyra told me about the songs she liked to sing with her mom, the books she'd read, and the games she played with someone named Spence.

Lost in my own thoughts, I smiled occasionally and nodded during longer pauses in an attempt not to upset her. How could my time with Torren have spanned only minutes?

Charlie came in after Mrs. Chapman had cleared our dinner dishes, pulling me from my thoughts and interrupting Lyra's chatter.

"You look so healthy, Lyra," he said happily. "Now all you need is a day in the sunshine. And Ari, you'd better find Edric. There's something he wants to talk to you about. He's in his office right now."

I grimaced. Edric excelled at getting in my head and making me question everything. "I guess I'd better get that over with. See you later, Lyra."

Hesitant steps moved me forward, and I closed the door behind me. Time with Edric was never anything I looked forward to.

A few rooms past the library, I knocked on the door to his office.

The door opened, and I took a step back in surprise as Thomas exited.

"Ms. Lunagarde." He curled his lips around my name like it was too sour to speak. "High Councilman wishes to see you."

"Yes, sir. Charlie sent me to speak with him."

Thomas sneered as he gave me a once-over with his eyes, then glided away muttering something about silver platters.

I'd barely interacted with Thomas. What could I have done to earn his disdain?

"Arisanna, have a seat," Edric called out from his desk, scribbling notes on a pad of paper.

I sat at the edge of the hard chair opposite him, knotting my hands in my lap.

"I'm worried for you." He set his pen down and pressed his fingertips against each other. "I'm afraid the boy's only going to cause you pain."

"No, sir. He's helping me. I'm learning so much from him. Part of me hopes he's going to remember me. I know it's impossible, but—"

"He *can't* remember you because, for him, none of it was real."

The punch from his words physically pushed me back. I took a deep breath. "Even so—"

"Everything he does is to benefit himself and his quest to lessen his guilt. His emotions from the Glass House are still raw and exposed. The guilt he must feel right now is likely exponential. That's why he's pretending to fall in love with you. You're his distraction."

"Sir, he's not—"

"Don't forget how he's treated you in the past. He's lonely and not allowed to leave yet. As soon as we release him, he won't look back."

"I...I think you're wrong, sir."

His eyes didn't leave my face, but he remained silent.

"May I go?" I needed to get away from him, and to my relief, he dismissed me with a wave of his hand.

I fled to the courtyard, my mind a jumbled mess. Could Torren be playing games with me like Edric insisted?

The water rippled as the fireflies that filled the evening sky dipped too low and skirted the pond's surface. I closed my eyes as memories of summer nights with Kai came flooding in.

Edric's voice slithered into my daydream. *"He can't remember you because, for him, none of it was real."*

I choked back a sob and opened my eyes. Every time I thought I'd figured something out, someone always cast doubt in my mind. How did I decide who to believe? Picking up a pebble, I tossed it across the pond.

"That's not how you skip rocks." Torren's crooked smile greeted me as I turned. "Want me to show you?"

"You already have." Despite what Edric said, my spirits soared when I had Torren by my side.

He raised his eyebrows as he chuckled. "I must be a terrible teacher."

A shadow of a smile graced my lips. "What are you doing out here? Shouldn't you be in your room?"

"Charlie sent me out. Said I needed to get some fresh air." He reached up and brushed a stray hair from my forehead. His fingers lingered against my cheek for a moment.

Edric's voice rose in my mind again, taunting me. *"Everything he does is to benefit himself. You're his distraction."*

I flinched away from Torren's touch, my doubts resurfacing.

"Did I do something to upset you, Ari?"

"No. I'm just confused."

Torren looked at his feet. "Because of Charlie?"

"What? No. It's Edric."

His head snapped up. "You like Edric?"

"Eww. No! He decided I needed a warning. About you."

"Me?"

I nodded. "He told me how the Glass House brings a person's heightened emotions to the top and that your strongest emotion was guilt."

"Okay…" Torren's eyes narrowed, and I looked away.

"He also told me nothing between us is real."

He placed his thumb under my chin, and I met his eyes. "How can you let him deceive you like that? Why can't you believe what's right in front of your own eyes?"

I jerked back at the comment. My lip quivered as my head and heart clashed with each other. Where I'd hoped for reassurance, I'd been insulted instead. Deceived?

"My mind's a mess. I've been thrown into a world I know nothing about and, as it turns out, is a large part of who I am." My voice rose with my frustration. "The only friend I've ever had has somehow forgotten all about me. Then, I come to find out he only became my friend because he just happened to be searching for his lost niece in my woods at the same time I'd been there. You told me you needed time. You said you didn't want to lead me on."

Torren's jaw set. "You said it yourself. My strongest emotion right now is guilt, and that's what you choose to throw at me? I'm sorry I can't remember our past. I'm sorry for any pain I might've caused you. But if you want to let Edric or Charlie or whoever else feed you your opinions, that's on you."

With that, he walked away.

I stood alone, his words sinking in. Did I make decisions for myself, or did I let other people's opinions influence me? I wasn't sure, but he didn't deserve the cruelty I'd thrown at him.

The holes in our past were still unfilled, but Torren—the Torren who didn't know me, didn't know the motivations of Kai—wasn't responsible for any of it.

I had to apologize. Leaving the courtyard, I made my way to Torren's room.

"Torren," I said, knocking on his slightly open door. "Can I come in?"

He sat at the table, his head in his hands. "I don't know, Ari. I'm kind of tired."

I hadn't expected that. He'd never really been upset with me before. "Um, okay. Well, I'll be in the courtyard for a while if you change your mind."

I walked back, my mind a swirl. I didn't know how to handle this situation.

When he didn't show up after an hour, I wiped my eyes and decided to go to bed. Maybe sleep would comfort me. I stood from my seat on the swing and turned to head back into Council Hall.

"Ari?" Torren spoke softly, faint moonbeams lighting his path toward me.

My heart rose. "Torren, you're right. I'm sorry for doubting you, and I'm sorry for blaming you for something you had no control over. You don't deserve that, especially from me. It's just—I don't know how to make sense of everything. Edric has this way of convincing me I'm wrong about you."

He looked into my eyes and smiled.

"What?"

"Get out of your head and listen to your heart. What's it telling you?"

"Torren?" I bit my lips together.

"Are you okay?"

I shrugged as I fought against the voices clamoring in my head. He didn't have to come back, but he did.

He pressed his palm to my cheek, and I leaned into the gesture.

"Torren, I'm the one who needs a distraction."

His breath quivered. "How can I help?"

I yearned to know more about this boy who had captured my heart as two different people. "Take me to your favorite place in the whole world."

He grinned. "Anywhere?"

I nodded.

He raised his eyebrows and led me under the willow tree. "Hold on tight," he whispered, "and shut your eyes."

We wrapped our arms around each other as we lifted off the ground, and he rested his head on top of mine.

"Keep them closed," he said, releasing me when the whisper of lapping water drifted in, and the song of the toads filled the air.

Shivers traveled through me as his fingertips brushed against my face. My heart tried to escape my chest as he moved behind me and placed his hands on my shoulders.

"Open."

The breath hitched in my throat as I took in the place that held so many memories between Kai and me. Moonlit dances. Forgetting the world with our toes dipped in the cool waters. Our first kiss. I was home.

Home. What would happen if I stayed?

"Why did you bring me here?" I whispered.

Did the memories flood in for him like they did for me?

"This is my favorite place in the whole world."

I spun to face him and tilted my head. "Why?"

His lips twitched into his crooked smile. "It's the one place in the world I feel free. No one judging me based on my mistake. There are no expectations for me to be somebody I'm not when I'm here. I'm just…" he closed his eyes and took a deep breath, "me. Completely me."

Our special place was still special to him.

My heart fluttered and a smile flickered on my face. He didn't remember me—us—but he remembered how he felt here. When he was with me.

Edric was wrong.

I couldn't stop the scowl that replaced my smile, and my palms burned.

"Hey." Torren pressed his forehead against mine, bringing me back to the moment with him.

As my anger faded, my hands cooled. Butterflies returned to my stomach when he leaned back to hold my face tenderly.

As the fireflies danced around us, he lowered a hand to the small of my back. Running a thumb along my cheekbone, he leaned in, and my eyes shut in response. His lips pressed softly against mine causing my heart to flutter again.

I had nearly forgotten what this was like. My hands traveled up his back, resting against his neck. My fingers weaved in his hair, and all at once, past and present came crashing together. I pulled myself closer to him, and his arms tightened around me as we melted against each other.

There was something new in his kiss. It was unrestricted. For the first time since we met, Torren was *only* Torren. There was nothing to hide. He was finally able to show me all of himself.

I lost myself within his embrace.

As we separated, the smile that ran across his face made me giddy. I couldn't stay here. I couldn't leave him.

"Wow," he said. "I can tell you one thing for certain."

"What's that?"

He gazed into my eyes. "*This* is real."

Chapter Twenty-One

Forced

"Can I tell you something?" Lyra asked timidly as we sat on the bench swing in the courtyard the next day.

"Of course." I pushed my feet against the ground, and we gently swayed.

"I think you're going to have a problem."

"You do? What might that be?"

"Well," Lyra sang. "Torren likes you, but I think Charlie does, too."

While I'd already made that assumption thanks to the hand holding, it surprised me Lyra had the same suspicions when she hadn't seen Charlie and I together in that way. "Why do you think that?"

"I can hear Torren in his sleep. He calls your name."

The heat rose in my cheeks, and I stopped swinging. "Oh."

"And Charlie won't stop staring at you. He's nice, but it's a little creepy." The way her nose twitched made me giggle.

"Charlie is a bit intense, but he has a good heart."

"Staring and looking are different, you know."

"Elaborate, mystery girl." I laughed to cover my discomfort at the truth in her blunt observation.

"The other day, when Charlie was in my room, you were asking him questions. He answered, but he wasn't really paying attention."

"He's a busy man."

"Yeah, but that's not it." She leaned back against the bench. "I don't know how to explain it. He watched you and answered you, but it's like he wasn't really there."

My eyebrow raised, and I chewed my bottom lip for a moment. "But Torren *is* there?"

"Oh, yes," Lyra said, brightening. "When you talk, Torren's whole self is paying attention to your whole self. Charlie only gives you his eyes. Torren gives you everything."

My stomach turned over uncomfortably, and Cade waltzed up to my side, forcing his muzzle under my hand. "That's not something I've thought about."

She speaks the truth.

The voice was so quiet I wasn't sure I'd heard her.

I glanced around. "Did you hear that?"

"Hear what?"

"I thought I heard someone, but I must've been imagining it."

"Watch it, or they'll put you in the hospital too."

I laughed for real this time.

"Well, who do you like best?"

I sighed and patted Lyra's hand. "I like Charlie just fine. But Torren..." After last night, I didn't think "friends" was the right word and hoped a reenactment might confirm my suspicion. Butterflies made rounds in my stomach. "I left him a note to meet me here later."

"Ooh," she teased.

"Really?" I laughed. "How are we involved in this conversation at all?"

"Lyra, it's time," Charlie called as he stepped into sight.

"Can she have five more minutes? I'll bring her back myself."

His face hardened so briefly I thought I must have imagined it. "No, I'm sorry. She may take the wolf for company, but it *is* time for her to go. I'll walk her back, but then I need to speak with you. Will you be here?"

"Yes." I thought of the note I left for Torren, bubbling with excitement at the thought of seeing him.

Lyra disappeared into the building with Charlie when again I heard the whisper of the voice.

Something isn't right.

She sounded distant this time, as though she wasn't talking to me, so I shrugged it off.

Charlie soon returned and sat beside me. He reached for my hand, but Torren's kiss last night made me withdraw. Charlie had told me it only meant what I wanted it to mean, but after Lyra's observations, I believed we interpreted the little touches differently.

"What's wrong?"

"Charlie, you know I enjoy spending time with you."

He stiffened. "It's not you, it's me. Right?"

"No, it's not even you. It's Torren. He kissed me last night. I think he loves me. Still or again, I'm not sure, but it's there."

"Oh, Ari," Charlie said gently. "Edric told me of your conversation last night. He was afraid something like this would happen."

"He was afraid Torren would fall in love with me?"

"No, that he would take advantage of you in a vulnerable moment. I'm so sorry." He reached for my hand again.

Confused, I let him fold my fingers into his palm while I fought with myself. Was I letting him feed me my opinion? Before I could dwell on it further, Charlie changed the subject.

"Edric suggested that you join a Council meeting."

I turned to him. "I got the impression Edric was upset with me. He wasn't exactly polite when I asked him questions."

"I'm always polite," Charlie responded, then covered his frown with a cough.

I looked at my lap, and soon he started tracing our hands with his fingers.

"I don't mean to sound like I'm bragging, but I pride myself on being respectful and considerate."

"Yes," I said, stretching the word. "But Edric brushes off questions I think are important." I carefully removed my hand from his and pushed my hair behind my ear.

"He's a busy man, you know," Charlie said harshly. "And he has to choose how to spend his time."

"You don't have to defend him. I understand he has a lot to deal with."

"Of course. I'm sorry. I didn't mean to offend you."

Be careful.

Nervous energy skated through me with the certainty those words were meant for me.

"What?" I asked.

"I said I'm sorry," he repeated, his voice soft. He reached out and cupped my face with both palms. "You're beautiful, you know, inside and out. I've never met someone quite like you."

"Charlie, don't," I whispered, my eyes wide.

"I have to."

"Please. I'm not—"

"Don't you think we have something special, Ari? Torren doesn't even remember you."

An arrow to the heart. "But our kiss…"

"It wasn't real."

Torren's words echoed in my mind: "This is real."

"Charlie, you and I don't have something real."

"Not yet, but we have a foundation. It's okay for us to grow what we have into something more."

"You don't understand," I pleaded.

"Shh," he whispered. His hands were still on my face, but he hadn't leaned in.

"Please...don't." I squeezed my eyes shut and stopped speaking.

Before I knew what was happening, he slid his hands down. With one hand, he drew me in at the waist, and with the other, he pulled my shoulders forward, holding me close.

I tried to fight against him, but he met my resistance with a tighter grip. My heart galloped in my chest as space around me closed in. I…couldn't…breathe.

He pressed his lips hard against mine, ignoring the tears that already spilled onto my cheeks and down my chin.

My stomach turned into a boulder and weighed me down. I needed this to stop. With nowhere for my hands to go, I reached for his hair to pry him away. My hands trembled so fiercely that his head didn't even budge.

When he pushed harder against me, I whimpered.

"Charlie..." A tear slid down my cheek.

"Ari?" Torren's voice cracked, laden with confusion and pain.

My stomach heaved.

Charlie stood, and I fell back against the bench with the sudden lack of resistance. "Torren, you're supposed to be in bed," he scolded.

Adjusting myself on the swing, I stared at the ground, twisting my hands and fingers together, a visible symbol of the knots in my stomach. I could barely get my words out. "I asked Torren to meet me here."

"I'll leave you two alone, then. I have some work to do." Charlie's footsteps faded as he left the courtyard, and the silence bore down on me.

I could feel Torren staring, but I couldn't face him. What must he have thought?

"Can I sit down?"

Numbly, I nodded as he sat beside me, the space between us wider than it appeared.

He cleared his throat. "You don't owe me anything. I have nothing to give you. It's not my intention to hold you back."

"That's not what I wanted."

"Ari, you don't have to pretend."

Pretend? My mind flitted back to our kiss, and tears stung my eyes. "Torren…"

"Look, I like you, and I know we had a history, but it's not *our* history right now. It's just yours." He reached out but then dropped his hand as I drew away.

"I told him no." My voice lowered, and I couldn't meet his eyes. "I didn't want that. I'm not in love with him."

He stared at me, his jaw set.

"You don't believe me?" My heart sank as I swallowed hard and wrapped my arms around myself. I felt so alone.

"I want to," he murmured, his edges softening. "Ari, you don't know how bad I want to believe that right now."

I held my breath so I wouldn't cry.

"Kissing you last night was a dream, but watching you reach out to him and call his name was a heart-wrenching nightmare."

Choking back my tears, I pictured what he must have seen as he witnessed my struggle. My throat stung as my thoughts shifted back to Charlie's hold tightening as I fought to get free. With my toes pressed to the ground, my legs danced with anxiety.

"Don't worry about hurting my feelings. I understand. You and I are in the past."

My heart dropped to my stomach as I gripped the edges of the swing so tightly, the tiny splinters of wood pierced my palms.

"Torren," interrupted Ms. Chapman. "It's time for your vitals. Charlie needs you back in your room."

"Of course he does," Torren mumbled under his breath, but he stood, and I was left alone with my thoughts as he disappeared through the arched doorway.

Taking a few deep breaths, I pulled out one of the library books to shift my focus. Fifteen minutes later, I'd read the opening page six times and still had no idea what it said because my mind was trapped in an endless loop of worries. Would Charlie come back and try again? My favorite place in Alterria was now tainted and left me vulnerable and exposed.

Where was the mysterious voice to help me now?

I stowed the book in my bag and swung it over my shoulder. I couldn't leave things like this. Torren *had* to understand what happened. I *needed* him to understand. He was the one person who made me feel safe, and while it hurt that he didn't believe me, I had to give him the chance to see the truth. I assumed by the time I got to his room, Charlie would be done with him.

I'd be okay if I never saw Charlie again, though that would be impossible if I wanted to keep seeing Lyra. And Torren.

Voices caught me off guard as I walked through the halls, and Ronin's name being hissed gave me pause. I glanced into the room, the door slightly ajar.

Thomas stood at the head of a table and spoke to a group of men, all wearing the Council uniform. "High Councilman has decided the traitor, Ronin, must be found and answer to his treason."

I gasped, and Thomas's eyes met mine, a smirk at odds with the glare he sent in my direction. I shifted my bag on my shoulder and walked at a hurried pace the rest of the way to the hospital.

As I neared the hospital wing, icy words grew into heated conversation. I looked toward Lyra's door to ensure it was closed before I cautiously approached Torren's.

"You're wrong, Charlie. She doesn't love you. She told me."

A knot formed in my throat. Charlie wasn't gone.

"Of course she would tell you that. She doesn't want to hurt you because she's not sure which one of us she wants yet. What do *you* have to offer her?"

Not ready to face Charlie, I turned to leave.

"A future," Torren said defiantly.

My heart skipped a beat, and I paused. Did he think we were supposed to be together?

"Based on a past that you refute. You can't blame her for looking elsewhere. I'm sorry you had to witness that…moment of passion…but there's no denying it was there."

My stomach churned, and my hands trembled. How could that have felt like passion to him?

"It wasn't passion, Charlie. It was pain, and you owe her an apology."

"Did she say I hurt her?" he growled.

Torren's voice slipped through clenched teeth. "Not in so many words."

Charlie's growl melted into wistfulness. "I'm going to relish this memory. A beautiful young woman welcomed me to her side with a smile meant for me alone. I took her hand and curled her fingers around mine. It's *me* she pressed against. It's *my* name she whispered, *my* hair she clutched. If you didn't see her pressing herself closer to me, you're blind."

I was going to be sick. I needed to go. A crash within the room made me freeze.

Charlie backed out, pressing his palm to his cheekbone, and shut the door. "Ari," he said upon seeing me stand there. "We need to talk."

I grit my teeth, my hands balled into fists at my side. "Not now, Charlie. I need some space." I turned back the way I came.

"Don't be so childish." He took hold of my backpack. "Let me carry this for you while we find a room."

I yanked it away, and fury boiled through me. My palms burned as I shouted, my voice hard and sharp. "I said not now!"

"Fine," he said, his tone mimicking Edric's confident arrogance. The spot he'd been covering had already begun to bruise. "I have duties to attend to. You may go."

The urge to run became too intense to ignore, so I turned on my heel and fled.

CHAPTER TWENTY-TWO

THE RIVER

I ran from Council Hall, tears blurring my vision. I followed the trail, kicking up dust from the dry summer heat. Though unsure where I was going, I needed to get as much distance between Charlie and me as possible.

I quickly approached the bridge that crossed the river. The bridge that could take me home. Somehow. I kept running, my destination in clear sight. My heart raced as my feet hit the wooden planks with a solid thump.

Board after board, I pictured my parents' faces and then froze just before I slammed through the glittering wall that separated my two worlds. I didn't know the way home from here.

I tried to call up the fog, but my thoughts were so jumbled I couldn't concentrate on a single thing.

The weight of my backpack crushed against my lungs, and I struggled for air. In a fit of rage, I tore it away from me and swung it as far as I could. With a thud, it landed at the edge of the bridge.

A pained scream ripped from my throat, and I dropped to my hands and knees. I punched the wooden planks with knuckles taut, feeling the skin begin to break under the force. Trickles of blood ran between my fingers, but I paid no mind. My screams rose in intensity. I wanted to cry, but the tears refused to come.

Exhausted from the strength of the fury flowing through me, I rested my forehead against the hot planks.

Charlie's coy smile as he dropped me against the bench at the sound of Torren's voice flashed in my mind.

My stomach tied into knots, and I screamed again to try to push the image away. I desperately wanted to go home.

Someone lingered behind me, and my body stiffened in response.

My breaths came in short gasps, and tremors shook me to my core.

Charlie must've followed me.

A hand rested between my shoulder blades, and I jumped to my feet, ready to run again. "Go away!" I screamed as I spun to face the unwelcome guest.

"Ari?" Torren's voice settled the flight signals running through me. "Are you alright?"

"Do I look alright?" I shouted, my hands clenched to my sides, and blood dripped onto the planks near my feet.

His voice was urgent and his eyes full of concern. "Your knuckles."

I inspected my hands, the skin broken and bloodied.

"Let me help you."

Sighing, I left my frustration behind and followed him to the riverbank.

He knelt at the river's edge and motioned for me to do the same. "Can I take your hands?"

I nodded.

He gently held my palm and drizzled water over the knuckles on my left hand.

I flinched at the sudden stinging.

"I know this hurts. I'll try to be quick."

Something had changed, but what?

"I don't understand. Why are you here?"

"Ari," he said, as he switched to my right hand, "we were interrupted at a bad place."

"You didn't believe me," I said through clenched teeth, turning away as the pain bit at my heart.

"I was wrong, and I'm sorry." He hesitated for a moment and let go of my hand. "Would you like me to go?"

The thought of being alone made my heart race and my throat burn. I gave a quick shake of my head.

"The way you fell back, the way you were sitting on the bench swing, your face pale…" He sighed. "Something about that didn't sit right with me. I believed what I thought I saw over my heart. I didn't listen to my own advice."

Lyra's words came to mind: "When you talk, Torren's whole self is paying attention to your whole self." She was right.

I bit my lip, my hands trembling. "But why are you here?"

"I heard you yell at Charlie and saw you run off. I *had* to make sure you were okay."

Jumping to my feet at the mention of his name, I searched the area surrounding us, but there was no sign of him. I swallowed the knot in my throat.

"Do you want to talk about what happened?"

Sickness overtook me again, and I shrugged.

"Whatever you say, I won't question you," he said, drawing an "x" over his heart.

My lower lip trembled. "I don't understand. I told him no. Just like I told him no the last time he tried to kiss me."

Torren's muscles tensed, and his jaw set. "He's done this to you before?"

"Last time he respected my no. This time…" I pressed my nails into my palms as my vision blurred and my stomach churned. "He really hurt me. I'm going to be sick."

He patted the space beside him. "Sit. Please. Before you pass out."

I sat by him with my head in my hands, thin rivers of blood and water trickling down my arms.

Torren rubbed my back gently, and minutes passed before I rested my hands on my knees. "Ari, these cuts are bad. You need—"

"Not a doctor," I said, panic crawling over my skin.

He closed his eyes while he sighed.

I started shaking again. I couldn't go back, not to Charlie.

"No. I'm not taking you back there. We'll figure something else out." He picked up a pointed rock from the edge of the water and attempted to sharpen it with another stone. "I'm going to take my shirt off for a minute. You can close your eyes if you want to."

Even in a moment of emotional turmoil, Torren could still find a way to make me laugh. I couldn't help myself. My nose was stuffy from my tears, and when I laughed, it came out as a cross between a cackle and a snort.

He laughed too, and I moaned in embarrassment. While he cut a strip off the bottom of his shirt, I bathed my hands in the water once more to clean off the blood as best as I could.

"Come hold your hands out for me." With a tender touch he used the ends of the fabric to dry the wounds, then wrapped the remainder around as a makeshift bandage. "It's not the best," he said, his t-shirt now several inches too short. "But it will hopefully protect them a little bit. They still need to be taken care of properly."

"I'm not ready to go back, and when I am, I'll take care of it myself." I sat near the river, the water lower here than it had been by the meadow.

Torren spoke gently. "Talking through what happened might help."

My shoulders stiffened. I couldn't stop the tremors that took over my body. "You're right, but I don't know if I can." I was frightened that once I let the monsters loose, they would become real.

Torren held his arms out to me. Despite everything we had been through, I still felt safe in his embrace.

"This isn't your fault, you know. Charlie is responsible for his own actions. You don't have to even look at him if you don't want to."

"I don't know what to do," I whimpered as Torren stroked my hair, his breath warming the top of my head. "I don't want to be there, but Lyra needs me. She would think she did something wrong if I didn't come back, and I can't do that to her. But with Lyra comes Charlie. I don't know how I'm going to face him after this. He saved you, and I owe him for that."

"You owe no one your heart, least of all Charlie."

I leaned back and looked into Torren's eyes. "I'm scared. I'm scared of what he might try next. 'No' doesn't seem to mean anything to him anymore."

Torren's jaw pulsed, and his voice was low. Deep. Serious. "I could kill him."

I brought my bandaged hands to his cheeks, and his jaw relaxed. "Hey, don't go losing yourself. I could never forgive myself for that."

He gathered me in his arms. "Only because you asked."

I saw a flash of the fierceness I thought had been lost. The part of Torren that tried to fight for me in the labyrinth. "Why are you so protective over me?"

"I'm not entirely sure myself. It just feels natural."

Charlie's face flashed through my mind. The smirk he wore once he let me go made my skin crawl.

Torren ran the back of his hand down my arm. "How can I help?"

His presence had calmed me, and I wanted to let thoughts of Charlie disappear. "You're helping me already."

"I should take you to Deborah. She could help you more."

It occurred to me how much he must miss his family, but it was too dangerous for him to go.

I glanced at Torren and shook my head.

When he nodded his understanding, my heart gravitated to the boy who had helped me through the labyrinth. Then he hit me with the crooked smile that won me over when I knew him as only Kai, and a dull ache settled in the pit of my stomach.

Were they really that different? I studied his face.

As Kai, his hair was shorter and his cheeks a bit puffier.

Torren's nose was a little slimmer than Kai's, but his lips were the same, aside from the missing scar.

I thought our kiss by the river had brought me resolution between my past and present, but I was wrong. *Kai* would have believed me without question.

Kai lived on in my heart, but I couldn't get Torren off my mind. The irrational feeling that I betrayed what Kai and I had by falling for Torren ate at me. Even if they looked different, they were the same person.

He brushed at his mouth. "Penny for your thoughts?"

"Just noticing a few things."

He wiggled his eyebrows. "Noticing the suave mustache? They won't let me shave."

I giggled. "The beard is nice, too, but no, just comparing the differences between your face and Kai's."

"You knew my grandfather?"

I scrunched my eyebrows together. "What? No."

A sad smile adorned his face. "I picked my glamour name in honor of my grandfather, Malachi. The scar on my lower lip matched the one he got in the war."

"I saw a picture of him," I said, recalling the frames on Celia's nightstand.

He paused and picked at a piece of grass. "When we knew each other, did I ever show you my real face? Or tell you my real name?"

I shook my head and stared into the water. My nose began to tingle, and I pressed my eyes closed. I wouldn't cry over this. Our past no longer existed for him, and we were building something new together.

"Well, for what it's worth, I'm *really* sorry." He gently touched my shoulder, and I opened my eyes. "I don't think the Torren that you knew as Kai would ever want to hurt you."

"What makes you so sure? Our last day together, the hurt seemed pretty intentional."

He answered quietly. "I wish I could take that day back."

"Why? You don't remember it anyway." My words came out in more of a whimper as I struggled to suppress the memory of that day. Despite my effort, a tear escaped and slid down my cheek.

He swiped my tear with his thumb. "Because it caused you pain. The girl I've gotten to know is amazing, and I'd have to be a fool to let you go."

My heart fluttered, not daring to hope. Not right now. He was a prisoner, and I... I sort of was, too. To lighten the mood, I leaned forward and splashed water at him.

"What was that for?" He laughed and wiped the droplets from his face.

I grinned. "No talk of what ifs and wishes. We can't change the way things are."

My gaze settled on the glimmering wall in the center of the river that extended as far as I could see on either side of me, seeming to separate Alterria and the Outside.

"Torren?" I turned, and his eyes met mine. "The war. I've read about it, but I'm still lost."

He tossed a flat rock into the slow-moving waters. It skipped right through the glimmer with no resistance. "What do you need help figuring out?"

"When you told me about my grandfathers and Robert, you mentioned their different opinions on the divide between Alterria and the Outside, but what created the divide in the first place?"

"No one knows for sure anymore. Some say there was a big power struggle between those with gifts and those without. But if that was truly the case, why wouldn't the giftless have been kept as servants or something?

"Callan says the real reason for the divide was to keep those without gifts safe. He used to tell Celia and me about this family, a mix of gifted and not.

"Mixed families were looked down on. People believed those with gifts and those without shouldn't combine for fear of losing gifts altogether.

"The husband was giftless but a talented alchemist. His wife could create barriers. Their oldest child was killed during a riot against families like theirs. It's believed the parents created the barrier to keep their children and the children of similar families safe. They didn't realize what would happen to those without gifts if they tried to cross the barrier." He chucked another rock across the river, watching as it hit the other shore.

"So not a power struggle but a way to create a safe space from prejudice?"

"Pretty much." He seemed miles away as he stared off into the rippling waters.

I rested my hand on his knee. "Are you okay?"

"Hmm, yeah. Just lost in thought. That's been happening a lot lately." He scratched the back of his head. "I have a confession to make. I stopped taking the medicines because I didn't like how they made me feel."

I felt the color drain from my cheeks. "How were you able to do that?"

"I didn't swallow them. Hid them once Charlie left the room."

"Don't you need them?"

"Nah. Pretty sure they're supposed to keep the memories from flooding back. To give your body time to recover from the torture of the mind."

"Are you remembering anything?"

"Ari, the only things I remember about you are from the moment I woke up in the hospital until now."

I squeezed my eyes shut.

Torren pressed his hand against my cheek, and I turned toward him, opening my eyes. "You have no idea how badly I want to kiss you right now."

My heart raced. "But?"

"I don't want to trigger anything for you."

I brushed my lips against his cheek and whispered in his ear, "Thank you."

Peace washed over me as my body filled with a natural calmness. I laid back on the grass and watched the clouds twist and shift into shapes and figures, like I used to do as a child back home.

Torren laid beside me and stretched his arm near my head.

Taking a chance, I nestled my head against his chest and concentrated on the steady beat of his heart.

He wrapped his arm around me and rested his cheek against my hair. "Is this okay?"

"Yes. This feels like home."

Home. The emptiness that came with missing my family churned inside me, and I realized Torren probably felt the same way. I took a sharp breath in.

"What's on your mind?"

"I meant to tell you I overheard Council members going over last night's meeting."

He narrowed his eyes. "Were you spying?"

"Of course not."

He ran his hand across my cheek, which usually made me smile but had the opposite reaction with the news sitting at the tip of my tongue.

"They're searching for Ronin. Calling him a traitor."

His body stiffened, and he sat up straight. "They called Brayden a traitor the day they threw me into the Glass House the first time. He fought against Edric, telling him I was too young to know what I did wrong. Brayden left Council and all of us that day. I think he was angry at Ronin for not fighting for me."

"Why did they send you there?" I sat up beside him.

"Apparently, twelve-year-olds needed to be chaperoned on the searches, but I went by myself. After the Glass House, they allowed me to continue on my own. Something about the transmissions proved I was just as efficient as the adults, or they were using me."

"I'm not sure what to say about a Council that approves of torturing children."

His face softened. "The original Council stood for more. There's something egotistical about the current regime. I always questioned whether the searches for Celia held a hidden agenda."

"Do you believe she's still out there somewhere, waiting to be found?"

He shrugged. "When I first woke up, I felt like I had been close to finding her. As this medication leaves my system, so does the hope I had. Right now, I'm stuck in an in-between. Part of me feels like she's still waiting, the other part…"

My eyes widened as realization dawned on me. "Torren!"

"Yes?"

"This isn't the courtyard!"

He smiled. "You're perceptive."

I pushed at his shoulder. "Not funny. You could get in big trouble being away from the hospital."

"I don't care. You needed me."

My cheeks burned. "We should probably get you back before they notice you're missing."

"Will you be okay going back?"

"I don't have much of a choice." The thought of returning made the pit that had taken up residence in my stomach grow. What if *he* was waiting for me. "Could you walk me to my room? I'll tell Edric I asked you to leave with me so you don't get into trouble. I just don't want to go alone."

"We could always fog in. Nobody would be the wiser."

I shook my head. Something about that plan kicked up a wave of anxiety, and I found myself unable to move from my seated position. "No. They likely already know we're both missing. Fogging in will make them suspect we're hiding something. We need to walk."

He smiled as he stood. "Let me help you?" He waited until I nodded before putting his hands around my waist and helping me to my feet.

I glanced around nervously while he grabbed my backpack from where I'd thrown it earlier.

We walked close together.

The corners of his mouth twitched, and his shoulders sagged a little. "You know, I can still help you with your studies if you want to keep hanging out with me."

My cheeks flushed. "Honestly, I'm not quite ready to go back to my room. I wouldn't mind some company in the courtyard if you want to join me there. Are you sure helping me study isn't too annoying? I feel like such a child with the questions I keep asking you."

"I enjoy sharing my years of Alterrian education with those less fortunate." He let out a gusty laugh.

"It's much easier hearing you tell me the history than it is to read it in the dry books from the library."

Too soon, we approached Council Hall, where Edric greeted us with a snarl at the entrance.

Chapter Twenty-Three

Official Tutor

My heart faltered as Edric's steely eyes burned into mine.

"What are you doing with the prisoner outside of Council walls?" His level tone sent trembles through my body.

I didn't trust that Edric would try to protect me from Charlie, so I hesitated in search of a response.

Torren placed his hand softly within mine and drew his shoulders back. He spoke with confidence. "I thought it may help Arisanna to learn by seeing the places she's reading about—to help her get a better understanding and feel for this world. I apologize for not requesting permission prior to leaving the grounds. But as you see, I have returned."

"Indeed." Edric's mouth twitched, and he set his lips in a firm line. "Is it as he says? Has the prisoner made your learning more efficient?"

I nodded and willed my voice to have the same confidence Torren had just shown. "Yes, sir. He turned the lectures into stories I could understand. If you please, I'd like him to continue teaching me."

"Have I not provided answers as you have needed them?"

"In all fairness, you've been quite busy, and I'd like to keep learning without having to wait for answers to clarify everything."

"Very well." His eyes flashed as he spoke. "But if the prisoner escapes, you will be held responsible."

"Of course." I nodded in deference.

He glared at Torren. "You will be sure to teach her the truth, no matter how awful it may seem."

"Thank you, sir." I attempted to smile, but Torren only nodded.

Edric grunted as he scrutinized Torren's appearance, his gaze settling on the torn edge of his shirt before traveling to my bandages. "Have Charlie examine your hands," he demanded as he retreated into Council Hall.

Torren grinned as he released a long breath. "That went well."

I couldn't control the laughter that erupted from me.

As we walked through Council Hall, he laid on a thick royal accent. "To the courtyard."

Although it had been my suggestion, I cringed. My favorite place had been tainted.

Not quite ready to face that demon, I paused outside the corridor that led to the hospital wing. "Actually, I promised Lyra I would check on her, and you need to change." My eyes rested on his torn hem.

"You're right." He dashed into his room while I tapped on Lyra's door and peeked inside.

To my relief, she was alone.

"Ari! You came back." Her eyes lit up as I walked in and pulled a chair to the edge of her bed.

"Of course. I promised I would." I brushed her hair back from her forehead.

The door swung open, and the sudden clenching of my fists split open the cuts from earlier. Red pools seeped through the makeshift bandages.

Inch by inch, I turned in my chair, my heart thudding against my chest.

Torren cupped his hands over his mouth. "I am so sorry."

I turned back to Lyra, resting my still throbbing hands on her bed.

"Ari!" Her eyes widened in horror. "What did you do to your hands?"

I withdrew them to my lap. "It's nothing. Don't worry."

Torren placed his hand on my shoulder. "We need to take care of them the right way. You need real bandages."

Carefully, I removed the wrappings from my left hand and tossed them in the red hazard bin near Lyra's bed.

"Not that bad," I said, showing off my wounds as though I wasn't lying through my teeth. The blood had begun trickling over my knuckles again.

Torren walked across the room to the sink and ran the water over a washcloth, and our eyes connected as he walked back to me. "Can I?" He held the cloth tentatively over my wounds.

I bit my lip and nodded.

The cool water calmed the pain as he patted the cloth against my skin.

I swallowed the knot in my throat. "Thank you."

He smiled and walked back to the sink to rinse out the washcloth.

Lyra ran her fingertips against the palm of my hand. "Oh, Ari. This looks like it hurts so much."

The throbbing seemed to ease up. "Actually, it's not hurting so much anymore."

"Ari?" Torren breathed as he sat beside me.

The gashes on my knuckles knit themselves closed. "How did you do that?" Trembling in my haste, I unwrapped and presented my other hand.

She repeated her gentle touch, the wounds healing before my eyes. Then her tiny frame sagged. "I'm so tired."

I brushed the hair from her cheeks and helped her settle into bed. Mimicking the memories I had of Mom tucking me in, I pulled the blankets to Lyra's chin and placed a soft kiss on her forehead. "Sleep well, little mystery girl."

Torren turned out the lights as we left her room.

As we walked down the hallway, I opened my mouth to speak, but he quickly pressed a finger to his lips. I nodded and laced my fingers within his, my mind wandering in daydreams until he led me into the courtyard and squeezed my hand.

"Ari…" A shimmering dome dropped around us when I stopped in my tracks, staring at the bench swing. "I don't know if you can avoid this place forever, and I thought it would help if we were together the first time you came back."

"Torren, I don't know if I can do this. It's so soon."

"I'm here." He enveloped both my hands in his, staring in disbelief at my knuckles. "I can't believe she completely healed you. She's an Outsider, and Outsiders can't have gifts."

Outsider or not, Lyra's touch had healed me. At what expense to her though? "Is she going to be okay? She got so weak."

"That's what happens as children learn their gifts."

"They pass out?"

He chuckled. "No. Using your gift takes energy. As you get older and practice your gift more, using it will eventually take less energy. Some gifts, like healing or soothing, will always take more since they transfer energy to another person."

As I was learning about Lyra, I learned about myself, too.

"Are you ready?" he asked as the dome dissolved, guiding me to the swing when I nodded and taking his seat where Charlie had been only hours earlier.

Overcome by tremors as I took my place beside Torren, my chin quivered, and my stomach twisted. I allowed the tears to flow as he placed his hands on mine.

"Hey," he whispered. He cupped his hands around my cheeks and brought his forehead to mine. "It's just the two of us here. Just you and me. We can handle anything."

The breath caught in my throat. He had said something similar back in the labyrinth. I glanced around, and the jitters intensified. "I don't think I can be out here."

Torren leaned back and rested his hands on my shoulders. "In the caverns, you were telling me about your abilities. Do you remember what you did to activate the Soother gift?"

Picturing Deborah as she transferred her calm to me, I took a deep breath and slowly exhaled. My heart rate slowed to normal, and the queasiness subsided.

"Feel better?"

"I do. How did you know that would work?"

"I didn't, but I figured it couldn't hurt to try."

"Can I ask you something?"

"Anything."

"What's it like, the medicine wearing off?"

He stared at his feet and cleared his throat. "Honestly? It's like I'm standing beside myself, waiting to be whole again. I keep hoping to feel something good, but even as the pieces fall back into place, I still feel…broken."

"And now I'm sorry I asked."

He waved away my worry, the hint of a smile on his lips. "Don't be. You might feel the same way once the lessons get going. Ready to learn more about your family?"

Unsure, I took a step back and twisted my hair around my fingertip.

Wrapping his hands around mine, he pressed them against his chest. "You can't complete a puzzle without all the pieces."

My heart raced, and briefly closing my eyes, I willed the calmness to replace the anxiety. "I'm ready."

"So, the Lunagardes and Morganfires were some of the most powerful and influential families in our world.

"Damond Morganfire—inventor and alchemist—had a unique gift. He could temporarily pull another person's gift from them and use it. He wanted to get rid of his gift as he thought it disrupted the balance, but it's rumored he found something more valuable, especially to Council."

"How is a rumor history?"

"A rumor isn't, but this one has circulated for so long that everyone here talks about it, so you should know, too. Anyway, it started because the prisoners, mainly people causing a boatload of trouble, were mysteriously giftless while incarcerated.

"Only one family line in known history had the ability to remove gifts. People began speculating that Damond worked with Council to remove them indefinitely. At least, that was the suspicion until the first rehabilitated prisoner regained his freedom and had full control of his gift again."

I studied him through narrowed eyes. "You're telling me my grandfather took away their gifts but was able to give them back?"

He smiled. "That's the rumor. And if it's true, your grandpa was hardcore."

I giggled. "Okay, so what happened to him?"

"He was injured and died right before your parents went missing."

My smile dropped to the floor, and I had to take a minute to process my thoughts. Maybe that was part of the reason Mom wanted to leave Alterria, for a fresh start away from sad memories. But it would still come across as odd to the people they left behind.

"Did Council search for my parents like they did Celia?"

He shook his head. "Brayden fought to find them. No one else agreed."

"That's right. He was friends with my dad."

"My brother and your dad were best friends. Those two and Ronin showed such potential that they were recruited to learn how to be Council members at sixteen."

"How does recruitment work at that age?"

"Well, they'd be trained, and when they turned eighteen, they could choose whether or not to join Council. My brothers both joined. Your dad decided to work with your grandpa and your mom."

"Didn't you say the Lunagardes and Morganfires were feuding?"

Torren nodded. "Then there was Cyran, who was also an alchemist. After his wife died, Lucian was all he had left. Another rumor suggests Cyran sent Lucian to spy on the Morganfires. Of course, that didn't seem as likely once your parents were married."

"Wasn't Cyran on Council?"

"Yes, and Brayden had been training to take over for Robert. That didn't sit well with Cyran. *He* desired the position."

"What happened to him?"

"He had a lot of enemies, so some suspect poison, but it's more widely believed he drank himself to death."

"Oy. You're right. This *is* a lot to learn. It makes me feel, not broken exactly, but disconnected from everything I thought I knew."

"I wish Brayden were still around. He really knew your dad. And Council. Council used to be amazing. High Councilman Robert would be rolling in his grave if he saw what it stood for now." He shook his head. "I shouldn't talk this way. Not here. Not to you."

My eyebrows scrunched. "Why not to me?"

"If Edric found out, I could be in prison for the rest of my life. Or put into the Glass House until it *actually* killed me."

"I'm not a snitch, and I would never let that happen to you."

He let out a small puff of air. "You wouldn't have much choice. Recruited Council members have no vote until they've been officially granted a position."

Movement caught my attention, and I focused behind Torren. Cade stood near the courtyard archway only ten feet away.

Ronin's words burned in my head: "He will betray you against his will."

I leaned close to Torren, and my mouth brushed his cheek as I whispered, "My wolf is behind you."

Torren's jaw tensed. "I have a bad feeling about any wolf that comes from Council."

"Why?"

Cade let out a short howl and trotted to us, his tail wagging. He lapped his tongue across my hand before retreating into Council Hall.

Torren released a long breath and scanned the courtyard before answering my question. "If you hadn't noticed, the High Councilman has a real dislike of the Lachloren family."

I waited for him to continue, but he didn't. "And what does that have to do with the wolves?"

"Next lesson. Wolves have been genetically modified to do Council's bidding. They can transmit any conversations they're close enough to." He wrapped an arm around me as I shivered at the thought of what Cade could have shared.

"There's more, isn't there?"

"They are super trackers. Whoever they're assigned to will never be able to hide from them. Make Council angry and the loyalty you think the wolves have for you can be flipped like a switch."

His words clamored in my head. I didn't know how long Cade had been standing there or how often he had been around Torren, but my heart dropped. "We need to get you far away from Council Hall. You can't stay here any longer."

"Here's the thing." He grasped my hand. "I may not remember our past, but every bit of my being is screaming at me to protect you. If I run, it'll mean trouble for you."

"I can handle it," I said more confidently than I felt.

"No way. Like it or not, I'm not going anywhere without you.

Chapter Twenty-Four

Lessons

With Cade nowhere to be seen, Torren and I headed out of the courtyard, away from Council grounds. Our quick steps turned to running until we found ourselves back at the river.

"Not even the wolves will be able to overhear us now."

"Good." I waited for my heart to slow before continuing. "Do you trust Edric?"

"In general? Not a bit."

"Why would he allow you to mentor me? He obviously has a lot of resentment toward you and your family."

Torren's mouth twitched. "I think he wants to keep you happy."

"What could he possibly want to keep me happy for?"

Everything Edric did seemed to center around Edric.

"If he has seen any bit of your gift…"

I thought of Edric chasing me down after I believed I'd killed Lyra.

Abruptly, Charlie's face popped into my mind.

My stomach flipped and sent waves of nausea through my system as my mind raced with thoughts of what he had done to me. The way his tight hold on me fell away as soon as Torren had walked into the courtyard made my head spin with sudden realization.

He wasn't ashamed to be caught kissing me. He wanted to hurt me, or Torren, or both of us. He'd gotten what he wanted, and I'd been nothing but a pawn in some game I didn't know we were playing.

"I can't get what happened out of my head," I said quietly.

Torren sat silent for a moment. "What can I do to help?"

"Teach me something."

"Anything in particular?"

My lips curled into a smile. "How do you control the fog? I wonder if I can use it like you do."

"Let's find out," he said, flashing a contagious grin. "We'll start with the basics. First, picture where you want to go as clearly as possible. Imagine a specific moment in that spot to help you get to the right place. If you imagine this old oak tree with no other identifiers, you could end up in a different country with a similar tree."

"Has that happened to you?"

Laughing, he brushed his thumb down the side of his nose. "A few times. Let's try something nearby. Close your eyes and imagine the bridge, the river running beneath it, the giant oak tree beside it. Picture as much of the surrounding area as possible."

Envisioning everything he said, I willed myself to end up on the bridge. Muffled pressure filled my ears for mere seconds, then the babbling of the river returned, and I opened my eyes to find myself in the center of the bridge.

Torren ran toward me, a huge grin spread across his face. "You did it!"

"I did it!" I met him at the edge of the bridge, giddy at the thought that I could control my gift instead of it controlling me.

He picked me up and swung me around before setting me down gently. Leaning his forehead against mine, he kept his voice low. "You should go home. You *can* now. You don't need me anymore."

But I did need him. I hadn't been myself since the day he walked away, but as I finally got to know the real him, I was finding those missing pieces. Helping him was mending my broken heart.

Overcome by intense dizziness, beads of sweat formed on my palms, and my knees wobbled. "I'm not feeling so well. Torren, what's wrong with me?"

He held me tight. "You've drained your energy."

"Like Lyra?"

He nodded. "Having multiple gifts and learning your abilities later than most Alterrians must drain your energy even faster."

"Why didn't this happen in the caverns? I used more gifts in there."

"The caverns and the labyrinth are different. They amplify everything, your gifts, your emotions. It's like your energy is on a constant charger."

Every muscle felt weighted down, and I began to sway, even as he held me.

He supported me as I collapsed against him. "Let's get you to your room."

I tried to stand, but my knees buckled. "I can't walk. Will you take me?"

He squeezed my hand. "Of course. Now picture your room."

"I thought you were going to do this." My eyebrows knit together.

"I am. I've never been to your room, but I can take you anywhere you can think of."

"Is that how all transporters work, just tell the person to think about where they want to go?"

He shook his head. "Not usually. I guess that makes us both a little unique. Even around here. Are you okay if I pick you up?"

"Yes." My eyelids became heavy as he lifted me into his arms, and I rested my head against his shoulder.

"Just close your eyes and think of where you want to go. I'll see what you see."

I pictured the stone floors, the large bookshelf, and the couch by the curtained window usually occupied by Cade.

Torren whispered, "Is this the right place?"

Opening my eyes, I smiled."Yes. Thank you."

"No trouble at all." He set me on the couch and took a step back.

"Not only for bringing me back. For helping me figure all this out. And for asking before you lifted me up, even though there was really no other option."

He raised a corner of his mouth.

"Would you mind checking the room? Make sure there's no boogeyman hiding." My voice teased, but I imagined Charlie peering around a darkened corner.

He chuckled and walked around the room.

Cade pranced behind him as Torren emerged from the bathroom. "All clear, aside from this mutt. Will you be alright alone?"

"I have to be. If you're gone from the hospital any longer, Edric will think you ran off." I smiled and pulled a blanket over my shoulders. "I mean it. Thank you for everything today."

Torren smiled back. "Any time. Until we meet again. Tomorrow?"

The breath caught in my throat as I nodded. Kai's greeting leaving Torren's lips brought me hope that even though he no longer had our past, our future was on his mind.

Smiling, he left the room, latching the door behind him.

Too tense to close my eyes, I trudged into the bathroom and ran a hot bath. I needed to relax.

As I melted into the heat and steam, a mess of emotions overwhelmed me. I wanted to know everything my parents decided I didn't need to know.

About who they really were. About who I really was. The daughter of the two most powerful families. Families that apparently hated each other.

I wanted to find a way out of this messed up world, back to the comfort of my own room. I wanted to go home—right after I helped Torren.

When the water took on a slight chill, I drained the tub, wrapped myself in a towel, and stepped out. My feet hit the cold stone floor and sent shivers through my body.

Writing on my mirror caught my attention: Meet me at the giant oak at nightfall.

The lack of dripping in the letters proved it had been written well before I was in the shower. Still, I shuddered at the thought of someone being in my bathroom. Who would sneak in like that? And why?

Was it Charlie? Could my parents have found me? Should I go? I wished I had a magic mirror to show me the future, the past, or anything at all.

I chuckled at the thought as I erased the message. I was trapped in a world filled with magic and even had a gift of my own. And I was wishing for even more.

I hastened to dress, then walked out of the bathroom to lie down.

Council accommodated their members very well. The room, although in a cavern, was bright and welcoming with a window to the outside. From the window, the tops of pine trees bowed toward Town Square, and from somewhere several feet below, a bird chirped a goodnight call.

Picking up a book, I stretched on the couch

Cade snuggled at my feet and fell asleep while my thoughts whirled.

After my conversation with Torren this afternoon, I knew Edric trusted me as much as I trusted him. Did Council need Cade to receive his transmissions? Was Torren safe? Did transmissions expire? My questions built a tower of worry higher for every moment I was on my own.

The sun began to set, and I waited.

A soft snoring vibrated from Cade's warm muzzle, and I covered him with a fluffy blanket.

Tiptoeing into the bathroom, I softly shut the door and closed my eyes, praying I could get this gift to work correctly.

I imagined the fog that crawled up my body as I was transported into this world. Opening my eyes, I saw the soft tendrils of white smoke wrapping around me. I closed my eyes again, holding onto the fog and imagining the giant oak tree Torren and I had been by earlier that day.

My head spun, and I reached out to steady myself.

A warm breeze wrapped around me, and I regained my sense of balance. My outstretched hands pressed against a rough surface and I peeked through narrowed eyes, afraid of what I might see.

I stood beside the exact tree I'd pictured, and a tiny squeal escaped my lips as I did a happy dance. I'd done it!

Mid-twirl, I caught sight of someone and froze. "Ronin!" I stepped back. "You startled me."

He smirked.

"You need to leave. Council's searching for you. Edric calls for the Glass House—indefinitely."

Ronin chortled.

Fury boiled in my veins, and I glared at him. "I hardly see how this is funny. I've seen what happens in the Glass House. To be trapped there permanently… you'd be insane within a few days. Dead in a week."

Laughter erupted from his chest.

"I try to warn you and you *laugh*?" Sparks danced on my palms, drawing Ronin's attention.

"I laugh, child, because I am *not* Ronin."

I gasped, and the sparks disappeared as my anger was replaced by fear. My heart sped, attempting to break free. I should've known this was a trap. Who was behind the Ronin glamour and what did they want from me?

"I have been watching you."

"Okay…" I stepped away from him. The fog enveloped my feet in lazy circles.

"You do not need to be afraid of me. I am Brayden."

My hands flew to my mouth to cover my gasp. "Your brothers think you abandoned them."

"I have been here all along. Protecting them to the best of my abilities."

"How could you have been there when they haven't seen you in years?"

"I have the gift of hiding in plain sight."

"What does that mean?"

"I can change the perception of the people around me. So, anyone who can see the oak tree right now will not see or hear us," he stated. "But where did you leave your four-legged friend?"

"Cade? He's in my room, asleep." My eyes widened, and my fingers trembled. "Why? What are you going to do to me?"

His mouth flinched. "First, I would never hurt you, and I am so sorry that the people you have met here have left you with so little trust. And second, your wolf could still transmit what we are saying."

"Then what do you want with me? And why meet here?"

"I asked you to meet here because I passed by this morning when you were with Torren. There are things you need to know that will help you better understand yourself and some of the people you have met."

"How do I know you'll tell me the truth?"

"Because Lucian was my best friend. I helped him and Izzy escape."

"But you fought to find them."

"Edric knew of our connection. If I had not fought to find them, he would have known I had something to do with their disappearance."

I sat on a bench that had appeared out of thin air.

Brayden chuckled and sat next to me. "My brother, Ronin, can do that trick. Make things appear as they are needed or thought of. We call it Manifestation. That is his gift. I am intrigued by you."

"You're not surprised?"

"I am still learning about you, but you seem to have a unique mix of your mother's and father's abilities. Some kind of amplified replication."

My heart raced. "What can you tell me about them?"

"There is too much to say, and your wolf will soon notice you are gone."

I shrugged. "I'll take my chances."

"Still, there is not enough time tonight. We cannot have you on the bad side of Council. Your position there could be needed. I will try to meet you again to tell you more."

I sighed. "I suppose that'll work. What did you hear this morning that made you come out of hiding?"

Brayden placed his hand on mine, and I briefly felt lighter than air. "You cannot share any of this with Torren. It would put him in danger. Do you understand?"

I nodded solemnly, acknowledging the importance of his warning. "I won't tell him."

"Torren told you about your grandfather and about the powerless prisoners."

"Rumors, he said."

Brayden snorted. "Not a rumor. Only three people knew about this agreement: Robert, Damond, and myself.

"Some gifts are too strong to leave unchecked, so Robert planned to temporarily remove gifts of criminals while they were imprisoned. Prisoners needed to go through rehabilitation and prove they were reformed before they would get their gifts back. There was a second-chance policy. If they ended up in trouble again, their gift would be permanently removed."

"Permanently? How?"

"Being a skilled alchemist, your grandfather created a potion to route the gift into an object. The potion worked off Damond's gift. Both he and the prisoner had to be in contact with the object that held the potion. Once the prisoner fully absorbed the potion, the object would hold the person's gift."

"Like pocket watches?" I flashed back to the scene from Edric's past.

Brayden smirked. "Exactly. Just any everyday object. The smaller the object, the quicker the absorption."

I furrowed my eyebrows. "Didn't anyone question why they were both holding this item?"

"I was working with them, too. I altered the perception, so the person thought they were the only one holding it."

"So, what happened to Robert? And my grandfather?"

Brayden heaved in a deep breath and dropped his shoulders. "That is the part of the story where everything changed. Edric claimed to have discovered an elixir to save any Outsider who may cross into our world. The rest of Council fell over his every word.

"However, Robert knew Edric was lying. Robert had the gift of Foresight but could not see his own future. He asked me to witness the meeting he scheduled with Edric."

"Did you go?"

"Yes. I concealed myself when Edric knocked. Robert confronted him with the truth right away. Edric's gift was so powerful that I did not realize in the moment he was using it. By the time I became aware of my mistake, the damage had been done."

He peered over his shoulder toward Council Hall. "You should leave soon."

"You haven't answered my question. What happened to Robert?"

"He made the announcement at the Council meeting later that week that Edric would be taking his position. That same night, Robert was found drowned."

My jaw went slack. "He killed him? What kind of gift is that?"

"Edric's gift is Manipulation. Everyone knew Robert favored me for the position. He had already begun training me. He never would have chosen Edric of his own accord. But we have no proof that Edric murdered him."

"Well, it seems kind of obvious, don't you think?" I scoffed.

"I certainly suspected. After Robert was found, I sought out your grandfather and told him what had happened. He went after Edric alone. With no one altering his perception, Edric must have known something strange was happening because he shoved your grandfather away before the transfer was complete."

I wrapped my arms tightly around myself. "Did Edric kill my grandfather too?"

"The night I helped your parents escape, your grandfather was murdered. Without proof, I can only suspect Edric's guilt."

I imagined my mother grieving her father and leaving her old life behind all at once. Then I pictured Edric's face when I told him my name. Fear gripped my heart. "Brayden," I said, my voice shaking. "Do you think he's going to kill me, too?"

Brayden shook his head, but my fear didn't subside. "I do not believe you are in danger. There is something he wants from you. I must warn you that because the transfer was incomplete, Edric did not lose all of his gift. It became weak, but it still worked for him six years ago."

"How do you know?"

"I learned from Robert's encounter that the person Edric used his gift against would forget the interaction. When the implanted idea returned to the person, they believed it came of their own volition."

"Forget? An entire encounter?" A sudden realization made me gasp. "Is he the reason you're in hiding?"

His eyes dropped to the ground. "When I stood against him— and the other Council members showed favor to my opinion— that frightened him. So, he threatened me. When that did not work to his satisfaction, he threatened my family.

"His Manipulation was still powerful enough that I could not fight against it. I had to make my family believe I no longer cared, that I had written them off, or they never would have stopped trying to find me. And *that* would have put them in danger. I used Torren's first stint in the Glass House as my breaking point."

I took a shaky breath. "This is a lot to take in."

"And I still have more to share, but you must return before your wolf awakens."

I didn't want to go back into that building alone, but I closed my eyes and allowed the fog to wrap around me as I pictured my bathroom.

When I opened my eyes, relief at my success surrendered to panic as someone began pounding at my bedroom door.

CHAPTER TWENTY-FIVE

RONIN

To make it appear as though I had just stepped out of the shower, I turned the water as hot as it would go. As billowing steam filled the room, I wrapped my hair in a towel and threw on a robe.

"Arisanna, I will enter if you do not answer," a man shouted from the hall.

Turning off the water, I yelled, "One minute please." I glanced in the mirror to make sure the message was gone. All that remained were the streaks from my hand.

I opened the door to the bathroom a crack, only to see the lock turn on my bedroom door. The red-haired man I'd seen in the room filled with listening devices stepped inside.

"Excuse me," I said, appalled. "Can I help you?"

"I'm sorry, Miss Arisanna, but we received a distress call from your wolf. When you didn't answer, we became concerned."

I nodded, repulsed by the fact that Cade could alert Council about anything. "I'm feeling unwell."

"Is there anything we can bring you to help you feel better?" Pressing onto his toes, he scanned the room.

"No, thank you. The shower helped."

"Shall I send Dr. Charlie to check on you?"

The mention of his name made my skin crawl. "There's no need. I feel much better now."

The man gave a curt nod and left.

I ran to re-bolt the door before collapsing on my bed. My body shook as tears overtook me. I couldn't help but chortle as I remembered Ronin's warning. "Protecting me yet unable to avoid betraying me, huh?"

Cade whined, nudging my hand for ear rubs.

Throughout the remainder of the night, the many questions Brayden left unanswered buzzed through my dreams. When I woke the next morning, I decided I needed to go back.

Reaching into my backpack to retrieve my water bottle, I discovered a new book, *The Faraway Princess*. I shrugged and stuffed it back in.

Perhaps Lyra would enjoy another story from Alterria. She loved the one I'd found a couple days ago so much she refused to let me return it.

I hesitated when I stepped outside my room.

Torren was probably waiting for me, but if I started there, I wouldn't want to leave.

I strode purposefully from Council Hall down to the river where I sat on the shore, leaning back on my hands and breathing in the fresh air. Each day brought so many new surprises, and now Brayden had me questioning everything I'd figured out. Could I trust him?

Sighing, I laid back on the grass only to be met by a smile similar to Torren's, one side raised a bit higher than the other. I gasped. "You startled me."

Brayden settled down beside me and smirked. "I did not intend to. I also did not expect you to return so quickly."

I sat up and crossed my legs beneath me. "I have so much I don't understand. I was hoping you could help me."

He looked into the distance. "Unfortunately, there is a lot you must discover on your own. I can only guide you in the right direction."

"Of course." I turned my attention to the trees on the other side of the river. The soft winds rippled through the leaves as I remained silent until Brayden's low chuckle pulled me back.

"If you do not ask the questions, I cannot share anything. What would you like to know first?"

"All right. Well, why can't I tell Torren you're here? I'm sure he'd love to see you. Your family misses you."

"My presence must remain a secret. The more people who know I am still around, the more danger our families will be in. But I can share no more about that for now."

My next question was prompted by Brayden's quick sobering. "Why is everything so ominous around here?"

His lips quirked up. "Not everything is. Did you find the storybook I slipped into your pile at the library a few days ago?"

I smiled. One mystery solved. "I read it to Lyra, the little girl in the hospital. She said her mom used to tell her a similar story."

He smiled. "Ronin told me about that day, the story of how they met. The book was supposed to be a gift, but I never got the chance to give it to Harmony."

"Ronin told you about that day? Wait—" I began putting two and two together but needed Brayden to confirm. "What happened?"

"I left out the part about Edric. They were friends once, you know. He was there that day, jealous of Ronin's happiness. But Edric did not know what to do when Alterria began to affect Harmony. He stood back and watched, but he did not forget."

"But the Ronin from the book is our Ronin, right?"

Brayden only laughed.

"Come on, Brayden. Don't leave me hanging. He married Harmony, didn't he? Did he leave Alterria then? If he did, why did he come back? Where's Harmony?"

"One question at a time. He did not live here, but he remained a member of Council, crossing the bridge daily to fulfill his responsibilities and visit his family. A few years after they married, he shared the good news that he and Harmony were expecting a baby. At that point, Ronin started spending more hours with Council."

"Wait. What?" I interrupted, confused.

"He sacrificed time with his wife in preparation for the long hiatus he planned to take when the baby was born."

"Well, where does Edric fit into this?"

Brayden sighed. "Ronin did not know that Edric had been making preparations too."

My heart sank, and my chest tightened.

"As the days stretched on, Ronin saw little changes taking place. He told me her smile was replaced by lines and shadows he had never noticed." Brayden paused.

I waited patiently for him to continue.

"On their last day together, Harmony waited for him at the door. Ronin said he ran to her shouting excitedly about how he would be home for weeks now that he had finished his project with Council. He picked her up and twirled her clumsily but had never seen her so sad. When he set her down, she backed away and cried."

I held my breath.

"She told him she did not want him to ever return. When he asked why, she told him the baby could not survive, and she could not bear the sight of him."

I couldn't help but cry, too—for her pain, his pain, the loss of the life that had never gotten to witness the beauty of a mother's love and a father's care. My assumption had been wrong. If the baby died, and Ronin and Harmony weren't together, the baby couldn't be Lyra.

"Ronin did not know what to do. Harmony had made it clear that her heart no longer belonged to him, so he walked away without a backward glance, not wanting to cause more pain than he already had.

"After Ronin came home, the bridge disintegrated. But then, inexplicably, years later, it began to rebuild. I suspected Ronin's gift had been at play and that he wanted to return to her. I decided to keep an eye on the bridge, waiting to see if my suspicions were correct. Hidden one day, I saw Edric cross, and I waited in the distance. He came back carrying the little girl, and there was nothing I could do."

The tightness in my chest changed, sadness replaced by anger. I didn't hide my disgust. "You didn't rescue her?"

"I had strict instructions, Ari. Like I told you, I can only share so much." His face paled. "Remember, Torren cannot know we have met or anything we have discussed."

I turned my face away, my jaw set. He wanted to justify his inaction and force me to obey his baseless rules. I couldn't understand Brayden's perspective, and my cheeks burned with the heat of words I wouldn't speak to him.

"Arisanna." Impatience tinged Brayden's voice. "You are still learning the history of our people and do not have the same knowledge or experience the rest of us have. Do not jump to conclusions about my motives."

I jumped to my feet. Being criticized was something new for me, yet the hypocrisy of his words took me aback. "You watched someone get kidnapped and did nothing. Nothing! And you want to tell me that because I haven't been here long, I should accept that that was the right thing to do?"

He grew quiet. "When you saw my little brother lying on the floor of the Glass House, tell me that leaving him there because your feelings were hurt was the right thing."

I staggered backward like I'd been stabbed. "You were there?" I whispered.

He ignored my question. "I saw my brother in that little girl's face. I knew right then she was Ronin's daughter. When I saw Harmony unable to follow her across the bridge, how could my heart *not* break?"

Still reeling from the truth behind the accusation he had thrown at me, it took a few moments until realization settled in. The baby had lived. Harmony lied to Ronin.

Brayden broke the silence, sadness in his voice. "I know what you must think of me. And believe me, I question my choice every day. But I wholeheartedly trust the plan I had been instructed to follow. I believed then, and I believe now, that things will work out."

"You couldn't even tell your own brother?"

"I tried to figure out a way to let him know without revealing myself, but I could not. And then he left soon after you arrived. I watched him walk over that bridge, and I knew where he was going. When he attempted to return, I suspected Harmony had filled in the rest of the story, but I had already hidden the bridge from him."

"You didn't rescue Lyra, and then you didn't let *her father* rescue her either?" My fists clenched in an attempt to keep the flames at bay.

Brayden stood, his eyes like steel. "I said I could not tell you everything. Ronin's return would have been dangerous for more than just him."

"What does that matter to you? You sat around hiding." It was cruel of me to judge him so harshly after what I'd done, but I couldn't help it.

He stared at me and shook his head. "I have set the wheels in motion. I did my best to send him a message. Harmony was with him, and she understood. I trust they have made it to their destination. The story is out of my hands now."

I looked at him with disdain, and he scowled.

"You have a lot to learn. If you hold people to a different standard of righteousness than you do yourself, no one will be able to help you." His words stung.

"I have to go," I said.

"Think about it, Ari," he said softly. "You have seen the evil with your own eyes, and not even you can fight this battle alone."

Chapter Twenty-Six

Lost Girl Found

My journey back to Council Hall was an assault on my mind. I turned over everything Brayden had told me. About Ronin. About Lyra. About Edric.

About me.

Had I been holding others to a higher level of righteousness than myself. Was I doing that with Torren, even now?

The entrance came quicker than I anticipated. With so much left to contemplate, I wasn't quite ready to be back.

I passed several rooms on the way to the courtyard but paid little attention until Lyra's name traveled from the open door on my left. Assuming this was the daily Council meeting, I slowed down and tucked myself against a wall, hoping to hear plans for her return home. As I listened, my stomach fell to my feet, and the blood drained from my face.

Thomas's voice rose above Edric's. "She's too young. You can't send her there."

"But she's Ronin's daughter," Edric boomed.

Dashing away as fast as my legs could carry me, I entered the courtyard in a daze.

Lyra and Torren were side by side, deep in conversation.

"Can it be anything?" Lyra asked, gazing at Torren with confidence he could answer any question. "Like can people fly?"

Torren smiled. "Not that I've seen, but—"

"What about moving things with their minds? I read a book like that once," she stated with a wiggle in her shoulders. "That was pretty awesome."

Without allowing her interruption to throw him, Torren gave credence to the possibility. "That definitely could happen, but gifts aren't necessarily broadcast. The only way people know what gift you have aside from outright telling you is if it can be used for their job."

Lyra plucked a rock from the ground and, flicking her wrist, sent it to the center of the pond, ripples spreading back to the shore. "That one worked, Torren!"

"Nice job, Lyra. Try another one."

"Let me find another good one. What's your gift?"

I smiled at the way she hopped between subjects, but Torren kept pace.

"Are you ready?" He waited for her to nod before transporting her across the pond and back.

"Again!" Lyra shouted, and after a second trip, she collapsed in a fit of laughter, and Torren joined in, propping his hands on his knees.

They still hadn't noticed me, so I headed for the bench swing to sort my thoughts. Pushing aside the image of Charlie and the remnants of nausea that refused to disappear, I focused on the rippling water while I rocked back and forth.

Another rock skipped by, followed by another squeal of success. Torren was bonding with Lyra, and he didn't even know she was his niece.

Alterria was home to many secrets, and now I was overflowing with them, too.

Torren's eyes met mine, and concern spread across his features. He leaned toward Lyra, and as he spoke, a smile spread across her face.

She waved before turning back to the pond to practice her newly learned skills.

Sitting beside me on the swing, he spoke under his breath, "What's wrong?"

"What happens if someone is put in the labyrinth when their gift is still brand new?"

"Well, it depends on the gift, I suppose. If they have no idea what gift the child has, there's no way to make preparations." Torren's face paled. "That wasn't hypothetical, was it?"

Shaking my head, I swallowed the lump that had formed in my throat.

His gaze rested on Lyra who giggled as more rocks plopped than skipped. "She's a healer, and no one knows aside from you and me. If she went in, she would need something to heal. Going in alone, she would end up getting hurt."

Ari, she needs to get home.

I froze, my fists clenching.

Torren placed his hand over mine. "Ari?"

"I need to think." I jumped to my feet and walked back toward the building, leaving a confused Torren on the swing. I had tried to speak to her before but received either no response or something irrelevant to my question. As I paced the walkway, I took a deep breath and spoke quietly, hoping she would respond, "I know, but how?"

Your gift.

I glanced over my shoulder to see both Torren and Lyra coming up behind me.

Lyra had her hand around mine in an instant and tugged. "Ari, what's wrong?"

Brushing his knuckles against the back of my hand, Torren fell into step beside me.

"Did you hear it again?" Lyra's whisper might as well have been a shout.

Torren stopped short. "Hear what, Ari?"

Taking a deep breath, I turned to face him. "It's nothing."

Lyra looked at Torren and shrugged. "She thought she heard someone yesterday. Maybe there's a ghost that likes to sit on the swing."

Why were little kids so honest?

"Is that true? Have you heard a voice?" Torren's eyes were wide.

I stared at my feet. "I don't want you to think I'm losing my mind."

"Nothing you say would make me believe that." He drew an "x" over his heart.

"I've been hearing a girl's voice since the night the fog brought me here." I covered my face, peeking through my fingers while I waited for his reaction.

His mouth hung open.

Dropping my hands, I twisted them together. "I knew it."

"Ari." Torren's soft voice captured my attention, and he laced his fingers with mine. With a gentle tug, he led me to the bench swing and asked me to sit beside him.

Lyra slid into the space on the other side of me.

"There's nothing wrong with you," he reassured me. "I heard a man's voice once. The day Celia disappeared. I thought *I* was the only one to hear someone speak inside my head."

My shoulders relaxed, and I tried to smile. "You told me about that once before, but I thought you were just trying to make me feel better."

He shook his head. "He told me she was safe and that I'd see her again…he lied."

I squeezed his hand and offered an empathetic smile.

"What did the voice tell you, Ari?" Lyra asked.

"That we need to get you home."

She bounced in her seat, a smile spreading across her face. "I'm going home? How?"

"Well," Torren said, stretching the word, "there are only two ways to the Outside. Transport and the bridge. Travel between the worlds is forbidden, especially since they stopped the searches for Celia. But we're more likely to be caught by Council if Ari and I walk out of here with you and head toward the bridge."

"So, fog it is," I said confidently.

"Don't forget what Edric said. You'll be punished if I leave. They watch my travel. If I leave this world…" He looked at the ground and swallowed hard.

A knot rose in my throat at the thought of how much he'd already been through, and nothing I said would change the truth in his unspoken words.

When he looked back up at me, the whites of his eyes were red, and he squeezed my hand tightly. "If anything happened to you because of *my* mistakes, I could never live with myself."

I brought my free hand to his cheek. "That's why *I* need to do it. She *needs* to get home."

"Taking another person by fog is different than just moving yourself."

"Tell me what to do."

"You can only start off transporting one person. Taking more people requires a lot of practice, and if you fail…"

My heart lodged in my throat. "Okay. So how do I take her?"

"Hold her hands and don't let go. You'll have to picture the fog enclosing both of you, and then picture where you need to go." He sighed and raked his hand through his hair. "But you can't because you don't know where she lives. You can't take her somewhere you've never seen."

"Where do we need to go?" I hoped the voice would answer.

To the place you first heard me.

I pinched the bridge of my nose. "How does that get her home?"

"The voice?" Lyra nodded an answer to her own question.

"Yeah. It doesn't make sense. She wants me to take you home. My home. We rarely left our property. Maybe once every few months for basic necessities. It's not like my parents would know your mom."

"She sells fruits and candies out in town. Maybe they saw her there." Lyra's smile didn't falter.

I smiled back. This was my chance to help Torren discover one small truth without breaking Brayden's confidence. "What's your mom's name? My parents always let me get a sweet treat when we went out. Maybe I've met her."

"Harmony."

Torren's hand tightened around mine again. "Harmony," he whispered.

"Are you okay?" Lyra stretched her arm over me and placed her hand on Torren's knee.

He stared at her little fingers. "Do you know anything about your dad, Lyra?"

She withdrew her hand, and her bottom lip popped out. "He had to go because of the bad man. Mama puts Daddy in my bedtime stories. Ronin the Brave. He's a knight, like Sir Lancelot."

My heart skipped a beat. "Torren."

He nodded. "Get her home, Ari. Keep her safe."

"Tell her."

Torren let me go and reached out for Lyra with both hands. She wrapped her fingers around his palms. "Lyra, your dad is my brother."

She gasped. "You're my uncle!" She jumped up and wrapped her arms around his neck. "I knew there was a reason I really liked you."

Tears pooled in the rims of his eyes.

"Lyra." I rubbed my hand against her back. "We need to go, but I need to talk to Torren first."

She glanced between Torren and me and grinned. "I'll go skip some rocks until you're ready."

I shook my head and smiled as she pranced over to the pond. "You've told me not to use my gifts here, but how else can we get her home? She isn't allowed anywhere but here and in her room."

"And the hospital rooms are under constant surveillance. We have no other options, but it will appear as though I'm controlling this, not you. You can use the willow tree as a cover, but someone could still see, and you can't give away too much of your gift."

"Why can't you send us?"

"I won't. Not after Celia." Torren stood, his hand extended for mine. He helped me up, wrapped me in his strong arms, and buried his face in my hair. "Be careful. I'm not ready to give you up."

I melted into him. "I have to go before they come for her."

He tightened the embrace before reluctantly letting me go.

Leaning toward him, I gave him a light kiss, and he pressed his fingers to his lips. I turned to Lyra. "Ready?"

She waved as I led her under the willow tree. "Bye, Uncle Torren."

"Hold on tight." I closed my eyes and imagined the picnic set for three and the shimmer surrounding it. The fog circled, enveloping us in its twisting fingers.

"Ari, don't come—" Torren yelled.

As I opened my eyes, he fell to his knees. My head spun, and I tried to reach for him, but Lyra's grip held me back. It reminded me that though my heart was divided, Lyra needed me most.

Back on solid ground, we were surrounded by the shimmering barrier. When I placed my fingers against it, sparks danced beneath my fingertips, but I couldn't break through the glowing wall.

I shook my head and whispered, "Now what do I do?"

It's her turn now. Give her the bottle with the pale green liquid.

I held it out to her. "Lyra, this is meant for you."

She spun it between her fingers, her lip curled up on one side. "What do I do with this?"

I tried to see through the barrier to the woods that were burned into my memories, but it was like peering through a glowing waterfall. Muffled conversation passed through, building in intensity as each second passed. Were there people in the woods? Were we going to get caught?

Have her pour a small amount into her palm.

"Pour a little bit into your hand," I instructed.

Lyra removed the cork and dripped the liquid onto her palm where it absorbed into her skin. The shimmer surrounding us flickered in front of her now-glowing palm.

"I have an idea. Bring your hand close to the light."

She bit her lip. "Is it going to spark like it did when you touched it? I don't want to get electrocuted."

I ran my hand through her hair. "I think that's something that happens only when I touch it. Torren doesn't get sparks when he does."

She let out a puff of air, her eyebrows drawn together. The wall of light responded to her hand by falling like the trailing end of a firework.

"Keep going," I encouraged. "You're breaking it down."

She took a deep breath and closed her eyes as she pressed her palm lightly against the barrier.

"Lyra, look up."

She opened her eyes, and her jaw dropped.

As the barrier trickled away, the muffled sounds became clearer. People were yelling.

CHAPTER TWENTY-SEVEN

AN EXPLANATION

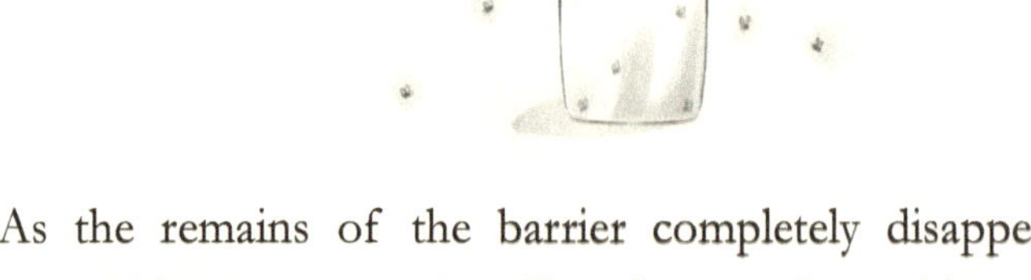

As the remains of the barrier completely disappeared, I was greeted by my parents' smiling faces and matching grins on the couple beside them.

"Mama!" Lyra bolted toward her mother's open arms with a shriek of joy.

"My darling!" Harmony didn't wait for her daughter. She met her in the middle, gathering Lyra against her and dropping tears into her hair.

Ronin approached with cautious steps, like moving too fast would chase away reality. When he reached them, he wrapped his arms around both of them repeating "my girls, my girls" as they fell to their knees in a mess of laughter and tears.

Their reunion after so many years brought a lump to my throat, though it was inevitable I'd cry when my parents met me in much the same way. In the comfort of their embrace, I began to sob. I was home.

"I'm so sorry," Mom whispered. "We shouldn't have kept any of this from you."

I laughed through my tears, the many unusual experiences I'd had flashing through my mind. "I wouldn't have believed you if I hadn't seen it for myself."

"Lyra," Harmony eased back from their embrace, eyes still shining as she shared a shy smile with Ronin. "This is your dad."

"Hi, Dad," Lyra said, causing us all to laugh happily at the joy in her voice as Ronin scooped her in his arms and spun her in a circle.

"And you must be Ari." Harmony stood next to her husband and daughter. "Thank you for bringing our Lyra home. I was so worried she was hurting. Or worse."

"I'm glad it worked. How did you get *here*, Ronin?"

"That's kind of a mystery. I found Harmony first, and then we received a cryptic message with this address." He looked back and smiled at my parents. "Found some long-lost friends."

I tilted my head and narrowed my eyes. "How did you get through the barrier surrounding our property?"

"Barrier? My brother, Brayden, can create barriers," Ronin stated. "There are no signs of their existence."

"She can see them, Ronin," Dad interjected. "I figured it out as she grew and asked about the sky sparkling every time we left the property. At first, I thought she was seeing a mirage, but she asked *every* time we left, even on days the sun wasn't out."

"There's a glimmer that covers our entire property like a giant dome." Everyone stared at me as though seeing a barrier was the strangest thing this group of Alterrians had ever heard. "I already know it's not normal to see them, but I also know that no one should be able to get through them."

Dad smiled. "He's a Lachloren. The barrier was created to allow our family and his to enter."

I shook my head with a smile. "That's how Torren was able to come through."

"Torren?" My dad's jaw set tightly.

"I told you I had a friend, Dad."

"You said his name was Kai. He was Torren all along?"

Ronin glanced around. "Where is he?"

"He stayed behind." I hoped he was safe.

"Then how did you get here?" he asked incredulously.

"*I* brought us."

Mom gasped. "You're a transporter? We've never had a transporter in our family lines. Have we, Lucian?"

"Never." Dad tousled my hair.

I grinned. "But I'm not *just* a transporter."

Ronin and Dad both stared at me. Their gazes held me in place.

"I can also make things appear as I need them and create fire."

"And you took my shakes away, Ari," Lyra popped into the conversation.

Ronin pursed his lips. "How is that possible?"

Mom shook her head, confusion sweeping across her face. "Honey, are you certain?"

"Yes. I've been able to do all that while I practiced with Torren."

"There's never been an Alterrian with more than one ability, let alone several." Dad rubbed his chin.

Ronin smiled with a sparkle in his eye. "We could be discovered if anyone else is able to break through the main barrier. That little picnic setup could give us away."

"Should we pick it all up?" I wished I could hide it from any prying eyes.

Ronin chuckled. "That's one way, but I'm pretty certain you've changed the perception of it."

Everyone gasped.

Lyra's mouth fell open. "It disappeared!"

"Ronin?" Mom breathed. "What just happened? Why can we no longer see the picnic?"

I glanced back. "It's still there."

"I'm guessing you've met Brayden," Ronin said. "It appears you have a unique ability, Arisanna."

Dad raised an eyebrow. "Why do you say that?"

Ronin started pacing. "If you recall, Callan has the gift of Flame, Deborah has the gift of Calming, I have the gift of Manifestation, Brayden has the gift of Perception, and Torren has the gift of Transportation."

My parents' eyes widened, and Dad spoke first, "Robert warned us Ari's gift would put her in danger. That's why we kept her hidden."

"She absorbs gifts." Mom sat on the ground and placed her head in her hands. "I'm so sorry, Ronin."

He laughed. "For what?"

"Didn't Ari take your gift from you?"

I froze, my mind spinning. "No, it doesn't remove gifts. Torren taught me how to transport. What exactly did Robert warn you about?"

Ronin looked at me. "High Councilman Robert believed that one day a child would be born with the gift of Duplicity. I believe that is you, Ari."

Dad ran his hand through his hair. "Wow. Just...wow. So, instead of her having *one* of our gifts, they merged into something new. An enhanced replication."

You must return before Edric notices you're missing.

Her instructions frustrated me. I had just gotten home. Why did I have to leave now?

But first, Lyra must complete the elixir. Tell her to stir the remainder with her finger and say 'facer enteiro'. Then give it to Harmony to drink.

I crouched near Lyra and pointed to the bottle in her hand. "I need you to stir that with your finger and say, *facer enteiro*. Then, Harmony, you need to drink it."

Lyra's eyebrow quirked as she stirred the liquid with her pinky. "Facer enteiro?"

The contents glowed for a moment and then faded back to a pale green.

"I don't know," Harmony said, wrinkling her nose. "What will that do to me?"

"May I see that?" Ronin took the bottle Lyra offered and held it up to the light before passing it to Harmony. "This is one of my elixirs. It's safe."

Harmony swallowed the elixir. "Did it work?"

"We aren't going to Alterria to test it right now," Ronin said, pulling his wife to his side.

"Daddy?" Lyra tugged on Ronin's hand. "I'm tired."

Ronin's face brightened when Lyra spoke his name, and he hoisted her onto his shoulders "Let's get you inside to rest. We can catch up later." Then, with his wife and daughter, he disappeared through the tall trees.

My parents came over to the picnic blanket.

"You've learned so much in such a short time, Ari." Mom beamed at me. "Not many people know that in alchemy, incantations are used like keys to unlock the full potential of a specific gift. The one you used means to make whole. Where did you hear it?"

"That's a bit difficult to explain, but I will soon." I inhaled sharply and wrapped my mom in a hug. "I have to go," I whispered.

"Bring us with you," Mom begged as Dad joined into our embrace.

You must go alone.

"I love you both, but I'm so sorry. I have to return alone." Stepping away from my family, I pictured Torren smiling by the giant oak tree. The fog swirled around and swallowed me within its tendrils as tears streamed down my cheeks.

When the ground beneath my feet solidified and the fog dissipated, I fell to my knees.

"It is alright, Ari," Brayden said, helping me to my feet and guiding me to the bench.

I slumped, my body weak from exhaustion. "I pictured Torren. I don't know why I ended up here."

"I am not sure exactly how transportation works, but I know you have spent time with him here. Perhaps that is why." Brayden suggested, shrugging. "Where did you come from?"

"Home."

"What happened?"

"I had to bring her back."

"Oh." His face paled as he sat beside me.

"What's wrong?"

He shook his head. "This could start a chain of unfortunate events."

"It would have been a more unfortunate chain had she stayed." I wasn't about to tell him about the voice. I stared at the leaves billowing in the wind on the massive oak tree. In the back of my mind, Torren's smirking face melted into Kai's.

"What bothers you, Ari?"

"If only a Lachloren could enter our property, why would Torren use glamour? Did he hide his true self because I was an excuse to escape from his guilt?" I knew Torren liked me for me, but I couldn't push back the sliver of doubt that Edric had planted.

"I sincerely doubt that. I have watched Torren for years, and I have never seen him happier than after returning from the woods."

I rolled my eyes.

Brayden rested a hand on both my shoulders, turning me to face him. "Besides, Torren never knew your family. He would not have even known there was a barrier. The glamour was protection for himself alone."

I fought the stinging tears threatening to escape from behind my eyes.

He spoke in a soothing tone, the corners of his mouth drooping. "Listen, the first year after Celia disappeared, he searched for her day in and day out. Little by little, he broke. I wanted to comfort him, but I could not let him know I was there." He dropped his hands from my shoulders and rested them on his knees.

I took a few shallow breaths. My heart ached for Torren and Brayden at the same time.

Brayden had hidden himself from his family for years. How lonely it must have been for him. "Why did you have to hide?"

"If Edric ever found me, my entire family would be in even more danger, as would yours. I am the only one, besides you—and now Ronin and Harmony—who knows your parents' exact whereabouts." His shoulders slumped, and he turned away from me. "I have a confession."

I swallowed, unsure I wanted to hear what he had to say.

"I am the one who told Torren to let you go."

"You? Why would you do that?"

"To protect your family. I had been hiding them for years, and your relationship with Torren put you all at risk." He paused and faced me again. "Torren was being watched. Thomas became so suspicious when he could not access your woods that he sent Callan to search the same area. That is why you two became linked the night you were brought here.

"Thomas is able to pull in any Alterrian within a certain radius. I watched as he sent Callan there and as he pulled him back. He did not know exactly where Callan was, so he cast out his fog and hoped for the best."

Brayden gave up everything to keep our families safe, and in turn, I had to give up something, too.

"Hiding us…" I breathed. The way my brows wrinkled gave away my confusion. "How? Why?"

"It all started with High Councilman Robert and his gift of Foresight. He saw your parents needing safety, so he sent me with a large sum of money to secure the land your parents own. He thought if they owned the woods that led to our world, they were less likely to be discovered. Still, as an extra precaution, he gifted Izzy a necklace that had the power to conceal. The power was strong enough to conceal an entire house."

"Once it's been used, what happens? Would the necklace or the power within it disappear?" I thought about Celia's cup and how it disintegrated.

He smirked. "No, that is not how it works. It contained the gift of a prisoner who had passed away. Your mother can use the gift because it was within the necklace, and she has the gift of Replication."

"Torren has a ring like that, but his gift isn't Replication."

"When Callan told us Torren could transport people to places he had never seen, Ronin and I knew we needed to protect him. Together, with his gift of Manifestation and my gift of Perception, we were able to create Torren's ring."

"So, the Manifestation created a ring with the ability to copy your gift, and the dome actually changes what people will see while he's enclosed in it?"

He nodded. "It only worked because we are twins whose gifts complement each other."

"About Perception, can you see the things you conceal?"

"They are just as invisible to me as they are to everyone else."

"And I'm guessing you don't see a shimmer where they exist, either."

"I do not. Do you?" His eyes sparkled as he smiled.

Ignoring his question, I asked another of my own. "Can you enter your own concealments?"

"Only if I create them with certain permissions, so to speak."

"Like the one over our property."

Nodding, he waited a few moments before changing the subject. "Did you get the book I left outside your door? It is a brief history of your parents' families and the roles they played in Council."

"Are you talking about the book with all the blank pages?"

"Yes. High Councilman Robert left me instructions to conceal its contents." He handed me a small vial of silver liquid. "I meant to give this to you yesterday. When you are ready, pour a little of this onto the pages, and it will all be revealed."

A nervous chuckle slipped through my lips. "I've used this liquid before. It's going to make me see things, isn't it?"

One nod confirmed my fears. "When you are ready."

My stomach was a sinking pit. Those visions took so much out of me. I didn't want to do this again. At least not alone. "I need to get back to Torren."

A howl rose in the distance, and we both jerked our heads toward the sound.

"You have been gone far too long." Brayden nodded toward Council Hall. "You must go before Edric wonders where you are. Especially with Lyra also missing."

As I walked back, remembering the way Torren fell to his knees as we left, my anxiety bubbled up. Was he okay?

Edric waited at the door again. His steely eyes narrowed as he saw me approach alone. A slimy smile slithered up his face. "Where is the prisoner, child?"

"I last saw him in the courtyard this afternoon, sir. I needed to take a walk to clear my head."

His smile faded, and his lips curled down at the corners. "Anything your little tutor has you confused about?"

"This entire world confuses me, but Torren is helping me understand it all."

His frown turned to a scowl. "Very well. You may want to get plenty of rest. I'd like you to join a Council meeting tomorrow evening. This one will be a little more intense than the last." He abruptly turned and disappeared down the dark corridor.

I released a long breath and walked toward the hospital.

Charlie met me outside Torren's door.

My skin crawled as he looked at me. I cleared my throat. "Excuse me. I'd like to speak with Torren."

Charlie smiled as he continued to block the door. "He had a setback."

"A setback?" I flinched away as Charlie reached for my hand. The pit in my stomach intensified.

His eyes flashed, and a smile seemed to snake its way up his face. It was eerily familiar but didn't belong to Charlie.

Chills raced up my spine.

"We found him in the courtyard screaming. We had to use a powerful sedative to get him complacent. You can visit him in the morning." He began to walk away and suddenly turned back toward me, his eyes narrowed. "You haven't seen Lyra by any chance, have you?"

The blood left my face, and I shook my head. "Not since this morning. Why?"

His eye twitched. "That is something Council will be addressing tomorrow evening, it seems."

"Oh." I watched as he walked away. How did Charlie know what Council would be discussing?

Once he was out of sight, I slipped into the hospital room.

Pulling up a chair, I sat beside Torren's bed and placed my hand on top of his. There was no response. "What did Charlie do to you?"

I stared at Torren, his body still. I considered returning to my room, but my heart fought against that idea. Instead, I stretched out beside him like I had many times in our meadow, my body fitting against his side like a perfect puzzle piece. Laying my head against his shoulder, his soft breaths lulled me to sleep.

A moment from my past slid into my dreams, hitting me hard and fast.

I was fifteen, and I hadn't traveled into the woods on my birthday since the girl had disappeared in front of me. A soft tune was being hummed, and I followed the sound.

Kai relaxed on his back, toes dipped into the flowing waters of the river.

"What are you humming?" I asked as I stopped just behind his head.

He tipped his chin up, the smile on his face brightening everything around us. "Just an old lullaby." His smile faded as he sighed and laid back against the grass.

"Are you okay?"

The corner of his mouth twitched. "I will be. This is a difficult day for me."

"Do you want to talk about it?"

He stretched his hand toward me and interlocked his fingers with mine. "I just need to forget the world today. Stay with me?"

Settling beside him, I rested my head against his heart and smiled when it began to race. I let silence lie between us, wanting to help him without being pushy.

It was peaceful, just being with him, the rhythmic rise and fall of his chest beneath my cheek. "Anything I can do?"

"I lost someone who meant the world to me. You being here helps."

I glanced up at him as he inhaled deeply.

His eyes fell shut, and a tear slid down his cheek. Pressing his lips against the top of my head, he whispered, "Thank you."

I woke short of breath. Had he been talking about Celia all along?

Chapter Twenty-Eight

Take a Chance

For a moment, I had forgotten where I was until Torren wrapped his arm tightly around me. I glanced up at him, a small smile toying at his lips.

"Are you okay?" I asked as he met my gaze, his eyes sparkling.

"I feel like I got shot with a tranquilizer gun."

I frowned. "What happened?"

"I don't know. One minute you were disappearing, and the next, I woke up here." He grinned. "With a beautiful girl sleeping in my arms."

I rolled my eyes and sat up. "Charlie said you were screaming in the courtyard."

Shaking his head, he tightened his hold on my waist as though he didn't want to let me go, then pushed himself into an upright position. "The medicine's completely out of my system now."

My heart skipped a beat, and my voice cracked as I spoke. "It is? And now you remember?"

His smile faltered, and he shook his head. "Some things...but not our past."

"Oh." I dipped my chin to my chest, not daring to meet his eyes. My spark of hope had burnt out, and I didn't want him to see my disappointment.

"The thing is…"

I snuck a glance at him from the corner of my eye, unable to predict the words he struggled to speak.

His eyes glossed over, and he looked away. "What we've been building the last few days is amazing, and I'm afraid I might completely ruin it with what I have to say."

My stomach twisted and my throat burned. Was I about to lose him again?

He inhaled sharply, his lips drawn down. "She's dead. She has to be. I kept going into the woods we played in as children, hoping to find a trace of her. A clue as to what happened. But I never did. I was just…alone. Still, I couldn't take away their hope. I'd already taken away Celia."

My heart sank as the sickening feeling faded. How terrible it must have been for him these last six years, not only knowing his niece was missing because of his gift but thinking he was also somehow responsible for her death.

"Torren," I said softly, resting my palm on his cheek.

He turned his face to me, his eyes rimmed in red. "You probably already knew, but I want to be completely honest with you."

My mind raced back to our time in the labyrinth. I had known he was keeping something from me then, and I understood now why he did. "No. I never knew. I wish I could erase your pain, but as far as what we've been building, nothing is ruined. I won't abandon you like the others did."

He let out a slow breath and closed his eyes. A small smile appeared.

I fought the tears forming, and my nose twitched. "Is there anything else you remember about the woods?"

His eyebrows drew closer together. "There's nothing more in my memories. The way we've connected, I *know* something's missing. I just don't know how to get it back.

Even after the medicine no longer affected him, he still couldn't remember us.

I knew what I had to do, and my heart raced in fear. I jumped to my feet, took a deep breath, and slowly let it out before speaking. "I want to help you."

"How? Lost memories don't appear out of thin air."

But they *can* play on a wall.

"The look in your eyes is scaring me." He chuckled nervously.

"We both need the truth. I don't know yours, and I'm not completely certain of my own. You can't complete a puzzle without all the pieces, right?"

"What do you need me to do?"

"Follow me." I led him to the place I feared more than any magical potion that could show me the past.

The corridor was dark and damp. The condensation dripped from the walls as I brushed by them.

As I opened a door and showed him inside, he hovered in the doorway.

"Why would you bring me here?"

"This is the Observatory. The Glass House has no effect on you in here." I walked up to the window overlooking the two-story-high cavernous torture chamber. "See? No transmissions."

He relaxed and cautiously walked to stand beside me, peering into the Glass House. His face paled. "I don't understand how this room will help me."

I reached for his hand. "I'm not sure it will, but will you give it a chance? For me?" My hands shook as I waited for an answer. I'd asked him to take a leap of faith, but I'd asked no less of myself.

His breath quivered, but his eyes searched mine, and my stomach fluttered. He had to see our past together.

Hopefully, it would help heal us both.

When he finally nodded, I dropped his hand and made my way to the the control panel.

I searched for the button Edric used to make the sound start and stop the day he convinced me of Torren's betrayal. Clicking one on a whim, the Glass House cycled silently through its sanitation process. My next attempt was successful as the sound of retreating water filled the Observatory. "Stay here. Please."

He pressed his lips together and clenched his fists at his sides, but he didn't move.

Closing the door, I took a shaky breath and drew my shoulders back. With my head held high, I walked toward the Glass House entrance.

Cade bolted to me and sat on the ground between me and the door.

"Where did you come from?" As I took a step forward, he bared his teeth, the hair on his spine raised, and his growl sent tremors through my body. I held my hand out to him, careful not to move too quickly. "I have to do this, boy."

He whimpered, and as he walked in beside me, I rested my hand on his back, glancing up at the Observatory window.

Torren pounded against the glass, his head shaking furiously. Horrified realization crossed over his face, but I turned away.

I had to do this. Resolved, I straightened my shoulders and took my place in the chair in the center of the space.

Cade sat beside me, resting his head on my lap. His soft whimpers sent tears down my cheeks.

Images bathed the walls, and voices flooded the room.

A humming, strong and clear, overtook my senses as my mother came into focus.

She sat at my bedside, holding my hand and
stroking my hair. My body was ravaged with

fever, and her lullaby soothed me to sleep.

The images shifted.

While chasing dragonflies, I was picked up, swung around, and set down on the ground again, turned in the opposite direction I'd been heading. I giggled as an older gentleman with eyes that reminded me of Dad's tickled my shoulder.

"Sweetheart, you cannot enter the woods without an adult."

I stopped giggling and searched his face. Wrinkles were etched into his down-turned mouth, and his hands shook. I pressed my tiny hands on his cheeks. "Why not, Papa?"

"The woods are so big, you could get lost." He kissed the top of my head, grasped my hand, and led me back home.

Papa. It was Cyran. Another shift.

I ran toward the trees as five people emerged. "Uncle Brayden!" I jumped into his arms, searching the empty woods behind him. "Uncle Brayden, where's Papa?"

Something was wrong. Brayden's eyes were red, and his smile was sad. He set me down, and his words were strangled. "Where are your parents, Rissy?" His hand tightened around a small burlap sack.

I pointed toward the house.

Deborah and Callan walked up behind him, each holding a small child.

"Torr! Ceely! I got new treats from the market. Want some?"

The image bounced, and I realized I must have been jumping up and down. My heart stuttered, and I gripped the chair's armrests. Torren and Celia used to visit? Why did they stop?

Torren and Celia wriggled away and ran up to me. Torren's bright eyes sparkled. "Last one to Rissy's bedroom is the smelliest!"

Celia smiled at me, and we gently pushed Torren back a bit before we took off into the house. We beat him by a toe. Celia stuck out her tongue. "You'd be the smelliest even if you won. You're a boy."

I started to hand out our sweets when a clatter from the kitchen startled us. We peeked out the bedroom door to find all the adults sitting in the living room.

"It is Cyran," Brayden choked. "He is gone. Edric knows."

Mom gasped, and Dad grasped her hand before pulling her close.

"Papa," I whimpered as I tiptoed out of my room.

Torren and Celia walked on either side of me, each of them gripping one of my hands. We stopped before reaching the end of the hall.

"What was his safeguard?" Dad asked.

Brayden opened the sack and handed each of the adults a vial filled with brown liquid. "It is a memory replacement potion. You are going to have to forget all your visits. And before you forget Cyran, too, he wanted me to remind you of his love."

"What do we need to do?" Callan asked.

"Drink it, and listen carefully to what I tell you. Deb, Cal, we will need to leave within thirty minutes."

"What about the children?" Mom sniffled.

Brayden shook his head. "There is no telling what it would do to their developing minds. They cannot take the potion. They are all young enough that, eventually, the visits may start to feel as though they were nothing but dreams."

The adults just looked at each other in the midst of the long silence that followed. As realization of what was about to happen sank in, tears began to flow, and they comforted each other with whispered words and shared embraces.

The vision became blurry. I must've been crying with my parents.

Little Torren appeared through the blur, swiping his arm across his eyes. Celia stood beside him, and tears filled her eyes, too.

"We're ready," Callan's voice boomed through the house.

The adults drank their potion, all except Brayden.

He cleared his throat as he put the empty vials back into the sack. "Your friendship is strong and will stand the test of time and distance. You have been using a communication potion for the last few years to stay in contact, but I have just warned you that your recent conversations have been intercepted and must be cut before Izzy's and Lucian's whereabouts are discovered.

"Arisanna must be kept safe. To do this, the kids must believe this was all a dream. Do not talk about the kids. They should not have reminders of each other.

"Izzy. Lucian. Cyran's love for you was deep, but unfortunately, his love of the bottle has claimed his life."

Brayden hung his head, waiting while the four adults sat in a trance-like state. As they came to, Brayden led Callan and Deborah to the front door. "Celia, Torren," he called. "Time to go. Say goodbye to Rissy and make sure to hug her really tight."

My heart had shattered at the finality of that hug. I hadn't wanted to let them go back then, and though I tried to hold on to that memory now, another shift ripped me away.

The cellar door was left open, and I'd never seen inside that mysterious room. The temptation was too much to resist, and I was bored, so I crept around the corner and down the stairs. Nothing but cubbies filled with random everyday objects covered the walls. I wandered the room inspecting its contents, wishing I could share this with my friends.

"There you are." Dad lifted me from the ground and pressed a kiss to my cheek.

"Daddy, when will Torren and Celia come back? It's been so long."

Dad's eyebrows drew together. "Sweetie, we've never had visitors."

Another shift. Celia's disappearance. I was nervous for Torren to witness this one. What if it trapped his mind in his own memories and guilt?

A small wolf pup trotted across the wall, a handkerchief pattern in the fur at the nape of his neck.

My eyes traveled to the golden-eyed wolf whose head now rested in my lap. "Cade! It was you."

The sound of a girl yelling filled the room, bringing my attention back.

> I saw the clearing, the root that caught my foot and sent me to the ground. Celia was there beside me. Then the light, and as Dad called for me, the light and Celia disappeared.

Another shift. I remembered this day vividly and smiled to myself as I relaxed into my seat. It was the day after my thirteenth birthday. I was allowed in the woods alone now, but only for short periods of time, and only if I marked my trails. I had gone in every day for the last year. No more flashes of light or a girl searching for her uncle.

> The babbling of the river called out to me. I wasn't supposed to go this far. I approached the river and slipped off my sandals. Sitting at the shore, I dipped my toes into the cool, churning waters.

> A soft crunch of twigs behind me startled me, and I twisted around to find a boy with messy brown hair and wide gray eyes.

> "I didn't think there would be anyone else here. I'm sorry if I scared you." He smiled as he sat, a small scar on his bottom lip stretching with the movement. "I'm Tor..." He nervously ran his hand through his hair. "Kai. I'm Kai."

> "I'm Arisanna—Rissy."

He stared as though my name was familiar to him, then scrunched his lips to the side. "Nah, you don't look like a Rissy."

"I suppose you could come up with something better?" I scoffed.

The left side of his mouth raised slightly higher than the right when he grinned. "Ari."

I didn't object. "Where are you from?" There was no sign of other homes as far as I could see.

He shrugged as he fiddled with a ring on his finger. "I live on the other side of the river."

"There's no bridge. How did you get here?"

He flashed his crooked grin. In front of his face, he waved his hands, fingers spread far apart. "Magic."

I laughed. "Okay, well, what brings you here?"

"Just needed a change." He smirked as he skipped a rock across the river. "You come out here much?"

I shook my head. "I'm not supposed to come this far."

"Why break the rules?"

"I guess I needed a change, too."

"Rissy!" My dad's exasperated voice echoed through the trees. "Riss, where are you?"

"I gotta go. I'm late, and he sounds upset."

"Wait." Kai caught my wrist as I started to my feet, and his eyes pierced into my soul. "Will you come back again?"

"Tomorrow."

"Arisanna!" Dad's voice grew louder.

"I get my free time after lunch."

Kai slid his hand to my fingers and lifted them to his lips. He brushed a soft kiss onto my hand and looked into my eyes. "Goodbye, Ari."

I ran to Dad, my heart thudding in my ears. It echoed in the Glass House.

"Where were you?" Dad's eyes searched me.

"By the river...I met a friend. Another kid."

"A friend?"

"Yeah. His name's Kai."

"Kai? Like the prince from your storybook?"

"I guess."

A long silence lingered comfortably between us as we walked home, but a new thought wriggled in my mind.

"Dad?" My voice was small. "Can you call me Ari now?"

A shift.

Kai's smile made his eyes sparkle as he brought me someplace new, a private meadow in the woods near the water's edge, where a picnic had been laid out. Covered glass containers dotted the red and white checkered blanket. Raspberries, blackberries, and blueberries filled some, while others held baby carrots, pickles, and sandwich fixings. To top off the display, a large basket with daisies poking out one side made up the centerpiece.

"What's all this?"

He grinned. "Did you forget again? It's our second friendiversary."

I snorted as I laughed. "I told you last year when you brought me the flowers. There's no such word."

"There isn't?"

I shook my head and sat on the blanket.

"Should we change it into a real word?"

"Like what?"

His cheeks flushed, and his voice was low. "You could be my girlfriend, and this could be our anniversary next year."

"We're fifteen, Kai."

"We spend nearly every day together already."

"So, what would change?"

He intertwined his fingers with mine as he leaned closer to press his lips against my cheek. "This."

Shift.

Kai approached me, his hand extended. "Come on, you don't want to miss this." He flicked a small piece of hair resting over his eye.

I reached toward him, and his fingers wrapped around my palm.

He pulled me to him and whispered in my ear, "Close your eyes."

I squeezed them tight and trusted him as he led me through the woods.

"Open." His grin held a mixture of pride and excitement as I loosened my eyes.

Mason jars with tealight candles inside flickered around the border of our meadow, and the river sparkled in the moonlight.

He slid his hands into mine and held me closer, our bodies swaying together. Fireflies flickered around us, and the forest creatures serenaded our moonlit dance.

"You ever had a dance like this?"

I shook my head and rested against his chest.

The rhythm of his heart matched my own.

Another shift. My heart clenched in my chest as the images changed. This part was going to break me.

"I can't be with you, Ari." Kai pursed his lips and swallowed hard, his face emotionless. "I don't love you anymore."

Chapter Twenty-Nine

REMEMBER

My heart shattered as I lived the betrayal all over again. I collapsed into a ball on the floor, and Cade ran from the room.

Next thing I knew, Torren screamed in pain as he pulled me into an embrace filled with the same desperation for comfort I needed in that moment.

The scene on the wall played out like a movie. I could see my own expressions merged into visions of an expressionless Kai as the wall replayed the day he left me.

He walked away from me, and when I ran back home, the vision shifted to his viewpoint.

"Until we meet again." Bringing a finger to his eye, he sniffled before turning back toward me. "I can't. This isn't right." He took a step forward, but the fog devoured him.

Shift.

A sharp howling filled the air.

"I'm too late," Torren whispered into the looming darkness, branches snapping as though he was shoving his way through trees. Fog formed at his feet and pushed out away from him. "No, you have to get this under control," he berated himself. He paused at the same time the howling intensified.

Moments later, a shimmering wall pierced the sky, and Torren shouted my name. He broke into a run, and the thud of his footsteps and small grunts of pain echoed in the dark.

The fog covering the ground crashed into him as though being pulled by a magnet. He was wrapped in white in an instant.

The next shift brought us back into the labyrinth.

Our fingers slid apart as the black and white fog engulfed him.

"Torren!" I yelled.

The curtain of fog slid away revealing the floor-to-ceiling bars of a prison cell. Torren gripped the bars in front of him.

"Send me back! I need to help Ari!" he screamed, but no one responded.

Footsteps sounded to the left, and Thomas slithered into view.

"That was a dirty trick you tried to play. I *know* Celia's dead." Anger laced Torren's voice.

"That was in your head, not mine." Thomas

smirked as he sidled up to the cell.

"And *your* fog took me away from Ari. What are you trying to do to her?"

"This isn't in my hands, and you know it."

"What does Edric want from her?"

Black and white fog obscured everything once more, and when it fell away, Torren was back in the Glass House, screaming to be let go.

It was me, *not* Celia. He was yelling to get back to me. "Torren?" Before I could say anything else, Edric's voice crept in.

"He *never* loved you. He wouldn't have left you if he did. Twice."

We watched the scene play out from my perspective.

Torren's body lay crumpled on the ground, the scenes of his past blurred in the background. Even as Edric spoke to me, Torren was my only focus.

"He wanted to protect me," I said uncertainly.

"You mean by using glamour to change his appearance?"

"Yes. That's proof."

"We all have that ability. That's not special. When you first came here, did it ever once cross your mind to pretend to be someone else? He wasn't protecting you. He was protecting himself.

That's not love."

Everything blurred.

A shift. This scene was after I had thought I'd killed Lyra. I squirmed in my seat as the memory played.

I sat on the bench swing in the courtyard, Cade perched at my feet. Charlie was seated beside me. Close.

Charlie inched closer as he talked to me. His hand covered mine.

"There's no one like you." Charlie leaned his forehead against mine and brushed his thumb down my cheek.

"No, Charlie."

When Cade howled, Charlie pulled back.

Torren's arms loosened as the scene shifted again.

Charlie sat across from me in the cafeteria, my vision blurring with tears.

I covered my eyes, and everything went dark. "I loved him."

"You *still* love him."

I dropped my hands and looked up. "He lied to me and used me, but all I can see is him lying on the floor of the Glass House. I won't be able to move on if I spend the rest of my life wishing I could save him."

Shift.

> Torren lay on the floor, face up.

> "It's not okay!" I moan. "He might've never
> loved me, but I can't take this. They're killing
> him."

Torren's embrace around me tightened as the scene shifted to the hospital and another stretched perspective played.

> "Torren," I said, my eyes searching his face.
> "Your love may have been a lie, but don't pretend
> you don't know me."

"It was never a lie, Ari," he whispered in a trembling voice.

It worked. He remembered me.

I twisted to face him, tears covering my cheeks. "You aren't supposed to be in here," I whispered.

Being held by him was so natural that I didn't question it. Now that he'd spoken, the realization that he was here with me struck fear into my heart. What would three trips in such short succession do to him?

He curled around me. "I've loved you since the first moment I saw you. The only lie was my name and my face."

"Torren, this place could kill you." I spoke harsher than I'd intended.

"I'd rather die with you knowing my truth than live a lifetime knowing you could never fully trust me."

Another shift forced our attention back to the wall.

> "It's the one place in the world I feel free. No
> one judging me based on my mistake. There are
> no expectations for me to be somebody I'm not

when I'm here. I'm just…" he closed his eyes and took a deep breath, "me. Completely me."

Fireflies danced around us as we came together, tangled up in each other's embrace.

"It wasn't the place. It was you. It was always you."
Our eyes connected, and my heart warmed with this beautiful memory. Against all odds, we had found each other once again.
The next shift erased Torren's smile.
My stomach flipped, and as I pressed my face into his shoulder, he rested his hand against the back of my head. I couldn't watch this.

"Please. I'm not—"

"Don't you think we have something special, Ari? Torren doesn't even remember you."

"But our kiss…"

"It wasn't real."

"Charlie, you and I don't have something real."

"Not yet, but we have a foundation. It's okay for us to grow what we have into something more."

"You don't understand," I pleaded.

"Shh," he whispered.

"Please…don't."

I could still remember the force with which he pressed against me. The determination in his kiss. I remembered fighting to push him away, but the way Charlie's name escaped my mouth sounded like I wanted him to kiss me.

"Ari?" The crack in Torren's voice tore at me.

Torren placed his fingers under my chin, guiding me to look at him. "I'm sorry," he whispered. "I wish I could figure out how to control the way this place pulls out memories."

Charlie's voice filled the room, and Torren's smile prompted me to turn back to the wall.

"What do *you* have to offer her?"

"A future," Torren said defiantly.

"Based on a past that you refute. You can't blame her for looking elsewhere." Charlie smirked as he walked toward Torren. "I'm sorry you had to witness that…moment of passion… but there's no denying it was there."

"It wasn't passion, Charlie. It was pain, and you owe her an apology."

"Did she say I hurt her?" he growled, and his eyes twitched.

Torren's voice slipped through clenched teeth. "Not in so many words."

Charlie's scowl melted away, and he closed his eyes with a smug smile. "I'm going to relish this memory. A beautiful young woman welcomed me to her side with a smile meant for me alone.

I took her hand and curled her fingers around mine. It's *me* she pressed against. It's *my* name she whispered, *my* hair she clutched. If you didn't see her pressing herself closer to me, you're blind."

Torren's fist raised and connected with Charlie's cheekbone.

Charlie stumbled back into the table with a crash. Straightening himself back up, he smoothed his coat and whispered, "Jealousy always gets them in the end." He backed out of the room with his hand pressed to his cheek.

I looked up at Torren, my heart swelling as another shift captured my attention.

Brayden sat beside me and placed a bottle within my hands.

This memory wasn't as difficult as the others had been, and I pulled back from it long enough to form a thought. "Torren, I need your help with something I'm not strong enough to do alone."

"Whatever you need."

When I whistled, Cade left his position at the door and ran into the room. "Help us out of here, Cade."

As he nosed us from the Glass House, a new scene played.

Mom's chin quivered, and Dad held her tight as the wall of fog separated us.

Had it only been a day since I brought Lyra home?

Without Cade's firm nudges, I would've stopped and stared. As it was, we trudged from the room.

Past the exit, the sensation of being watched settled over me, and as I looked back, a shadow slipped away from the Observatory window. Could it be remnant effects from the Glass House, or was someone actually there?

I shivered, but it didn't matter. We were free from the chamber of torture, and one thing filled my mind: Torren remembered me.

I was elated and overwhelmed, still trying to breathe out the vestiges of the Glass House depression. The trembling started with my legs but quickly moved up my entire body.

"Ari?" Torren spoke my name, and I leaned against him. "Just think where you need to go." He swept me into his arms, and all I could do to help was picture my room.

Chapter Thirty

Visions

As the fog thinned, Torren and I stood in the middle of my room, my strength returning as he held me tight.

I couldn't escape the Glass House memories, and the longer he was silent, the more nervous I became. My mind had been on full display.

Torren shuffled his feet. "Ari, can I ask you something?"

I nodded.

"You were ready to walk away. Twice. Why stay? You must have doubted my love enough to leave it behind."

"I told you I needed the truth."

He let go of me and stepped back, shaking his head. "There's more to it than that."

"I couldn't get home without you." I dropped my chin to my chest, ashamed.

"There it is." The sharpness in his voice cut me, and my head snapped up.

"Torren, I—"

"You didn't have to get close to me again if you'd given up. But you did. Why put me through all those feelings and make me fall in love with you all over again?"

The weight of his accusation crushed me.

"You're right. I *was* ready to walk away, and I'm so sorry. I know now I was being controlled by someone else." My lungs refused to take in enough air, as though I was being smothered, and numbness tingled the tips of my fingers.

"When I was under my own free will, I went back for you. And when I saw you—" thinking of him lying there, the water flowing over him, choked me. I swallowed hard and tried again. "When I saw you there, broken, my heart broke, too."

He wouldn't meet my gaze, but his eyes glistened. "You said yourself that you wanted to rescue me so you could move on." He dropped down on the edge of the bed. "I hadn't forgotten you yet. Why would you have wanted to move on?"

My heart was bursting. I had so many emotions battling to escape, to explain why I did what I did, but I hesitated. "I was hurt." I looked away in shame again. "You left me in the labyrinth for the promise of Celia. I was standing in front of you, and you didn't choose me."

He shook his head. "That wasn't my fog."

My voice wavered as I remembered his conversation with Thomas. "I know that *now*."

"You didn't have to fix me," he said under his breath.

"You were hurting. I had to try something."

"Why?"

"Because I love you."

At that moment, our eyes connected.

Jumping up, he gathered me in his arms. "You said love." He spun me around, an intensity I had never seen before burning in his eyes. "You still love me after all we've been through?"

"I never stopped." I trailed my finger along his bottom lip.

"You miss it, don't you?"

"The scar? A little. It's a part of the face I fell in love with." I giggled. "Is it strange that I feel guilty right now? I love you. I know that. But Kai..."

He laughed. "I'm Kai."

"I can't seem to merge you both in my mind, and I feel like I'm betraying him when I admit my feelings for you."

He sobered up at the earnestness in my voice. Shutting his eyes, he transformed. "I can be him forever," he whispered.

I brushed my hand through his hair like I'd done so many times before.

This was the face I fell in love with.

My heart clenched.

But no, I didn't fall in love with Kai's face. I fell in love with who he was, and that was Torren. I'd been loving Torren all along, and he was willing to change who he was—for me—forever.

Ever so slightly trembling, I traced the scar on his lip. My heart was full of awareness for the sacrifice he offered. A sacrifice I wouldn't—couldn't—let him make.

I shook my head. "It's you I fell in love with. Just be you."

Torren's crooked grin never changed as the scar faded, and I could have sworn he stared into my soul.

"What?" I asked, my cheeks burning.

"It's just..." He grasped my hands. "I need you to know. In some of the darkest parts of my life, you were my only light."

A passion sparked in my heart with his words. I pressed my lips to his, and electricity spiraled throughout my body.

He wound his hands into my hair and held me tighter.

This was different. Our past as Ari and Kai and our past where he was Torren and I was a stranger collided at this very moment in our present. We were finally whole.

When we pulled apart, my heart fluttered, and we stood there drinking each other in.

Torren broke the silence first. "I love you so much that I could stay like this forever, but you said you needed help with something. What can I do?"

Reluctantly, I let go. "Will you grab the book from under my mattress and put it on that table?"

"I've heard of a pea but never a book." He laughed.

Lifting the crystal bottle from the nightstand, I twisted it between my palms. "This is where I need your help. I don't know if I can do this."

Taking hold of the bottle I held out to him, he studied it. "This is from Brayden, isn't it?"

"I wanted to tell you, but he said you'd be in danger if you knew he was still around."

He shrugged. "Okay. So, we're supposed to ruin this book for what reason?"

"Let's find out."

He opened the book and poured a drop of the liquid onto a page. A soft haze rose over the top, and two men appeared within it.

"Damond, what you've discovered is incredible." Robert held up a glowing toothbrush.

Damond took the toothbrush and set it on an end table. "If this potion ended up in the wrong hands, it could be disastrous. It's incredibly powerful and should not be used foolishly."

"I understand, my friend. I know you don't want a seat on Council, but perhaps your discovery could be used in the aid of justice. To balance out the good and bad here in Alterria."

Damond shook his head and chuckled.

"You're persistent, Robert. How may I assist? And why a toothbrush?"

"Every prisoner needs one, and they are easy to replace."

The mist flickered, and a new scene appeared. "Wait. What's Brayden doing there?" Torren asked. "Shh," I said with a smirk. "I'm trying to listen."

"How will we accomplish this, Robert? They'll know something's off when their toothbrush is glowing." Damond paced the room.

Robert nodded toward Brayden. "That's where he comes in, my friend. He'll mask the glow. After I've replaced the toothbrush, store it in your cellar."

Damond sighed. "I fear this may not end well."

"Once the prisoner has been rehabilitated, they will be eligible to have their gift returned." Brayden placed his hand on Damond's shoulder, and his pacing stopped.

"Very well," Damond replied.

Flicker.

"Cyran," Robert said, placing a firm hand on the bar counter. "We need to discuss your son. I see great potential in him, but he seems disinterested in pursuing a Council seat."

Cyran tipped his head back, making the amber liquid from the short glass disappear. "Filthy rat. Thinks the Morganfires walk on water."

"What makes you say that?" Robert took the seat beside him.

"He married that Isadora, you know. He'll never join Council. Wrote me off, too." He pulled a small vial from his jacket, rested his elbow on the counter, and swirled the brown contents. His words slurred. "He'll forget why he ever betrayed me. He'll forget her soon enough."

My mind was torn. How could this be the same man from my memory in the Glass House?

Flicker.

A smile snaked across Edric's face as he walked beside Robert. "I am the better choice for High Councilman. Don't you agree, sir?"

Robert spoke as though in a trance. "Better choice."

Edric's smile grew. "At the meeting next week, you will name me your successor. Effective immediately."

Flicker.

Robert approached Brayden, a large envelope in his hands. "You must secure land on the Outside for Lucian and Isadora Lunagarde. They're key to bringing back a just Council and restoring Alterria. They need our protection."

Brayden scrunched his face. "Sir?"

"Dark days are nearing. You must prepare in haste. I won't be around much longer."

"Is this because of what Edric said to you this morning about the High Councilman position?"

Robert glanced up at Brayden. "You know I favor you as my replacement. That's why you're the only other person to know of the rehabilitation program. I did not speak with Edric this morning, certainly not about anything related to the High Councilman position."

Brayden's lips turned down, but he didn't argue. "I will secure the land."

Flicker.

"Damond, you have the objects that contain the relinquished gifts. Is there a way to transfer those gifts into another person?" Robert looked at his friend with a hopeful smile.

"The only way a person can obtain another's gifts is if they have the gift of Duplicity." Damond frowned and added a drop to the small bottle he held.

"That's only a legend. There's been no Alterrian in recorded history with such a gift. Yours and Izzy's gifts are the closest I've seen."

"Yes, but Replication and Duplicity are vastly different. With Replication, we can remove and use the gift of the person we are in closest proximity to, but only for a short amount of time. Duplicity learns the gift and can retain the use of that gift indefinitely, without removing it from the other person."

Damond frowned and surveyed his cellar. "I'm playing a dangerous game keeping all these gifts here. Aside from all the prisoner's toothbrushes, there are objects from people who donated their gifts. Someone will discover our arrangement soon."

Robert sighed. "My friend. Please use my gift. As you know, I'm unable to see my own future, and something doesn't feel right."

Damond nodded and closed his eyes. Confusion crossed his face, followed by astonishment, horror, and resolve. "Robert," he said, opening his eyes. "I fear you must disappear. An evil is coming for you. If you don't take precautions, Alterria will be lost in darkness forever."

Flicker.

"Damond, I need your help. Can you create an object that copies someone's gift without removing it completely?" Robert paced the floor. "I feel I'm running out of time."

"I can. Who needs such an object?"

"Alterria." He handed Damond a piece of paper. "Once the object is complete, present it and this note to Deborah and Callan Lachloren."

Flicker.

"Handing Council over to Edric? What have I done?" Robert held his hands behind his back as he paced along the river. The crickets chirped as the sun sank behind him, bathing the trees in a pale pink glow.

He pulled a vial from his pocket and sat on the riverbank. "I hope you were right. Good luck, old friend."

Robert opened the vial and tipped back his head, swallowing the contents. His head drooped and his body sagged until he collapsed completely.

The mist died down, and Torren spoke first. "Now what?"

Chapter Thirty-One

Sentence

"I need to think," I said, closing the book and stashing it back under my mattress with the remainder of the potion—in the nick of time, too.

Heavy footsteps pounded the stone floor outside my door.

"Arisanna," Edric called. "Are you there?"

"Yes, sir," I responded, waving Torren back as I headed toward the door. I waited for him to slip into the bathroom before I faced Edric.

"Why have you not prepared for the meeting?"

"Prepared, sir? It's not until this evening."

He pushed past me and slid my curtain open, revealing the setting sun. How had that happened?

"I'm sorry. I lost track of time. I'll dress now."

Edric scanned every corner of the room.

"Sir? I can manage to change on my own," I said with a light-hearted smile, motioning my head toward the door.

He pursed his lips and turned on his heel.

I ran to the bathroom the second the bedroom door shut and whispered, "It's safe." When my light knock was met with no response, I pushed open the door and confronted an empty room.

My heart weighing me down, I slipped the Council robes over my clothes and made my way to the meeting.

Edric was seated in the head chair and directed me toward Ronin's place. No sooner had I sat, Edric stood.

"Tonight, we reveal a crime," he said to Council members and the townspeople that were gathered, their voices ceasing almost immediately.

I searched the crowd and found Callan and Deborah standing in the same place as the first Council meeting. I sent a wavery smile to the back of the room.

Deborah winked.

"As you all know," Edric announced, "we've had a visitor for several weeks, one whom we as a town have adopted as our special guest."

A wave of nods flew around the room. Callan whispered into Deborah's ear, and she looked at him with a bright smile.

"What you may not have known," Edric continued, "is that I have perfected the elixir to send her home to her true family."

A gasp and murmurs replaced the nods, and someone near the center shouted, "Hooray!"

Edric's face grew grim. "As I entered her hospital room yesterday afternoon to share the good news, I found it empty. The doctor searched everywhere. She was not with Arisanna, our Council member in training who had been guiding the girl. She hadn't seen her since earlier that day. Isn't that right, Arisanna?"

I nodded slowly, unsure where this was going.

"In fact, with all the staff accounted for, Arisanna included, the only person housed at Council Hall who could have given us answers was also unaccounted for. Torren Lachloren, our recent hospital-arrest prisoner, went missing around the same time."

Anger boiled within me. Torren wasn't missing. He'd been knocked out.

"Arisanna," Edric turned to me again. "You were responsible for watching over the prisoner during his recuperation. Do you have an alibi for him?"

My stomach churned. If I wanted to hide the truth, I'd have to implicate the innocent, the one I yearned to protect. My breath came in shallow bursts, and the room full of eyes burned into me. I tried to catch Callan's attention, but he turned toward the far side of the Council table. I couldn't seek even unspoken advice.

"Well?"

"Perhaps," I said, meeting Edric's eyes, "she left the same way she arrived."

He sneered before turning away. "Council members and fellow Alterrians, I had hoped in Arisanna we would find a strong future. But when an innocent girl is brushed off as finding her own way, without concern for what danger she might truly be in, I'm afraid I may have been mistaken in my initial assessment. If one child is forsaken, how can we trust her vote when the town's best interest may be at stake? The way I see it, this Council seat is cursed. It's time to reduce our numbers to be more concise."

The fewer Council members there were, the closer Edric would be to an iron-fisted rule of Alterria, a place I was growing to love despite my trials. I stood without another thought. "Let me prove his innocence before you minimize Council."

Edric turned around. "Prove his innocence?"

"I will find him."

Near the dark, endless hallway, fog curled in from the stones, and Torren stood in its midst. "I apologize, High Councilman, for my tardiness. Someone neglected to invite me to this party."

"Come here, Mr. Lachloren," Edric commanded with a scowl.

Torren obediently walked to Edric's side.

"Where is the girl?"

"Which girl?" Torren responded with an arrogant toss of his head.

"I'd say Celia," Edric said heartlessly, "but you haven't answered that question for six years."

Torren's lip curled. He gave no other indication that Edric's words hurt him, but by the way Edric's smile grew, he knew he'd struck Torren's sore spot.

"No matter. I won't play games." Edric turned to the crowd. "From both his history and his entrance today, we know this man is capable of the crime in question. However, perhaps our prisoner is innocent. A guilty man may have run."

Torren stood with his shoulders back, head held high, fists clenched at his side.

Edric looked Torren up and down. "Still, we must take precautions. The Glass—"

"NO!" I jumped to my feet.

"How dare you speak out of turn?" Thomas demanded when Edric simply stared.

Instead of shrinking back into my seat, I stood firm. "He cannot go back there. No person should ever have to go there again. Lock him up if you must," I winced, the weight of the words sat like a boulder in my chest, "but you will *not* sentence him to the Glass House."

The way Edric dropped my gaze told me he'd consider my proposal but only on his terms. "She's right," he spoke to the townspeople. "After all, that particular discipline has lost its power over Mr. Lachloren. For the time being, he will be put in a high-security cell."

"And Cade," I added.

"Cade?"

"The wolf. He can guard the door to assure there's no escape."

Edric's smile seemed genuine, and he nodded at me once in approval. "There's promise in you yet, Arisanna, and *you* will find the true criminal. That is your task."

I lowered myself, refusing to respond. I tried to meet Torren's eyes as guards grabbed his wrists and led him away, but I didn't succeed.

The rest of the meeting slid by in a blur. Callan and Deborah didn't stay when it was dismissed. In their eyes, what I'd done to Torren must have seemed cruel.

Shuffling down the hall, I removed my Council robes and draped them over one arm, focusing on the stones on the floor as they passed under my feet. Turning a corner, I ran directly into Charlie. This day just kept getting better.

"Ari, I'm so glad you bumped into me," he said. "I've been meaning to talk to you."

"I'm not interested." I stepped to the side, and he mirrored my movement.

"It was a kiss. Don't deny you enjoyed it a little. I heard you."

"I told you no. What you did was cold, cruel, and vile." When I tried to move past him again, he grabbed my arms. Though fear hammered my heart, I shook him off. I wouldn't let him see that he could affect me that way.

"I didn't mean to hurt you. I wanted what I wanted, and you gave me signs that we were on the same page."

I jerked back in revulsion. "I did no such thing."

He adopted a new, sorrowful tone. "Then it was a misunderstanding. How can I make it up to you?"

"Make it up to me? I trusted you."

He hung his head. "You always loved him. I never had a chance."

I refused to fall into his trap. "I *have* always loved him."

Charlie loosened his grip on my arms, grabbed my hand, and yanked me in the opposite direction. "I know how to fix this."

Tell him to let you go.

"Let go," I said, digging my heels into the ground.

He ignored me. "You're going to love me for this."

"Charlie, let me go," I repeated more sternly.

"It's too late, isn't it?" he asked, coming to a halt. "You'll never even give me a chance."

I shook my head and glared.

He opened his mouth as if to say something, but instead finally let me go and walked away.

I watched him until he rounded the corner, and then I turned and shuffled toward my room, my energy depleted.

"Thank you," I whispered to the voice, but she didn't answer.

A few turns shy of my destination, I saw someone about to enter one of the many doors in the hall. "High Councilman!" I exclaimed.

He looked up and waited for me. "Arisanna," he said, his voice sharp. "I owe you an apology."

I stopped short. "What?"

"There's an air of distrust seeping into our village. It mostly stems from a few families, but some people have been asking questions no one knows how to answer. Tonight, I thought I had a solution. I was even willing to sacrifice you." He hung his head. "I'm not fit to be a leader, and I need to consider my options."

"Wait. You agree with me?" I asked. "You know Torren is innocent?"

"I suspect, but I needed to provide an answer tonight. Someone had to pay. It was you or him. And I'm sorry." He had taken the weight of a whole town on his shoulders, and I found myself pitying him, unsure what I might do in that position.

"I forgive you. But Torren *is* innocent and doesn't deserve to be locked up."

Edric stood tall. "You're right. Let's go."

"Go?" I asked.

"Torren doesn't deserve to be locked up."

The night was not turning out as I had expected. "Sir," I said as we walked, "when the townspeople find out that you're willing to admit your mistakes and maybe even ask for help…"

Edric scoffed.

"No, really. A leader who can accept blame as well as praise is someone to be loved."

"Thank you, Arisanna. I may not believe your words, but I appreciate their intent. Here we are."

Cade sat outside the open door of a cell.

"Where is he?" Edric roared, any lightness he'd displayed gone in an instant.

A guard scurried out from a few doors down. "What's the problem, sir?"

"Where's the prisoner? I had him sent here under the highest security. How could his cell be empty?"

The guard's mouth opened and closed. "I don't understand, High Councilman. Dr. Charlie said the prisoner should be freed on your word."

Charlie. He'd helped Torren escape.

Edric faced me. "Did you have something to do with this?"

I shook my head, and the guard backed away into the other room.

"You must leave." Edric didn't sound apologetic now.

I blinked. "What?"

"You must leave. As I said, he's your responsibility. When you've found him, you may return. Others will also be searching, and if they find him first or catch you running like your mother, you will be punished."

My heart sank.

This is an opportunity.

"I will do my best, sir," I said.

"Take your wolf."

Cade strode to my side, and I rested my hand in his fur, once again finding comfort.

I didn't know if or when I'd return to Council Hall, so I packed my meager possessions into my backpack. In case I might need it, I tied my robe to the outside.

Cade stayed close, panting near my legs.

I knelt down and gave him a good scratch around the ears. If Edric wanted him with me so badly, I had to leave him behind. "Stay, boy," I whispered with a final pat on the head as I closed the door behind me.

I didn't know how long I had until Cade would alert someone of my absence, so I hurried to the Council Hall entrance. It wasn't easy to miss, the large drawbridge pointing the way out. Without a glance behind me, I headed into the darkness.

Chapter Thirty-Two

Finding Home

I followed the road to Callan's house, stopping every few minutes to listen. I imagined footsteps pattered on the path behind me, but only the wind whistled by when I paused. Chalking it up to nerves, I continued on.

The walk was longer than I remembered, but eventually, the dilapidated cottage loomed before me. The lack of light in the window triggered an ache in my heart that I hadn't expected.

Lowering myself to the porch steps, I gazed at the bright moon dancing between thick clouds before it disappeared behind them. The wind blew strands of hair across my face, and I shivered.

Knock.

I shook my head at the instruction, recalling how Callan had turned away from me. I couldn't bear another rejection.

Knock.

The porch creaked when I stood. A light flicked on, and I scrambled away, only turning back once I was hidden in the shadows. Even if Torren was with them, they were probably all angry with me. The light went out, and my ache grew.

The meadow was the next familiar landmark, so that's where I went. When it came into view, I stopped and spread out the map I had confiscated on my first day in the library.

"Where do I go from here?" I whispered.

Willow Lane.

"Thank you," I replied, grateful she spoke to me even though I'd ignored her instructions.

As I walked through town, shadows moved behind curtained windows, but the streets were bare.

Mrs. Jones' house was dark except for one bright light in the kitchen. She lay with her head on her arms. From my vantage point, it appeared as though photographs were spread out on the table around her. She held one in her hands, and my heart ached for what she must be going through.

At the edge of town, the road turned into a dirt path, and too soon, that disappeared.

I pressed on with no guide and only the moon to light my path. Within minutes, I had come to a clearing. In the center grew a lonely willow. This must be the place. I slowed my pace and approached the willow cautiously. Nothing happened. What did I miss?

The Glass House took a lot out of you. Concentrate.

Like the first time I had seen it, the willow disappeared. In its place was a field of ruins. Something beautiful had once stood here. What had happened?

I walked over to what appeared to have been an arch and raised my hand to touch it. It was cold and black, except for a six-inch square bearing a worn engraving—D. Morganfire.

This was my grandfather's home, my mother's home. The connection between this horrible mess and my mother knocked me back. I fell, and the ruins were replaced by the willow and a shimmering wall.

"Who are you? Why are you here?" a man shouted.

I crawled forward, placing myself back under the concealment. Hidden, I was able to get a closer look.

Callan stood in front of the willow tree, his arms folded across his chest.

"I'm sorry, Callan," I said, standing and stepping back into view, as dim as it was.

"Arisanna? Oh, thank goodness. We've been so worried about you." He closed the space between us and pulled me into a hug.

"I thought you hated me." I was afraid that saying it might make it true, but I had to know.

He leaned back. "What made you think that?"

"You turned away from me at the Council meeting when I didn't have an alibi for Torren. I should've fought for him."

"When I saw what Edric was doing, I knew Deborah and I would have to pretend to want nothing to do with you. Our family is under constant scrutiny, and we didn't want to put you at risk. If I'd guessed you were in danger, it would've been a different story."

"Why didn't you ever come visit me?" I asked.

"We tried every day, but they always turned us away. Thomas started sending us home personally."

My heart lightened knowing I'd been wrong. "Then they must've stopped you from seeing Lyra, too."

"Who?"

"Callan, you don't know! Lyra's the Outsider in the hospital. Ronin's her father."

"No." Callan's mouth went slack. "Harmony told him she lost the baby."

"I don't have the details, but I know Lyra's back with her parents."

"Ronin is safe?"

"They all are."

"And he has a daughter?" The happiness in his voice was almost tangible.

"Yes," I laughed.

"And Torren?" His question tamped out the brief ray of joy.

"He's not with you?" My glimmer of hope extinguished, too.

"Of course not. You had him locked up."

I flinched.

His voice softened. "I didn't mean it like that. Your decision saved him from more torture. Everyone in that room today knows that."

"Maybe." I sat and crossed my ankles in front of me, resting my head in my hands. I was so tired. "I don't know where Torren is," I admitted. "The doctor set him free."

"Why would he do that?"

"Charlie's twisted games make no sense to me." My voice conveyed no gratitude to the doctor despite his good deed. "But I have to find Torren. I'm not sure exactly what will happen to me if I don't, but it can't be good."

Callan put his arm around my shoulder. "Ari, you're not alone."

I had to focus to keep his fatherly affection from opening the floodgates. The fear and loneliness I'd been feeling begged to be poured out, but I fought them back. "How did you find me?" I asked, my voice tight.

"With what happened to Torren, I thought Deborah or I would be the next targets. When I heard someone on the porch, I followed them. Had I known it was you, I wouldn't have been upset, but my question stands. Why are you here?"

"I'm not sure. I set out to find Torren but was afraid to knock on your door. I should've known better, and I'm sorry."

"Don't apologize."

"What do you see?" I gestured toward the tree.

"A weeping willow." A knowing smile flashed across his lips. "What's really there?"

"Ruins," I said, disgust dripping from my voice. "I don't understand how something like that could happen. It had to have been deliberate, a way to chase my parents away."

I grew indignant on their behalf. "I wonder what my life would've been like if none of this had happened. My family could've been whole again. And Torren would've *always* been Torren."

Callan took a deep breath. "I wish you knew how present you've been in our hearts all these years, even though we couldn't have you present in our lives."

I remembered what I'd seen with Torren earlier that day, or was it yesterday? "You *were* present."

"I can't explain it, but I feel the truth in your words. Torren and Celia used to ask for you when they were younger, but they'd never met you. It was the best way we knew to protect everyone."

Callan stared at the willow. "Deborah and your mother have always been best friends. Neither of us would do anything to hurt you. Did you know Deborah was the first to know about Lucian? Believe me, she questioned that choice. We all did. We liked Lucian well enough, but his family…"

I crossed my arms. His family was my family.

"That didn't cause us to dislike him. His father caused us all, your dad included, to fear for your mom's life. And that's where tough choices came in."

"What kind of choices?"

He waved his hand in front of him. "These ruins. *I* burned down the Morganfire home."

"What?" I couldn't believe my ears.

"Brayden concealed me so I wouldn't be caught, but yes. I started the fire."

"Why?"

Callan took a moment to answer. "It's a long story, and I'm not sure where to begin."

"If it helps, I've learned about my grandfathers and their gifts."

"That does help. Lucian and Izzy didn't have a lot of time to collect their belongings or even decide which things were most important. They took what they could."

"Couldn't Brayden conceal the house without the fire?"

"The concealment came later to protect the ruins from anybody digging through them, especially Edric. We didn't know what, if anything, had escaped the blaze. If he couldn't find the house, he couldn't steal whatever may have remained. But this is the part I'm ashamed of." Callan paused.

"You were all very young, and you must've been scared. I don't blame you for the choices you made back then."

Throwing me a grateful glance, Callan continued. "We hoped to frame Edric for the fire."

I blinked, taken aback.

"It would've gotten him in the trouble he deserved, knocked him off his throne, so to speak. We knew he hadn't been truthful about how he rose to power, but we had no evidence. Brayden knew Edric would come snooping, and with so little time to come up with something better, we decided everything had to be destroyed."

"But Edric told people it was arson."

"Yes. We didn't see that coming. He told people the fire was set as a distraction to give Lucian and Izzy time to escape. He used the truth to hide his lies."

The wind picked up again, whirling around me.

"Callan."

He turned slowly, his jaw dropping as he studied the new arrival's face. "Brayden?"

Brayden approached and embraced his brother.

Callan clutched him back, the moonlight highlighting the emotion on both their faces. "Where have you been?"

"I have been around, watching over you. I have been doing my best to maintain the safety we all worked together to provide all those years ago."

"Why didn't you tell us? We would've understood."

Brayden shook his head. "You could not know. Edric would do anything to glean information that might aid his selfishness, and I was not willing to take that risk."

"What brings you back now?"

"I am following instructions, but I am not leaving."

"Brayden, Torren is gone," I said, pleading in my voice.

"He is safe. I have hidden him. He is not happy about it, but if his presence jeopardizes the rest of you—especially you, Ari—he will not put you in danger."

"But his *absence* puts me in danger." I rolled my eyes when he remained silent. "You can only share so much, right?"

Brayden looked at me sorrowfully. "I have delivered my message and must depart. I will see you again."

Callan and Brayden clasped their arms around each other, sharing a determined glance before they stepped back.

Brayden walked away, and the darkness swallowed him.

"Ari, let's go home," Callan said.

You must find one item before you leave.

"I can't," I replied.

"You can't come with me?"

"I have to find something."

"What do you have to find?"

You'll know it when you see it. It once belonged to me.

"I'll know it when I see it," I repeated aloud.

Callan frowned. "How can I help?"

"You can't, but will you wait for me?"

He nodded, and I strode back toward the willow tree, which transformed into the ruins of my mother's home. Taking my time, I walked the perimeter until I kicked aside a large chunk of rubble that caused the ground to give way in front of me, revealing a staircase.

"Here goes nothing," I whispered to myself, descending the staircase, my hands grazing the earthy walls leading down.

Below the surface, glowing blue lamps on opposite walls illuminated a whole room full of tall shelves, each housing a variety of objects and books. One nook housed a large pile of toothbrushes covered in a thick layer of dust. A pair of goggles sat atop a leather-covered book on a tall wooden table, a pile of pens to the side.

Ash covered everything near the entrance. This must've been my grandfather's workshop where he created his inventions. Were these the objects he practiced housing gifts in? I was intimidated by the gifts that might still be in this room. But what was I searching for?

Do you see it? This is the key to revealing truths and regaining freedom.

Near the top of the tallest shelf, the dim glow of a white object caught my eye. I carefully wrapped it in my robe and placed it in my backpack. My head grew heavy. I hadn't had a decent night's sleep in days. I needed to get out before I stopped thinking straight.

"Ari," Callan said, relieved, as I came back to him.

"I'm exhausted. I need to go."

"Yes, home. With me." Callan offered his arm. "I truly wish things had been different."

"Mm," I said, leaning against him. It had been a long night. I was too tired to transport us both, and it felt nice to lean against someone who reminded me of family. "I miss my mom and dad."

Callan gave my arm a squeeze and chattered on the way home.

I couldn't focus on what he was saying, but "Torren" and "Celia" slid into my brain often enough to perk up my mind and keep me upright.

Like the first day we'd met, Callan led me into the kitchen where Deborah waited.

She jumped up and held me close the second I walked through the doorway. "Ari, you're safe!"

I hugged her back briefly and then lowered myself onto a chair.

Callan and Deborah joined me at the table.

"What did you have to find?" Callan asked.

My eyes blurred. "The key to revealing truths and regaining freedoms. That's what she told me." I laid my head on the table.

"Who told you?" Deborah asked.

"The voice in my head. She's been talking to me since I met you, Callan. She said it was hers." My words slurred as they left my mouth.

"Sweetie, please wake up for a moment," Deborah begged. "What voice? What's hers?"

I mustered the energy to sit up and pull the object out of my backpack. Seeing it on the table, I fully awakened.

We *were* friends, in a way. I'd been hearing her this whole time. It was *her* cup.

Ari, Celia whispered, *will you send a message for me?*

Callan twisted the cup between his hands. "I don't understand. It's Celia's."

"She needs me to bring her home."

CHAPTER THIRTY-THREE

CLUES

"Thank you for letting me stay last night." I brushed the crumbs from my toast over my plate before I stood, and Deborah's hand caught mine.

"Of course. You've always been welcome here." She gave me a quick hug, and I saw her eyes shining before she turned to busy herself at the sink.

"Morning," Callan mumbled as he walked in, his eyes glued to the cup in the center of the table.

Deborah and Callan hadn't just made me feel welcome in Alterria. They assured me I belonged, and their pain ate at me.

"I'm going to figure out how to get her back."

Callan cleared his throat and tugged the corners of his mouth upward. "Just knowing she's alive brings us such relief." His arms surrounded me and—in contrast to the intimidation I'd felt standing toe to toe with him—I could practically feel my dad's hug within Callan's embrace. His breath warmed the top of my head. "And absolutely no one expects you to figure it all out on your own. We'll find her together."

"Don't go back to Council. Stay here with us." Deborah sniffled as she wrapped her arms around the two of us.

I couldn't help but giggle as they both seemed to struggle with breaking their embraces.

They each dropped their arms and took a small step back. Deborah's eyes were red and puffy.

"Fine. You win. I'll be back as soon as I'm done." I grabbed my backpack from the corner of the living room and threw it over my shoulder. I glanced back at the cup before meeting Callan's gaze. "I feel like this may be safer here."

Callan's mouth stretched into a thin line. "I'll come with you. I can help protect you."

I grabbed his hand and squeezed. "I know you mean well, but if anyone sees you with me, I'm afraid of what that would mean for you…" My breath quivered. "And Torren."

Callan gave a quick nod and left the room.

A light smile grazed Deborah's lips. "He doesn't like to show anyone when he gets upset."

"I understand."

"Where are you going? That way I can send Callan to find you if you don't return before dark."

I smiled. "I'll be okay. It may be best if no one knows where I'm going. At least for now."

Giving her a small wave as the door shut, I pictured the willow in my mind. Soon, the smoky fingers fell away, and I was back at the ruins. While it had looked like a wall in the moonlight, in the daylight, the glimmer actually surrounded the entire area. I took a deep breath and whispered into the air, "Celia, can any other Alterrians see the glimmer?"

What glimmer?

"Never mind." My thoughts shifted from the glimmer to the glow around her cup last night. "Why did your cup disappear when your dad broke that bottle over it, and how did it end up here?"

When it disintegrated, it returned to its place. It served its purpose.

"What purpose?"

A chill traveled up my spine as Celia warned: *Someone's watching.*

"Watching me?"

I don't think so. I can see the shape of a person… she slowed her words, and the sudden sharpness in her voice sent shock waves through my body. *Go past the willow tree. They can't follow you there.*

Dashing past the tree, I took a deep breath to calm my shaking muscles, then walked toward the remains of my grandfather's house with light steps.

What are you looking for?

Quickly, I approached the cellar. "I'm not entirely sure. I've had this feeling all night that I needed to come back here." I walked down the stairs, eager to peek inside the leatherbound book I'd seen last night. Removing the goggles from the cover, a flash of light blinded me, and I dropped them to the side. My heart sank as I thumbed through the pages of the thick journal. They were all blank.

I closed my eyes, and my shoulders slumped. "Oh no."

Placing my backpack on a rickety stool, I unzipped a small compartment on the inside of the bag and twisted the cork out of the bottle of blue liquid. "Here we go again."

What are you going to do?

I wrinkled my brow. "Haven't you been watching me all the time?"

No, I could only see when we were able to connect.

"Well, then you're in for a show." I opened the book and dripped a drop onto the page. As the mist danced above the book, I capped the bottle and placed it back into my bag.

Celia gasped when Damond's face came into view, and I couldn't help but smile.

My grandfather seemed to be looking right at me.

He glanced around before he spoke, his deep voice hushed. "My sweet granddaughter."

My breath hitched in my throat. How?

"If you're seeing this message, that means what I foresaw using Robert's gift has come to pass. I hope you have learned of our family history by this point, or what I tell you next will make little sense.

"You're safe in this room. It has been concealed from all except Robert and those in the Morganfire and Lachloren families.

"The objects that remain here are relics of my work with Robert in creating a rehabilitation program for those who misused their gift. These objects retained a prisoner's gift until they could prove they were reformed and would use their gift for good.

"Our program was on the path to success. Most people changed and were able to regain their gift. Many of the objects you see are nothing more than mere objects. Unfortunately, our plan was forced into defeat.

"Council is rotting from the inside, and you are the key to change.

"My child, there are several items around my workshop you must obtain. The list of what you need is in the *Book of Records*. It's an inventory of objects that still retain gifts and to whom they belonged. Good luck."

His face faded and another appeared in his place. Celia gasped. *Robert!*

Robert smiled. "I apologize for all the cryptic messages you've received. If all has gone according to plan, a friend of yours is trapped between worlds. I'm hoping I have been a guiding force for her.

"Cedric, a powerful portal maker, created a space to keep me hidden while I awaited the child. I foresaw her exit from the portal but must not reveal more. The more a person knows of the future, the more the future will change.

"There's one more message for you within the pages of the *Book of Records* stored in this cellar. You are the change."

The mist disappeared, and I stood staring at the journal for several moments. I had met Cedric in town.

Ari, you need to find the book.

"Of course."

A shelf in the corner filled with dust-gray books towered over me. Speckled air swirled in the dim light when I blew on the books, and the only one without a title on its spine piqued my curiosity. Sliding it away from the others, I discovered *Book of Records* embossed across the cover in gold.

What kind of records?

I paged through the book, maybe an inventory of some sort, full of lists. None of them appeared helpful, and I was about to return the book to its place when I found an envelope doubling as a bookmark. *Unreturned Gifts* labeled a three-columned table that filled the page with a list of names, some familiar. Several of the names were scribbled out, but five remained.

Name	Gift	Object
Cedric Valencia*	Portal Maker	Will meet him
Talia Lachloren*	Disintegration	Metal hair clip
Calypso Einar*	Seer	Goggles
Unknown Lachloren	Time Control	Cup
Edric Agnar	Manipulation	Pocket watch

* Gift willingly given up. Former holder not a threat

I transferred my attention to the envelope I held tightly between my fingers. The writing scrawled across it read: *Young Lunagarde*. I opened the envelope, my heart thudding against my chest. I took out the letter from Robert and read it with trembling hands.

You have come so far in your short time here in Alterria. I apologize for any hardships you have come across during your adventures. The page marked by this letter reveals the objects you must locate. If I'm correct about you, the donated gifts willingly given over will be of great use for your journey. I leave you with these final words:

Little girl lost...

Deep in the meadow where the willows whisper,

Friendships: past, present, and future.

Bound together, intertwined,

Lost with hope, cloaked by love, and untold power combined.

The song of childhood to pull her back.

"What does this all mean?" A deafening silence surrounded me. "Celia? Are you still there?" No answer.

I stuffed the letter into the envelope and returned it to its place. Shoving the book into my backpack, I tentatively grabbed the goggles off the shelf, but there was no flash this time. When I held them up to my face, the cloudy lenses made it impossible to see much. How could these help me?

Another search of the room yielded the metal hair clip haphazardly placed beside some of the books I had knocked off-kilter looking for the *Book of Records*. As I picked up the clip, a tingle ran through my entire body. Stowing both the clip and the goggles in my backpack, I searched the shelves for the pocket watch, but it was nowhere to be found.

As I made my way out of the cellar, a glow shining from tiny cracks within the wall at the top of the stairs caught my attention. Was this another concealment?

Upon a closer look, I found the cracks were actually a hinge to a stone door that covered a nook. I pulled it open and discovered a faintly glowing pocket watch that seemed to laugh at me from its hiding place. I reached for it nervously, and as I picked it up, a pain momentarily pierced my temple. Inhaling sharply, I made my way back to where the willow hid the ruins of my family history.

I twisted the chain to the pocket watch within my fingers. "What am I supposed to do with these things?"

Celia remained silent.

Suddenly, a white light again blinded me. It didn't go away this time, so I concentrated on the moving pictures that ambushed my vision.

> Three people stood in a circle, all holding
> onto an item in the middle of them. Then I saw
> the meadow where Torren and I spent most of

our time together. Lyra's hospital bed came next, followed by a vision of my mother tucking me into bed, silently singing my lullaby. Finally, a blue light began to swirl, and a girl was removed from within it by whisps of fog.

The visions disappeared as quickly as they began, leaving me disoriented.

I pressed my palms against my eyes and exhaled slowly. "If that was some sort of gift I've learned, I hope I don't experience that again."

Soon, I approached the willow tree. With my head lowered, I drew in a deep breath and stepped through the invisible shield back into the open. As I looked up, I came face to face with a wide-eyed Charlie. Gasping, I placed my hands and the pocket watch behind me and backed up, but not far enough to re-enter the concealment.

He shook his head slowly. "Where did… how did…" His mouth hung open as the words refused to leave.

If he hadn't jolted me with his presence, I might've laughed at his expression. Instead, I scrunched my nose. "What are you doing here?"

"I could ask the same of you." His voice was cold, and it put me on guard.

With no way of knowing what his gift could be, I shrugged and sidestepped to go around him, hoping he couldn't see past the concealment.

He spun on his heel and fell into step beside me. "I've been coming here several times a week since the place burned down."

I froze, my face bunched in confusion. "Why?" The word escaped sharper than I intended.

"I'm fascinated by its history. I always hoped that one day, I may be able to get past that darn tree façade and figure out what happened here. Maybe even find some old forgotten treasure."

"What kind of treasure could you possibly find?" I stopped and faced him, clasping my hands tighter around the watch behind my back.

His eyes sparkled as he spoke, and I couldn't look away. "I know all about the secrets of the Morganfire family and how they stole people's gifts."

I glared. "Stole gifts?"

"They had a special gift that could borrow another's gift while in their presence, and the old man figured out a way to hoard them inside everyday objects. If only I could find one."

"What would you do with it?"

"Try to figure out the magic that keeps the gifts locked away." His lips twisted into a snakelike smile.

Chills ran up my spine, and I instinctively wrapped my arms around my chest. The pocket watch slipped and dangled by the chain wrapped between my fingers.

Charlie's face shifted momentarily as his eyes landed on the watch. "Where did you find that?"

Celia's voice broke through. *RUN!*

I took off without a second thought, regathering the chain and clutching the watch to my chest as I attempted to outrun Charlie.

What? How does that help? Celia's voice was strained. She wasn't making any sense.

I could feel Charlie gaining on me.

Drop the watch? Celia didn't sound very confident. Was she with someone else?

I shook my head and possessively tightened my grip.

Ari, Robert wants you to drop the watch.

I tripped over my feet. Robert? He died. Didn't he?

Charlie closed the gap between us.

DROP IT! Celia screamed.

I flung the watch away from me and called upon the fog, picturing Deborah's and Callan's welcoming arms.

"Finally!" Charlie yelled. He scooped up the watch as the fog swallowed me whole.

CHAPTER THIRTY-FOUR

TRAITORS

I dropped to the ground with a thud, landing on my knees. Something was wrong. I had pictured Deborah and Callan, but I was surrounded by darkness…no. As I became more aware of my surroundings, I realized light shone weakly through the thick cover of leaves above me.

"Ari, are you hurt?"

"Torren!" I shouted joyfully as I jumped to my feet. "Brayden!"

Torren spun me around with a hug. When he set me down, he glared at Brayden and held up his right hand. "Excuse me. We'd like some privacy." He twisted his ring, and I couldn't help but laugh at the incredulity plastered on Brayden's face before the shimmering bubble closed us off from the world.

"Now what?" I asked with a flirtatious grin.

Torren lowered his eyes as he stepped closer to me.

My heart sped up. We were alone, together. What was he going to do?

He took another step.

I pulled in my lower lip, my breath now shallow. He was going to kiss me. I *hoped* he was going to kiss me. His arms circled my waist, and when he pulled me against him, I could feel his heartbeat racing as fast as mine. He grinned and dipped me gently as I looped my arms around his neck.

I closed my eyes and drew in a quick, jittery breath before he pressed his lips to mine.

We melted together, and I knew in his arms was where I belonged. I never wanted to give that space up. The kiss continued even as he raised me upright. For once, all was right in the world.

But it couldn't stay that way forever. I nipped his bottom lip before pulling away.

"We should probably check on Brayden," he breathed as he pressed one last kiss against my neck, then twisted the ring to make the dome disappear.

I leaned against Torren as he slid his arm around my waist.

Brayden's eyes traveled between the two of us, and he smirked. "I do not have Robert's gift, but I called this."

"Me using the ring to kiss my girl?"

Brayden chuckled. "No. Ari being your girl. You were inseparable when you were toddlers. Poor Celia, always chasing after the two of you."

Torren laughed. "Toddlers? Brayden, we met when we were thirteen."

I rested my hand on his arm and shook my head. "Didn't you watch the entire time I was in the Glass House?"

Torren's eyes widened as he thought back over my transmissions. "My memories of you didn't return until I saw us meeting in the woods. That flash from us as preschoolers didn't click until just now."

"Brayden, why did you all stop coming? I was so lonely."

His smile dimmed. "Edric figured out your grandfather planned to leave Alterria. He wasn't about to let Cyran be happy. So Edric killed him. Cyran's dying wish was for your safety. He gave his life to protect you and your parents."

"He was coming to stay with us?" My heart yearned for what could have been. "I thought he didn't like my mom."

"He realized how much he missed out on by cutting his son from his life." Brayden stiffened and leaned away from us as though straining to hear something in the distance.

"What made him change?" I asked.

Brayden returned his attention to me and smiled. "You did."

My heart glowed, shining through my smile. Love was powerful. And apparently, it manifested in unexpected ways, Brayden's decisions included.

"Brayden." I paused, choosing my words carefully. "I understand why you disappeared after Torren's first experience in the Glass House. He had similar memories, didn't he?"

Brayden nodded.

"You *had* to leave. To protect all of us. You said Edric threatened your family, but they figured out you knew where my parents were. That's what you meant by protecting your family and mine."

Torren shook his head. "Why don't I remember seeing these memories?"

"The Glass House is traumatic, and you had bigger events that took up the majority of your mind. Your earlier memories with Ari were nothing more than flashes, but enough to show we had been in contact with the Lunagardes." Brayden stiffened again and took a step away from us. He pressed a finger to his lips.

Suddenly nervous, I held my breath.

"What's wrong?" Torren whispered, stepping protectively in front of me.

Brayden held up his hand and moved away cautiously. "I thought I heard a howling." He disappeared within the trees.

Torren turned, pulling me close, and I nuzzled my nose in his neck. He held me briefly before leaning back and holding my shoulders.

"He's put a dome of his own around us. We can't be found. But we do have a problem. Charlie has had it in for you all along, but now that he's found what he's been searching for, you're not safe."

"But I'm here with you, Torren," I said, confused. "I am safe."

Ari, please listen to him.

"Torren. Celia's alive!" I clapped both my hands over my mouth at my outburst.

Torren scoffed. "I don't know what makes you think that, but she's definitely not."

"She is. I've spoken to her."

Torren stared at me and shook his head. "Where is she?"

"Where are you, Celia?" I waited, but there was no response. "I don't know. She doesn't always answer."

"Celia's alive?" His eyes widened, and he whispered. "And that's whose voice you've been hearing?"

I nodded.

A grin slowly spread across his face, and he trembled as he enfolded me close. When he leaned back, happy tears colored his cheeks, and he planted a kiss on my forehead. "I can't believe it. I thought she died a long time ago. I thought I'd killed her."

"She's the one who told me to drop the pocket watch. Charlie has it now. I don't know how he knew to find it there. I suppose that's—wait." I interrupted the words that poured from my mouth. "Torren, I pictured Deborah and Callan, but I ended up here. How could that happen?"

Torren appeared mystified. "Ari, it's dangerous. Who knows where you could end up. You have to picture a location."

I shrank back. "You said to picture moments. Moments include people."

"I told you to picture moments in a location to solidify the place."

"I've been lucky then. After I took Lyra home, I pictured you and wound up at the river with Brayden."

Torren closed his eyes and exhaled slowly. "Extremely lucky. It's a good thing I was able to interrupt you this time."

"How? You weren't anywhere near me."

"We were there. Brayden concealed us, but Charlie was prowling the area, and we didn't want to get too close to him. When we saw you start to run and throw the pocket watch, we knew we had to get you out of there."

"Last time we transported, we were touching."

He grinned. "Was I going to give up a chance to hold you?"

"Torren, stop teasing," I said, feeling my face redden.

"I sent you to a place of my choice, so I didn't need to make contact. If you want me to take you to a place of your choice, we have to be touching." His smile dropped and he shifted to the side. "Brayden?"

"I am here." He stepped into the clearing. "We have to—"

Torren cut him off. "Celia's alive. Ari can hear her."

Brayden put his fist up to his heart and closed his eyes, a smile tickling the edge of his mouth. "I am glad, but now is not the time to discuss. The watch—"

"We have to find her," Torren interrupted.

Brayden turned to me, his brow wrinkled. "Is Celia in danger?"

"She didn't say she was."

Brayden appealed to us with stubborn insistence. "Then we must address other challenges first. The pocket watch is in the wrong hands."

"Then let's go get it." I spoke with false bravado that was a far cry from the unease that twisted inside me.

Brayden shook his head. "It is too late."

Torren turned his back and kicked a root sticking up from the ground. "Then what do we do?"

"I do not know, Torren," Brayden said quietly. "But..."

In the distance, wolves howled, and all three of us snapped our heads toward the sound.

Brayden swore.

A sudden bright burst of light blocked my reality. "Oh no," I breathed, bending my knees as I reached blindly toward the ground.

"Ari?" Torren's arms wrapped around me, and I leaned into his embrace, relaxing as the visions began again.

> Brayden stood in the clearing, staring into the distance. Torren sat beside me on the ground, holding me tight, his face warped in concern. Slowly, Torren and I rose to our feet. Cade strolled up to Brayden, sniffed his legs, and then pranced over to me. Three men appeared before us with Thomas directly in front of them.

> Torren hung his head behind bars, iron bracelets adorning his wrists. From the other side of his cell, I wrapped my hands around his bracelets and rested my head against his. When I stepped away, the bracelets had disappeared.

> The hospital room that Lyra once lay in came into focus. The cabinet I had bumped into was wide open, and Edric rummaged through the contents. Bottles clinked together as he pulled out item after item. The pocket watch swung from his hand. Edric stilled and carefully clicked the doors shut.

Another flash of light and my sight returned.

Brayden stood motionless, staring off into the distance. His sudden instructions cut into the thick silence. "We have to leave."

I rose to my feet, and Torren followed my lead, refusing to let go.

He held my elbows and turned me so I looked at him. "What just happened?"

"Brayden's right. We need to go. Now." I moved to the side.

Torren dropped his hands and stood beside me as another howl broke through much closer this time.

The blood drained from my face. "It's too late. They're coming."

Brayden nodded, not moving from his position. "When?"

Cade emerged from the trees, tongue lolling from his mouth as he bounded toward me. He slowed when he reached Brayden, circling him once while sniffing his legs. Cade's slobbery huff indicated he'd found no danger, and he resumed his excited prance toward me.

I greeted him with a scratch behind the ears when he rested his front paws on my shoulders.

Any other time, I would've giggled, but a knot was growing in my chest. I stroked his head, trying not to let my fear show, and he licked my face, howling in excitement. My heart raced. "Now."

Brayden shifted, his back foot searching to gain traction behind him. "I cannot hold the concealment. Someone is breaking down my power."

Torren took a step closer to Brayden. "How did they find us?"

I repeated Ronin's warning, "He will betray you against his will."

Cade nuzzled Torren's hand in response.

"Unique gifts are Edric's secret weapon. He tends to collect them. Apparently, he has one that can break down barriers." Brayden stiffened as three men appeared in front of us.

Torren wrapped his arm around my waist, bringing me closer to him.

Thomas stood front and center. His snaky smile sent shivers up my spine. "No need to fight, Ronin." He turned to Torren. "We've been searching for you. You need to come with me. You too, Arisanna."

"But I found him," I protested.

"Not soon enough. You will be punished. Don't try to whisk her away, Torren. Your gift won't work here either."

"Thomas," Brayden's voice dripped with ice. "This is unnecessary."

Thomas grinned. "I was mistaken. Of course the barrier was yours, Brayden. It's been too long, old friend. What a shame we don't have time for a longer reunion." Thomas's eyes slid to me, Cade smiling by my side. "Three will fetch a better response from High Councilman."

Cade nosed me away from Thomas as he inched toward me.

Brayden stepped between, his body inches from Thomas's. "Will you ever stop getting your hands dirty for Edric?"

Fire rose in Thomas's eyes. "Step aside."

Brayden smirked. "I am guessing your gift has also been disabled, Thomas, or we would already be in Council Hall."

Stepping backward, he joined us

"It's not working," Torren hissed. He looked at me, pleading in his eyes, and whispered, "You'll have to try."

"But…"

"Please. It's our only option." Torren glanced at the line of men.

None of them moved, and my nerves set on edge.

With a quick nod, I rested my hands against Torren and Brayden's wrists and called up my fog. It crawled around my feet for a moment before climbing around Torren and me. I stomped my foot and tried again. This time, it slid around Brayden and me. I let it go and shook my head.

Thomas's chuckle escalated into roaring laughter. He turned toward the three men behind him and nodded to the one on the end. "Elden."

Everything faded to black.

My head grew heavy as I blinked, the bright lights burning my eyes like I'd stepped out of a hazy daydream. Chained at the wrists and standing in a shallow pit between Torren and Brayden, anxiety clawed at my chest when Council Assembly Room came into focus.

Council bench loomed over us, and my ears rang with the chattering of the townspeople who filled the room.

Brayden glared at Edric, who stood firm at the cavern's entrance.

I turned to Torren, my heart lodging in my throat until he weaved his fingers within mine, his lips curving slightly upward.

The chattering died down as Council members entered the room, and took their seats at the long table.

Thomas stood and allowed several moments of silence before his voice thundered through the cavern. "All rise for the Honorable High Councilman, Edric Agnar."

Edric sauntered into the room, shoulders back, head held high. He never shifted his eyes away from his chair at the long table, ensuring he never made eye contact with a single person. Until he stopped and faced us. He and Brayden locked eyes.

Brayden scowled.

Edric's smile snaked across his face as he took his seat, and the rest of the Council members followed suit.

Edric cleared his throat. As he spoke, his voice filled every crevice in the cavern. "Welcome. As you can all see, we have a few to judge this evening. Our former Council member, Brayden Lachloren, has returned from his six-year sabbatical. However, he has been confirmed a traitor. His list of offenses is long. He is guilty of removing and aiding a prisoner from Council grounds, covering up a crime scene, and implanting a spy into Council ranks. He's been attempting to destroy Council inside and out for the past twenty years.

"Torren Lachloren is guilty of escaping imprisonment and assisting in the disappearance of the Outsider child.

"And finally, our former recruit, Arisanna Morganfire Lunagarde, has been arrested for her crimes against Council, including aiding and abetting an escaped prisoner and espionage." Edric's eyes sparkled as a collective gasp and an uproar filled the caverns.

"Settle," Thomas spoke, and the cavern fell silent.

Edric nodded and stood. He casually approached us. "The prisoners have been silenced. They would only fill your ears with lies. I have worked hard to create a strong Council to keep Alterria pure and our citizens safe. These criminals have tried to throw a wrench into the safety of Alterria, and our Council will not stand for such traitorous actions."

He turned to face Brayden. "For our former Council member, I sentence him to public execution."

"NO!"

I searched for the source of the few voices that seemed to bounce off the walls.

"The execution will occur tomorrow morning at the center of town square. As for the remaining prisoners, they shall be incarcerated until after the execution, after which time, a trial will be conducted to review possible sentencing."

Edric turned his attention to Thomas. "Council Member Thomas, please send the prisoners to their cells."

REVEAL

Black and white smoke wrapped around each of us. When it dissipated, we were all in separate cells.

In the cell directly across from me, Brayden walked to the bed and sat on the edge. The confident man I had met by the river was now a crumpled shell.

"Torren," my voice squeaked. I cleared my throat and tried again. "Torren?"

"Ari? Are you okay?" Torren answered, slipping his hands through the bars of the cell beside Brayden. Our chains had been removed, but the iron circles that wrapped our wrists remained.

My heart raced, and my palms were sweating. "For the most part. I'm a *little* scared, if I'm being honest."

He glanced at me, and helplessness filled his voice. "I wish I could comfort you."

I was caught in my lie. I was *terrified*, and he knew it. "Torren? Can you get out of here?"

Brayden chortled, the gruffness startling me. "These new iron bracelets we are all sporting are dampeners. They render any and all gifts completely useless."

"Oh," I whispered as my stomach clenched. I twisted and leaned against the cold, damp wall, sliding into a sitting position.

Drawing my knees to my chest, I wrapped my arms around them and laid my head in the empty space between.

"Ari?" A familiar voice cut through my defeat.

"What are *you* doing here?" Torren's voice boiled with hatred and anger.

I raised my head to find Charlie standing outside my door.

He met my eyes with a shake of his head. "I never wanted you to end up here."

"Well, here I am," I said, my voice tight.

Charlie grimaced. "Edric has requested I bring you to the hospital for evaluation. He believes you are somehow being manipulated."

"That is a funny thought, coming from the king of manipulation," Brayden spat as he spoke. He now leaned against the bars, one arm extended above his head.

Charlie turned to face Brayden, the backs of his ears cherry red. "You will do well to hold your tongue, sir. Speaking ill of the High Councilman has dire consequences."

"Worse than death?" Brayden scoffed. His eyes seemed to sparkle as he spoke. "I think I can say whatever I please at this point."

Charlie turned his back on Brayden as he pulled a set of keys from his pocket and unlocked my cell and dampeners.

"I don't understand." I rubbed my wrists as the dampeners fell to the floor.

Shaking the door to his cell, Torren yelled, "Run! Ari, get out of here! Go!"

Charlie's face turned red, and he stalked toward Torren's cell.

I scurried to Charlie's side and pressed my hand against his shoulder to slow him down. "Let me calm him, please."

Charlie paused, rubbed his chin, and then nodded his head in Torren's direction. "Don't try anything funny or Edric will have no problems hanging more than one Lachloren boy tomorrow."

Unsure which one of us the threat was directed at, I closed my eyes briefly to calm my shaking breath. Deborah's gift flowed through me, and I hurried to Torren's cell. "Give me your hands."

His eyes were wild, searching my face.

I pressed my fingers to his temples, transferring the calm to him. "It's okay."

He pushed his hands from his cell, and I gripped the bracelets on his wrists before sliding my hands into his. "If you can get away, don't come back for us. Just run," he whispered.

I glanced down, and Torren mimed me, his eyes widening. The way the bracelets disintegrated, falling to the floor like sand through an hourglass, made me believe the gift I'd just used was the one from the hair clip.

There was so much I wanted to tell Torren, but no time to do anything but rest my head against the bars and brush a kiss upon his lips. "Take Brayden to my parents. Safety," I whispered, stepping away from his cell as he backed up against the wall.

"Ari, no," he whimpered.

With tears in my eyes, I went back to Charlie. "I'm ready."

I trailed behind him out of the prison, staring at the ground as we walked. I didn't notice exactly when Charlie fell into step beside me.

He placed his hand on my back, and I stiffened in response. "I knew you weren't like them. I felt it when I observed you in the labyrinth. I believe you have a unique gift."

My heart stuttered, and I stopped walking. "Why were you observing the labyrinth?"

There was an unnatural hesitation before he responded. "I'm the doctor. What if a child's power is too strong and they get injured?"

I started walking again. "I guess that makes sense."

He led me into the room Lyra had occupied when I first stumbled into the Council hospital and pointed to the bed.

I sat and willed Deborah's calmness through my shaking limbs. This was a good gift to have.

Charlie stared at me with a raised eyebrow. "Firestarter and Soother. Interesting."

The sound of his voice sent a shiver up my spine.

He walked closer and placed his hands on either side of me before leaning uncomfortably close. "Have you been taught the skills of your grandfather?"

I shook my head slowly.

"No matter. Whatever your family's history, you're different. It's you I care about."

"Stop." I closed my eyes to escape the discomfort of his nearness, and he laughed.

As his laugh changed, I opened my eyes. To my horror, Charlie was gone, and Edric stood in his place, wearing Charlie's coat.

I shoved myself backward from beneath his lean, kicking him in my haste. My stomach clawed its way into my throat, and fear beat my heart.

Edric stood and brushed his hands against his pants.

I rolled off the other side of the bed and pulled myself shakily to my feet.

Where had Charlie gone? How had Edric taken his place so quickly? Had they been plotting against me all this time?

I took a deep breath and bit back the tears climbing to my eyes.

Edric sneered, and as he rounded the bed, he caught one of my wrists between his thumb and forefinger. Towering over me, large and intimidating, I couldn't even use my gift to get away without bringing him with me.

"Don't be frightened, Arisanna. I'm here for one thing."

I couldn't breathe. Thoughts of Charlie tortured me. That kiss. It had been Edric all along. *Edric* had pulled me into his arms. *Edric* had pressed his lips against mine. *Edric* had used me.

"You." My fear turned to anger, and I tore away from his grasp.

He took a step back.

"You stole from me. I never gave you permission."

"I stole? I?" He slammed his hand on the wall next to the bed. "Child! Don't play me for a fool. I know you have power like your grandfather. You steal gifts." He shoved his hand inside his pocket and removed the watch, shaking it in my face. "Why doesn't this work?"

Squaring my shoulders, I took a step toward him. "After what you did to me, why would I answer any of your questions? Who do you think you are?"

We faced off. Though he stood close to a foot taller, my anger gave me power.

"Arisanna, I want my gift back," Edric snarled with the same expression and tone he once used to tell me that Torren's love was a lie, but today his bag of tricks came up empty.

"My grandfather was no thief, and I never took anything from you."

"If you recall, that vial I planted in the cabinet at the library showed your crook of a grandfather stealing my gift with *this* watch."

"I do not steal gifts, nor do I know how."

"Don't lie to me," Edric shouted, snatching my wrist again. "I have worked too hard on you. You're not going to evade me again."

"You've worked too hard on me?" I asked, aghast. What work? He'd never answered a single question, not in a way I could trust.

"Why else would I ask you to join Council? You hold answers, and I needed to keep you around. But just like Harmony, you made things difficult for me."

I tried wriggling away while encouraging him to continue talking. "Harmony? What does she have to do with you?"

Edric's chest puffed up. "Why do you think she wanted Ronin to leave? She preferred the time I spent with her."

Another attempt to lie, but for what purpose—his own egotistical tendencies? I glared at him. "That's not true. She didn't."

Edric scowled at me. "And that's why I had to threaten her. Little did she know I always planned to come back. That girl's genes were too tempting to leave unstudied."

That girl's genes? A cold wave of understanding flushed through me. Alterrian blood coupled with that of an unwelcome Outsider. "You kidnapped Lyra?"

"Of course. She was nearly ten. She would either be exceptionally gifted or just a common Outsider. I had to find out if she could benefit me."

My chest heaved with the injustice this man had imparted on so many people.

"She's safe now. You can't harm her anymore."

"Never mind that. I have you now, and you've given me nothing but trouble, especially when that boy complicated things. He *just* wouldn't leave. You kept drooling after him, and not even Charlie could sway your attention. What was wrong with Charlie?"

I pursed my lips. "Charlie never got to know me like Torren did."

"Charlie tried to get close to you. You wouldn't let him."

"Charlie didn't want to get to know me. He only wanted to touch me."

Edric shrugged. "That's what Torren wanted, too. I saw you together. Even after I made him forget you, he was watching… waiting for his moment."

My mind caught hold of just one portion of Edric's speech, and it echoed:

I made **him** forget **you.**

I **made** him forget you.

I made him forget you.

"You...did...what?" I seethed, my nails biting into my palm.

Edric glared at me, his eyes cutting. "I did what I had to do. It was a sacrifice for me to keep him around, but I did that for you. And yet, you have refused to give me what I want."

As his fury grew, I held onto my indignation at his confession and resisted the inclination to shrink back. Suddenly, the anger drained from Edric's face, and his shoulders slumped. "Please. Find a way to restore my gift. That's all I want."

The knot of outrage blocked my throat, but I was taken aback. I had never seen Edric vulnerable.

He dropped my wrist, defeated, but when I rubbed the feel of his hand away, he straightened his shoulders and sneered. "Let me rephrase. You *will* figure out how to restore my gift to me, or your little boyfriend will go back into the Glass House."

I staggered back. "No," I whispered. "That would kill him."

Slime dripped from his voice as he stepped closer. "Precisely. And you will watch him die."

No. I wouldn't let Edric affect me like this anymore. My palms burned as I summoned my courage to push him away.

He stepped back willingly, his eyes full of confusion, when my hands singed his shirt, leaving pale tea-colored prints.

A burst of strength flowed through my veins. "You misunderstand. Your threats have no control over me anymore."

He stood his ground with nothing but a fleeting backward glance weakening his resolve to make good on his threat.

My jaw clenched, and a venom toward him raced through my veins as I met his eyes. "You will not put Torren into the Glass House *ever* again."

He blinked hard and cocked his head. "The noose then. Makes no difference to me." He stuffed the watch back into his pocket. His lips were thin lines of white. "I have arrangements to make. You are free to go." He strode toward the door.

Somehow, I'd beaten him at his own game. Despite what I'd just learned, a glow of victory washed over me, and I lifted my chin.

I inhaled deeply, intending to release the riotous emotions that had overtaken me, when suddenly Edric turned back.

No.

The breath sputtered from my lungs.

Charlie turned back, grabbed my face, and kissed me directly on the mouth. Releasing me like he did on the courtyard swing, he ran from the room.

I dropped to the chair, shaking, and scrubbed my lips with the hem of my shirt. I grew tense when footsteps echoed in the hall.

Mrs. Chapman walked by, not seeing me, and I realized something important.

Charlie—Edric—had left the door open behind him.

Chapter Thirty-Six

Choices

Taking a deep breath, I ran to the closet across the hall and latched the door behind me. As the darkness enveloped me, a chill ran up my spine. It was spookier without Torren.

Torren.

My heart sank. I hoped he had gotten Brayden to safety. I had to believe he did.

With my eyes squeezed shut, I pictured the cozy kitchen. The love of family. Deborah and Callan. My feet drifted from the floor for mere seconds before returning to solid ground once again. Before I could even open my eyes, the comfort of a warm embrace held me close.

"How?" Deborah stepped back without letting go of my shoulders.

Callan stood an arm's length away, bathed in an eerie glow from the setting sun's red hues. "Torren? Brayden?"

I bit the inside of my cheek. The fragrance of freshly baked bread meant welcome and comfort, but my news only brought uncertainty and fear. "I can't know for sure. I'm choosing to believe they're safe. They have to be."

Deborah tilted her head. "What do you mean you can't know for sure?"

"Charlie," I choked on the name, "he said Edric needed to talk to me. That he didn't believe I acted on my own accord. I hope I got Torren free. I told him to take Brayden."

"But you didn't make sure?" Callan asked.

"Charlie brought me to the hospital. Edric is—" I shook my head. Speaking that truth out loud was more than I could bear. "Edric thinks I steal gifts."

"How did you get here?" Deborah asked meekly.

"I was left alone, so I came here."

Callan stiffened. "You didn't check to make sure my brothers were safe?"

"I couldn't." I swallowed the lump rising to suffocate me. "There were guards at the prison. And wolves."

Deborah sat in the chair at the table, her face pale. "Why didn't you just go home? Why come to us?"

"Charlie threatened all the Lachlorens. If Torren and Brayden escaped and Council can't find me, they *will* come after you two."

Callan must have recognized the truth in my warning because he closed his eyes and set his jaw. "What's the plan?"

I tried to mask my worry with a smile but bit my bottom lip instead. "I can't transport you both at once, but we need to get you out of here."

Deborah's eyes were wide. "You're a transporter? Like Torren?"

I shook my head and held my palms up. I thought back to the anger that boiled in my chest as Edric threatened to throw Torren in the Glass House again. Flames danced across my palms.

Deborah's breath hitched, and Callan let out a gruff laugh.

"Ronin called it Duplicity." I thought of Torren's crooked smile, and the flames disappeared.

"Duplicity?" Callan ran his hand through his hair and took a step back. "It's real?"

"It is, but we don't have time for this."

"Take Deborah first."

I shook my head as I threw my backpack over my shoulders. "He threatened you, not Deborah."

"Deborah goes first."

"No, no, no." Deborah shook her head insistently, tears streaking her cheeks.

Callan wrapped his wife in a tight embrace before pressing her hand into mine. "I could never live with myself if something happened to you. Go."

I closed my eyes and pictured my home, the large house set alone in a small clearing, surrounded on all sides by trees. As the fog lifted us, the sound of wolves filled the air. I opened my eyes and saw Callan's back door fly open just before the fog swallowed us. The howling rang in my ears even after the fog faded, and Deborah and I stood outside my house.

"Go in," my voice cracked, and my heart raced as I dropped my backpack. "I need to go back for Callan."

Deborah grabbed my wrist and shook her head as the fog formed at my feet. Her eyes glistened. "It's too late, Arisanna."

"It's not. I can get him." I tried to pull away from her, but she wouldn't let go. "Please," I pleaded and dropped to my knees.

The screen door slammed against the side of the house. Voices surrounded me as my head began to swirl.

I drifted on a cloud, my body a boulder on the ground. I stared at my hands, flames flickering to life. The fog continued swirling, flashes of light assaulted my vision, and faces flickered in and out.

I blinked hard a few times as Torren cupped my cheeks. My senses returned, and I stared into his eyes. Was he really in front of me? I placed my hands on his. "Torren, we need to get Callan," I whispered as I collapsed against him, and he held me close.

Deborah sat beside us. "I saw them go into our house. They've got him. If any of us return now, we'll be taken as well." She paused and grasped my hands. "We're no good to him captured. I have faith all will work out as it's supposed to."

"Ari?" Dad spoke like he stood in the middle of a dream, but Mom rushed toward me with open arms.

I fell into her embrace, and Dad joined us a moment later. Tears of joy overwhelmed me and slid down my cheeks as my smile grew. It was so good to be home.

I stepped back and took in everyone around me. Ronin, Harmony, Lyra, Brayden, Torren, Deborah, Mom, and Dad. Everyone except Callan. "We have to try," I squeaked. The fog swirled again.

Torren spun me around to face him. "Ari, we need to make a plan. It's too late to go back for him."

My hands curled into fists, and the fog faded away.

Brayden rested his hand on my shoulder. Cool metal brushed against my neck, the dampeners still adorning his wrists.

"Brayden, why do you still have those on?"

Ronin cleared his throat. "I tried. I can't manifest a key for a lock I can't see."

I furrowed my brows and drew my lips to the side. "Give me your hands."

He lifted his hands level with my opened palms.

"Let's see if I can do this again." I closed my eyes and pictured the bracelets disintegrating beneath my touch. When I opened my eyes, Brayden and Ronin exchanged a glance while the bracelets disappeared completely.

"Where did you learn that?" they asked simultaneously, then looked at each other with twin grins and chuckles.

The air around us filled with laughter, including my own as I picked up my backpack and shuffled through the items until I found the metal hair clip. "I picked up the gift from this."

"May I see that?" A note of curiosity tinged Brayden's voice, and he held out his hand.

Ronin stepped to his brother's side. He must have found it familiar because he leaned in for a closer look. "Is that..."

Brayden confirmed my suspicion when he nodded. "It belonged to our mother."

He didn't wake up. Celia's soft voice trembled.

I walked several feet away from the group, slinging my bag over my shoulder before stopping on the outskirts of the woods. "Who?"

Robert. I don't know what to do. I can't breathe.

"Try to calm down and tell me what you see. Is anything different?" I didn't know what compelled me to ask, but it felt imperative.

She gasped. *It's just like the day we met. The blue circle.* She began pulling in breaths quicker than she should've. When she spoke again, her whispered words had a shrill edge to them. *Ari, it's eating everything. The field, the animals. They're disappearing.*

I twisted my hands around each other and paced the tree line. "What do you mean?

That blue light. It's not growing...it's shrinking!

Torren fell into step beside me and slid his hand into mine, easing the pounding of my heart with his presence. His eyes were fixed on me, but I concentrated on Celia.

Her scream pierced my mind, and I doubled over, though pressing my hands to my ears only amplified the sound.

I don't know how much longer I'll be able to keep it open. It hurts. Her voice faded. *Help!*

"Celia?" When she didn't respond, I gripped Torren's shirt. "We need to save her."

"Where do we need to go?" Torren's breath warmed my neck as the group joined us.

"To the picnic, where you saw that wall of light. That's where she disappeared."

"I want to go on a picnic," Lyra said.

"I'm sorry, Lyra. Someone's hurt, and Torren and I need to go get her. We'll take you on a picnic another time."

"But if she's hurt, I can help. You said that's my gift," Lyra insisted.

"Gift?" Harmony looked at Ronin. "Gifts don't come to children of cross-world couples."

"Lyra's a healer. That's why she was able to complete your elixir." I turned to Torren. "We don't have much time."

Lyra stood next to Ronin, her pout and folded arms expressing her displeasure at being left behind.

Torren encircled me in his arms when I started calling up my fog "Save your energy. You picture it. I'll get us there."

Why hadn't I asked him to teach me how to transport more than one person? I could have saved Callan, too.

"Hey," his gentle voice calmed me. "Push those thoughts aside and picture the picnic, not my kitchen."

I sighed and nodded, clearing the thoughts from my head and remembering the details of the picnic. The checkered blanket, the glass bottles, the clearing surrounded by trees.

Torren pressed closer to me just before we lifted off the ground.

Ronin shouted, but I was concentrating too hard to hear what he said.

In a few seconds, the earth solidified beneath my feet again.

"Lyra, that was *very* dangerous," Torren said sternly.

I put my arm around her when she shrank back. "Now isn't the time, Torren."

He turned to me, raising his voice, "There's a reason you can't transport with more than one person yet, Ari. You need to be fully aware of everyone you're transporting as well as the place you're going. If I hadn't realized she grabbed onto me at the last second and compensated for it, she could have been hurt, or worse."

Remorse flashed across her face, and I swallowed the lump that jumped to my throat.

He hadn't yelled exactly, but the combination of fear and frustration in his voice solidified how serious Lyra's action could've been.

Thank goodness I hadn't attempted to move Deborah and Callan together. At least he was alive...for now.

Torren sighed. "I need to take you back, Lyra. Your parents will be worried sick."

"I thought you might need me." Lyra's chin trembled as her eyes filled with tears and she kicked the grass.

Celia's last words echoed in my mind. She could be hurt.

"Torren, she's right. Besides, we're out of time."

His eyes darted to Lyra, then back to me before he sighed. "Okay. What do we do?"

Swinging my backpack in front of me, I crouched on the picnic blanket to remove the Council robe. Carefully, I unwrapped the cup from the folds of fabric.

Confusion colored Torren's face. "That's Celia's."

I nodded and motioned for them to join me.

Lyra knelt beside me and studied the cup. "How does this work? Is she in the cup?"

"No." I chuckled.

"Tell us what to do." Torren helped me to my feet.

"I don't know." Closing my eyes, I urged the flashes of future to take over my sight and provide me with answers.

Lyra and Torren remained silent, waiting patiently for me to give them instructions, but my imagination sparked to life with images of what might be happening to Celia, to Callan.

Pressure built in my chest, making it harder to breathe, and the panic brought a picture of Charlie to my mind. My breath hitched, and the pressure burst forth in a choking sob. I covered my mouth, trying to hold it in.

How was I supposed to save everyone with a robe and a cup? I wasn't strong enough to hold back the weight of everything I had to confront, and tears spilled from my eyes.

I gripped the cup, and Torren placed his hand on mine. Opening my eyes, I saw Lyra resting her tiny fingers on Torren's. We were in a circle, all connected to the cup.

In a hushed voice, Lyra began singing the song of my childhood, the lullaby. As her voice rose, the weight I'd been feeling lifted. Lyra, lost within Alterria yet always filled with hope. I closed my eyes and let the song comfort me.

> *The mist and the meadow, whenever they do meet*
> *Speak of the young, dancing and free*
> *Glamour in the moonlight, true love so sweet*
> *Sharing ambition, never meant to be*

Torren joined in. His memories of love had been hidden. But he was here with me now, just like before. The promise of the future we had once talked about lay before us, and I knew everything would be okay. His deep voice harmonized with Lyra's, and my heart grew even lighter. I dried my eyes.

> *The forest calls my name, I must leave it all and go*
> *In the shadow of the leaves, past the river I will roam*
> *Others will not understand, I can't teach what they don't know*
> *Forever with my guardian, the forest is my home.*

Robert's words came back to me. Friendships, past, present, and future. The time was here. Powers untold. This is what he meant. I smiled and joined in.

Born of this world but not within, missing link from far away
Faith expands, protection grows, whatever price must be paid
A power once thought lost revealed, Enlightenment dawns today
From a world once dying to itself, a new life will be made.

I thought of the blue light that captured Celia's attention all those years ago. The way the light grew the longer she stood in front of it. And the flash that made them both disappear.

A ring of blue light, resembling a rabbit hole, appeared in front of us. I placed my palm flat against it, and it began to swirl.

Lyra spoke softly. "Ari, what is that?"

"I think it's a portal."

"Where did it come from?" Torren asked, mouth agape.

"It's always been here," I said, remembering the day mine and Celia's paths first crossed. "But I think I just opened it."

I dropped the cup and pushed my hand into the center of the blue light. At my touch, it expanded, showing a girl crumpled on the ground. I reached further in to try to make contact with Celia, but a shock made me withdraw and shake my hand. The portal began to shrink. I turned to face Torren, his eyes wide.

"Ceely?" When he leaned toward the portal, I pulled him back.

"It's dangerous to get too close." I placed my hands on his face, guiding his eyes to mine.

"She's not breathing," Torren cried.

"I need you to listen to me. It's collapsing on her. We need to get her out, but we can't go in."

The last glimpse of hope drained from his eyes.

I could only imagine the years of guilt that must be piling on top of him right now. "If you can see her, can you transport her?"

I took the slight raise of his chin for a nod.

"Torren," I said, stroking his hand with my thumb. "There was absolutely no way you could have found her until this exact moment. And now, it's up to you to save her."

He inhaled sharply and focused on Celia. Fog slithered inside the portal, filling the space that continued to shrink before our eyes. The wispy fingers curled around her body, enfolding her in a hug that took her from our sight. The next moment, smokey tendrils formed beside us, and we waited with bated breath. As the fog dissolved, Celia's body lay still on the blanket.

Torren stood, frozen, staring at her lifeless form. "I was too late."

I covered my mouth in horror. How could I assure him this wasn't his fault when "too late" echoed through my mind too?

While Torren and I battled our fears, Lyra wasted no time dropping to her knees. With confident fingers, she ran her hands over Celia's ribs, whispering, "You can do it," until Celia's chest rose and fell in a natural rhythm. A tight smile flashed across Lyra's face, replaced by a shadow when Lyra moved her hands along Celia's face, arms, and legs.

She'd done it. That fragile little girl I'd found trembling in a hospital bed had saved a life.

My heart leapt in joy, then dropped again when I took in Lyra's pale face.

"Torren, I—"

Before I could finish my sentence, Lyra collapsed.

Chapter Thirty-Seven

Reunited

The fog dropped away, and my heavy heart forced me to my knees, Lyra's limp body like lead in my arms.

Ronin came running from the house, Harmony hot on his heels, sharing a look of unknowing fear about their daughter's fate, and I couldn't reassure them.

"She collapsed," I said before anyone spoke, but neither of Lyra's parents seemed to hear me.

Pulling her from my arms, Ronin cradled her as Harmony folded against him and stroked Lyra's hair from her face.

From the ground, I found it impossible to ignore the way the rising moon highlighted the family of three in the midst of their suffering, surrounding them with an almost mystic glow.

"Is she okay?" Harmony clasped her daughter's hand and looked to her husband for comfort.

"She's breathing but weak." He turned to me. "What happened?"

"She collapsed when she tried to heal Celia."

A sigh of relief escaped Ronin's tightly pressed lips. "Gifts require energy, and healing takes more than most. She needs to rest but will soon be back to her normal self. What about Celia?"

Scanning the area and finding no sign of Torren, I shook my head. Where were they?

Ronin smiled grimly and nodded. "Let's get her inside, Harmony."

As they disappeared into the house, Deborah supported herself against the doorframe, hands wringing the hem of her shirt. She looked around, her eyes wide and wild.

"Torren?" My voice cracked as tears flooded my eyes. I'd go back for them. Before I had a chance to call my fog, a pillar of smoke dropped Torren on his knees in front of me with Celia clutched against him.

He lowered her to the ground and hung his head .

"Is she…" My words refused to leave my mouth.

He glanced up at me, the shine absent from his emerald eyes. "She's still not moving much."

I knelt beside him, pressing my hand against her forehead. "I can try, too."

Beside us in seconds, Deborah gathered Celia's rigid body into her lap before I could do anything, humming the lullaby in a wavery tune. Tears streamed down her cheeks as she stroked Celia's hair, and though I'd experienced the effects of Deborah's gift, I marveled as I witnessed her energy transfer to her daughter.

As Celia relaxed, Deborah began to slump over.

And so did I. I'd used so many gifts in such a short period of time. How much further could I push myself before I was drained like Lyra? Still, I couldn't give up. Resting my hand on Deborah's shoulder, I whispered, "Can I help?"

Tears slipped down her cheeks as she nodded.

I placed my hands against Celia's temples and squeezed my eyes shut. I pictured her soft gray eyes, so full of wonder, and her sweet smile as she stared into the portal. I imagined her running with Torren, chasing him into the woods. I imagined her healed and happy and here.

"Mama?" The voice that had lived in my head was beside me. And everyone could hear her.

I opened my eyes and fell back, exhausted.

Deborah gasped and pinned Celia to her heart. "My girl! You're alive!" Sobs wove in with laughter in a tapestry dotted with the kisses Deborah placed all over Celia's head, never loosening her embrace.

Torren observed the happy scene, a smile toying at his lips.

A hush shuffled through the trees, and I brushed my hair from my eyes as I gazed at Torren. Why wasn't his smile bigger? Celia was home. If this was his dream come true, why did he stand there like an invisible force held him in place?

I mustered enough energy to stand beside him, and he folded my hand into his with a light squeeze.

"She's home?"

"She's home," I assured him.

Then Deborah, still overcome with emotion, beckoned him to her.

"Go." Releasing his hand, I gave him a nudge.

With hesitant steps, he made his way to his family and dropped to his knees, wrapping Deborah and Celia in his arms. It hit him then—that she was really there—because his body began to shake as he held them like he'd never let go.

Feeling like an intruder during their special reunion, I took a step toward my house, but Torren caught my wrist and tugged me down into the embrace.

"Torren, this is *your* moment."

"We wouldn't have this without you, Ari." Celia smiled.

Deborah sputtered incoherently in agreement before lifting Celia gently. "Let's get you inside."

"Could you send my parents out here?"

"Of course." Deborah nodded at me, then turned to walk into the house.

Torren and I sat a few moments longer, our hands joined together. "I thought I'd killed her. The guilt that weighed in my heart and mind was drowning me. Then I met you. You showed me that even in the darkness, there was still light in the world.". His eyes had regained their brightness, and he smiled at me. "You brought her back. I'm going to spend the rest of my life trying to figure out how to thank you."

"Then I'll need to do the same because you found me at a time I longed for something more than unchanging days. Your friendship opened up an entirely new world."

"Friendship?" Torren spun his ring. The corner of his mouth raised as he slid his grip from my hands to my waist and pulled me onto his lap. "Is that all this is? Here I was hoping we'd progressed a little further than that."

I smiled and folded my arms around his neck. "Oh, did you now?"

His lower lip jutted out briefly before transforming into his crooked grin. Wrapping his arms tighter around me, he pressed his lips to mine.

I tightened my hold around his neck, wanting to stay in this embrace forever, but we couldn't. As much as I hated to, I pushed away.

"Torren. We have to go." I planted a kiss on the tip of his nose as I stood.

"I know, but I couldn't resist."

My cheeks heated up as he spun the ring to make the dome fall just as my parents approached.

"Mom, Dad, you've met Torren, but he's also Kai."

Mom chuckled, shaking her head. "Of course he is."

"We want to show you two something." I grinned as I turned to face Torren.

He stood between the trees, his hand held out to me. Our fingers weaved together, and I led us down the heart trail.

Before entering our little meadow—the piece of the woods that used to belong to only us—Torren squeezed my hand.

Mom's fingers pressed against her lips, and her eyes watered. "Oh, Ari."

"You've shared this place with us. A few times. Always talking about this friend of yours. We never saw him, so we thought you were so lonely that you'd made someone up." Dad shook his head and focused on the ground. "And Celia. I thought you'd imagined the entire thing because of the bump to your head. The way you explained what happened and the book you were reading that day..."

Mom picked up where he left off. "We were so confident in Brayden's barrier that when you started talking about things that sounded Alterrian, we brushed it off. If anyone from the Lachloren family had come through, they would have come to see us."

"But no one did. We believed that *you* believed it but couldn't quite believe it ourselves," Dad added.

Mom reached out and squeezed Torren's hand. "And we missed out on meeting such an amazing young man. If we'd have thought logically, we'd have known you had to be a Lachloren. We knew who could enter the barrier, yet we ignored all logic because of our fear of the unknown."

"Everything worked out. We wouldn't have gotten Celia back if none of this had happened." I wrapped my arms around Torren's waist, and he held me tight, pressing a kiss to my cheek.

"We should probably head back. I can get us there in just a few seconds." Torren called up his fog and brought the four of us to the front door.

Torren and I walked hand in hand into the house and were overwhelmed by the scent of freshly baked cake. We followed Mom and Dad into the living room where my eyes landed on a knee-high box of keys in the middle of the floor.

Ronin glanced from the box to my face. "I told you I tried."

I raised an eyebrow and laughed. "You certainly did." I took a seat on the floor, and Torren followed my lead.

Our couches were filled for the first time I could remember, making my heart soar. My fleeting joy dissipated with the ache from Callan's absence. Despite being together for the first time in years, tension filled the room.

Torren cleared his throat. "What are we going to do about Dad?"

"That is for the adults to figure out," Brayden said, meeting Torren's eyes.

"I've been an adult for months now."

"Two," Deborah chuckled. "You've been eighteen for two months."

Torren folded his arms across his chest like a child being told he couldn't have dessert. "Exactly. Months."

I wrapped my arm around Torren's elbow and rested my head on his shoulder, and he lay his head against mine.

When a timer cut through the stillness in the room, Mom and Deborah jumped to their feet and scurried to the kitchen. They reappeared several minutes later carrying a sheet cake covered in glowing candles.

I had lost track of the days in Alterria, but had I actually forgotten my birthday?

They set the cake down on the coffee table in the center of the room. It had been decorated for two, each half holding the same number of candles. "Happy birthday" tilted across the top of the cake in Mom's fancy cursive, with "Celia" on the left and

"Arisanna" on the right. My mouth dropped, and chills ran up my spine. "We have the same birthday?"

Celia only had time to smile and nod before Brayden belted out the first words of the traditional birthday song. Everyone else joined in, and Celia and I blew out the candles. She got all hers on the first try, but I missed one, much to Lyra's delight.

Torren stood behind me, his breath warming my ear. "You never told me today was your birthday."

"I didn't know it was today."

"No. I mean, you *never* told me."

I bit my lip. "Except for the cake, birthdays weren't a huge deal. Besides, you were always so sad that day. It didn't feel right to insert my birthday, so we just laid by the river."

"You could've told me." He pressed his lips to my temple.

"Pretty sure you never shared yours, either." I said, bumping my shoulder against him.

"I guess birthdays were a little depressing after Celia disappeared on hers. Never felt right celebrating *me* when she was missing."

I gave him a squeeze.

As Mom dished out the cake, I glanced from Celia to my slice and back again.

She chuckled. "Is there something you want to say, Ari?"

I pressed my palms to my cheeks, attempting to hide the growing blush. The tips of my ears burned. Traitors. I placed my hands in my lap. "Yeah. But if you're too tired…"

She raised an eyebrow.

"Fine." I squeezed my eyes shut and blurted out my question. "How were you in my head?"

Celia giggled. "I thought that was weird, too. He said that when we first met, the sparks and the burning just before the portal opened somehow linked us. When you returned and fell into the same place where the portal and the concealment came together, that activated our connection."

"Will we stay linked together?"

She shrugged. "I don't actually know."

"You weren't always there."

"I tried to start the connection so many times, but you had to be willing to listen and let me in. He said not only were you struggling with the new world you were thrown into but also with your own mind."

I pulled my lips between my teeth, and Torren ran his hand down my back. "Okay. You were warning me and guiding me. How did you know what to say?"

Her eyes glistened. "Robert."

Gasps around the living room reminded me the three of us weren't alone.

"Robert?" Brayden's voice cracked. "Robert is still alive?"

Tears spilled from Celia's eyes, and she struggled for the words. "No...he...that's..."

I went around the table and wrapped my arm around her. "He passed away. That must be why the portal collapsed."

Celia buried her head against my shoulder.

"The land, the cup, the hiding, the cryptic messages," Brayden spoke as though trying to work through the limited information he'd acquired. "He always said that she would be protected and returned one day. He must have staged his own death to provide the protection Celia would need."

Deborah tilted her head. "The cup. Ari froze when she held it, but the liquid Robert sent along with it made it disappear, and she could move again. And then you found it, Ari. Where?"

"My grandfather's cellar."

Mom smiled. "My dad created a potion to put an item back where it belonged."

"Celia," I asked softly, "what *is* your gift?"

Deborah answered as Celia sniffled. "We were never able to figure it out. Sometimes she would just freeze."

"No, that isn't it." I thought back to the time I spent with Torren, wishing for more. "Torren, remember when we went to the caverns and you were nervous we'd been gone too long?"

He nodded, eyes narrowed as though unsure where I was going.

"Did you know we were only gone for half an hour?"

"Not possible. We were there for at least two hours."

Celia lifted her head and used the palms of her hands to dry her cheeks as her tears subsided. "Robert called it Time Control, and he helped me to understand it. I wasn't freezing. I was making the time around me speed up or slow down. I slowed it in the labyrinth while you translated the symbols. I couldn't hold it for too long because I wasn't physically there."

"Why'd you slow time down there?" I asked.

"You would've been in danger if I hadn't. They would've discovered your gift was more than just fire. You disappeared into a cavern that didn't exist moments before. When I slowed the time, they couldn't see that."

"Why?" Deborah's voice cracked. She cleared it and tried again. "Why did Robert take you?"

"He said the labyrinth would have killed me because I didn't have control of my gift."

Torren's hand curled into fists, and his jaw tightened. "But why keep you all this time?"

Celia dropped my hand and nodded toward Torren. She'd been my friend for such a short time, but I found it easy to read her intentions.

Scooting back to sit beside Torren, I placed my hand on his and smiled at how well Celia still knew him. The moment I touched him, he relaxed and twined his fingers in mine.

Celia gave a satisfied nod before she answered his question. "Just because the Ceremony passed didn't mean the danger did. Edric had begun collecting children who showed special gifts. Robert tried to find a way for me to get home and avoid the danger, but the visions never changed."

"We could've protected you," Ronin spoke in a low firm tone, careful not to disturb Lyra, who was sleeping on his lap.

"You'd have lost *me* either way." Celia met Torren's eyes. "This way, you were able to find *her*."

"There really wasn't anything I could do to save you?" His hand tightened around mine like he feared I'd vanish, too.

"Nothing anyone could do. Those were the only options."

His crooked smile made my thudding heart take flight. "Then I'm glad it happened this way. I don't think I could live in a world that didn't have her in it."

For a moment, I worried Celia might take that the wrong way, but her smile proved my concerns were baseless. "She helped you to heal."

"Did he keep you all that time so I could find Ari?"

"So you could find true love?" Celia giggled, and all eyes fell on her. "No. That was merely the catalyst. Without Ari, the portal never would've reopened. Cedric shared his gift with her."

"Robert arranged all this to save you?" Deborah whispered.

Celia shook her head. "To save Alterria from the corruption that's been eating away at it from the inside for the last twenty years."

"I need some air." Brayden stood, his footsteps heavy as he walked out the front door.

"Is he okay?" I asked, turning to Ronin.

He shifted Lyra and slid from beneath her. "He bears the weight of those words because he was chosen to follow in Robert's footsteps, then watched as Council crumbled from the glory it had been. Excuse me. I've stood against my brother one too many times, and that's something I don't intend to continue." He stood and followed Brayden's path.

Mom smiled and locked eyes with Dad before he followed them.

"Why didn't he warn anyone?" I asked softly.

"The thing about knowing your future is you can't do anything to prevent it. Robert saw paths. In his mind, he would change certain events to see which way the paths would diverge. Ari, when you fell in the woods and our hands touched, that changed our path. It gave us a connection once you were ready to accept it."

"That spot. It's the same place my parents placed the picnic."

Celia nodded. "The picnic setup is why Robert chose to have the portal there. He saw the portal and concealment clashing together, creating a physical marker to guide you back when you were ready."

"You said Robert's visions never changed. Does that mean you're in danger now?" I asked.

Celia's smile was contagious. "When you two met, he finally saw a path that would get me home safe."

Torren's hand squeezed mine. "How?"

"Robert said you were the mentor she needed to grow into her gift. If she'd ended up in Alterria without having you, her gift would've destroyed her."

A tremor ran through me. "What makes *me* so important?"

"Duplicity. Robert wouldn't share any more than that."

I yawned, my eyelids getting heavy.

"And with that, it's time for bed," Mom said, walking to the linen closet to stack comforters and pillows in her arms.

Deborah fell into step behind her. "Let's get you kiddos settled for the night. I hear there's a room for everyone."

"No, I want to have a sleepover with everyone," Lyra said as she sat up, then sniffed the air. "Cake?"

Harmony giggled and handed a piece to Lyra, which she devoured in three bites. "Alright. Go with Celia."

Celia offered her hand to Lyra, and together they made their way to my room.

Finally alone, Torren and I hovered in the living room a little longer.

"Torren, we have to save Callan," I whispered.

Torren opened his mouth to speak just as Dad came back inside.

"Where's everyone headed?" he asked.

"To bed," Mom called from my room.

"Don't you think you should follow, Ari?" Dad raised his eyebrow, then glanced between Torren and me. "Maybe you should stay out here, son."

"No way!" Celia yelled. "I just got him back."

Dad straightened his back as Mom came out to persuade him.

"Lucian, his nieces are also in the room. Let them spend some time together."

"Fine." His locked jaw and narrowed gaze contradicted his response.

Mom patted Dad's chest. "Come with me to the attic. We finally get to use those cots we've been storing all these years."

Torren and I shuffled toward my room. He leaned in close, his breath tickling my ear. "Since the adults are so adamant that we can't help, we'll plot once Lyra's asleep."

Chapter Thirty-Eight

Town Square

The four of us hunkered down in my room for my first sleepover. I smiled at the thought of what we had managed to accomplish today. We did it together.

Celia was home.

Lyra jutted out her bottom lip as she scanned the chapter books jammed into my bookshelf. "I wish you had a bedtime story here."

I smiled and walked to my closet, pulling the storybook from my bag. "I have one right here. I found it the same morning I brought you here."

She gasped and took the book from my hands, grasping it to her chest. "Uncle Torren, can you read me this story before bed?"

Celia's face brightened, and she bounced on her toes, a teasing lilt to her voice, "Oh yes, Uncle Torren. Please."

Torren smiled through gritted teeth and sat cross-legged against my headboard, his eyes shining with mirth. After so long without her teasing, Torren clearly welcomed its return. "Let's see that book, Lyra."

She whispered, "Yes," and pumped her fist before snuggling onto his lap.

Celia took her place beside him, resting her head on his shoulder, and I couldn't help but drink in the peace that washed over him.

"Someone's missing." He interrupted my thoughts and flashed me *that* grin. "Not starting 'til you join us."

I took my place on his other side and relaxed against him as he began to read.

"The Faraway Princess.

Once, a very long time ago, there lived a beautiful princess named Eulalie. Eulalie's kingdom was comprised of people with all kinds of abilities. Some had magical gifts while some did not. The mix of people kept the kingdom balanced.

Princess Eulalie was one with a special gift. As she grew, her parents became frightened by its power. While those with gifts only had one ability, the princess could hold many. Fearful of what they believed to be a curse on their kingdom, they locked Eulalie away, vowing to keep their people safe from her overpowered ability.

One day, a handsome young man rescued Eulalie from her prison.

"To whom do I owe my gratitude, good sir?" Her eyes sparkled as she spoke, and her smile lit up her face.

"Princess Eulalie, I am Edmund, but I am afraid your rescue is not for a joyous reason. Since your parents have passed, your people have become unwell."

"Unwell, Edmund? How so?"

"The balance between them has begun to tip as fear has overcome the kingdom. Some with gifts have begun to see themselves as superior and have taken those without as servants. Many of the gift-less have fled the kingdom in fear."

"And what am I to do, Edmund? My own parents saw me as a curse and locked me away in my own home. How can I help my people when I have been unable to help myself?"

"Hope, your highness."

"Hope?"

"Meet the people. Assure them they still have a ruler and that everyone has value, no matter their ability."

Princess Eulalie followed Edmund to the town square. Walking through the crowd, she became overwhelmed as she bumped into the people, terrified by the uproar within her kingdom. They were miserable and quarreled in the streets.

She took to the raised podium and called for the attention of her people. One by one, they lined up to air their grievances to the princess. As she offered solutions, the people would thank her by taking her hand and kissing her fingers. She noticed some contact would feel different than others. One man caused her to feel as though she was floating. Another made her feel as though she could no longer move.

By the time she had seen each citizen, exhaustion overwhelmed her. She swayed upon the stage and collapsed into Edmund's arms. He brought her back to the palace and watched over her as she slept.

When she finally awoke several days later, she could not control her gift. She would suddenly disappear, her eyes would randomly cloud over, and little bursts of flame would shoot from her fingertips.

"My princess, what has happened to you? I have never met a person with multiple gifts." He gazed into her eyes. The sparkle had disappeared entirely, as though she was no more than a shell of her old self.

Through tears, Eulalie confided in her companion. "It is not a gift but a curse. When my parents discovered I could acquire new gifts, they had me locked away. I am a danger to my kingdom and our people."

Edmund grasped her hand. "You are no danger."

"There are too many gifts within me, Edmund. I fear I cannot hold so much at once. I can feel myself breaking down the longer I am filled with all this power.”

“I am an alchemist. I will find a way to help you.”

Eulalie drifted into another long sleep. Her body, ravaged with power, thrashed around restlessly.

Edmund worked day and night to come up with a cure. When she finally awoke, he presented her with a potion.

“Drink a little of this each time an unwanted gift activates. It should remove the gift from you.”

“Thank you, my friend.”

As the day went on, Eulalie drank a bit of the potion each time a gift activated. Edmund watched as life returned to her eyes, little by little.

When all the unwanted gifts were gone, Eulalie proved to be a fair and wise leader.

The end.”

Lyra’s nose scrunched. “Why was that fairytale so sad?”

I swallowed hard and walked to my window, staring at the moon with my arms folded across my chest. A tear slid down my cheek.

Torren came up behind me. He wrapped his arms around my waist and rested his chin on my shoulder.

“Eulalie had the gift of Duplicity,” I breathed. “Is that going to happen to me?”

He kissed my cheek. "I don't know, but I'm going to protect you with all I have."

"Ari, you have all of us." Celia stood beside me.

"If anything happened to you, I would heal you."

I smiled as I patted Lyra's hand. "Thanks, guys. I'm glad to have you all in my corner."

Lyra yawned and stretched as she chose a camp cot from the three my parents had set up as we were reading the story. She was asleep in minutes.

"So, what's the plan for tomorrow?" Celia's smile spread across her face.

Torren shook his head. "You need to stay here. Keep Lyra safe."

"I'm going to help." She glared at him. "Ari needs both of us."

Torren slumped against my back. "Ceely," his voice cracked, "I'm so sorry, but I can't risk losing you again. My heart couldn't handle that."

She raised her eyebrow, her arms crossed. "But your heart could handle something happening to *her*?"

"I never said that. But we don't need to risk any more of us than necessary."

"And what do you suppose her parents will say if you and Ari are missing?"

"I offered to help, but they turned me down. What are they going to do without me? Walk?"

"Celia," I said softly. "We need you here. My parents won't understand, and they'll be angry. If you and Lyra are still here, that will ease a lot of unnecessary tension."

She scoffed and rolled her eyes. "Fine. I guess I'll cover for you criminals." She walked to the cot and laid down, pulling the blankets over her head.

Torren swayed back and forth, and my eyes grew heavy. "You need sleep. We have a big day tomorrow." He guided me to my bed, but when he tucked me in and stepped away, I reached for his hand.

"Please don't go." *Not tonight. Not now.*

"I'm not going anywhere, Ari. I'll be right beside you."

The cot was inches from my bed and somehow miles away.

I shook my head as I folded back the blanket. "You make me feel safe. Stay with me. Please."

"For some reason, I don't think that would make your dad too happy with me."

"You're probably right." I lay staring at the ceiling, Eulalie's story looping in my mind. Princess Eulalie was an oddity just like me, and her gift nearly killed her. I was about to go into a public place, surrounded by a lot of people. Would I pick up more gifts? Would they kill me too?

My fears grew, and even with everyone in the room, I still felt alone. "But the monsters aren't as scary when you're right beside me. Besides, we're just sleeping."

He searched my eyes before lowering himself onto the bed to lay beside me.

A calm even stronger than Deborah's gift comforted me, and I sighed in contentment as I turned to look at him.

His eyebrows scrunched close together.

"What's wrong?"

"I don't know what's going to happen tomorrow, but I'm worried about your gift." He hesitated. "Have you ever tried to use two gifts at once?"

"I hadn't honestly thought of the idea before."

Refusing to meet my eyes, he stared at the ceiling. "I shouldn't have said anything. I saw how much transporting exhausted you. Each time you use a gift, it takes energy."

"So what makes you worried?"

He spoke quietly, "No matter what, don't try to use more than one gift at a time. Who knows what that could do to you." He moved a little closer and wrapped his arms around me.

I couldn't make a promise if I didn't know I could keep it, so I closed my eyes and squeezed his hand.

"Goodnight, Torren." I curled against him and fell fast asleep.

***

The morning had come fast, but Torren and I managed to get out before anyone else woke up. We stood at the edge of the town square, sheltered by the trees, discussing our plan to save Callan.

"Want to try that glamour one more time, Ari?"

Looking at Torren's face—now Kai's—I bit my lip and closed my eyes, picturing a face other than my own. Eyes wider and golden brown, hair shoulder length and blonde, chubby cheeks, full lips. I opened my eyes and wishfully ran my hand through my long hair. It hadn't worked. I let out a small puff of air, and my bottom lip stuck out slightly.

Torren kissed my cheek, and I couldn't help but smile. "It's okay. That's why I grabbed this from your library. You have quite the collection." His voice soothed me as he dug a shoulder-length blonde wig from my backpack and placed it on my head. "Just as good as glamour."

Giggling, I readjusted it so it would pass as semi-natural. "Thanks, but not even close to the drastic changes everyone else can make."

He chuckled and placed his arm around my waist. "Stay as close as possible. I don't want to take any chances of you bumping into anybody in a crowd this size."

I recalled Eulalie's story and grasped his hand. My heart sped up. Staying close wouldn't be an issue.

Weaving through the ever-thickening crowd, my stomach lurched at the thought that these people were all gathered to watch someone die. "This is sick, Torren," I said, my lip curled. "Why so many people?"

He nodded toward a wooden board erected along the side of the road: Mandatory.

"What do you think would happen if we went home?" a man in front of me said.

"I don't know, but I don't want to find out," the woman beside him replied.

The heat around me rose with my mounting anxiety, and I gripped Torren's shirt.

"We're almost there," he whispered.

A voice behind me said my name, and I froze. "I met that sweet Arisanna. Espionage? There's no way. She has Lucian's wisdom and Izzy's heart. I don't believe a thing High Councilman says against her."

I glanced over my shoulder, and Mrs. Jones's weary eyes met mine. Her encouraging smile boosted my confidence in a way I hadn't expected. One near stranger's support meant more than I could've guessed.

Torren guided me along until we got close to the center of the square. We stopped beside an older couple and a young woman.

"I can't believe it." The younger woman shook her head back and forth. "I never would've suspected Brayden to be a traitor."

"I *don't* believe it." The older woman beside her scoffed. "Robert saw such potential in him."

"I wish Robert were still around," the older gentleman beside the women spoke up. "Public executions never would've happened under his regime. High Councilman Edric has another thing coming if he doesn't believe this event will cause an uproar. No one agrees with this."

The two women glared at him.

The younger woman spoke in a hushed voice, "Keep speaking like that, and you may find yourself on that stage today."

I leaned into Torren. "Where's Callan?"

"I don't see him."

Edric took the stage, front and center. "My fellow Alterrians, our execution today will play out a little differently than originally planned." He scanned the crowd, compelling Torren to avert his eyes until black and white fog captured Edric's attention.

Torren's face became strained as he waited for Callan's inevitable appearance.

The wait wasn't long. A hiss of discontent rippled through the crowd when they realized who stood before them.

"Silence!" Edric roared, and the crowd swallowed back their objections.

"Are you close enough?" Torren's eyes were fixed on the platform.

My heart raced, hoping we'd be able to pull this off. "I think so." I closed my eyes, willing time to stretch out. Everyone around us appeared to be frozen. Even Edric was silent.

Torren smiled and shook his head. "I'm not going to stop being surprised by you, am I?"

"Did I slow *everyone* down?"

He showed me his watch. The hands were hardly moving. "You sped us up." He grinned. "This is our chance. I'm going to send Dad now. As soon as he's gone, we go, too."

Fog crawled up Callan's legs at a snail's pace. Too slow. My palms became clammy, and my mouth went dry. I looked to Torren. "It's not going to work, is it?"

"I don't think so."

"What if I tried?"

He grasped my hands. "You can't. What if you accidentally sent Callan to a different realm like Celia? I can't let you live with the guilt that I have."

I willed time to return to normal.

A collective gasp sounded as Callan disappeared with Torren's smoke.

Edric smiled as our eyes connected. He anticipated this.

My heart faltered as black and white wisps slithered toward us. I turned and kissed Torren. "I love you," I said as I thought of home.

His eyes widened, and he shook his head when my fog surrounded him.

"I always have and always will."

Once he realized what I'd done, he'd certainly come back, but I hoped he wouldn't.

Edric wanted something from me, and I was of no use to him dead. The same couldn't be said for Torren or any of his family.

Torren disappeared in front of my eyes just as Thomas's fog reached me, and I was dragged away from the crowd before I could protest.

Edric gripped my wrists, his face set in triumph. "Ah, our rogue recruit. Looks like we'll still get our execution."

"No!" To my surprise, Brayden, not Torren, appeared in a cloud of white fog at the foot of the stage. He grabbed my hands, and a ring of blue light formed beside us.

I pressed my palm against it, and the light began to swirl. When I pulled him into the portal with me, the blue ring faded, and we were standing toe to toe in a vast white space. I glanced around. "Where are we?"

Brayden stared at me. "Come into contact with a portal maker recently?"

"*This* is where Celia was all that time?" She had to have food to survive, so there was more to this gift than I knew, though I didn't have the time to figure it out now.

A quirk of a smile appeared with my question but was soon replaced with a grave expression. "You must send me back. I will not allow you to take my place."

I grabbed his hands. "Brayden, you don't have to do this. You're not thinking clearly."

He turned to me, his eyes sparkling. His face seemed to have aged overnight. "Arisanna, I have spent my life protecting my family. I am not about to stop now."

"But I'm not your family. You don't have to sacrifice anything for me." I angrily wiped at the tears streaming down my cheeks.

Brayden hugged me tight. "And that is where you are wrong." He held my shoulders and looked into my eyes. "I trust you will keep that little brother of mine out of trouble. This is the way it was always meant to be. Robert told me I would die protecting my family. Send me back."

I stomped my foot and set my lips in a firm line. "Fine. We'll go back." I wound my arms around his waist and summoned the fog before he could argue.

A door slammed open as the fog slipped away.

Torren crashed into us, wrapping us in his arms. "They're back!"

I smirked and let go of Brayden.

He shook his head as we were surrounded by both our families. "This is not how it is supposed to be."

"You spent the last six years of your life alone, protecting everyone you loved." Around us, everyone's eyes shone, some with tears, some with gratitude, some with the relief that lost years could finally be restored.

"The difference today is that you're no longer alone. You have a family to fight beside you."

CHAPTER THIRTY-NINE

TAKE A STAND

As the moon rose in the cloudy sky, a howl shattered the silence of the night. Everyone stiffened and leaned toward the window, and I wondered if it could be a figment of our combined imaginations. Another long howl sent us all out the front door.

I stood beside Torren, gripping his arm. His muscles were taut.

Callan placed his hand on Torren's shoulder. "Don't."

I glanced down, following the fog's languid climb up Torren's legs. My heart raced. "Listen to him, Torren."

He sighed, and the fog disappeared.

I relaxed a little until the howl got closer and dragged out for a full minute.

Brayden's voice cut through the tense air. "Everyone in the house. We need to put protections in place."

Dad shuffled everyone back inside.

I tried to pull Torren back as he inched toward the edge of the trees. "Please come inside."

His eyes connected with mine, and he wrapped his arms tightly around me. "Ari, I need to see what's going on so we can be better prepared. I'll stay hidden."

"I don't want to lose you again."

He lifted my chin and ran his thumb along my jawline. "I'll come back to you." He pressed his lips against mine, and tears spilled from my eyes as he disappeared.

Worry ate at me while I walked back to the house, and as I entered the living room alone, all eyes turned to me.

Callan jumped to his feet. "Where's Torren?"

My chin quivered, and I inhaled sharply to keep the tears at bay. Would he be safe? What would he find? "He said he was going to see what's happening."

Ronin rose to follow Callan to the front door, and Brayden's voice filled the living room.

"Brothers! You will do more harm following him. We must prepare for the worst. Edric has Barham on his side."

Dad spoke through gritted teeth, "Who is Barham?"

"Barham is a Disabler. He can render other gifts useless and destroy barriers." Ronin's face had gone pale.

"That's not good," Dad muttered.

A sense of urgency pressed down when Brayden took charge. "Deborah and Harmony, you will stay in the house with the girls. I will conceal it to keep you protected. Izzy, you will likely be targeted for your gift and knowledge of your father. It would be best for you to stay as well." He turned toward me. "You will stay, too."

I shook my head. "Not with Torren still out there."

"Ari." Dad gripped my shoulders, and I knew what was coming. "You've faced what you've been handed with so much strength and courage."

Mom stepped in when he sighed. "What your father means to say is we trust you to make your own choice."

That's not what I'd expected at all. I embraced them and whispered, "I love you."

Brayden pressed his lips into a thin line. "I think this is a mistake, but if you insist, follow me."

Ronin, Callan, Dad, Brayden, and I took our places alongside the garden behind the house. The drought had prevented the rose bushes from flowering over the summer, leaving a wall of dried thorns. We were just outside the woods, and amidst the growing humidity, a sense of pride in the men beside me filled my heart. Even though we were facing a challenge, I had faith that together we could beat the odds.

With another long howl, Cade burst through the trees. He bounded toward me, his tongue hanging from the side of his mouth.

"Hey." Dad ran his hand through Cade's thick coat. "This little guy reminds me of a wolf my dad used to have. She was always fiercely protective of him. If I didn't know any better, I would think he's one of her pups the way he seems drawn to you."

My momentary joy at seeing his playful prance disappeared as a line of men, each flanked by a large wolf, emerged from between the trees. Until that moment, I hadn't realized how much danger we were truly in.

"Brayden, do you see Torren?" I searched the shadows, hoping to catch a glimpse of his face.

Brayden struggled against an invisible force. "No, but Barham is here. Brace yourselves. Our cover is about to be blown."

My heart dropped to my feet. "Does that mean everyone at the house will be exposed?"

"My concealment is like a barrier. He would have to destroy each individually."

"Can I help?" I asked, trying to summon up a shield.

"Save your energy," he said softly.

Thomas stood mere feet away, his smile growing as Brayden's concealment fell and exposed us all.

I scanned the faces in front of us, my eyebrows knitting together. "No Edric?"

Thomas's laugh filled the empty spaces between the trees and sent a shiver up my spine. "You'll have to ask your boyfriend what happened to him."

As if on cue, the men and wolves at Thomas's sides charged. Ronin and Brayden disappeared from my sight. Dad and Callan had been pushed far beyond the dried rose bushes and were surrounded by a trio of men. Everyone was being forced away from me.

I tried to move toward my dad, to help if I could, but my feet were anchored in place—powerless against the attack on my family.

Callan held his palm up to reveal a baseball-sized sphere of flame, which he pitched toward an approaching man. Judging by the look on Callan's face when he missed by mere inches, that was only a warning.

Too bad his opponents didn't heed it.

In a flash, Callan was ready again. This time, Dad placed his hand on Callan's shoulder until the sphere had tripled in size like it was a miniature sun. Before Callan had a chance to release his weapon, Thomas called my name.

"You are precisely the person I hoped to see." His voice made my skin crawl. "Catch me if you can." Thomas's black and white smoke covered him, and he disappeared.

Discovering I could move again, I scanned the trees, hoping to find Torren safe and simultaneously willing him to stay away. All my search turned up was black and white smoke beckoning me into the woods.

The wolf that had accompanied Thomas walked beside me with a slow step. He sniffed at my hand, dipped his large head, and lobbed away.

"Traitor." Thomas's gravely tone sent shivers up my spine.

Glancing around the vast darkness, my heart sank.

His voice rose behind me, the heat of his breath brushing against my neck. "Hoping to find your boyfriend? I'm afraid he's been…detained."

The way he hung that last word made my stomach roll, and I swung around to face him. "What did you do to him?" Tingling flames grew until they burned my palms. Though it went against my nature, I had no choice if I wanted to protect my family. As I collided with Thomas, I pressed my hands onto his cheeks.

He howled as he threw me to the ground, and my flames died out. "You will pay for that, girl."

A blur of movement distracted me. "Dad!"

Dad heeded my warning and spun, his powerful right hook connecting with Thomas's eye.

Without a second's thought, Thomas held out his hand, and black and white smoke twisted around my dad.

"No!" I wrapped myself in my fog and appeared beside Dad, but I was too late.

Thomas straightened up, his eyes lighting. "Edric was right. You do have more than one gift." He turned and took in my yard that had been transformed into a battlefield. His lips curled into a smirk as fog swirled around his legs. "One down. Let's see how well you can keep up."

I searched for his mist, waiting for his next move before making mine.

A tall man with dark hair approached Ronin from behind.

Too far away to be heard, I did the next best thing. My fog dropped me close enough to get Ronin's attention.

The wolf at the man's side waltzed toward me, heeled at my side, and licked my hand before disappearing into the woods.

Ronin spun around as the man raised a knife over his head. A shield materialized at just the right moment and the clang of metal against metal rang in my ears.

Black and white smoke gathered at the edge of my vision, the telltale symbol of Thomas's imminent arrival that enabled me to meet him as he reappeared.

"You're good, but not good enough." He cackled as he disappeared again.

With no patience for Thomas's games, I turned in place to take in my surroundings. I needed to help where I could if Thomas only wanted to play hide and seek.

Barham crowded beside Brayden as though they were having a conversation.

As I ran toward them, the wolf accompanying Barham pranced up to me, raised himself onto his toes, and sniffed the air before running his wet tongue across my cheek.

I wiped at the goo and watched as he joined the other two. What was going on with these wolves?

Thomas appeared behind me again, his hot breath brushing against the damp spot on my cheek. "One doesn't notice how quickly the fatigue sneaks up on them when they are new to their gift. Not until it's too late. And the fatigue from multiple gifts? It's unprecedented."

I twisted to meet his eyes, but he had already fled. Movement by my garden shed made my throat tighten.

Callan waited near the shed's flimsy walls with no protection but his fist full of fire as his opponent closed in.

With Thomas nowhere to be seen, I used my fog to drop near Callan, certain I could help him.

The wolf beside the enemy froze and sniffed the air. He approached me and nuzzled against my hand before heading the way Thomas's wolf had.

I blinked in confusion. Were the wolves planning their own attack?

In an instant, Callan's fireball lit up the surrounding space. "Ari, move!" He launched the fireball past his opponent just as I threw myself to the ground.

The flame grazed the man's arm, and he backed away toward the edge of the woods.

Black and white smoke on the ground in front of me was my only warning before Thomas grabbed a chunk of my hair and yanked me up. "How're you feeling, little mouse?"

I screeched in pain as I tried to disentangle from his grip. Metal glinted in his free hand as it collided with my exposed arm. The knife tore my skin as he slid it down my forearm. I screamed and kicked my legs toward him.

Callan appeared with the steel spade Mom and I used in the garden. He wielded it with ease, and as he approached, I twisted my body away. The collision of steel against bone seemed to echo in my ears.

Thomas roared but didn't lose his grip. Before he could move, voices rose behind us.

"No. Ari will get hurt."

"She already is."

I couldn't tell the twin voices apart, but the chain that appeared around Thomas's feet had to be Ronin's doing.

Thomas's legs gave way beneath him, and he landed on his injured elbow. His grip didn't loosen.

The twins closed the gap between us. Ronin pried Thomas's fingers from my hair, and then Brayden grabbed my hand to pull me up.

Though blood still dripped from my arm, I was finally free and enclosed inside Brayden's protection.

But Ronin wasn't. He too became a victim of Thomas's talent.

"Arisanna," Thomas sang out, cradling his arm against him. "The people you love are sacrificing themselves for you. Two down. Two to go. Then, we find your mom. I know where she's hidden, and I can get in."

"Do not fall for it, Ari," Brayden whispered. "The girls are safe, and Lucian and Ronin can handle themselves."

"So we just stand here and wait?" I hissed back, busy pressing my gaping wound. The pain seared through me and made me double over. I whimpered and closed my eyes, focusing my energy into removing the pain and stitching the cut back together well enough to keep the blood from seeping out.

"You need to get out of here. I cannot hold this anymore." Then the safety net fell, and we were exposed.

Barham looked at us with regret as he backed away into the woods.

I glanced around. None of Thomas's men remained.

"Go, Ari," Brayden commanded, rushing at Thomas. This time, the fog took both of them, but before they disappeared, Brayden shouted, "Callan, make it rain!"

A huge fireball shot into the sky, exploding into a slow, fiery drizzle, and I turned toward it.

Callan fell on his knees, nearly spent. Behind him, Thomas appeared gripping the spade.

I couldn't stop the inevitable, but I had to try. Determined to take him far away from here—from the girls—I concentrated on my fog as I walked.

Before I reached Thomas, he swung out at Callan, the metal making a sickening thud as it collided with the back of his skull. Callan toppled forward, unmoving.

Thomas smiled condescendingly at my white smoke that now swirled around the two of us. With his good hand, he whipped the knife from his belt and aimed it at my heart. His swollen eye and broken elbow didn't slow him down.

I panicked, losing control and stopping in my tracks. My gift was similar to Thomas's, but he'd had more practice and was more powerful.

Taking advantage of my hesitation, the black and white fog swirled at my feet, holding me in place.

Cade bared his teeth as he charged toward Thomas, causing him to lose his focus and release his hold on me to protect himself.

As Cade clamped down on the wrist that held the knife, Thomas's wolf pushed to his feet as though trying to decide which side to join. Cade thrashed his head around until the knife flew from Thomas's grip and landed at my feet.

I used my fog to send the knife deep into the woods where no one but I could find it.

The moon slipped behind the clouds and bathed us in darkness as a roll of thunder shook the ground.

Cade whimpered as Thomas crowed, and my heart sank. What happened to Cade? Where was he?

My eyes adjusted to the darkness, but I couldn't see him anywhere, just the disappearing telltale black and white fog.

Thomas glared as he advanced toward me, bleeding from the deep gash Cade's teeth had torn on his wrist.

I backed against the wall of rose bushes until thorns stabbed into my legs, and Thomas smiled when I winced.

"You should have gone home when I told you to. It didn't have to come to this." He gripped my arm tightly, digging into the barely healed wound, and whipped me to his side.

I yelped in pain, wishing a moment too late that I'd remained silent.

Heat lightning illuminated Torren as he emerged from the darkness of the woods for mere seconds while he searched for me. Then in a wisp of smoke, he was by my side, the wrath in his eyes a warning that he would risk everything to keep me safe.

"Let her go," he said, voice rumbling like the thunder I'd heard moments ago.

Thomas swung me in front of him. "I'll let her go. You'll just have to figure out where."

My mind went into overdrive imagining where he had sent Ronin, Brayden, my dad—where he planned to send me. "No," I shouted. "Torren, stay back."

Thomas yanked my arm and jerked me around to face him. "Shut your mouth!" He slapped me across the face. Hard. I bit my lip from the force and cried out.

Torren charged forward with Thomas's distraction and wrenched me from his grip.

Thomas gritted his teeth and snarled.

"We need to get out of here." Torren wrapped me in his arms, but there wasn't enough time.

"Look out!" I shouted.

Torren's grip loosened as he spun around, and Thomas's fist connected with his lip. Torren fell to the ground, a cloud of dirt settling onto a thin layer of perspiration. Pressing a fingertip to the cut on the edge of his mouth, he jumped to his feet and stood facing Thomas.

My cheek throbbed from the slap, and I pressed the palm of my hand to cool the fiery sting. Fire. Callan's fire had served a useful purpose tonight. Could mine?

"I spent twenty years at Edric's side, nothing but loyal. I've worked my entire life to get to the position I'm in, and you've been given all the privileges of a Council member without putting in the work." Thomas stared me down as he spoke.

"I heard your plan. You won't win." Torren wiped the blood dripping from his lip with the back of his hand. His eyes flashed with fury, and he took measured steps toward Thomas. This wasn't going to end well if I didn't intervene.

I cupped my palms together, feeling the heat intensify. Tearing my eyes away from the scene before me, I concentrated on concealing the fireball as it formed. Successful, I called out, "Torren, come back to me."

Thomas sneered, watching Torren back away. "Aww, true love wins after all. And to think, all the trouble Edric went through to keep you two apart..."

I thrust my hands toward the thorny bush behind Thomas. Almost instantly, the wall of thorns burst into flame. As Thomas whipped around, Torren and I disappeared.

I brought us to the meadow outside Callan's house, and the thunder rumbled closer.

Torren held me away from him, his eyes landing on the dried blood over the scar on my arm. "You're hurt," he whispered.

I shook my head. "I healed it."

Rain poured down on us, and the way blood trailed his lip reminded me of the boy I first loved. I gently ran my finger across his lips, the wound closing up, but it was worse than I thought. There might be a scar.

Memories bombarded my mind. Kai. Our first kiss. The courtyard. Torren. Building our love again from scratch. The rain washed the dirt down his face in muddy tears, and he gathered me into his arms.

"What happened, Ari?"

"I didn't listen to you." An ache in my head weighed me down. "You told me not to use two gifts, but I did."

"What did you do?" he whispered into my ear.

Darkness closed in from the edges of my vision as the storm swept overhead. "I concealed the fireball before I threw it into the thorns." It became increasingly difficult to breathe.

"Keep talking. We'll be home soon." He lifted me into his arms, and I slumped against him.

"It took time to enclose us both, but it worked. I did it."

His voice thickened. "Did what?"

"Concealed my fog."

Torren's was the last face I saw before all went black.

A sense of weightlessness overtook me, as though someone held me while I soared through the air. Voices filtered into the darkness, followed by flickers of memories.

Kai's smiling face flashed in front of me. No, not Kai. Torren. And he wasn't smiling. He was screaming.

I tried to speak, unsure if any words were actually formed.

"Not again!" Torren yelled as the warmth of his arms disappeared and the damp ground cradled my body, droplets of rain splashing against me. "She needs help!"

Footsteps quickly approached. "Torren, what happened?"

"I don't... she's hurt. I tried... Lyra... I couldn't..." His voice cracked and his words faded in and out, as though he shifted his head back and forth.

"Torren, you must calm down or you will be unable to help her. Go into the house and get Deborah and Lyra. I will protect her." Brayden's voice was calm, but I could hear the rise of concern. Following a sharp intake of breath, Brayden spoke again. "I have a barrier around the perimeter. No one is getting in who is not already."

"I'll be right back." Torren placed a gentle kiss on my forehead and ran off, his calls for help getting further by the second.

"If you can hear me, Ari, please stay where you are. Trust that I am nearby, and no harm will come to you." Another set of footsteps moved away from me.

My eyes were heavy, but I forced them open to find myself back where we began, alone. Had I blacked out at some point and everything after had only been in my head?

Flames danced within the dried bushes several feet in front of me, the rain working to smother them. That *had* happened.

I pushed myself up, and my knees wobbled beneath me. Scanning the area enclosed in Brayden's glimmering barrier, my heart thudded against my chest. Was Thomas trapped inside with us, lingering in the shadows for the perfect time to pounce?

As though he could read my thoughts, Thomas emerged from behind the fiery bush, his singed skin still smoking. A glint of metal in his right hand. He was out for blood.

Mine.

I focused what little energy I still had into one last trick. He needed to freeze. Or at least the time around him did.

As Thomas's feet slowed, Brayden rushed toward him.

Flashes assaulted my vision, and I began to sway.

Thomas's face morphed, a Cheshire grin replacing the frustration as he regained mobility and spun around.

The metal blade glided into Brayden's chest. Brayden fell and Thomas turned, coming straight for me.

Around us, a chorus of wolves closed in.

"Ari!" Torren's arms were around me, catching me as my legs gave out beneath me.

The wolves howling turned to vicious growls, and Torren's body went rigid.

"Stay with me, Ari." His voice splintered.

I tried to fight the weakness that overcame me, but I could feel myself slipping away in his arms as everything went silent and the flashes stopped.

CHAPTER FORTY

LUCKY

The only light that greeted me when I forced my eyes open filtered in from outside my cracked door. Fingers jerked between my own, and I turned my head slightly.

Torren sat in a chair pressed against my bed, his torso slumped over and arm curled beneath his cheek, his slumbering form highlighted in the moonlight that shone through the shades in sharp slices.

He had been my constant, even when he could no longer remember me and our past. He kept the promise he'd made in the labyrinth without intending to. He didn't leave my side.

If anyone had asked me two weeks ago, I never could've imagined that my love for this man would've changed in any way, but it had.

My heart swelled. The love I'd held for him as Kai had grown and become stronger when he no longer hid his true self. Torren, with the same crooked smile and bright eyes I fell in love with in the woods. Torren, the goofy guy with a huge heart. Torren.

I lifted my free hand and ran my fingers through his hair.

His head jerked up, and I was met with red-rimmed eyes. "Ari," he whispered. He jumped up and shouted toward the door.

"She's awake!" He turned back to me. His bloodied lip had already scabbed over.

I ran my thumb over his healing wound. "How long have I been asleep?"

His chin quivered, and his voice cracked. "Five days."

My parents came rushing into the room, and light flooded in from the hallway. Mom came to my bedside and sat near my knees.

"Is everyone okay?" I took in the faces surrounding me.

Mom, Dad, Callan, Ronin, and Torren wore matching expressions and tear-stained cheeks.

In the dim moonlight, I'd missed the stains on Torren's cheeks. "Why do you all look like you just came from a funeral?"

Torren's eyes glossed before he wrapped his hands around mine and hung his head. His shoulders shook as tears fell onto our joined hands.

My heart sank. Another secret lay just beyond my reach, a secret I didn't want to know but couldn't help but ask. "What happened? Are the girls alright?"

"They're fine. Everyone's asleep." Ronin shifted uncomfortably in the doorframe.

I scanned the room as I tried to sit up. A pit formed in my stomach. "Where's Brayden?"

"Honey." Mom took a shaky breath. "There's no easy way to say this—"

"So don't," I choked, feeling like a small child. If it wasn't spoken, it wasn't true.

Dad stood behind Mom, fresh tears racing down his cheeks. "Sweetie, he didn't make it."

"You're lying. He's fine. I saw him…" my words trailed as I accessed my last memories from the fight. I did see him. Before I lost consciousness, Thomas stabbed Brayden. A cold wave traveled through my body, causing me to shudder. Thomas used the knife he'd intended for me. I squeezed my eyes against the memory and shook my head.

Torren wasted no time wrapping his arms around me, and in the protection of his embrace, my tears flowed.

"But Lyra..."

The lines around Ronin's eyes etched into his skin, drawing down his cheeks to a broken-hearted frown. "His injuries were too severe."

Another cold wave traveled over me, but I willed it away, my knuckles turning white as I gripped my comforter. "Couldn't Celia pause him until..."

Torren settled his head against my neck. Tears fell onto my exposed shoulder. "Ari," his voice was strangled, "no one could help him."

"No."

Brayden was gone, and it was *my* fault. He told me to save my energy, and I failed when it mattered the most. Thomas had sent everyone else away. I was Brayden's only chance.

"Wait. How did you all get back?" I asked.

Callan grinned. "When we were kids, Lucian, Brayden, and I got lost in the woods after dark. We couldn't find our way home, so Brayden told me to send up a signal. It worked, and our dad found us. We used to joke about it growing up, and it came in handy again. Brayden suspected Thomas didn't have enough time or energy to send anyone too far. They were all scattered in the woods. To get back, they only had to follow the light."

"Then Cade's back too? He always finds me."

Torren stiffened and slid his hand into mine giving me a gentle squeeze.

Dad shook his head. "We couldn't find him."

"He could've wandered off. We don't know," Callan added.

It was sweet of Callan to try to make me feel better, but hope was pointless. Cade would've found me if he could.

I focused on Callan, the white gauze wrapped around his head capturing my attention for the first time. Letting go of Torren, I reached out to Callan. "You're hurt. Let me help you."

"No, no. It's nothing I can't handle. Thomas didn't do me as much harm as he hoped."

My pulse quickened as I glanced at the scar down my forearm, remembering the way he grinned as he cut me open. Was he still out for my blood? I braced for the worst. "Where is Thomas?"

"After Brayden went down, the wolves came out of the woods. We were afraid they were going to attack us, but instead they became our protectors," Dad said.

"How?" I asked.

"They formed a barricade, blocking Thomas from us. When he tried to break through, his own wolf attacked him. He sent himself away. Ronin found him dead from his injuries in the hospital the next day. With the doctor all but disappearing, Thomas stood no chance."

The doctor. Charlie. My stomach twisted, and I fought back nausea. Did *anyone* know who he truly was?

"Thomas can't hurt you anymore." Torren brushed his hand across my cheek, and I relaxed with his touch. "No one can."

"What about Edric?"

"He's being held. Torren sent him to the Glass House." Ronin stepped closer to me. "I saw his transmissions, and there's something we need to talk about."

Torren sat up straight and interrupted with a growl in his voice. "This can wait. Let her rest."

It didn't matter. I knew exactly what this was about. "You saw what happened in the courtyard." I twisted my hands together, fearing his judgment, but it never came.

Instead, Torren covered my hands with his, and my nerves settled as I wove our fingers together.

Ronin waited until I met his gaze, and then his eyes held mine. "Ari, none of it was your fault. Edric has always been Charlie. He was an adult who preyed on the vulnerabilities of a child who didn't understand our world."

A fresh set of tears flowed from my eyes. The betrayal, the hurt that Edric caused. And for what?

Torren's jaw tensed as he swallowed audibly before exchanging a grim look with Dad.

Dad patted my knee as he attempted to soften the anger in his tight expression. "You need to rest. Both of you."

My lip quivered at the thought of being alone. "Dad, please don't make him leave. I need him here."

"Wouldn't dream of it." Dad stood and paused. "But the door stays open."

Mom leaned over and kissed the top of my head before following the others out.

When Torren and I were alone, silent tears spilled from our eyes. We held each other in mingled grief, finding comfort in each other's presence.

Torren made an effort to cheer me up, but his crooked smile was broken. He fell into my open arms and nuzzled his face into my shoulder.

The floorboards creaked just outside my door, and our attention turned toward the noise. Celia's wide eyes met mine, and my heart faltered.

"Are you okay?" Torren asked, an edge in his voice teetering between fear and confusion.

Tears settled on the rims of her eyes, and she lowered her head to stare at her toes. "I dreamed of him. Of Robert. We had a conversation a long time ago, and the dream reminded me of his words. Words that made no sense to me back then, but now..." Her head jerked up, and her gaze shifted between Torren and me. "They have overcome one hurdle, but their troubles are far from over."

I drew my eyebrows together. "What's that supposed to mean?"

She shook her head. "He saw something. Something meant to tear you two apart, but he could never see a clear outcome."

My chest rose and fell rapidly. What could be worse than what we had just gone through?

"I'm so sorry," she whispered before turning on her heel and heading back the way she came.

"That was a bit ominous," I breathed out. "I need to get out of here."

"Okay." Torren stood and reached out his hand to me.

I shook my head furiously. "I can hear them out there. I can't walk past them and be ambushed anymore this morning."

Torren sat beside me and gathered me into his arms. "Show me where you want to go," he whispered.

I pictured our meadow, the place we grew up together, the place we rediscovered our love for each other, the one place that was ours alone.

He smiled against my cheek. "Hold on tight."

I knew it wasn't required, but it helped to ease the pain and anxiety that had settled into my bones. I relaxed into his hold as I breathed him in.

Torren was still here beside me. He was real.

The air around us shifted, and the warm summer breeze ruffled my hair. My body trembled, and the pain poured from my eyes. We were safe, but I'd failed my family. I'd failed Brayden.

Torren pulled back without losing contact. Worry danced in his eyes.

"I'm so sorry I didn't save him, Torren. I should've saved him. I could've sent him away, but I didn't. I used the rest of my energy to freeze Thomas, and we lost Brayden because of it."

"Ari, no." With tears streaming down his cheeks, Torren placed his hands on either side of my face. "There was nothing you could have done. There was nothing any of us could've done. Thomas was too quick. If you would've tried to send Brayden away, Thomas would've sent you away and we'd still be in this same place. Except, we may not have been able to find you in time, and we could've lost you both."

His words made sense but did nothing to ease the guilt that had made a permanent home in my chest.

I turned my head away and watched the water ripple beside us as the sun rose. All those years spent separated from Alterria by a river, and I found myself wishing it could've remained that way because then maybe Brayden would still be there, watching over his family in the shadows.

Then Lyra's bright smile filled my mind. She wouldn't have lasted much longer had I not shown up.

And Celia, what would have happened to her?

And Torren—my sweet, funny, loving Torren. We never would've found each other again.

"Hey." He placed his thumb under my trembling chin and guided my eyes to his. "What's on your mind?"

I pressed my lips together before responding. "The last couple of weeks have been so much. Everything that's been thrown our way. Torren, what if this isn't the end of it? What if the world keeps trying to find ways to tear us apart? Or worse?"

"If I've learned anything during this, it's that you're strong. So strong. And no matter what gets thrown our way, they can't break us. Even if I can't remember you, I'll always fight for you."

"And I'll always fight for you." I brushed the tears from my cheeks before lacing our fingers together. "I'm so lucky you stumbled into my woods five years ago."

"Oh, Ari," he said, his voice still choked from his tears, "I'm the lucky one."

"How so?" I sensed something more behind his anguish, and my stomach filled with butterflies.

He pressed his forehead against mine and gazed into my eyes. "I got to fall in love with you twice."

ACKNOWLEDGEMENTS

First and foremost, this book wouldn't have come together without our husbands. Michael Kampa and Jason Aumock gave us the gift of support. Not only did they encourage us to take our twice-a-year weekend getaways to write together, but they also stepped in to manage the home and family while we spent hours on phone calls and video chats.

Thank you to our children who pitched in to help while we worked and who celebrated with us as we reached milestones along the way. Not even a million pages would be enough to describe the blessings you are in our lives.

Our parents, particularly our moms, also played a huge role in making our dream come true. For starters, they each took on a bonus daughter, and let us be kids in a world where everyone was growing up too fast. Cindy and Sheryl, our first cheerleaders, our first fans. Hearing "I'm proud of my girls" from both of you meant the world.

To our fellow WordWarrior Princess, Heather, a special thank you for putting up with our tangents and interruptions on Wednesday Write Nights, getting us back on track, and reminding us that every new word is a step closer to making this book the reality it has now become.

Thank you to our first readers who encouraged us that this was worth sharing with the world. Many of you were complete strangers, and your love for our characters gave us the push we needed to keep going. A special thanks to Jim, Nancy, Joyce, Kaitlyn, and Kay whose comments helped reshape our story.

Our editors, Holly Stoddard and Tracey Barski, thank you for your keen eyes and attention to detail.

Madison Szmurlo, our brilliantly talented cover artist, we are thrilled you were open to our request because we cannot imagine anyone else being able to bring our visions to life the way you do.

Last but not least, of course, our biggest thanks to God. Without His plan for our lives putting us in the right place at the right time so that we would meet—in addition to the talent He gave us both—none of this would exist.

To all who have been part of our journey, thank you for your love and support. We hope you've enjoyed the world we've created. There's more to come!

Welcome to Alterria!

-Aimee and Missy

Friends come, and friends go. That's just how life is when you're twelve. As seventh graders, neither Aimee nor Missy ever imagined that the nice girl from French class and choir would  become a lifelong friend, let alone that they would write a trilogy together.

Passing notes after* class, editing each other's junior high newsletters about their favorite sitcoms, and writing an article for their high school yearbook turned into encouraging each other to write stories and poems.

The plethora of sleepovers they used to enjoy turned into phone calls and texts as they graduated high school, married their soulmates, had children, and moved far away from each other, but they never lost their connection. Loyal friends are a treasured gem, and they both recognized they'd been blessed to be part of each other's lives.

Twenty-six years after they first met, Aimee and Missy began a new journey together, trading sentences across nearly 200 miles until Divided, the first book in the Alterrian Gifts trilogy was born.

Everyone has a gift, and they agree that one of the greatest gifts they have received is the gift of Friendship.

---

*After class—never during, of course! How else would they have been able to pay attention to the English teacher?

Sway

Enjoy this unedited sneak peek into the continuation of Ari and Torren's story. Sway, book two of the Alterrian Gifts series, is set to release February 2025.

The curse had been mostly silent while Celia and I worked on the elixir, but when my days stretched out before me, it began to rumble in the dark spaces of my mind, clawing its way back to the surface.

I sped through the familiar paths in the woods, running from the darkness that waited for my defenses to lower. In no time, the meadow spilled out from the tree line, and sun sparkled on the river. The shoreline called to me, and I slipped off my shoes to dip my feet into the flowing waters. Laying back on my elbows, I closed my eyes and let the serenity of nature flow over me.

The bright warmth of August carried away thoughts of my curse, and the only shadow that crossed my face turned out to be my favorite person. "Torren!" I giggled. "You're blocking the good sun."

He chuckled, planted a kiss on my forehead, and plopped down at my side. His shoes and socks joined mine, and he bathed his toes beside me. "You looked so cute, I couldn't resist. It reminded me of the first day we met. Well, the second time, I guess."

I curled into his embrace when he stretched out his arm to hold me close. *I* couldn't resist either. "I remember. I came here after searching for the clearing where Celia had disappeared the year before."

His heart beat against my fingertips, calming the worry that had clenched my thoughts most of the morning. Moments like that never failed to make my heart light, and I had no doubt he felt the same.

"And I showed up because I was the only one in my family no longer searching." He plucked a long piece of grass from the ground and twisted it between his fingers. "If we would've searched together here, I wonder if we could have found her sooner."

"No. The portal wouldn't open until I learned that gift."

He kissed the top of my head and held me tighter. "You're right. I really need to work on stopping those what-if scenarios from clouding my head. She's safe and I have you back. Everything is great."

The darkness slithered in like a shadow in the night, ambushing my consciousness.

Everything's great...for now. What happens when he decides there's nothing more you can offer him and he leaves you?

I shook the unwelcome visitor from my head, refusing to listen to the seed of doubt it tried to plant. I knew Torren. It was this curse that was foreign.

"What brings you to this spot today?"

"Besides my beautiful girlfriend?"

I blushed as his words brought me affirmation. No matter how often he called me that, it felt brand new, and the butterflies inside flurried in circles.

"Your mom sent me to find you."

Mom had rarely even sent *Dad* to find me, both of them knowing how I liked to explore, so her request was unusual. I pushed up to face him, the worry again clawing at me.

He brushed my hair from my cheek, and his emerald green eyes sparkled. "She thinks she has it figured out. You can go whenever you're ready."

"Really?" I managed to choke out. I'd been waiting for that moment, but my heart pounded in fear.

You'll regret it.

Torren nodded and reached for my hands. "Ari, you can learn to control it."

The boy makes a good point. Think of all we could accomplish together.

I shook my head. It had to go. No matter the cost. "It's too dangerous."

"We can work together to make it something you can manage."

The earnestness in his voice surprised me, and when I sat all the way up, he followed my lead. Had the curse wound an idea of its "usefulness" into Torren's mind? Could it make *me* forget the encounter as well? "Why are you fighting for me to keep it?"

"You are the first Alterrian with Duplicity. What if this cure removes your gift entirely?"

"I lived almost eighteen years without one. It really wouldn't be a huge sacrifice if I lost it all."

You're wrong. You'll sacrifice everything. You'll lose the last part that keeps Torren beside you, the connection to his brother.

Torren sighed and squeezed my hands.

"I would hate to lose the connection I have to Brayden, but Torren, you have no idea how terrible Edric's gift is for me."

He looked me in the eyes. "Tell me."

I swallowed hard against the knot forming in the base of my throat. "It makes me think awful things, but my mind tries to fight against it. It is exhausting to fight that kind of war with myself. I feel like I'm losing my mind."

I waited for it to say something, but the darkness remained silent.

Torren pulled me close again and was quiet for a moment before he spoke. "You need to do what you feel is best for you."

Relief flooded through me. I'd already made the decision, but his understanding made it easier. "It needs to go, and if that means I'll lose everything along with it, I'm willing to take that risk. I don't think I can handle this gift much longer."

"Do you want me to come with you?" Torren stood and helped me to my feet.

The evil returned. **Let him come. He'll save you from the excruciating pain when you rip your gift away from your soul.**

"Actually, I'm a little nervous about how this will all work." I brushed off the back of my pants and reached for my shoes. "If it seems like something is hurting me, would you try to interfere?"

"Of course. I never want to see you in pain."

I smiled. "Then I need to do this alone."

The look of confusion that crossed his face quickly gave way to comprehension, and he kissed me gently. "I'll walk you home and then go hang out at Dad's. Come see me when you're done, please?"

"Where else would I go?" We slipped on our shoes, then walked hand in hand in complete silence. When we reached my front door, he kissed the back of my hand before calling up his fog and disappearing before my eyes.

My fate lay on the other side of my front door, and though the risk might be worth the reward, the consequences were a mystery.

You're making a mistake.

"No, I'm not."

I took a deep breath and walked inside.

To follow Ari's journey into Alterria, join us at
Morning Stories Publications

@morningstoriespublications

@morningstoriespublications

@morningstories97